COLOSSUS

COLOSSUS

ALEXANDER COLE

CORVUS

First published in trade paperback in Great Britain in 2014 by Corvus,
an imprint of Atlantic Books Ltd.

10 9 8 7 6 5 4 3 2 1

A CIP catalogue record for this book is available from the British Library.

Trade paperback ISBN: 978 0 85789 115 0
E-book ISBN: 978 0 85789 120 4

Printed in Italy by 🦁 Grafica Veneta S.p.A.

Corvus
An imprint of Atlantic Books Ltd
Ormond House
26–27 Boswell Street
London
WC1N 3JZ

www.corvus-books.co.uk

This is for my dear old mum. It seems more than appropriate as I finished the last pages of Colossus *camped by her bed while she slept through the last week of her ninety-two years. Thanks for all your love and support in your good and long life. Wherever you are now – in Heaven as you deserve, or in Fiddler's Green with the rest of the card players and sherry drinkers – this one's for you.*

RIP Doris Bowles 1920–2012.

CHAPTER 1

Babylon

'KILL HIM! KILL the monster now!'
Colossus has sent everyone scattering. He has ripped the stake out of the ground and the heavy iron chain now trails his hind leg as light as a flower garland, bouncing this way and that. He has pulled down a small building at the edge of the enclosure by ramming it with its head and shoulder. A *mahavat* lies stricken on the ground nearby.

Someone has scared him. He is screaming with rage.

He picks up another of the *mahavats* with his trunk and swats him like a fly. The man rolls across the ground like tumbleweed and thuds into a mud brick wall. Colossus finds a straw cart and stamps on it leaving behind just splinters. The captain of the elephants has lost his fine turban and his swagger. He is panicked and his face is covered with dust and sweat.

The captain is deciding where to place his spear but it is not easy to kill a fully grown elephant. It takes an army and a forest of darts. Even without armour there are not many places a man can strike with a spear and even offend an elephant much, let alone kill him. He must somehow get underneath the beast, avoid his tusks and feet and strike upwards. To do that the beast's attention must be distracted and Colossus is not of a mind to take his cold red eyes off the captain of the elephants for even a moment.

The fool tries to run around him but whichever way he turns, Colossus turns too. It is clear now that he is the target for the animal's fury. Gajendra supposes he has been beating him with the *ankus* again. How many times has he told him not to do that?

Colossus tramples down several tents and knocks over another cart. It is pandemonium. The other elephants are agitated now and if someone doesn't do something they will stampede. Gajendra doesn't like the captain and will happily see him squashed like a beetle, but someone must help him, for the sake of the entire regiment.

So Gajendra steps out in front of Colossus.

The world stops. He can hear only two things now: his own blood pounding in his ears and his Uncle Ravi shouting at him to come away. He hears galloping horses on the road, sees a hawk soaring high overhead.

He cannot let them slaughter Colossus. The beast just needs someone who knows how to handle him, that's all. If someone put that bull hook up the captain's ample fundament instead everything would be all right.

He stands in front of the big bull and Colossus bellows, trunk raised, ears flared. The tusks are terrifying. He once saw a man gutted and near torn in half by one of those. He still remembers the inhuman cry as the bull tried to shake him off.

Never mind the tusks, just watch what he does. The

tusks are the least of your worries. He can just stamp on you if he wants, leave behind just a red stain and a few stringy fibres like betel nut.

Colossus swings his front foot, a sure sign he is going to charge. He starts at a gait, trunk curled. The ground shakes under his feet. The captain of the elephants screams and tries to run but he trips in his haste and falls flat on his face in the dirt.

Hold your ground now. Go down on one knee like Ravi showed you. Don't let him see you're afraid even though you're near pissing yourself. Remember what he said. 'On one knee and point to the ground.'

'*Hida, Hida!*' Lie down!

The effect is dramatic. His ears crack out and he unrolls his trunk. He shakes his huge head, showering Gajendra in a cloud of sand, and backs off a few paces.

Impressive. He has only once before seen an elephant break off an attack at full speed. On that occasion it was Ravi who was standing in front of the elephant.

'*Hida!*'

Colossus is slow about it, but he does it, settling into the dust.

The captain runs forward with his spear. Gajendra sees what is intended, and throws himself at the captain, taking him in the midriff, knocking the wind out of him and sending him sprawling on the ground. The spear bounces across the dirt. Colossus gets back to his feet, picks it up with his trunk and tosses it casually over his massive shoulder. He does not see where it lands.

Greece, perhaps.

*

After all the trumpeting and screaming the silence that follows is eerie. A shadow falls across Gajendra's face, and he hears the jangle of trappings, realizes that a horse and its rider have stepped up to him. The rider has his back to the sun and Gajendra must shield his eyes to look at him.

'Well, that was smartly done,' the newcomer says. He sits on a huge white Arab stallion. The captain of the elephants scrambles back to his feet and almost immediately puts his head back into the dirt, this time without the assistance of one of his own elephants.

The rider steps his horse forward and turns to the officer beside him. 'I can make an oriental kneel, but this one makes an enraged elephant grovel. Which of us is greater, do you think?'

The rider slides from the saddle and stands, legs apart, surveying the scene. Gajendra finally realizes who it is and gasps and falls to his knees behind the captain.

'Oh, don't bother with all that now,' Alexander says and grabs him by the tunic and pulls him back to his feet.

Gajendra is surprised to find that the great Alexander is shorter than he is. Squat, golden and broad, his legs are bowed from spending his entire life in the saddle of a horse. And yet he feels as if he is standing next to a giant. He had heard legends of his general long before he was conscripted into Alexander's army. It is like standing next to the sun; how the energy burns off him.

Alexander nudges the captain of the elephants with his foot. 'What's your name?' He has a high-pitched voice, this lord of war, it grates on the nerves.

'Oxathres, my lord,' the captain says, without raising his face from the dirt.

'You might as well lick his boots while you're down there,' Alexander's lieutenant says and then guffaws when Oxathres actually does it. Apparently, it was just a joke.

'You're a fool, Oxathres. What are you?'

'A fool, my lord.'

Alexander winds up and kicks him hard in the ribs and then turns to Gajendra and asks him his name.

'"Gajendra",' Alexander repeats, when he hears it. 'It sounds a little like my own name. Gajendra the Great!' he says and his lieutenants laugh, which is why he keeps them with him, Gajendra supposes.

He nudges the captain of the elephants with his boot a second time as if it is something in his path that he is unsure about. 'You're in charge here, am I right? How did this come about?'

The captain says, 'Beg pardon, my general, but the beast is mad. It should be killed immediately.' He wipes the sweat off his face and smiles up at his general in an ugly way, something like a grimace. 'The animal is a menace and will not be properly trained.'

Alexander starts to laugh. He throws back his head and roars. Even Oxathres starts to laugh, not yet party to his own joke. Now the lieutenants on their horses laugh as well; even one of the horses seems to snicker. Then Alexander draws back his boot and kicks Oxathres in the ribs again. It is a terrifying sight because Alexander is still laughing as he does it.

'Who made you captain of these beasts?' Kick. 'Was it me?' Kick. 'I shall have to put myself on a charge for incompetence. What was I thinking? I must have been drunk!' Kick, kick, kick.

The captain of the elephants starts to cry. The fault is not his, he grunts in between having his ribs tickled. The beast is unnatural. It will not submit to direction. Forgive me. I am Alexander's most faithful soldier. I would follow you to the ends of the earth.

'Only to the ends of the earth?' Alexander says. 'But I've been there. I need somewhere to march that is more of a challenge!'

He suddenly loses interest in his captain of the elephants. He seems as easily distracted as a child.

'Well, look at this,' he says and walks up to Colossus and stands in front of him with his hands on his hips. Gajendra watches Colossus carefully; the imperceptible flick of the pink tip of its trunk, the slow blink of his eye. No sudden movements please, my lord, he thinks, or you will follow the captain's spear over that wall.

'What is his name?'

'Fateh Gaj – it means Victory Elephant. But your soldiers have called him by a different name.'

'And what is that?'

'Colossus, my lord.'

Alexander laughs. 'Yes. Colossus. It suits him.'

Gajendra approaches, so that he can intervene should Colossus take exception to his general's behaviour. Colossus reaches out with his trunk and touches Gajendra's head and face. He makes a deep rumbling in his stomach as he does this.

'He is the biggest beast I have ever seen; even at Gaugamela I never saw the like,' Alexander says. 'How did you tame him?'

'I spoke to him.'

Alexander walks around the grey mountain of leathery flesh. Colossus has tufts of greyish hair all over him and ears as big as a man. Alexander folds his arms and frowns. 'You're not telling me this beast can talk?'

'No, but he can understand.'

'And what's that language you use?'

'It's the language of elephants, my lord.' He cannot explain to him that it is the language Uncle Ravi spoke as a child.

Alexander gives him a pained look. 'And why does this special language make a difference?'

'He is trained to obey certain commands and that is the only language he understands.'

'Does that imbecile…' he indicates Oxathres with a dismissive nod of the head, '… does he know that?'

'I have tried to tell him, but he pays no attention to me.'

'Are you Indian? You don't look Indian. You look Greek.'

'My mother was Persian.'

'What was your father doing with a Persian? Besides making you?'

'The Rajah gave her to him. As a gift, for his exploits in battle. He said he was the best *mahavat* in his whole army. But then he was wounded and he could not be a soldier any more. He turned to farming.'

'The son of a hero!'

'I suppose.'

'So you are telling me that you are the only one who knows how to control this animal?'

'It would so appear.'

'So if you are the only one here who knows how to

control the beast, why has it done all this?' He looks around the enclosure. Two men lie motionless in the dirt, two small buildings are partially destroyed and three carts are now only of use for firewood.

'I believe the captain of the elephants took to him with a bull hook. He doesn't like bull hooks.'

'Where were you?'

'I was mucking out the straw.'

'But isn't this your elephant?'

'He won't give me an elephant. He says I'm too young.'

Alexander sighs, theatrically puffing out his cheeks. He walks over to Oxathres, who is still curled up on the ground, clutching his ribs. This has not been a good day for him and it is about to get worse. Alexander grabs him by the hair and cuffs him smartly about the ears. 'You're stupid. Say it now. Come on. You'll feel better once it's said.'

'I'm stupid,' the captain of the elephants sobs.

'Why are you stupid?'

'I don't know.'

'You're stupid because you don't know how to use your resources to their best effect.' He picks him up by the collar and drops him back into the dust. He kicks him again, much harder than before. 'From now on, this boy here... what was your name again?'

'Gajendra, lord.'

'Gajendra is this animal's *mahavat*. Now I want no more trouble.' He nods to his lieutenant. 'Give the boy five of those new coins I had minted yesterday.'

Even the lieutenant seems surprised. 'So much?'

'Just do it.'

The lieutenant gestures him to approach. Gajendra gapes; it is as much money as he might make in a year.

Alexander turns around and takes a last look at Colossus, who is still kneeling, playfully blowing at the dust with his trunk, mild as a kitten. Alexander shakes his head.

Then he looks at Gajendra and grimaces with distaste. 'You're covered in elephant snot,' he says.

Gajendra looks down at his tunic. He is indeed covered in slime, half a pint of it from where Colossus has expressed his affection.

'We have known each other a long time. He is fond of me.'

'I should not like anything to be that fond of me,' Alexander says, and then gets on his horse and rides away, his lieutenants in tow.

The captain of the elephants gets to his feet. His ear is bleeding. He tries to straighten up but his ribs will not let him. He looks at Colossus and then at Gajendra. He points a finger at him.

'You're dead, boy,' he says and staggers away.

Gajendra looks over his shoulder at his elephant. All the madness has gone out of him. He flaps his ears and tastes the air with his trunk. Now that Oxathres has gone, he seems perfectly at ease.

'Now look what you've done,' Gajendra says to him. He taps the *ankus* behind his tail and Colossus does as he asks, and trails him across the enclosure, leaving the waterboys to clear up.

CHAPTER 2

THE MOON IS tentative, slipping in and out between dark clouds. The night wind collects the fallen leaves and whispers them along the trail that winds along Elephant Row.

He cannot sleep tonight, not after all that has happened. It's not just the excitement; he also wonders if Oxathres might slide a knife across his throat in the dark.

He gets up to check everything is all right. A few of the elephants are asleep, others sway in the darkness, still awake; he can feel the rumbling from their stomachs through his bare feet. A lone waterboy is about his work.

He has been around elephants since he was nine years old. Uncle Ravi made it his job to talk to them, to rub their bristly hides and the smooth hindside of their ears, then feed them melons and whisper to them that one day they would grow up and be talked of in the same breath as Ganesha himself.

The torches are sparking. In his mind he goes back to being nine years old, walking into the Rajah's camp for the first time, Ravi's hand on his shoulder, the hard faces of the other *mahavats* scowling at him. Ravi says: he is my new waterboy. Just like that. Overnight he changes from the boy who cries for his mother when he falls in the river to a soldier in the Rajah's army.

Gajendra has an *ankus* in his right hand. It has a small blunt hook. Some other *mahavats* sharpened the hook to a point but Ravi told him that a good handler would never do that.

'It is just for guiding him,' he said, patting Colossus high on his bristled foreleg. 'A good *mahavat* makes his elephant do what he wants with his voice. The elephant should obey because he loves you, not because he is afraid of you.'

A massive shape looms out of the dark and the rumblings grow deeper. It feels like an earthquake. He hears the tinkling of the bell Colossus has around his neck. They all have one; when you are working around animals the size of a house you need to know where they are all the time. Especially this one; a man would have to stand on another man's shoulders just to reach the top of his head. Ravi could walk under him without even touching his belly.

Colossus finds him with his trunk and explores his head and his chest. There are fibres all along it and the tip is wet and soon he is covered in slime. Gajendra tries to push him away, for all the good it will do. Now he'll have to bathe in the river before bed or sleep on his own in the straw.

He finds a melon with his foot and rolls it over, picks it up and tosses it into the great pink maw. Look at him, playful as a kitten now. But two men are groaning in the hospital tent because of him.

'What did you think you were doing today? You've got to keep a rein on that temper of yours. Be clever about these things. I know the captain's a dog, I know he beat you with the hook. But you learn to bide your time. You wait for your moment, you give it back just when they're not expecting it.'

He finds the puncture marks the bastard captain has made with the *ankus*, in his knees, the base of his trunk. It's not supposed to do that, you test your hook on your own finger, and if it draws blood then it's too sharp. The captain must have been sharpening his.

Now Colossus is done with the melon he searches Gajendra out with his trunk again. It looks like affection but Gajendra supposes he just wants something else to eat. Colossus sneezes in his hair; now he is covered in a nice mess of melon and grey snot. The rumbling gets louder.

Well, Ravi and the others won't let him near them now, not like this. He finds some straw next to Colossus and settles down on it; it's safer here anyway, no one's going to stick him with a knife with the big fellow standing guard. Besides, sometimes he prefers the smell of elephant to the smell of other men. With the tuskers at least you know where you stand.

Colossus keeps at him with his trunk, nagging him for another melon, but finally gives up and lets him sleep. Gajendra sleeps sound. He knows Colossus won't step on him in the dark. Even the biggest tuskers are strange like that. They never hurt anyone by accident.

But when they set out to do harm, a man had better watch out.

The next day he takes Colossus down to the river, watches as he splashes water over himself with his trunk. There is a basket of apples on the bank. Colossus decides on one and places it in his mouth with great delicacy, like a courtier selecting a grape. He swings his trunk from side to side. He appears happy.

Nothing like a good scrubbing bath. Gajendra uses his *ankus* to scrape the mud off his back. He talks to him the whole while. He is so engrossed he does not see Uncle Ravi until he is almost at his shoulder.

He calls him Uncle, but there is no blood tie. He was nine years old when the old *mahavat* saved his life and brought him into the camp. He has looked out for him ever since and taught him all there is to know about elephants.

He has no idea how old Ravi is; Ravi himself does not know. He has always looked the same: hard, wiry and nut brown. He says he is from the south, but he left there so long ago he can't even remember the name of the place. He only has one arm, lost his left arm at the elbow in some battle a long time ago.

'Uncle! I didn't hear you.'

'I've been watching for a while.' He scratches his head and says in a whisper: 'Do you trust him?'

All the *mahavat*s, even Ravi, talk in whispers around Colossus.

'I trust him more than the captain of the elephants. At least this one is entirely predictable. If you hit him with a hook, he'll kill you; if you don't, he won't. He likes the apples you found for him.'

'He eats as much as a regiment every day.'

Colossus reaches into the basket of apples again and tosses several aside until he finds one that suits him. Then he reaches out with his trunk and tosses one at Gajendra's feet.

'Did you see that?' Ravi says. 'He's giving you an apple.'

'He dropped it. He wasn't giving me anything.'

'No, Gaji. You and him have the same ghost. You're half elephant and he's half human. Here, I brought you something to celebrate your promotion. You're one of us now.'

It is a bull hook, made of teak root, as long as a man's arm. The end piece forms two dull points, one straight, one curved back towards the handle. It is trimmed with silver and copper, the shaft inlaid with sculpted silver elephants. There are a series of engraved initials of the *mahavats* who have owned it before.

'But this is your *ankus*,' Gajendra says, bewildered.

'And now it's yours. One day you'll pass it along, just as I'm doing now.'

'I can't take it.'

'You'll have to, because I don't want it any more. No one else can handle this elephant, you're the only one. You've earned the right to have this.'

Gajendra laughs in surprise. He shows it to Colossus. 'See, I'm your new *mahavat*,' he says to him. 'I'm the boss now.'

Colossus watches him with mucus-rimmed eyes and selects another apple from the basket. Gajendra knows what he is thinking: if you're the boss, why are you the one scraping mud off my backside with your bare hands?

The captain of the elephants appears on the bank. He keeps his distance. Colossus sees the bull hook at the captain's side and his eyes turn cold.

Oxathres can't shout because his ribs are still paining him. Why would he come near Colossus again holding a bull hook? His stupidity is alarming.

'Get him out onto the *maidan*,' he croaks. 'We are having a drill.'

It takes a long time to get the elephants ready, even without the paint and the sword tips on their tusks, which they would need in a real battle. First there is the armour: a metal sheath for the trunk and the head, then a camel-hair blanket must be thrown over the beast's back before the heavy timber *howdah* is mounted in place with the aid of broad straps of woven hemp. Colossus bears it but he doesn't like it; he bellows and thrashes around.

It is a long and exhausting process, and today it is taking far too long. 'Hurry!' Gajendra shouts at the handlers. His voice sounds shrill, even to him. The waterboys are not accustomed to being bossed around by someone quite so young, and grumble about it.

It is not Colossus's fault that he is the last to be ready. They are still securing the wooden *howdah* onto his back when the others are already filing out to the *maidan*.

Oxathres marches over, tapping the bull hook on the ground; he clearly wants to smash someone with it and he doesn't mind who, but he would rather it was these two. His face is purple. This is what he wanted, has been spoiling for it since he woke up this morning with his sore ribs.

'Why are you not ready? Everyone else is set for the drill.'

What can Gajendra say to him? He might have authority

over the elephant but these other men are not as accustomed to his commands. They are sullen now and on the captain's side. 'We are almost finished,' he says.

'What good is "almost finished" in battle? You are not ready to be a *mahavat*!'

'Alexander thinks I am.'

At the mention of Alexander's name he goes berserk. He screams at the man tying the ropes of the *howdah*; he screams at Gajendra; and then, for good measure, he screams at Colossus and strikes him a glancing blow on the hindquarters with the bull hook.

He thinks he's beating a carpet. Doesn't he realize what he's doing?

Colossus screams, red-eyed with rage, and lumbers to his feet. The boys scatter. This is what happened last time, you'd think Oxathres would learn. You can be stupid or you can be vicious but being both is something Gajendra just can't understand.

A chain is attached to an iron stake in the ground and that's supposed to hold Colossus; it will, when he is calm. But when he is angry he forgets he is tethered, he forgets everything. He whirls around and the stake skitters across the dust like a twig. It hits one of the boys on the legs and he goes down howling.

Gajendra leaps at Oxathres, and knocks him to the ground. The bull hook bounces in the dirt. Gajendra jumps to his feet, throws it as far away as he can and turns around.

'*Hida! Hida!*'

Colossus shakes his head, ears standing straight out, his eyes pink, wide, terrifying.

'*HIDA!*'

Oxathres staggers to his feet. 'You assaulted your senior officer!'

'I saved your life.'

'I'll have you bullwhipped!' he shouts, but Gajendra doesn't think so. Not if Alexander hears what has happened.

'You can't beat him. Not this one. You just have to talk to him.'

'He's out of control!'

'No, I can control him.'

Colossus looms over them both, stock still, not even his trunk moving. This is like no elephant I've ever seen, Gajendra thinks. While I'm here, he holds back. A truly mad elephant would have run over the top of both of us. Right now this one looks like he is doing something a wild animal can never do.

He is considering.

'That elephant is a menace and a threat!' Oxathres looks at the bull hook lying in the dust.

Gajendra follows his eyes. 'You pick that up and he will tramp us both into the *maidan*. Is that what you want?'

The captain hesitates. The boy with the broken leg is still howling. Everyone else is staring, unsure whether to laugh or to run. The captain of the elephants has been humiliated twice in two days now.

This cannot end well.

Oxathres is so red he looks as if his head will explode. 'Get your elephant to the drill,' he says and walks away.

Colossus stands at Gajendra's shoulder.

Gajendra feels himself relax. A rubbery trunk nudges

him in the back, knocking him off balance. He looks over his shoulder at a mountain of grey flesh. Colossus picks up some dust in his trunk and blows it over him.

He is as calm as a lapdog again.

The boys finish roping the *howdah*. They have carried away the one with the broken leg.

Gajendra climbs on his neck. 'We're finished, you and I,' he says to Colossus. 'You know that, don't you? That dog Oxathres will kill us both, sooner or later.'

Colossus hoists his trunk and bellows. Everyone scatters, thinking he is crazy again, but then he settles into a slow walk, the *howdah* swaying wildly on his back. It's almost as if he understands.

The purpose of the battle training is simple: to make the elephants accustomed to the horses and make the horses accustomed to the elephants. Horses despise elephants and it takes many months of patient training before they will approach one.

The elephants, for their part, must grow accustomed to all the noises of battle. Most of the tuskers come from India, from Rajah of Taxila, and only a few have been in a battle, like Colossus. They are like men, and all have their different temperaments. At first some will run, while others will wade into the fight wholeheartedly.

The infantry are formed up into ranks, the cavalry on each flank. These are some of the best cavalry in the world. Their horses are beautiful, steel grey, but they are high, prancing and nervous with elephants around. They have been working with the elephants for months now and they are still shy when they come too close.

Gajendra recognizes the commander; it's Nearchus, the lieutenant who was with Alexander the day Colossus went berserk, the one who gave him the five silver coins. How fine he looks in his red cloak, cocksure, joking with the front row of infantry.

He sidesteps his grey towards them, along the line of elephants, controlling his stallion with his knees, his hands resting on the withers. He shouts his orders but Gajendra cannot hear a word he says above the bellowing of the other bulls and the rush of the wind. There's grit in his eyes. He wishes just to get it over with.

The cavalry ride in pairs to the heroes' wing, on Gajendra's left. The infantry put on their helmets, pick up their shields and weapons and get ready for the drill. The tuskers around him scent the air with their trunks, flaring their ears and trumpeting, frightened by the noise and the confusion. Only Colossus is quite still.

Gajendra wonders if this is what it feels like, the real thing; they said that in any battle the Indians were the first to die. Kill the *mahavat* and you kill the elephant. But I'm not going to die, Gajendra tells himself. I am going to charge to glory.

I will show Alexander what elephants can do, that's my destiny.

Nearchus's equerry waves a short staffed flag in the breeze, and the cavalry charge over the plain; he can feel the concussion of their hooves even up on Colossus's neck. The infantry advance also, beating their swords against their shields making as much noise as possible; they give their battle cry, in unison, and it is like there is no more air left to breathe.

The cavalry close in first, dust rising from their horses' hooves in a brown fog. They reverse their spears and swarm in, poking and jabbing the tuskers on the legs and flanks. Some of the horses have broken away, but most of these greys keep up the attack. Gajendra feels Colossus twitch. He kicks him behind the ear to set him going. They will meet the charge head on. He screams at the archers in the *howdah* to hang on; not that they have a choice.

Some of the elephants have broken away already and the cavalry chase them, whooping, into the river. One goes down, crushing its *mahavat* and sending the *howdah* with its archers spilling into the dirt. Just because it's a drill does not mean you can't die.

Colossus coils his trunk and flares his ears. He's game for the fight; he charges the phalanx. But the soldiers don't want to tangle with him, not even for a drill. They saw him in the *maidan*, and they know what he can do.

The archers on the ground aim without arrows; he sees one of them wave to him, letting him know that if it was real he'd have an arrow in his neck right now. He looks back at the men in the *howdah* but they would be useless in a fight with Colossus running full tilt. All they are able to do is hold onto the sides to keep from being pitched out.

Gajendra cannot see anything. The dust kicked up by the horses and elephants has obscured everything. A rider goes down right in front of him and scrambles back into the saddle as soon as his Arab is back on its feet; Colossus would have gored them both but Gajendra kicks him hard behind the ears to stop him.

He hears the boom of a drum, the signal for the manoeuvre to end.

His heart is hammering, he is covered in sweat. He has no idea where the rest of his squadron has gone. All their battle plans have been forgotten in the chaos.

Is this what a real battle will be like?

He yells for the boys with the wineskins. As the dust clears he sees that only five of the twenty elephants are left, the rest have run off into the river.

Nearchus rides through the lines, a spear overhead, held level, to signal that the two sides are to pull back. The soldiers throw down their weapons and flop down to rest.

Gajendra turns Colossus towards the river, finds the waterboys with the melons and wineskins. Colossus lets him down and follows him into the water.

Oxathres appears, ranting again. What did they all think they were doing? Nearchus is most unhappy. If that was Arabian or Numidian cavalry they would all be dead.

You will all stay out here in the sun until you find some semblance of order.

Gajendra and Oxathres exchange a glance. For all his cant, the captain of the elephants would have enjoyed it if Colossus had been one of the tuskers to run. Colossus ignores him, happily spraying water over his back.

The sounds of trumpets and horses and drums haven't frightened him at all. Gajendra watches the other *mahavats* fighting over the wineskins but he stays in the river with Colossus, patting his trunk and telling him how his mother would have been proud. Colossus may not know the words, but he knows what he's saying, Gajendra's sure of that. He tips in another watermelon. They wait for the next drill.

The elephant's trunk and face plate are smeared with watermelon pulp. His eyes sparkle behind the iron mask. It's as if he can read your mind.

CHAPTER 3

Carthage 323 BC

'YOU MUST THROW the baby into the pit.'
She is standing before the well, swaying slightly on her feet. Her eyes are turned to the side, but sightless. She sees the past, a time when the child was alive and warm in her arms. She is unsteady; one gentle push and she will topple forward into the oblivion also.

The child is mottled and grey. A girl. She is wrapped in a shroud, but Mara has pulled the folds aside so she can look one last time at her face. A tear falls on her cold cheek.

Mara takes a deep breath and sighs. She arranges the linen neatly around the child's face, so it will not trouble her in death. She wants her to look at her best in the afterworld, neat and well attended.

'No,' she murmurs, though inside her head it sounds like wailing. The priestess glances at her father. What shall I do? the look says. We cannot stand here like this forever. He gives an almost imperceptible shrug of his shoulders as if to say: I am a soldier not a devotional. This is your problem.

She puts a hand on Mara's shoulder to encourage her, but Mara does not move.

While she holds her, her daughter yet lives. She tugs at a fold in the shroud and takes out the child's hand and holds the small fingers. When she is gone there will be nothing left. For now this is enough. If I can hold her like this forever she will not be gone. The wind roars inside the well. It could be that the goddess is growing impatient. In a moment she will come up and take the child herself.

The priestess nods to her. 'See, child, the goddess wishes to take her now. She will be safe with her. She is a good mother and a kind one. There is no pain down there.'

Mara shuffles forward, a half step, another. Her arms are locked and she cannot unbend them. She strokes her baby's cheek. She imagines how cold her breasts will feel when she is gone. What is a mother without a child? Who will suckle the milk? Who will hear her whispered song?

'You must let go now.'

Mara lowers her face to the shroud. She doesn't smell like her baby any more. How did she used to smell? She tries to remember. She was all curds and warmth once. She starts to shake. The priestess guides her forward another step.

She hears her father say, 'Do it.'

At his command, she drops her baby into the well. Then she screams and falls to her knees. Her father catches her. Grief swallows her up and she screams for hours until she loses her voice.

CHAPTER 4

ALEXANDER HAS ORDERED that his pavilion is guarded by elephants in full battle armour. There are two hundred elephants and they work in shifts through the daylight hours, with canopies to shade them from the blazing sun. It is not necessary; a handful of bodyguards who know what they're about are as much deterrent as any would-be assassin needs. Gajendra supposes that he does it to intimidate visitors with the sights and the smells.

But it is how Gajendra first sees Zahara.

Alexander leaves his headquarters to make a sacrifice at the temple of marduk. His whole court is with him. He has more arse lickers than anyone he has ever known. Perhaps they go around and sweep up his dung after him, too, like the waterboys with the elephants.

Gajendra feels like he knows him now and almost expects a cheery wave. Alexander is in full regalia, the sun shining off his burnished ceremonial armour so that Gajendra must shield his eyes.

He is mantled in gold, edged in silver. He sits squat in the saddle, jaunty and smiling; Nearchus rides just behind him with Ptolemy and Perdiccas and the others he calls his Companions. They say that should Alexander die – an improbable thought, when one considers his history

– then one of these will be his anointed successor. His bodyguard rides behind, all ostrich plumes and iron, trappings jangling.

Alexander's harem are with him, mostly Persian princesses and concubines. They say he has not much use for them himself, that he uses them just for show and for bribery. He hands women out like markers: here take one, it's a favour, now you owe me. Gajendra has heard that Alexander would rather drink or fight than screw, and even then he prefers boys to girls, like most of these Macedonians – Macks.

The woman are veiled, as much to protect them from the sun and the dust as the hungry eyes of men. But the wind takes the scarf from one of them and Gajendra catches a glimpse of the most beautiful woman he has ever seen. In that instant he understands what jealousy is.

The procession passes, and he watches her until she is out of sight, a splash of violet lost in the dust thrown up by the rearguard. He closes his eyes, commits to memory the black eyes, the haughty look, the imagination of perfection.

'Did you see her?' he asks Ravi later that day, when they are relieved and washing down Colossus and Ran Bagha in the river. Ran Bagha is Ravi's elephant, smaller than Colossus and with only one tusk. The Macks think it is hilarious: a one-armed *mahavat* with a one-tusked elephant.

'What are you talking about now?'

'Did you see that girl riding behind Alexander? Could you imagine having a woman like that?'

'What woman?'

'The one with the dark eyes.'

'They're Persian. They all have dark eyes!'

'Did you see the way she looked up at me? I am going to have her one day.'

Ravi shakes his head, feeling sorry for him. 'Why would you even think about something like that? He's marrying off his harem to his officers. They're not for the likes of you!'

'Why is he giving them away?'

'Reward for services. For keeping the Macks from mutiny.'

'Mutiny?'

'Don't you ever listen to anything anyone says? The elephants know more of what's happening than you do!'

'Why would the army want to mutiny against Alexander? He's the greatest general in the world.'

'Not the army – just the Macedonians, the ones he relies on most in a fight. They're sick of it, Gaji. Some of them are old men now. They've been campaigning for years. They want to go home.'

Gajendra doesn't understand it; but then he has no home to go back to. It seems to him that the Macedonians are formidable on the battlefield, clannish and tough as spit. But they are a miserable lot when they have no one to fight, they sit with their scars and their silence, hating everyone with their eyes. They are a mountain people, raised in high valleys they call creases, which they talk about as if they are a Rajah's pleasure gardens, when it seems to him that what they really miss is rolling about in mud and conjugating with pigs.

They grumble constantly that there are too many foreigners in the army now.

Foreigners like me, Gajendra supposes.

If that's their mettle, then Alexander is better off with exotics, strong brown lads who are hungry and up for it, not these three-fingered old hacks.

'Alexander wants to march on Carthage.'

Gajendra wonders how Ravi hears these things so fast. He has a fly on every wall. 'How do you know this?'

A shrug. 'I thought everyone knew.'

'I thought we were aimed at Arabia.'

'He has to keep the Macks happy. Carthage is his compromise. He has told them they can go back if they help him take Carthage on the way. He'll sail them back from Sicily. He tells them it will be easy and there's profit in it.'

'Is it true?'

'I don't suppose so, but you know what he's like. He won't stop until he has been to both ends of the world and back and then he'll start thinking about conquering the sky.'

'Then I want to go with him.'

'Be careful what you wish for! Rise too high and the gods will knock you down!'

They start back toward Elephant Row with Colossus and Ran Bagha trailing behind. 'The gods like a man who believes in himself. Like Alexander. If you believe it can be done, you can get whatever you want.'

'You frighten me, Gaji. It scares me what will become of you if you keep talking like this.'

'Do you remember in Taxila? That archer. What was he called?'

'Mohander. And he wasn't an archer, he was an officer in the cavalry.'

'He saved the Rajah's life at the river crossing. As his reward he gave him the most beautiful girl in his harem.'

'And what good it did him! Three months later he got an arrow in his thigh and he died screaming at phantoms. Karma is karma. You can't change it.'

'I'll make my own karma, Ravi. That's what a real man does.'

But what if you don't? he thinks. What if you finish your days an elephant boy, or die in the next battle?

Well, dying is better than living afraid.

Anything is better than living afraid.

That night they sleep in the straw. Gajendra listens to the elephants and wonders what it is like to sleep next to a princess. He imagines sliding a filmy gown off a bare shoulder, the feel of satin skin, a woman smelling of jasmine and oils.

Then he imagines riding a white horse like Nearchus does, moving with speed and intent, not swaying on top of an elephant. He thinks about holding a sword, wearing armour and a red cloak; looking brilliant, purposeful.

An officer, a lion.

He stares wide-eyed at the stars and thinks about the little boy he left behind almost a decade ago. He supposes that the dacoits left him alive because it amused them better than leaving him dead. There was no other explanation for it. He feels no especial pity for his younger self, just a kind of bitter impatience.

It is only when he revisits the memory of his father dying, shivering shouting at ghosts, that he experiences a hollow anxiety. Perhaps Ravi is right, a man has his karma and there is nothing he can do about it. It is the way of the world; you catch a fever; you are left unprotected when the bandits come; you marry a princess or you sleep in the straw; luck, the fall of the stars.

But how can a man feel safe in a world where the gods control everything? Look at Alexander, he thinks. He rules the world and makes his own luck. He has become a god himself. That is the only way you can stop it, the only way you can rid yourself of this unholy dread.

You make yourself divine.

He remembers how his mother held out her hand to him as she died. The bandit who had raped her was still lying between her legs when he stuck the knife in. *Help me*, she mouthed at him. *Help me.*

He rolls on his side and tries to sleep. In his dreams he crucifies the men who did it, watches them turn black in the sun and die by inches. In reality he supposes they are still out there somewhere, laughing around the slow coals of a campfire.

The stars wheel above him, thrown across the sky like diamond chips towards Carthage; to the temple of Tanith and the general's sad-eyed daughter. He and the woman wait for Alexander to come, for if they but know it, it is only a god that can break the spell they are all under.

CHAPTER 5

Carthage

Hours later, days later, weeks later; Mara is propped on cushions in her bed. Hanno, her father, is standing in the doorway with his hands on his hips. He has two of his sergeants with him. He shakes his head. 'Look at you.'

'Just go away.'

He bawls for the servants, cuffs the first that arrives for her negligence. 'Why did you not send for me before? What sort of creature are you?'

She knows how she must look from the way he stares at her. He has that same face when he comes home from a campaign or an execution.

He grabs her chamberlain by the ear. 'Look at her. Have you been bathing her, feeding her? She looks like a body on the street. Why did you not send for me?'

'She forbade it!' the old man protests, but he doesn't hear it for he has already booted him out of the door.

'It's time to get yourself back on your feet,' he says and throws open the shutters. She winces at the light.

He gets her maidservant to fetch water and turns his

back while she washes her. He folds his arms and gives directions. *You will do this, you will do that.*

I don't care, she thinks. I would not care if the Shades rose up now and dragged me down there with them. I have not strength for anything.

How long has she been like this? he demands of the servant girl.

Even Mara does not know. It's not the servant's fault, she wants to say. Every time they came in I screamed abuse at them and told them to get out. I threw a chamber pot at one of them and it was full.

The only difference now is they are more afraid of you than they are of me. Anyway, it's not their fault, it's yours. You went to Lilybaeum the day after I gave the last surviving piece of my life to Tanith. If you want to yell and shout at someone, find a deep pool and take a look at yourself. You think more of Carthage than you do of me.

But then, she knows he blames himself too for the state she is in. But he cannot ignore his employer's demands. He may be a general but they can just as easily turn on him. He lives as much on a sword's edge as any of the city's enemies.

The girl lifts her from the bed and carries her to the hip bath, now warmed with scented water. She is surprised that she can lift her so easily, the maid is a sturdy girl but not that strong. Am I so thin now that even a woman might carry me? She rests her hand on the girl's shoulder. It is difficult to breathe. She starts to cry and the girl rubs her back and tries to console her. She would like to rest her head on her servant's breast, like an infant.

When she is done the maid wraps her in a long towel

and her father takes her. He is still angry and will not look at her. This is what he is good at: being angry and taking charge.

'Where are we going?' she says.

'You will come and live with me. I will make sure you are looked after.'

'Why don't you just let me be?'

'Because you are my daughter. I will not stand idly by while you do this to yourself.'

There is a litter and bearers waiting in the court.

'There is no need for this,' he tells her. 'You will love again. You are young. You turned men's heads once. You shall again. I will not let you give up on your life.'

Was it how he got over the death of her mother? Dusted off his hands and straightened his tunic once she was cold. She had never seen him grieve.

The chamberlain rushes after them across the court-yard, calling her name. He holds in his hands a ring and a small blanket. He hands them to her and she accepts them, gratefully.

'What are they?' her father asks.

She does not answer so he asks the chamberlain next.

'The blanket is the one she used to wrap her babies when they were born. The ring was given her by her husband before he sailed to Panormus with their son.'

Her father wrenches the blanket free and throws it in the sand. The ring she has already put on her finger. He struggles with her and works it loose. She is so thin now that it no longer fits snug. He hurls it away. She sobs.

'You do not need to be continually reminded of the past! Let it go!'

She silently appeals to the chamberlain but he shrugs helplessly and does not move. He thinks her father would cut him down if he did and perhaps he is right.

'There is no sense to this continual grieving. They are gone and they are not coming back! We must live and carry on!'

He sees one of the maidservants scrambling for the ring in the sand. 'What are you doing, girl?' he bawls at her in frustration.

'She will want it back, sir.'

'Leave it be! She is never getting it back. All of you, listen to me! Your services are no longer required. I will find you all new masters. You have failed me and you have failed her. Now go! Get out of here, all of you!'

The lush suburbs of Megara are out past the great triple city wall and overlook miles of vineyards and farms where goats stand in the black shade of olive trees and red water gurgles between date palms.

Her father brings her a broth and feeds it to her himself. She shuts her eyes so she does not have to meet his eyes.

He settles on the revision of her future; a new husband, new babies. He is going to take a broom to her grief. Tidy it away and assign it to the whimsy of the gods. She hears him form up his philosophy and would like for a moment to reach inside and transfer a little of her grief into him, watch him shrink and wither also, as if he had put his hand unexpectedly into a fire. But the effort of contending with him is too taxing. She nods as if she agrees with his summation of life and fate and loss.

Her heart is disjointed and it is easier that way.

'You are looking better,' he says when he has fed her the broth. He stands up, satisfied. She feels like one of his soldiers: there, you have lost an arm and a leg and your manhood, but never mind, some rest and some of my excellent soup and you'll be as good as new.

She puts a hand to her breast. They should be swollen with new milk. She feels as withered as an old woman.

'You cannot just give up,' he says again.

But he fails to add a reason. Why can I not just give up? My children are gone, my husband also. I might be consoled by my sister, if the gods had not been lonely for her too.

I wish I had his stout courage; the way he forms up his troops, reorganizes the ranks after every bloody defeat, straightens lines, makes new strategy. Life surrounds him in better tactical position and he shouts bloody defiance and charges its flanks.

I am not like him. I would rather lie here in the middle ground and wait for the final sword thrust with the rest of the maimed and wounded.

He stands there, massive and helpless. He has the salt and pepper hair of a survivor and there are few enough of those among the generals of Carthage. Unlike him, I have no sense of tactical withdrawal. I have committed all my troops to a man who is lost at the bottom of the ocean with all hands, he is gone along with the children he gave me. A good soldier would never find himself cut off like this, with no means of retreat.

'Tomorrow I will take you for a walk in the garden,' he says and his voice breaks. It startles her.

The moment passes. He straightens, gives her a smile like a rallying cry. 'Yes, a walk in the garden will make you feel better,' he says and marches out before he breaks ranks and weeps.

Peacocks call from the darkness beyond the silvered lawns; the sound of the cicadas is deafening. She lies on a fresh linen sheet in a strange bed.

Her father's servants feed her and wash her while he hovers, worrying that she is still too thin; he sends musicians to play music, takes her for long walks in the garden, always tiresomely cheerful.

She hears him berating the servants; can you not make something more appetizing for her than this? Do not go in there scowling like that! Smile, be cheerful! She wonders he does not berate the birds outside her window for not singing loud enough. Tree, can you not provide better flowers?

Her arms feel empty. She thinks about soldiers she has seen begging in the street without limbs. Do they feel like this?

The servants whisper about her. She has gone mad, she hears the chambermaid say to a serving girl. She lost her husband and her children and her sister all inside a few months and it has turned her mind.

Have you seen how thin she is? the other whispers. She looks like a skeleton. And so pale! The cook says she cannot keep her food down.

And they say she was a real beauty once! I wish she would get better or die, for she is driving the poor master mad like this. And we are the ones who pay for it!

*

36

The lawns of her father's villa stretch down to the sea wall where the fat boles of the palm trees plump themselves in the sand like old women out for some sea air. From her bed she watches a slave pruning an ilex tree. Her limbs are black and shine in the sun.

She decides to go downstairs and surprise her father at his breakfast. His face registers astonishment, then delight. He thinks she is better, and his long campaign against doom is won. 'Well, look at you. I do believe you've put on a little weight.'

She sits down. 'Thank you for all you have done.'

He stops chewing and throws the hunk of bread on the table. He senses from her tone that a pronouncement is coming and he doesn't like those. 'You're not anywhere near ready to leave.'

'I've decided what I'm going to do.'

'I'm your father. I'll decide that.'

She shakes her head.

'What does that mean?'

'I am going to devote my life to the service of Tanith.'

He laughs, then sees that she is serious. 'I will not allow it.'

'Then I will stop eating.'

His shoulders sag. His force of will has carried battles and councils but he cannot overrule shattered hopes.

It's too soon to decide things, he says. He has a big house and all these servants; why doesn't she just rest, take her ease in the garden and listen to his lute player and pray for his success when he goes to Sicily to fight the damned Greeks in Syracuse?

'We should think about this.'

'For weeks now I have done nothing but think. My mind is made up.'

'But the priestesses are all women without hope.'

'As am I.'

'I will find you another husband.'

'I do not want another husband. If the gods wanted me to have a husband why did they take the one I had? I'll never find one better so I really do not see any point in it.'

'You can't just give up.'

'I am not giving up.'

He slams his hands on the table, startling her. 'Right, so shall we understand this then? The gods play fast and loose with my daughter, tear out her heart and take away everything she lives for, and so after she has dragged herself back to the land of the living she says she will go and light their incense every day and clean their statues and say their prayers for them?'

'We cannot fight the gods.'

'Watch me,' he growls, with a tilt of his chin.

She touches her belly. It feels so empty. She misses her baby's little kicks. She liked to put her hand there and imagine she could feel her daughter's heart beating through her skin.

She once thought of climbing to the rooftop and leaping off but even dying requires a certain strength that she no longer possesses. And what if the roof were not high enough? She could not bear to die slowly. That is the trouble with the faint-hearted, she thinks, cowards endure more pain than the brave.

Her father hides his face from her. He is calling for reinforcements he does not have. She understands how much he loves her but it is not enough. She wants only what she had before.

In truth, he has lost as much as she. She imagines the life he should have had also: children running around his knees, a large family gathered around his long table, piles of bread and steaming meat, shouting and laughter, he at the hub of it.

Instead here he is at the head of an empty table, with fresh baked bread he has no appetite for, arguing with a recalcitrant daughter who will not join him at the barricade in his rearguard struggle against circumstance.

Woodenly, he gets to his feet. He leans on the table with his knuckles. 'Why? Why would you do this? There have been widows before and there will be widows again.'

Mara considers his question. Why does she miss her husband so much? She recalls how, after her sister had died, he took her head in his hands and kissed the top of it, not saying anything, his silence as reassuring as any consolation. Unlike her father, he had never tried to take away her sadness, only reshape it.

She had leaned her head on his chest with her arms at her sides. Feeling sad with someone you loved was the greatest strength there was. He had reminded her of the palms along the road to the port, all of them bending with every breeze so that they would never break.

She wondered if he had fought when his ship had capsized. She imagined rather that he had just shrugged when he saw the sea rise up and slid in without even a splash. The waves would have been disappointed with him.

'We will talk more about this. You are not in your right mind.'

'Thank you for what you have done for me. I am sorry I have caused you such pain.'

'You will come around, you'll see. You just need time. Sometimes life takes us along strange and painful byways to help us find the things we need, even though they are not the things we want.'

She bows her head and does not answer. There is no point. She knows what will happen. She will be ordained at the temple. At first, he will miss her, and then he will be angry. Then he will join his army again. He will go on.

'What made you think of Tanith?'

'She has my baby. If I am at the temple every day I will be near her.'

'Your baby is gone.'

Mara shook her head. 'Sometimes at night, when it is quiet, I can still hear her heart beating. Do you remember how big her eyes were?'

'I will not allow you to do this!' he says, still shouting defiance, and storms out. 'We will talk more about this.'

She sighs. Now her future is decided she feels better. The goddess will know what to do with her. It is the struggling that's hard; once you accept that you cannot have what you long for, then life becomes so much easier to bear.

At the temple, at least, she will be safe from life.

CHAPTER 6

Babylon

BY AUTUMN ALEXANDER is ready. They are going to march north-west to Tyre, then down to Egypt and along the coast to Carthage. The men don't like it; the murmurings that Ravi had told him about are no longer secret. The men shout their discontents at Alexander as he rides past.

Alexander appears untroubled when he addresses them. There is not a city or state he has not conquered, a battle he has not won. The word is that he will not be content until he has the entire Mediterranean in his jaws.

Gajendra says to Ravi, 'They have never seen elephants where we are going. We will carry the day everywhere and one day I will be captain of the elephants!'

Ravi seems alarmed. 'Let the gods decide, Gaji.'

In public Alexander's generals are all smiles, riding behind him like peacocks. But rumour has it there have been drunken arguments in Alexander's pavilion, food thrown, daggers produced. Everyone knows how Alexander once put a handy spear through one of his best friends when he dared to challenge him. He is dangerous sober. In his cups you might as well bait a tiger.

The worst of it, the Macedonians say, is that their great king has gone native.

Did they go to all this trouble defeating these pansies and Persians just to have them take over their army? There are even Persians among his own Companion Cavalry now. And what do they need with barbers and bathmasters, wine stewards and pastry makers? Alexander even has a night porter now. And look at all these fops with greased ringlets and perfumed beards hanging around the court, it seems he's taking a liking to all their bowing and scraping.

What will they make of us back home if they could see us?

To head off trouble Alexander has sent some of the more disaffected of the Macedonians home with Kraterus. When he gets there Kraterus is to assume the regency from Antipater, who currently rules in Macedon in Alexander's place. Antipater has been ordered to Alexander's side with fresh troops to assist in his current campaign. Everyone knows what that means: soon after he arrives, Antipater will end up on a cross and turn black in the sun. No one knows what he has done to offend Alexander; become too efficient perhaps. No king can afford able princes in times of discontent, even one old enough to be his father.

Two of Antipater's sons are already in Babylon; Iolaus is already Alexander's cupbearer and another, Kassander, arrived just a few weeks before to plead his father's case. Apparently the audience did not go well. Kassander left the pavilion with blood on his face.

Ravi looks doleful when he recounts Alexander's plans. 'You cannot take elephants across the desert. They will all die and most of us with them. He is mad!'

'All gods are mad,' Gajendra replies.

'The Macks say they have had enough.'

'Enough of what? Enough of winning battles?'

'You only say that because you have never been in a battle yourself. Some of these old goats have been with him for years, since he first came to Persia. What's the point of winning all this loot if you don't live to spend it?'

But Ravi makes no sense to him. He cannot imagine living without the stink of the elephants, the anticipation of the next city. They have been in Babylon a year now and already it seems an entire history.

'I have heard there is a plot against him,' Ravi whispers.

Gajendra moves closer. 'Against Alexander? What have you heard?'

'One of the Macks said that Alexander will never leave Babylon.'

More likely they would pull Zeus out of the sky and kick him to death. It is a bizarre notion. 'He is immortal,' Gajendra says.

'So is every king. Until he dies.'

Ravi tells him what others have said. The country called Egypt was once ruled by a race of kings called pharaohs. Alexander has installed his satrap in their place, and has named a new capital after himself. It is a dark place, Ravi says. The people eat the brains of the dead and keep their vitals in jars. Then they wrap them in sheets and put them in coffins that look like women.

And Carthage is a long march across the desert. They will only be able to take a handful of elephants, because there is not enough water, and when they get there the city is guarded by three walls, high as ten men and almost as thick. The Macks all say that Alexander will die there.

Gajendra shakes his head. A soldier opens his mouth and the wind blows his tongue about. 'I did not join this army to march elephants up and down the *maidan*. No soldier ever found his destiny in peacetime.'

That night in his sleep he goes home. His mother is outside with his sisters pounding the rice, he hears the rhythmic *tonk-tonk* as they work in unison. They are talking and giggling as girls do, his mother is chiding them for being slow.

He hears men approaching on horseback and he runs outside. They are silhouetted against a copper sun. He feels the earth shudder under his feet.

Then he wakes. The sweat has risen on his skin, like a cold grease. Unable to sleep, he checks the patrols on Elephant Row.

He finds Colossus in the straw. He will not rise no matter how he chides him. It is early and the boys are still asleep. He lies there like a grey, heaving mountain. His trunk flicks feebly at the dust. It occurs to him that the horses he thought he heard in his dream was actually Colossus, struggling to breathe.

'So we must fetch an elephant doctor now?' the captain says the next morning, and he positively glows with satisfaction.

Ravi and the boys stand around, helpless. They bring Colossus water, and apples, which are his favourite, but nothing will tempt him to rise or show interest. A scour runs out of him. He stinks.

Gajendra sinks to his knees. How could this happen?

'What about the rest of the elephants?' he asks Ravi.

'All the others are fine. It's just Colossus.'

Gajendra feels Colossus watching him with his small, flat eye. He looks bewildered and betrayed. But an elephant can't feel those things. It's just his imagination.

Gajendra does not sleep that night. He talks to his elephant. He tells him he's going to be all right, tells him how they will build a statue for him one day, right in the main square in Carthage, then one in Alexandria, in Athens, in Macedon; that he will be the most famous elephant in the whole world.

He feels as if Colossus can understand him, though he is only an animal. His eye follows him as he moves around, though he cannot move that massive head. Death pours out of him in a dark brown stain. The flies torment him. Gajendra fans him with a palm leaf, keeping them off as best he can. He supposes they sense a great feast here in a day or two.

He tries to remember the things his uncle taught him about elephants and their ailments but he has heard of nothing like this.

Ravi is awake early and comes to sit by him. They watch the great creature suffer. Ravi breaks a twig off a nearby tree and places it inside his trunk to keep his airway open. 'I wish my uncle were here. He would know what to do.'

He has tried Soldier's Friend, dried yarrow petals, used to stop bleeding and for fever, but how much do you give a tusker the size of a house? He puts a handful in a bucket of hot water, but getting Colossus to drink the mixture is a labour that takes him half the day. It does no good anyway.

They seek out one of Alexander's physicians; he knows something of animals, and fries the leaves and flowers of the Beni Kai plant. It makes a sort of potion and he tries to get Colossus to drink it but when he's lying on his side it just dribbles out and he's too weak to stand up and drink it, even if he has a mind to do it.

Gajendra imagines the massive workings inside, lungs like bellows as big as a man, labouring to push that massive chest up and down; a heart as big as a chariot hammering the beat like a slaver's drum but slowing with every strike.

He goes back to Alexander's physician, looking for another remedy. There is this, he says. I brought it back with me from Taxila, one of the Rajah's doctors gave it to me, but the dose is uncertain. Give a man too much and it kills him anyway.

'How much do you give an elephant?' Gajendra asks him.

He just shrugs and gives him the powder, tells him to mix it with warm water.

Gajendra sniffs at it and winces. 'But how can I make him drink this? It's foul.'

'It's not for drinking,' the old quack says, grinning. 'You have to find some other way to get it inside him. Strip down and get to work!'

So now here he stands up to his elbows in elephant shit, pale and drained from lack of sleep, and Oxathres walks in. He takes one look at Colossus and frowns as if he is asking himself: why isn't he dead yet?

'We move soon, with or without him. Alexander's orders. If he is too sick I will replace him with Asaman Shukoh.'

'We cannot leave him behind.'

'It looks like we have no choice. The other beasts are better managed than this one.'

'He's the best warrior elephant we have.'

'Not any more, he's not,' Oxathres says. He wrinkles his nose. 'You like sticking your hand up an elephant's arse, son?' he says and walks out again, laughing.

'Don't listen to him. I won't let you die,' Gajendra promises. 'I won't let them leave you behind.'

Occasionally he bellows, a pitiful sound that leaves them all covering their ears. 'He is dying,' Ravi says. 'He is scouring from the inside. There's something in his vitals. Something he has eaten. What can we do?'

'While we have breath in us, we keep going. And so will he.'

He imagines his father sitting with him through the vigil that night. 'The resin will settle him,' he says. 'If he can see his way to the morning, your old tusker will be all right.'

CHAPTER 7

GAJENDRA WAKES TO a shadow across the moon. Colossus is standing up. He waves his trunk weakly side to side.

See, you thought I was done for, didn't you?

He wants to laugh out loud. Instead he runs down to the river; the important thing now is water. He kicks the boys awake, gets them to fetch buckets of apples. Another few days before they are set to march and Colossus has to have his strength back by then. What had seemed impossible is now merely difficult.

The next morning a young Macedonian officer arrives, on his horse, self-important and sweating. Alexander himself is coming to visit. He is concerned at the news he has been hearing. Is he to lose his best elephant?

Gajendra sets the boys to scouring him, using rags to remove the stains from his hindquarters, others to paint him with henna, make him look fierce. Soon he is polished like a newborn and caparisoned in red and ochre.

He stands before the animal himself and issues new instructions. I want him looking ready for the charge! Gajendra tells his boys. Set to on the ivory, paint the tips scarlet. Braid his tail!

Colossus looks baleful.

'Don't look at me like that. If he sees you stagger he will leave you behind or carve you up for beef. Bellow at him. Stamp your foot. Don't let him see you weak. He despises weakness. He once fought a battle with an arrow through his chest!'

Alexander stamps in, in his golden armour. 'I heard the beast was dead,' he says.

'As you can see, my lord, rumours of his end were greatly exaggerated.'

Oxathres stands behind their king, looking very unhappy indeed.

'I don't want to lose him. They don't have these where we're going.'

'He will kill ten thousand of your enemies on his own,' Gajendra says. He looks at Colossus, who sways dangerously, like a tree about to come down. Their eyes meet. He swears the animal winks at him.

Alexander turns on his captain of the elephants. 'I suspect that you have risen above your ability,' he says and walks out.

That's it. The audience is over. They are all going to Carthage.

Gajendra finds a melon. Colossus opens that huge pink mouth. Gajendra tosses it in and laughs out loud. He wants to hug him.

The look on Oxathres's face.

CHAPTER 8

EVERY GIRL IN Babylon, once in her life, is required to offer herself to the goddess. It is a sign of great piety to offer Mylitta her virginity.

So the courtyard temple is always packed with women, sitting in sombre rows, separated from each other by scarlet cords. The first man who tosses a piece of silver into her lap can have her, and it is her duty to the goddess not to refuse.

No woman is too fine to overlook her obligation; no man so low that he might be rejected. Princesses sit on silk cushions, perspiring with exquisite delicacy while their slaves stand to the side with fans; next to them peasant girls with calloused hands and sun-hardened faces sit glum and alone on the baking marble.

Men stroll between them as if they are at a horse fair. They might as easily find a lady today as a farmer's daughter. It is all there for the taking.

Some of the less favoured girls sit there for days on end, just waiting. A beauty might not be there long enough to warm the stone.

Gajendra has Alexander's silver and he plans to use it well for his first time. They are heading to Carthage in a few days. Who knew if a first time might also be the last?

He arrives at the temple just after dawn, hoping to avoid the crowds. He wishes to do this with dignity, not get into a shoving match with a drunken ferryman over who saw who first. He strolls along the lines, trying to avoid outstretched hands. He is flattered that he is so sought after; he supposes that being young and better favoured than most, the girls would prefer him to some ditch digger with bad teeth.

And then he stops, has to catch his breath. It is *her*, the girl he saw riding behind Nearchus in Alexander's procession. She is just as exquisite now as she was seen in a blur of dust over the heads of the other gawpers. She appears surreal in a long white diaphanous gown. It has a wide scarlet belt with a gold chain dangling from the buckle. Her blue-black hair is braided down her back.

She has just arrived; she has two slaves with her, one to choose the perfect place for such a delicate bottom to rest, another to fan away the flies. The other girls eye her bitterly, jealous of her looks and her wealth. There is a commotion all around her; it will be a while before she is settled. As if she thought it might take so long!

He experiences panic; he has to get there before any other sees her. She has her back to him, is waiting for her slave to finish brushing dust from the marble and set out her pillows.

He takes Alexander's silver siglos from his leather pouch, hurries over and holds them out to her. 'May Mylitta prosper you.'

She raises her eyes. They are a stunning violet colour,

and her casual glance leaves him gawping like a bumpkin. She cups her hands for the coins then passes them to one of her slaves. Later she will offer them to the goddess, and her duty to the temple will be done.

She gives a little tremulous sigh and holds out her hand.

He leads her through the temple, past the glares of the less favoured. 'She didn't even get to sit down!' he hears one of the girls hiss as they pass. She walks with her eyes down, but there is no humility in it; she might have been going to her own coronation. Her pride excites him.

'My name's Gajendra,' he tells her.

Not even a nod. It is as if she had not heard him.

'What is your name?'

'You have paid for my virginity, not my conversation,' she answers, and that haughty reply is what changes his mind and makes him do what he does.

She keeps her eyes to the ground once they are inside the grove. A pair of hairy buttocks writhe in front of them, a carter skewering some poor girl against a fig tree. They almost fall over another coupling on the ground. She does not comment. Her hand feels cool in the morning heat.

Over there a man is at it like a dog, taking his choice from behind and making a sound very much like howling. Gajendra is disgusted. He looks for a quiet spot, finds a little shade, secluded by bushes.

He lets go of her hand. She gives another forbearing sigh and waits.

He takes her chin and tilts her face to look at him. 'Listen to me, there's something I have to tell you.'

She still looks faintly bored.

'My name is Gajendra. Remember my name, and my face. Gajendra. At the moment I am just a *mahavat* in Alexander's army, but one day I will be counted among his finest officers. Nothing will stop me from achieving that aim, nothing.'

Still no response.

'I know I could never possess a woman like you as I am. I do not want a moment's pleasure up against a tree, that is not why I chose you. What I want from you is not something I can buy for a few pieces of silver. I want you for my own, forever.'

Her eyes widen a little. She doesn't look bored now; just scared.

'So you can leave the grove with your duty to the goddess done and your maidenhood yet intact.'

She frowns, not quite understanding.

'Remember me. Gajendra. *Gajendra.* One day you will be mine by right and for always.'

And then he turns and walks away from her. For a moment there is pure exhilaration. And then he almost doubles over with the horror of what he has done. He wants to beat his head against a tree.

'You idiot!' he mutters, as he fully realizes his loss. 'You idiot!'

He has just surrendered his chance to have the woman of his dreams. What was he thinking?

Yet there is another part of him that remains calm and resolute. He has set the stakes; he has now made his dream real, has declared it aloud in front of the gods. The only thing to do now is to perform the impossible as Alexander has done. To conquer the world, to marry a princess; a man must first believe it can be done. He has come close enough to touch his dream, to feel her sweet breath on his cheek. He will move heaven and earth to have her as close again.

One day she will say his name. Gajendra. *Gajendra.*

And she will say it with a sigh.

May the gods bear witness.

The camp is like a small town and gossip travels fast: Alexander has decided to delay the march to allow Colossus time to recover. He has never done anything like this before. Well, that is not quite true; he once threatened to lay waste an entire country after someone stole his horse, even though the beast was old and practically lame in one leg. He wept like a boy when the tribesmen who took it brought it back.

The morning clatters on; men playing dice; a clash of swords from the practice yard; the boys mucking out the yard where they keep the beasts. Colossus sways his trunk as he dips into the apple barrel, trumpeting loudly. Two days ago he could not even find his feet.

He has put a guard on him. *No one is to feed him unless I am present*, he has told them. *No one!*

There is a hazy sun. The trees are a lurid green, the wind picks up a gritty sand that stings the eyes and sticks in the throat, everything smells of the shit the locals use as fertilizer. He will be glad to get away from here.

'I know who did it,' he tells Ravi.

'Who did what?'

'I know who poisoned Colossus.'

'You don't know it was poison. He got sick just like

a man does. It is a foul humour that brought him down.'

Gajendra shakes his head, swearing under his breath when he sees the captain of the guard go by. 'What if I did it now? Just put a knife between his ribs right here in the yard. What do you think Alexander would do to me?'

'You know what he would do. Let it go. Do your friend Ravi a favour instead.'

'You need money?'

'I'll pay you back.'

'Why do you need money to pay other people when you owe me so much? Or is that what you do all day, go around begging money in a great circle?'

'Just two siglos.'

'Two siglos! You lose that much at dice?'

'It's not so much. I saw Alexander's lieutenant give you *five* from his purse.'

'I spent it.'

His interest is piqued. 'On what? On a whore? What tart charges that much?'

Gajendra doesn't answer.

'Was she a virgin then? Must have been a pretty one. What was it like?'

'It was fine.'

'Fine?'

'Fine.'

Ravi puts his face in Gajendra's. 'Fine? You get yourself a girl at last and that's it, *fine*.'

'What do you want me to say?'

He narrows his eyes. 'You didn't do it, did you?'

Gajendra looks the other way.

'So where's the money?'

'I told you, I don't have it.'

'You couldn't get it up and you still let her keep the money?'

'I can get it up.'

'I don't believe you.'

'I don't care what you believe. It's none of your business. I have to go into the town.'

'You can't go. There's a drill.'

'Colossus is not well enough for the drill. I'll be back later.'

'Where are you going?'

He doesn't answer. He walks off, leaving Ravi staring after him, bewildered.

Babylon means Gate of God; they said the black walls had been built by a king called Nebuchadnezzar when Alexander's ancestors were still living in caves and eating each other. They look like cliffs and there are over a hundred gates of solid bronze. It would take a man two days to walk around them and return where he had started.

There is a hot dry wind, ideal for flying kites. They love kites here, or anything that snaps in the wind; every noble house has its own standards, irrigation huts fly rafts of banners, every building in the city has some sort of bunting. Out on the *maidans* kite masters fly extravagant creations of pressed flax dyed to dazzling colours, and every imaginable shape – there are swallows, butterflies and carp. The more kites a man has, the higher his station. It makes for great spectacle, though it didn't help that much at Gaugamela.

You go in by the Ishtar Gate, all gold and lapis, after you have paid your coin to the ferryman to take you across the Euphrates, cramming in his water taxi with the lovers and the merchants and the hawkers. Gajendra looks up at the towers, burned brick and bitumen so high they merge with the sky. They say from the top you can see all the way to Macedon.

Inside the gates it reeks of incense; the people love their gods here. And they love plants too – the city is a riot of greenery, everyone has a roof garden. It is a city fired and glazed in colour, where they jabber to each other in Sumerian but will take your money in any language you care to choose.

The shops in this city cater for every kind of depravity. These Persians would rather fuck than fight, or so Ravi says, but Gajendra is not so sure after seeing this. He gapes like a farmboy; do they need these whips and phalluses between dusk and dawn? Perhaps when the appetite grows jaded, he supposes, though he cannot imagine growing so old there should ever be a time he would find the need for an olive wood penis.

He asks some hook-nosed hustler for an apothecary. There are two worthy of the name, he is told. It takes him all morning to find the first, but when he tells him what he needs the man laughs at him and says that it's impossible.

The second shop is no more than a hole in the wall. Inside there are shelves lined with jars and flasks. A crocodile gapes its jaws at him, terrifying even though long dead. There are dead men's skulls, a still, a set of scales. It smells like a tomb.

The shopkeeper is cautious. He has a certain look about

57

him; if he is not guilty of the crime against his elephant, then he is guilty of many other things, he can tell this much by looking at him.

When Gajendra tells him he wants white hellebore, he becomes suddenly wary. 'Why do you want this?'

'But you can get it?'

'It will be difficult.'

'Come on, don't tell me you can't. You got it for my captain!'

The apothecary's eyes drop. He looks around the room, either for a weapon or a route of escape. 'I don't know what you're talking about.'

Gajendra grabs him by the throat and pushes him against the wall. The apothecary would like to scream but he can't get his air. 'Now listen,' Gajendra says and lodges his knee into the man's groin to sharpen his concentration, 'all I want from you is the truth. Otherwise I'll slice you up and put you in a jar up there with the snake's droppings.'

His eyes acquiesce. Gajendra releases his grip on his throat but only a little. 'Tell me what happened.'

'I only supply. It is not my fault what a man does with such things.'

'Didn't you ask him what it was for?'

'He said he wanted it as a purge. I told him to take care with it, that he should not use more than a pinch each morning. Has he done murder with it?'

'He tried.' He releases the man but his legs won't hold him and he flops onto the floor.

So it was Oxathres, just as he thought.

He reaches into the apothecary's belt and takes out his

purse. He extracts five silver coins and drops it back into his lap. Then he steps over him and goes to the doorway.

'Wait! You are robbing me? Is that what this is all about?'

'I'm accepting a loan on very favourable terms. If I ever see you in the street I will slit your throat.' He leaves.

Now for the captain of the elephants.

CHAPTER 9

HE STANDS AT the waterfront, among the bustle of hawkers and shovers and pickpockets and merchants and procurers; he smells spitted meat and baking bread and his stomach growls but he cannot eat. There is too much murder in his heart.

I have to do something about this. It is him or me now.

But when he gets back to Elephant Row he cannot find the captain. The waterboys say he disappeared after the drill that morning and they haven't seen him since. It is toward evening when someone points to him heading out of the camp. Gajendra follows him.

He looks furtive and Gajendra takes pains not to be seen. A Macedonian officer is waiting for Oxathres near an olive grove and there is something about the way they are talking that makes him cautious. They make their way along one of the irrigation channels to a hut used by the government officials whose job it is to inspect the complex system of waterways. They go inside and he hears them bar the door.

He takes off his sandals and climbs up the wooden ladder at the back of the hut and onto the flat roof. A hole has been cut for a cooking fire and if he lies beside it he can hear them talking below.

'You look like you have the flux,' a man's voice says. 'Get a hold on yourself, man, or we'll never get this done.'

Then Oxathres: he'd know that grating whine anywhere. 'My lord, you don't understand the risk I am taking.'

'You think the danger is any less for me? I'll die with you if we're discovered.'

'I won't betray you.'

'Of course you would, if his torturer is at you with his knives and irons.'

Death? Torture? This is bad business they're about. The gods have shaken the tree and let the captain of the elephants fall in his lap. This is not about elephants; Oxathres has more on his mind than murdering Colossus. He wonders if they can hear his heartbeat down there. It sounds too loud to him. Any moment they will look up and wonder who it is pounding on the roof with a stave.

It is getting towards evening and the sun drops behind the city. With the twilight the mosquitoes are out and swarming. He dares not swat at them. They buzz impudently in his ear as if they know his predicament. Look at me, I shall bite you on the eye and you cannot do a thing about it.

'You have the poison?'

'I had an apothecary in the town make it up for me.'

'And you have tested it?'

'Well enough.'

'It must be slow. If he dies quick it will raise suspicion and give his friends reason to accuse me.'

'They say it resembles a fever, like the one he had in India. Once it takes hold a man dies measure by measure, from the inside out.'

'You had better be right. We cannot fail at this.'

'You have the means to deliver it?'

'My brother is Alexander's cupbearer. What do you think?'

The itching on his bare legs is unbearable; yet he must bear it. Start slapping away at these midges now and they will be up here with their swords out to fillet him. They have said enough yet he wishes they will say something more; he has enough for accusation but not for proof.

The first stars are blinking above the desert.

'It is harsh to kill him this way.'

'I would rather he died frothing than drag me across that fucking desert for yet another campaign. Our men will laud us as their saviours. They want to go home.'

They have lit a candle in the room. He resists the urge to peek down. He remembers the captain's fellow conspirator well enough: reddish hair, broad shoulders in a red cloak, the bearing of a general. He believes he has seen him before, in a procession; it is Kassander, the son and envoy of Antipater, who rules Greece in Alexander's absence.

'You will remember me when all is done?' Oxathres says.

'You will get your reward, never doubt that.'

They leave separately and he listens till their footsteps have receded before he dares a glimpse above the parapet. They are silhouetted against the evening headed in different directions and on foot. At last he can take his revenge on the midges, one of them so fat with his blood that when he squashes it, he looks as if he has been knifed in the leg.

Almost night. Above him the stars are swinging across a deepening sky. Only the gods that ride them know their future promise. If he gets back to the camp alive he at least knows what they foretell for himself and for the captain.

Alexander no longer sleeps alongside his men. Gajendra comes from a place where you would expect nothing less of a Rajah. But the Macks are in a froth about it. It seems the general can do nothing these days without the phalanx muttering into their beards and spitting into the fire.

A sense of paranoia has overtaken the great Alexander; he has abandoned the grand pavilion he captured from the Persian king, Darius. It is the size of a parade ground, you could stable horses in it. But he now prefers the palace and leaves his soldiers to sleep on the other side of the river. He fears assassins, some say; others think that as he now considers himself a god, he believes he should live like one.

Guard dogs yelp and growl behind the palace gates. A sentry looks him up and down and laughs at him when he requests entry.

'What the fuck have you done to yourself?' the guard asks him. 'What's wrong with your face?'

'I was bitten by mosquitoes.'

'You look like you've been in a fight.'

'I have to see Alexander.'

'Who the hell are you?'

'My name's Gajendra, I'm a *mahavat* with the elephant squadron.'

'Well, see here, Gajendra. Fuck off.'

'But I must see Alexander.'

'Leave a petition with his scribe in the morning.'

The gatehouse door slams.

He hammers on it with his fist. The guard comes out again, asks another guard to hold his spear and then kicks Gajendra across the street. 'Look here, lad, I won't have this. If you do that again, I'll grab your ankle and bash you up against the wall like a cat. Now get out of here.'

But the commotion has woken the captain of the guard. He storms into the torchlight, still buttoning his tunic; he has been screwing a servant girl and the commotion has put him off his stroke. 'What's going on out here?'

The guard snaps off a salute. 'We have here a skinny little gyppo. He wants to see Alexander and won't fuck off when he's told.'

'I'm not a gyppo. I'm a *mahavat* with the elephants, his finest.'

The captain's face is a study. All his men have to do is guard the door and only open it to a password, not get into brawls with elephant boys. It seems a simple enough task. 'What are you doing here?' he says to Gajendra, still buckling his sword belt.

'I have to see Alexander. There is a plot against him.'

'What's a young lad like you got to do with plotting?'

'I overheard two men speaking. I know one of them, I saw him riding with Alexander in procession. He plans to poison him.'

The captain stands there, considering. Gajendra feels blood trickle down his forehead where the guard has struck him.

'How did you come by this information?'

Oh, you know, by chance. I was out looking for the captain of the elephants, planning to bash his brains in with my *ankus*, throw him in a ditch, hope no one notices and then here he is, plotting to kill our king. 'I overheard him speaking. The plot is real. He fully intends to carry it out.'

The captain grabs the guard by the tunic and pushes him out of the way. His dilemma plays on his face: there's a promotion or a horse-whipping in this.

'You'd better come with me,' he says to Gajendra.

They go deep into the palace, the captain's studded sandals echoing on the stone. Torches flare in brackets on the walls. Gajendra counts six gates before they get to the final one. Once all there was between Alexander and his army was a strip of canvas and a guard's good morning.

He is shocked by the change in the King of Asia, as he now styles himself. Alexander is sprawled on a chair surrounded by his generals. He is dressed in a white robe and sash with the royal purple at its border; he even has a blue and white diadem. A Persian nobleman would just look like a fop, which most of them are, in Gajendra's opinion. On Alexander, such a dress looks outlandish.

Even some of his Companions are dressed the same.

Alexander does not have his usual bounce; he is yawning and bleary. Gajendra glances at the silver goblet on the table. He hopes they have not poisoned him already. It would be easy to do when he is in this state. He glances at the men hovering around him. I wonder which one of you is the assassin?

Only Alexander smiles at the captain's approach. The silence and hard stares of the others terrify him.

'Who is this?' Alexander says to the captain. The glittering eye and curling wet lip are not what the army see.

'This man came to the gate saying he needs to see you

urgently. He claims he has information of a plot against your life.'

'Another one?' one of the generals sneers. It is Nearchus.

'What's your name?' Alexander asks him.

'Gajendra. I am a *mahavat* in the elephant brigade.'

'A jumbo fucker,' another one growls. 'What's he doing here?'

Alexander rouses himself from his stupor. He swings his legs around and gives the captain signal to leave. The man looks disappointed. He had hoped for commendation. He gets none.

'I've seen this one in action before, haven't I? He talks to elephants. And they seem to understand him.'

'Does he trumpet at them with his pizzle?' Nearchus says. 'I should like to see that.'

The other Companions enjoy his ribald choice of imagery. Only Alexander does not laugh. 'What do they say about me among the troops?' he asks Gajendra.

This is unexpected. He did not expect to be interrogated about general morale. He is being tested before he has even had the chance to tell his news.

'I don't pay attention to the talk.'

'Well, you should. A man who does not pay attention to the talk around him cannot use it to his advantage.'

There, you see! Gajendra thinks. You knew it was a test. He wants to see your mettle away from the elephants. That glittering eye is on you and you had best speak up, there is no point in being mealy mouthed in this company.

'Some adore you and would follow you to the end of the earth. But you know this already. Others say that you have gone too far and that conquest has gone to your head, that you have forgotten your crease. Forgive me, but I am from Taxila. I have no idea what that means.'

The lip curls in the torchlight. 'A crease is what we call the valley where we are raised. They mean to say that I have forgotten my own people. What else do they say?'

'That you are mad.'

There is an audible hiss as everyone catches their breath. Alexander just smiles. He still has a face like a boy's. 'Madness is divine,' he says. 'All gods are mad. Didn't you know that?' He stands up. He is not unsteady, despite the wine that is spilled across the table, soaking like a bloodstain into the wood. 'And what do you think. You think me mad?'

'I think you are all that I should like to be.' He has spoken without thinking. There is a moment of stillness, then Alexander throws back his head and roars with laughter. He stabs Gajendra in the chest with his forefinger. 'Who is this pup? Tell me again why he is here.'

Gajendra addresses Alexander directly. 'I overheard two men plotting against you. They will put poison in your wine.'

'Which men?'

'One is Oxathres, the captain of the elephants.'

'Well, of course it is,' Nearchus shouts. 'This ragged-arsed little fucker is out for his own advancement. If you listen to every calumny that comes wheedling up to your ear we shall have the whole army settling scores by way of promotion.' He turns on Gajendra. 'Look at him. He comes in here, stinking of elephant, with yet another poisoner's story.' He reaches out and grabs Gajendra by the jaw. 'He doesn't even shave yet.'

'He's a wondrous turn with an angry elephant.'

Nearchus stands up close and Gajendra can smell the wine on his breath. 'Sold your arse to a corporal yet? Pretty boy like you, there must be a copper or two in it.' He turns to his fellows. 'They all do that, these Indians. Did you fight against us at the Jhellum River?'

The calumny is ringing in his ears. The hypocrisy – being accused of buggery by one of these big-nosed Greeks – is more than he can bear. But he manages a suitable reply. 'I would not sell my arse to a corporal,' he says, setting his shoulders. 'Nothing less than a captain of cavalry, thanks. But most of them are spoken for.'

Alexander laughs. He is enjoying this. Until now he was growing bored with the company.

Nearchus is irritated. 'Who *is* this?'

'I got him and his fellows as part of the truce with Porus. I asked for a core of his war elephants and the handlers to manage them.'

'Well, this one's no use to you. No hair on his balls yet.'

Gajendra flinches again at these insults but doesn't take his eyes from Alexander.

'You heard what he said. Speak up for yourself.'

'I was just thinking that I'm older than you were when you fought against the Thracians and that you'll be happy to smell my elephants when there's a squadron of enemy cavalry at your right and centre and your own line's ready to break.' He rounds on Nearchus. 'Let's see if my elephants don't smell as sweet as patchouli to you then.'

Nearchus looks suddenly too hot in his clothes. His face is red from drink and bad temper. Alexander decides to intervene. Another time he might have let his general skewer him for his impudence but tonight he will be impressed with the lad's spunk. 'Don't mind him,' he says to Gajendra. 'He lost his nephew to an elephant at Gaugamela.'

He puts a hand on his shoulder and leads him away from the others. 'So tell me about these men who conspire against me. One was the captain of the elephants. Did you recognize the other?'

'Yes. He is sitting right there.'

He points to one of the couches but it is now empty. One of the guests has slipped away during the arguments.

'Kassander!' Nearchus hisses.

Iolaus, Alexander's cupbearer, springs forward and grabs Gajendra by the throat, calls him a toady and a serpent. Alexander pulls him off and tells the others to find Kassander. They believe him now, even Nearchus, who was in better humour when he thought him a liar.

Everyone is in uproar except for Alexander, who looks delighted. 'Rouse my torturer. Tell him the captain of the elephants needs stretching and twisting a little. If there's any truth to this tale, we'll hear it from him.'

The company is dispersed. At last only Alexander remains behind with Nearchus and Gajendra. He sits down and pours wine into his goblet from a flask. He grins. There is red wine on his teeth, making him look bloody. 'So shall we ask how you came by this information?'

'I was following the captain.'

'To what purpose?'

Gajendra considers a lie, but an instinct tells him the truth will serve him better, incriminating as it is. 'I was set to brain him and leave him in a ditch.'

'You see?' Nearchus says. 'This is just revenge, not information.'

'I might agree with you,' Alexander says, 'except for the empty chair at the end of the table. We'll soon get to the bottom of this.' He resumes his slump and regards Gajendra with a lazy grin. 'Well. What a useful lad you're turning out to be!'

By the time he gets back to the straw, it seems the whole army knows what has happened. News travels faster here than fire through summer grass. Ravi rushes over to him, face creased with worry.

'What has happened?'

'What are people saying?'

'Oxathres has been arrested. Some say you were part of the plot and are to be crucified in the morning. Others that it was you who denounced him and that Alexander has promoted you to general and given you a palace and your own harem.'

Who starts such talk? Gajendra wonders. 'The truth lies somewhere in between.'

'I was afraid for you,' Ravi says.

He puts a hand on his uncle's arm. 'I was afraid for me, too.'

Something hits him hard on the side of the head. He looks up. Colossus has taken an apple from his barrel and blown it at him, using his trunk. Ravi shakes his head.

Gajendra pats his tusker's head. He is mollified, but only after Gajendra feeds him a watermelon.

Ravi shakes his head again. 'I swear he's almost human sometimes,' he says.

*

Over the next few days the stories flow thick and fast. It is like an army of old women, all gathered by the well. It amuses him to hear the stories repeated back to him in different ways: that Kassander paid Oxathres to make Colossus run amok in the *maidan* and trample Alexander; that he made a poison from elephant bile on the general's orders so that he might take over the army; that all of Alexander's Macedonians had turned against him and were preparing to rebel the moment he fell sick and Oxathres was to lead a charge against the palace with the elephants.

When you know the truth, lies become astonishing.

'I almost feel sorry for your friend Oxathres,' Ravi says. 'You should have seen him when they dragged him off. He was crying and slobbering, and they hadn't even done anything to him yet.'

He might feel sorry for him too, but then he reminds himself that Oxathres did not blanche at torturing Colossus with the hook and then the poison.

'Kassander planned it all,' Ravi goes on. 'They found him halfway to Sidon and have dragged him back here to face Alexander.'

Three days later there are executions. The captain of the elephants is first. It is a chill morning, the men stand around huddled and shivering, warmed by the prospect of hearing somebody scream. Alexander strides from his tent in his golden armour, mounts his horse and parades in front of them. He does not speak. He rides up and down the lines, his horse skittish, flicking its tail and twisting its head.

Then Oxathres is dragged out, or what Gajendra believes is him. He has been badly used. He cannot stand, either from fear or from their tortures; his guards must drag him towards the cross that has been prepared. A rope of saliva spills from his mouth. He is screaming, but there are no words, just a high-pitched wail.

He has on only his tunic, and there is blood matted in his beard. Listen to him, someone says, he is crying out for pity. But no one can really understand what he is saying.

Two of the men behind Gajendra make a wager; one says he will be dead by the morning, the other bets a siglo that he will still be groaning when the crows take his eyes out.

A man standing behind Gajendra leans forward and squeezes his shoulder. 'This must be a good day for you,' he says.

A good day? Four days ago he wanted to pulverize this man with his fists and feet; but that was different. He wanted to do murder, but not this. 'What did they do to him?' he asks Ravi.

'Hot irons and a turn on the wheel. They say he gave it all up before they started but Alexander insisted they make him scream anyway, he said it would help his digestion.'

They strip him. There are lesions all over him. Gajendra swallows down the acid in the back of his throat. 'I hated him,' he says to Ravi. 'But I never hated him this much.'

'Why should you care? He did this to himself.'

The executioners are expert, they have performed the task before. They hold him down on the cross as they apply the nails, first the wrist bones and then the ankles separately, the legs pinned either side of the stanchion.

They have dug a hole in the ground ready to plant the base of the cross, and they haul him up. It isn't very high from the ground, Alexander's horse could look him in the eye. Gajendra flinches and cannot watch. Could they not just kill him and be done with it?

To hear a man scream like this in the silence of a shuffling parade ground is a sobering proposition. He tries to remember Oxathres lashing at Colossus with the bull hook to make himself feel better about this.

The next wretch is brought out, Iolaus, Alexander's cup-bearer. He looks as well as a lad might who has been flayed with horse whips. Gajendra thinks he sees Alexander staring at him, but that's impossible because even their great king could not make out one face in this crowd of thousands.

The boy is similarly prepared and hoisted up. It takes longer because he faints when they bang in the nails and Alexander insists they wake him with buckets of water so he can better enjoy the experience.

He supposes no one here this morning will be in a great hurry to be next to try and kill the King of Asia.

Alexander wishes to make his point. He spurs his horse to the front rank of soldiers, until he is close enough that they can feel his horse's breath in their faces. Then he slowly rides around the entire parade ground, as if he is looking at each man in turn, until he has completed an entire circuit of his army.

The sun rises over the eastern hills. It is going to be a hot day. The man behind him taps him on the shoulder again. 'A fine day to be out in the sun. His skin will be black by sunset. Two siglos.'

Gajendra shakes his head, declining the wager.

It is Kassander's turn last of all. Gajendra wonders how

it might have turned out if he had kept his nerve that night and bluffed this out. Would Alexander still have believed him if the son of Antipater had looked him in the eye and denied everything?

When he is brought out it sets up a murmur among the Macedonians. Alexander flicks at the reins and his horse spins around to face them. He sidesteps his Arab right to the first rank. The murmur dies to silence.

Unlike the others Kassander walks with his head held up. Behind him comes a squadron of a dozen archers, marching single file.

They chain him to a post facing the Macedonian ranks. It is clear Alexander wants them all to have a good view. Kassander spares a glance for his two fellow conspirators gasping on their trees. He appears contemptuous. You have let me down, the look seems to say.

'Look at their faces,' Ravi said. 'The Macks do not adore Alexander as they once did.'

'He'll bring them around,' another man said. 'He always does. When he takes Carthage, they'll be fighting over each other to kiss his arse.'

The archers arrange themselves in a line, facing the post, and about twenty paces from it. Alexander walks his horse towards them and with a grand gesture withdraws his sword from its scabbard. The archers each select an arrow, and raise their bows in unison.

Gajendra holds his breath. Kassander starts to make a speech and Alexander hits him around the head with the flat of the sword and he slumps in his bonds. 'I have decided to be merciful,' Alexander says. 'Cut him down.' He looks at Oxathres and Iolaus. 'Not those two.'

Oxathres starts weeping again, not from pain, Gajendra supposes, but from envying the other's fortune. The passage of a single day is nothing when you are in a pavilion by the river, eating sesame seeds with honey. When you are hanging on a splintered cross in the desert sun, it may as well be a hundred times a hundred years.

The army is dismissed and shuffles back to the camp, unusually silent. Gajendra turns to Ravi. 'Have you ever done something and you're not sure afterwards if it's a good thing or a bad thing?'

'No.'

Gajendra stares at the two men on their crosses. The cupbearer is trembling but Oxathres is quite still and he thinks that by some miracle he has died. But then he raises his weight on his skewered wrists and takes a long trembling breath before sagging to hang limp on the nails again. He wonders how many times he will do that before his strength and his will give out. He hopes the man who wagered him still alive by the morning will lose all his money.

'Do you think Alexander will give them an hour or two and then order them killed? He won't let them hang there all day, will he?'

Ravi shrugs. 'What do you think?'

'I think it unlikely.'

'So do I. They plotted to kill him. You saw the look on his face. Do one thing for me, Gajendra.'

'What is that?'

'If you ever rise so high that you are just like him, and I try and kill you for it, don't hang me on a cross.'

75

Gajendra laughs, uncertain.

But Ravi is deadly serious.

'That could never happen,' Gajendra says.

'Oh, you never know,' Ravi says.

'You must get them back to their drills,' Nearchus tells him. 'We can't have another debacle like last time. If it wasn't for your big tusker it would have been a disaster.'

It seems he has been promoted from being a gyppo to Nearchus's second in command, though no announcement has been made.

'Can you do that?'

'It should be Ravi. He's the most experienced. I'm just his apprentice.'

'Which one's Ravi? I don't know the names of all these fucking Indians. You don't look like an apprentice. They listen to you. That elephant of yours is the best we have. Just do as I say.'

'All right.'

Gajendra is rewarded with Oxathres's position as captain of the elephants; he is even offered a place in Alexander's outer circle. He feasts at the long table with the other junior officers of Alexander's army. His general announces that Nearchus has been promoted in rank to Elephantarch. It is a new position, invented just for him, the first time a Macedonian general will be in command of an elephant squadron.

It demonstrates to everyone the importance their general places on his new weapons of war.

Gajendra tries to catch Alexander's eye. He has felt a

supernatural bond with him since that first day in the yard when Colossus went berserk. Or did he just imagine it? He is just another elephant boy, a minion and a foreigner, and all the Macks except Alexander hate foreigners.

He watches him embrace Nearchus. One day that will be me. For now let the sun shine on his favourite general, but soon it will shine on me, and I will blind this whole army with my brilliance and bravery.

I will never be a nothing ever again.

CHAPTER 10

Carthage, 322 BC: Temple of Tanith

H<small>E IS SURPRISED</small> at the change in her. Hanno had always thought of her as a little girl; a father always does. It is not a physical change in her so much. She is beautiful again, but then she was always beautiful, even near death; but now there is a light in her again. Not a raging fire, to be sure, but after so long even candlelight will do.

She treats him with formal respect, like the head of his household giving the weekly report. He would hesitate to rebuke her now. Her serenity is intimidating. As they walk in the gardens of the temple her talk is of prophesies and the downfall of the city, which she tells him was foretold by the oracle, and will now happen with or without his army's intervention.

He doesn't believe in prophecy, except for political purposes. The oracle only says what they all fear: that they will not be the first to stop Alexander. News of his advance along the coast came months ago.

He is marching west from his new city of Alexandria in Egypt, building a road as he goes. He could have come by sea and landed at Cape Bon, if he had wanted to play the invader. He has constructed a vast fleet of one thousand warships in Cilicia and Phoenicia but instead he is laying a trans-African road.

It seems he comes to colonize, and is taking his time about it.

But all is not well in Alexander's Empire, his envoys tell him. Antipater has fomented rebellion in Macedon and has found a willing ally in Antigonus the One-Eyed, the satrap of Turkey. Alexander has sent one of his favourites, Kraterus, to deal with it, along with ten thousand of his veterans from Babylon. There are reports of the two armies massing in Tarsus.

Antipater had no choice really; Alexander crucified one of his sons and has imprisoned the other over yet another poison plot. He is glad he is not Macedonian. You dare not eat anything over there unless you pick it fresh off the tree or throttle it and cook it yourself.

It is one thing to be forewarned of Alexander's intention, it is another to prevent it. He is a vast storm building on the horizon. You cannot stop the weather either.

His spies tell him that it is not the same army that he took against Persia.

There are weaknesses, or perceived ones, at least. He has Scythians and Bactrians in his cavalry, wild tribesmen with tattooed faces and bedecked ponies; his archers are Indians, his lancers are Parthians and Syrians, his light infantry Greeks and green Macedonians, just arrived and never seen a battle. He has another twelve thousand Egyptians and Persians in training with the sarissa, so they tell him. One infantry phalanx is entirely Persian.

For the first time there is discord in Alexander's army. He will also have to leave perhaps fifteen thousand troops stationed in Babylon with Meleager to guard his rear and enforce his rule there. Hanno estimates he will have perhaps five thousand horse and a little over twenty-five thousand infantry by the time he arrives. He will be heavily outnumbered, of course. But when has that ever troubled him?

Not even half the army remaining are Macedonians. Yet the core of his strength is still there. He has his Agrianian javelineers, wild men who fight with dogs and can take the eye out of a lizard at a hundred paces. Some of them came out here with their grandfathers. He still has his Companion Cavalry, though that too is reinforced with Persians and Syrians. Most telling of all, he still has some veterans with him, fifty- or sixty-year-old veterans who were fighting battles when most of the population here were still suckling at their mothers' teats. These are the men who will make the difference, hardened by years of campaigning, with iron discipline and versed in weaponry and tactics. They are the best soldiers in the world.

Day by day Alexander gets closer. What frightens Hanno is not the battle but the inevitability of his defeat. Alexander has never lost; he knows it, and his army, who are mostly mercenaries, know it too.

'You have been charged with the defence of the city,' the Council have told him. 'You have superior numbers. He will be exhausted after a long march. This Alexander is not invincible.'

Not invincible. Really? Many think he is. Being invincible has nothing to do with numbers. It has to do with attitude and with cunning and with fortune. But what was fortune but the invisible hand of the gods? Hanno suspects that his daughter, privy to the private mumblings of the divine, now knows more about life than he does.

'We must get you away from here.'

'My place is here in the service of the goddess. I cannot leave.'

'It is not a request. It is my express command.'

'You cannot command me, Father. My only authority now is the goddess herself.' She speaks quietly and without resentment. She states facts, and the fact of her being so reasonable makes him bridle.

'What will you do if the city falls and you are made a slave?'

'Accept it.'

'A daughter of mine cannot accept such a fate! I order you to leave the city.'

She smiles, which only infuriates him more.

Once she would have defied him, now she slides either side of him, like waves around a rock. He sees now how she has changed. 'Why should I leave if you are defending the city for us? Do you not believe you can win?'

'I wish to be assured of your safety in all eventualities.'

Rumours have run all down the coast. They say Alexander has elephants with him that he has trained as warriors. He owns two hundred, his spies say, which seems an impossible number, a certain exaggeration. But he has only brought three score, as the rigours of the desert road across Libya would tax even a camel.

How does a soldier fight an elephant?

The Council have argued among themselves: should

they meet him on the plain or prepare for siege? A siege would be better. Alexander will always outwit you on a flat plain.

The Council choose the plain. He suspects they will have boats waiting should the fight go against them. They say the weather is better in Spain at this time of the year.

She says, 'I will not break my vow to the goddess. I will stay here.'

He approaches her. He has never told this wisp, this fragile wonder, how much he loves her. A sinew jumps in his cheek. He thinks of perhaps arranging an abduction, sending her to Lilybaeum. 'Do it for me, then.'

It is the first time he has ever asked her for anything.

Her serenity fractures. 'Father, I cannot. You have your duty. Allow me mine.'

Once, as a child, he found a pup that had been abandoned by its mother. Its eyes had not yet opened and it squirmed warm in his hand. He placed it on a cushion in his room and tried to feed it ass's milk with a spoon. He had even slept beside it that night, murmuring encouragement. He blew on its face and whispered about the rats they would catch together when he was grown.

In the morning it was dead. That was the way of it. You did your best to love something, but Mara was right, in the end it was the gods who decided.

CHAPTER 11

A SKY LIKE PEWTER, air so thick he can hardly breathe. Sweat crawls over his body. Yet Alexander looks fresh and spirited. It might be a dewy morning in the mountains.

The generals are there, Lysimachus, Ptolemy and the rest. Nearchus stands in the corner with his arms folded, like a predator, wondering which of the company he might like to consume. His eyes fix on Gajendra.

He will snarl at anyone who asks; these fucking Indians, these pretty boy foreigners. It is always the same old cant. He is Macedonian, like Alexander, thinks that mud wrestling pigs in his youth is a sign of aristocracy. It seems to Gajendra that every true-born prince in that country fucks a goat by the time he is twelve years old and considers it a sexual conquest.

The generals resent these Persian princes who now make up half their king's Companions; they resent that they have conquered half an empire and cannot go home and watch it crumble away again; they resent that they have elephants but must employ the Rajah's men to ride them, even if they may win the next battle for them.

Alexander claps his hands and laughs as if they are all about to open a new flask of wine or go into a brothel. He looks at his generals; his generals look at him. He is dressed in full armour, the gold polished like a mirror, and there are greaves on his legs. His thighs are the size of tree limbs and look about as hard.

His height is no impediment to the force of his personality. 'So,' he says, 'are we ready to take Carthage?'

Not yet dawn and Alexander's tent is full of generals and marshals, brigade commanders as well as the chiefs of wild-looking tribesmen in fox-skin caps. They stink to heaven. The fear is palpable though none wants to show it. The wind has come up, and the concussion of the tent flaps is deafening.

Alexander wears the armour they say once belonged to Hercules, the metal greening with age, a leopard-skin cloak over it. Under his arm is a gold helmet with the wings of a bird set in white gold on either side. The dawn catches the purple silk of their general's tent and colours them all in blood.

There is a parchment on the table, held down at the four corners with stones. Alexander points out the enemy's defences; Hanno has the sea on his left and the lake on his right. 'They have sixty thousand infantry and six thousand cavalry. Their infantry, however, are made up of recruits who do not know which end of a lance to hold, and mercenaries from Gaul, Greece and Iberia. They have some Numidian cavalry, bare-arsed gyppos in leopard skins. As one Macedonian is worth ten barbarians, I calculate we outnumber them five to one!'

The generals laugh. The Persians frown at each other.

'Hanno has taken up a defensive position with his infantry in the centre, his cavalry at the wings. He is showing us what he thinks are his strengths: his massed infantry, a flanking left wing. So we already have the advantage. We can change our plans as we see fit. He has already indicated his intention.'

And Hanno's intention is clear. There are staked timber palisades in front of his infantry; he wishes to fight the battle on the wings. They have never faced elephants before, and it is clear from this deployment just how greatly they fear them. He has placed the Sacred Band, irregulars from the city itself, behind the main army, in reserve.

Alexander tells them how they will win. His philosophy is simple; to win a battle you do not have to prevail at every strategic position, or even at most of them; an army needs only to win at the most telling point. In every case, it means ignoring the limbs and going to the heart.

'We must ask ourselves with our every stroke how our foe will counter,' he tells them. 'All our tactics shall seek to provoke a breakthrough in their line.'

He turns to Nearchus; as Elephantarch he now has the responsibility for the most unpredictable element in his army – the elephants.

'We will hypnotize them with our tuskers. We will wave them in front of their faces like a cobra while we strike elsewhere. They are well drilled and rested after our trek from Egypt. The effect will be terrifying.'

The Persians look at each other; they are terrified of the elephants themselves. They call them *ahrima* – demons – and refuse to go near them.

Alexander should be looking to me for this, Gajendra thinks. I will be the one on Colossus's neck; if Colossus stands firm, so will the rest.

This plan is one that Alexander has used before, at the Granicus River. Hanno has superior cavalry numbers and will try to exploit it. So Alexander will use specially trained javelineers he calls stingers against him. Perdiccas has been charged with several squadrons of cavalry to hold the left flank.

The elephants will attack the centre of their line; the first time a man faces an elephant in battle he is tempted to run. Even the Silver Shields still shudder when they talk about Jhellum. At some point the line will break, and Alexander will exploit it.

'It is not about numbers,' he reminds them. 'It is about bringing utmost violence to their most vulnerable point with the greatest speed. Speed is the key to all martial success.'

Gajendra goes back to Elephant Row, listening to the beasts trumpet to each other as the waterboys paint red circles around their eyes to make them look fierce. That night not one of the elephants sleeps. He watches the water ripple in the troughs from their rumblings. They are talking to each other. It's as if they know.

CHAPTER 12

The Battle of Carthage, 322 BC

GAJENDRA HAS NEVER been in a battle before.

As he rides Colossus through the phalanx he sees one of the young recruits vomit on his boots. The veterans are having a joke of it. Their sergeant pushes the boy back into line and orders the rest to silence.

The plain rings to the slap of leather and armour as the regiments jog into place. It is a close morning, the air like treacle. The colours of the army are muted. Yesterday's overcast has been replaced with a fierce yellow sun and white hot sky. Armour is scalding to the touch. Men are eager to be at it, anything than stand around waiting in this heat.

Gajendra sits astride Colossus's neck, sweat running down his face from under the headband. His arm muscles ache from holding the quiver of javelins and his shield.

The elephants will not take much of this. They do not like to stand out in the sun. They are dressed in thick, quilted armour, they are boiling up. Colossus fans himself with his ears and trumpets his disapproval. Gajendra pulls an ear over his eye to protect it from the blazing sun. 'Not long,' he says to him, though in truth he does not know how long it will be before Alexander starts the attack. Boys with skins of river water pour them into pots between each pair of elephants. It is quickly gone and they rush back behind the lines to get more.

Ensigns snap in the wind; a squall dances on the pan. A sand-coloured murk obscures the horizon. It will disguise our feints. It seems the gods are on the side of Alexander once more.

He hopes he will prove valiant. This is the moment he has waited for, the brief chance for glory in front of Alexander. He is at the centre of the line. Each elephant has a squadron of Persian slingers and archers between them, as protection.

There are more light infantry to guard Colossus's legs.

The Agrianians are out there in front. They have no armour, no helmet, all they have is a cloak and a shield and steely nerve. They fight in pairs, father and sons, brother with brother, a wolfhound to shield them if they go down. It is a beautiful and terrifying thing to see them hurl a javelin so straight, playing the wind. It takes years of practice, so they say; they must use a finger sling, learn to apply the right spin to the shaft. The older man is always the hurler; the younger will spot the targets and pass the javelins.

Gajendra finds himself praying. *Ganesha, let me be bold and fearless and lucky today.*

Alexander rides out. He holds his sword in his right hand, and with the sun blazing on his armour he looks like a god. His helmet is in the crook of his other arm.

Behind him his generals wait in a tight group, their horses high with excitement. They look impatient to be done with this. Only Alexander seems unhurried.

He walks his massive Arab along the line.

'Men of Macedon! They do not wish us to enter Carthage. Do you know why? Because the city is a treasure house. They have all the wealth of Iberia and Africanus in there. Riches that will soon be yours! We are on our way home, brothers, but we will not go back empty-handed. Anything we have won so far will seem like mere trinkets compared to what we will find when we ride into Carthage. You left your crease as men and you will return as gods!'

The army cheers him, though only the Macks can understand what he said. His rallying cry was meant only for the veterans, for he will rely on them when the battle reaches its pinnacle. These are the men who will not break, who will always hold their lines.

He stands in the saddle, his sword raised, and a roar ripples over the plain. They would hear it in Carthage.

Someone has brought a ram. Alexander jumps from his horse, expertly slits its throat. He butchers it, holds its still beating heart to the gods, the blood running down his arm. The army roars. They are following Zeus's son into battle. How can they lose?

Hanno watches the army come; it looks too small. The battle is unfolding as he imagined it. This seems too easy.

Alexander has advanced on the oblique, trying to draw Hanno's forces away from the centre and his war elephants. He himself is crossing to the centre; Hanno had seen the flash of his gold armour, the fluttering standard.

His army is too small to overcome them – if they hold their line. But his generals are panicking about the elephants. What if their hoplites cannot hold them?

They have the advantage on the other flank. One bold sweep from their heavy cavalry and they will have Alexander's army surrounded. Alexander seems to be inviting him to do it. This is why Hanno hesitates.

One after another his generals urge him to attack. Now the elephants start to move forward. Dust drifts over the plain and soon it obscures everything. He can hear them coming but he can see nothing. The imagination can have you slaughtered or victorious depending on which way the wind blows. He fidgets in the saddle and waits for his outriders to return and tell him what is happening.

His generals scream at him to hurry. *If we lose this opportunity and those beasts from the devil break our line, we are finished.*

The horses are so high they can scarce be contained. How does a man direct such confusion? Where is Alexander now? How far are the elephants from the lines? Have our Numidians broken through or did they meet unexpected resistance?

If only someone could tell him what is going on.

We must do it now, they are screaming at him. *Commit our cavalry to the right flank.*

Do it now.

We must do it now.

No, he tells them. Wait. If we hold our line, we can contain him.

But if we attack now we can crush him.

He looks around for one dissenting voice. The wind blows grit in their faces. If only he could see what is going on.

An outrider rushes in. The enemy are weakened on their left flank. The captain wants your permission to attack.

None of them has ever faced elephants before. He does not know what to expect. His instinct tells him to hold his cavalry in reserve. Yet he has the numbers, so the obvious move is to attack Alexander's left. But if Alexander invites you to attack him at a certain point, is it better advised not to?

He turns to a captain. 'It seems too plain.'

'We should take the advantage now!'

'I had expected something more… complex.'

Finally he gives the order and his courier gallops away, ordering his right wing into the attack.

He experiences a tide of misgiving. He tries not to think about his daughter. Thousands dead on the battlefield if he is wrong, perhaps even a great city ruined and ransacked. Yet what troubles him more is thinking of the harm that might come to Mara.

He finds himself praying to his gods; has she not suffered enough at your hands? She has lost a husband and a son and a daughter, all in the space of a year. Yet if we win this battle I might yet find a way to persuade her to give up the temple and return to the life she was born to. She is still young. She can have more children. If you, the gods, will just let her be and pay back what you have done to her and to us. Give me this victory today and we will see what is to be done.

He spits the dust out of his mouth. Ravi is pointing to the left, where the Numidian cavalry are coming on, near naked, the only colour the leopard-skin cloaks they wear across their shoulders, like a sash. The best cavalry in the world, apart from our own.

The line is so thin on the left. If they get in behind them, they would be cut off.

Gajendra is shaking so hard he thinks he will drop his *ankus*. What he wouldn't give for a flask of water right now. The Carthage line glitters in the sun, a thin silver line spread across the horizon. Colossus throws up his trunk and bellows again, staggers to the side, rocking the *howdah*. The soldiers scream curses at him. Not his fault, he's hot, he needs to move or get out of the sun.

Silence, just the wind blowing grit in their faces, the muted roar of the battle far along the left flank. The dust obscures everything, which is worse than seeing a rout. Gajendra looks over his shoulder, looking for a rider, hoping for the order to withdraw. The archers in the *howdah* would get out and run if they were not so far from the ground.

Colossus is eager now, the sun burning on his armour; the bronze face plate and the massive chest protector are heating up and he bellows in protest again.

The brigade commanders have rallied to the colours to receive their orders; behind them the master sergeants are reconfiguring their line; the order finally comes – advance. They start to beat the drum, pounded out with a mallet to set the cadence, the sergeants bawling out orders.

Colossus curls up his trunk and flaps out his ears as he lumbers forward, gaining speed with every stride. Gajendra looks over his shoulder again. The peculiar character of the elephant's gait makes a ride in the *howdah* an unsettling experience. An elephant will only raise one foot off the ground at a time, and puts it down before raising the next. Those on its back receive four separate shocks with each stride, and when it happens at speed, as it is now, it is as much as a man can do to keep from toppling out.

The infantry follow behind, a terrifying sight. They have formed into a rectangular formation, marching in locked step. The sarissas are sitting upright, twenty feet in the air, shafts swaying, a bristled row of serried steel points.

Then the dust obscures them too.

Arrows rain in from the other side of the palisade. He holds his shield above his head and arrows bang in one after the other. He sees them bounce off Colossus's front corselets. The elephant ignores them and sets to work ripping out the stakes from the ground in front of him. If Colossus is hurt or frightened he knows only one way to react and if he gets through this desperate line then someone is going to pay.

The noise hurts the ears; the horns, the drums, the screaming of wounded men. Already Colossus's armour is bristling with arrows. Gajendra sees the Agrianians running back to their own lines, their ammunition spent.

What was easy on the drill ground is now a blur. It is hard even to think. Everything is instinct; he hunkers behind his shield, he prays, he urges Colossus on. He is convinced he is about to die.

CHAPTER 13

'*DERI, DERI!*' HE shouts.

Colossus needs little urging. He hurls the stakes from the palisade aside as if he is stripping branches off a tree. Soon there is a gap and he charges through, the hoplites following. A few brave men rush out to meet him but they have no expertise for this. One of the Macks might have told them how to do it, but then they had learned the hard way at Gaugamela and the Jhellum River.

The best thing is to attack the *mahavat*. But they cannot get close enough, the guards around Colossus's legs keep them at bay and his big tusks keep them so occupied with defending themselves that they forget that without me he is deaf and blind.

He sees two men dash out, both looking like Zeus himself. They have gold shields and their helmets have cheek pieces embossed with stylised curls. They look utterly magnificent for a few moments, until they disappear without fuss beneath Colossus's charge. His tusks have been replaced with razor sharp iron. He is difficult to resist.

When the men from Carthage see several more of their own hurled into the air like dry leaves or gutted like goats on the iron tusks of a charging elephant they all lose appetite for the fight. One thing to see your comrade fall with an arrow; another to see his limbs torn off by a wild beast. To defend against fellows like Colossus it takes discipline and icy nerve and the fellow at your shoulder has to stand firm also.

These boys aren't trained for it; they run.

The line shivers and breaks. What starts as desertion soon turns into rout.

Gajendra's instinct is to follow, and it is Colossus's instinct too. But without infantry an elephant is too vulnerable and so he signals Colossus to stop, even though he is in a rage.

Alexander thunders past them in his golden armour with his bodyguard cavalry behind. It is the very moment he has waited for. He will hit the Carthage centre and drive a hole through it.

As the phalanx comes up, Alexander is already lost in the dust. The moves and counter moves are done.

It is then that Nearchus appears. He rides across our front with his spear held at the level to signal that our attack has stopped. More cavalry thunder past, with the Silver Shields following behind.

They are like starfish left behind by the tide. The battle has swept on past them; he can hear it raging on either side but can see nothing. He feels Colossus beneath him, trembling. Then he raises his trunk high in victory.

As the murk clears he sees that there are only a dozen elephants alongside him; the rest have run to the rear. He stares at the litter of bodies, and is relieved he is not one of them. He is at last a soldier. He feels more like a god.

His mouth tastes foul. He realizes with some surprise that there is an arrow in his arm. How long has it been there? He stares at it in astonishment.

He heard one of the Macks talking about wounds once; they said that any wound that would not kill or maim you was something you were proud of. Ravi walks alongside, on Ran Bagha. 'Look,' Gajendra says grinning and shows him the arrow in his shoulder. And then he faints, sprawling across Colossus's neck. If Colossus had not felt him start to fall, and immediately dropped to his knees, Gajendra might have broken his neck.

CHAPTER 14

Two months later

CARTHAGE BAKES. In Megara a palm tree lies where it has fallen across a stone staircase; lizards sun themselves in the dried fountains and from his window he can read obscenities scrawled in dried excrement on the walls of his neighbour's villa. Everyone is blaming each other for this.

In the Parliament the Hundred howl at each other like dogs across the speaker's staff. Dignitaries with oiled beards and long ringlets curse each other for fools. Militiamen doze beneath makeshift awnings.

They are making swords in the temples. At night he lies awake and listens to the hammers. He has packed his crate of dress uniforms ready to depart. His study, once so precise he had been complimented by a visiting mathematician, is now piled with discarded maps, dispatches and letters.

The Council thought themselves secure behind their triple walls, even after the army was defeated. But Alexander has not even tried to breach them. He has built his camp, cutting off their land route and crucifying anyone who tries to break his blockade. But instead of trying to breach the unbreachable, he has secured the isthmus to the south and begun construction of a mole to block the harbour mouth.

At first it seemed impossible. The townspeople had stood on the walls and jeered at his efforts to fill the sea. It is a hundred, two hundred paces from the beach to the harbour walls, Tyrian galleys could pass each other abreast there. The channel is too deep, too wide to ford; their mathematicians calculated that it would take ten years, twenty to fill it.

Six weeks later Alexander is halfway there. It seems that 'impossible' is not a word that Alexander knows, or it has never been successfully translated for him in any language from the Indus to Africa.

Grass seeds drift across the inner harbour where a rusted iron chain is mirrored in the black water. Rubbish is piled up in huge mounds along the docks. A green slime has attached itself to the sea wall.

Once it was the busiest port in the whole world, a forest of masts, three deep with corn ships. Now look what one man has done.

The last of the blockade runners are gone, sunk by Alexander's warships or wrecked on the chain he has thrown across the harbour mouth of the Coton. The masts and sternposts of sunken ships rise above the water. Even the fishermen are gone; it is safer for them to sell their fish to the soldiers in Alexander's camps on the other shore.

The heat mirage makes it appear that Alexander's navy is floating in the sky. Another miracle; the man has one for every day of the week.

A line of ox carts, laden with stone, trundles out to the

deepwater channel. Another load crashes into the water. He has almost completed the causeway along which he can bring his troops and siege equipment to batter the harbour fortifications.

Huge wooden towers edge out, taller than the city walls. If you raise a helmet on a stick above the parapet wall it invites a hail of stones and bolts from his slingers and archers. The helmet will go spinning across the barbican in a shower of sparks, damaged beyond all repair.

Their onagers – huge stone throwers – have left the ancient wooden lighthouse a sprawled ruin. Round artillery stones as large as a man lie everywhere; one monstrous boulder lies embedded in the paving outside the corn warehouse, some poor wretch leaking from under it.

The rolling siege towers loom larger every day. Men crawl across them like ants. They have started hurling burning pitch over the walls.

The city is full to bursting with refugees swarming in from the countryside. Alexander is burning all the coastal towns, murdering as he goes.

The man is pitiless. The whole world is not enough for him.

Catharo walks in and stands there, looking around as if he is expecting a fight. He doesn't look much like a brawler at first glance, for he is scarcely taller than a child. It is only on closer examination that he appears terrifying. His head looks as if it's been kicked about in the yard by small boys. On first meeting people think he is black; it is just the tattoos on his face. The only bit of his face not inked in are his eyeballs.

He waits for his orders. Get a goat from the market, strangle someone, it's all the same to him.

Hanno goes to the window. Those who can get out are already gone, several of the city fathers among them, just after they expressed full confidence in his ability to save Carthage. We'll organize a great ceremony for you, a great honour! Then: where's my slave with the baggage and the boats?

Catharo has been his creature for many years now. Every general needs men like this, someone out of the chain of command whom you can trust with grubby details. He is unswervingly loyal; a hard thing to come by in any age.

Catharo peers at the chart spread open on the table. 'Is this your battle plan?'

Anyone else and he would have them tied to a cartwheel and whipped for their insolence. Instead he joins him at the table.

'What's this?' Catharo says. 'And this? And this?'

'This is Alexander's army. This is the isthmus. This is Carthage. Here is the Coton, the military harbour, there the outer harbour. It is called a map. What you would see if you were a bird and could fly above it.'

'If I were a bird I'd shit on Alexander's head.'

He laughs. 'I should like to see it. But we need more than bird shit to save us now.'

'There's the temple. There's the Parliament.' Catharo has the delight of a child in finding things for himself. Finally: 'What's this square here?'

'His war elephants.'

'Where does he get elephants?'

'From India. He brought a squadron back with him. I hear he has been training with them all through the last winter in Babylon.'

'I have never fought elephants.'

'Nor will you now. I have a different job for you. One that is much more important.'

He rests a hand on Catharo's shoulder. He rarely touches his men; this is an honour. 'This will require all of your ingenuity. It concerns my daughter, Mara.'

'She's become a priestess.'

'Yes, she has dedicated her life to the goddess Tanith. She refuses to leave the temple, though I have told her she is not safe there.'

'You want me to get her out?'

'You are to go there and watch over her. Perhaps fortune will smile on me and I will find a way out of this mess. Who knows? If not, then you are to save her life any way that is necessary. No one and nothing is to stop you.'

'It will be done.'

Other men may have raised objections. But I will be defiling the temple; but how might it be done if Alexander defeats you and decides to lay waste the city; what if she refuses my protection? Not this one.

'We may not see each other again.'

'When do my orders terminate?'

'When your last breath leaves your body. Until then, I charge you with her life.' He gives him a purse containing a fortune in gold. Enough for Catharo to buy himself a house and set himself up as a money lender in Syracuse.

No more is said. Catharo bows and leaves. He'll do it too, he thinks. Another man might wait to see the way the wind blows before deciding whether to risk his life and the money. Not this one.

CHAPTER 15

THERE IS NO race in the world that can drink like these Macedonians. They slop around in Alexander's pavilion ankle deep in wine. They remind him of his tuskers, standing in the river spraying water over each other, trumpeting and barging everyone else aside.

Alexander does not look like the conqueror of the world when he is in his cups; except, Gajendra thinks, there is always such a fierce cunning in that flat eye, it never rests. When he laughs it sets a chill through the room.

He killed one of his childhood friends, Black Cleitus, at a gathering like this. Took a spear from one of the guards, they said, here may I borrow this, and straight through his guts. Griefstricken the next morning. Black Cleitus was still dead, though, for all his wailing.

Gajendra likes the way everyone fears him.

His Companions crowd around him, laughing too loud, spilling wine, telling war stories. But for all their high spirits there is a shadow over tonight's proceedings. There is news from Greece: Antipater has made a treaty with Athens, now he has the Greeks and their navies fighting for him. He has offered them autonomy if they help him keep Kraterus out of Macedon and secure him the throne. Now Corinth has been dragged in as well. Alexander seems unconcerned, even jovial. My own countrymen have rebelled against me? Oh well, never mind, I'll go and invade them. When I have a spare moment.

The soldiers Antipater was supposed to send to Alexander have now been recruited for his own army. The tyrants in the Greek city-states are likewise being wooed with promises of autonomy; if they decide to stand with Antipater they will soon be fighting on two fronts.

Alexander reclines at the centre of a half circle of couches with silver feet. He holds out his arm and a cringing cupbearer hands him another. Then he stands and declares lifelong friendship for Nearchus, and gratitude for his valour at Carthage. Gajendra seethes. What did he do? He told us when to attack, when to withdraw. He spent the battle astride his horse, somewhere behind us.

I led the charge.

Everyone is laughing and slapping each other on the back but he sees the looks every time one of the Persians goes near their king. The Macks don't like it when they get on the ground and bow to him. He can see what they're thinking: if he is no longer King of Macedon, then what are we fighting for?

The old timers will have none of it, they still call him Alexander and there's none of this getting on the ground, King of Kings or not. Alexander bears it but you can see he's getting to like all this toadying. He would like to take issue with the old men. The Gentlemen of the Bodyguard have prudently removed his sword.

Gajendra slips away, unnoticed. He is staggering from the wine. He smells perfume on the wind. Alexander has brought with him the great pavilion that once belonged to

Darius and he uses part of it to house his seraglio. Zahara will be over there somewhere.

Soldiers are silhouetted against the rubbish-fires on the beach. Gusts of sparks are driven on the night wind.

He hears two guards grumbling; they are cold and tired and waiting for their relief to arrive. They are guarding a cage and at first he thinks by the smell it is some wild animal they have in there. It is too dark to see.

'What have you in there?' he asks them.

'Better not to ask,' one of the men grunts and that is all the answer he needs. Alexander has brought Kassander all the way from Babylon in that cage. He cannot believe he is still alive. How much more torture will Alexander put him through before it is enough?

He finds Colossus, a massive presence in the dark. His wounds have been healing well. An arrow found its way through his quilted armour and lodged in his shoulder. 'Even your wounds are the same!' Ravi had shouted.

'How are you doing, old friend?'

Colossus shifts in the dark, there are the usual rumbles and squeaks. Gajendra feels the ache in his arm; it had not caused him much pain on the battlefield but every night since it has left him in a lather of sweat. The joint has seized and he cannot raise his hand above his shoulder. He has told no one about this, for fear they will not let him fight again.

Later he finds Ravi bundled by the fire. He is still awake.

'You still sleep with us mere mortals then, general?'

'Don't mock me, Ravi. You never thought I'd ever be captain, did you? Maybe I *will* be a general one day.'

Ravi chuckles.

'All the talk was of Nearchus tonight and what a hero he was at Carthage. I was the one who led the charge!'

'No, Colossus was. You might as well make Colossus the new Elephantarch as you. Look, Gaji, Nearchus is one of them. You're just an elephant boy. What did you expect?'

'I tell you what I expect. I expect to be as good as any of them. God grant us good battles so I can prove it. I may not have a fine Arab stallion but I have Colossus and I have courage and my will. One good battle and I shall be standing next to Alexander at the next feast and he will be lauding me!'

'One good battle? You had one good battle! A good battle is one that you live through and don't come out without an eye or an arm or your balls. You can be as brave as a tiger but it's the generals who get the credit. That's the way it is.'

'I will not be nothing all my life.'

Ravi sighs and rolls over. Soon he is snoring but Gajendra stays awake, staring at the stars. He tries not to think about Zahara, tries to forget the scent of patchouli and those fathomless black eyes.

The temple had been outraged and Alexander is still not within sight of the walls. The high priestess says to her, 'Your father is a barbarian.'

Mara is lighting copal at the feet of the goddess, part of her morning's duties. She has no idea what she is talking about. 'My father?'

'Men are not allowed here.'

'He is *here*?'

'He has sent one of his villains.'

Mara gets up and follows her out to the courtyard.

The temple entrance is flanked with huge pilasters, the courtyard divided by an altar and podium. A small statue of Tanith, carved from black onyx, has been placed there. Her eyes, which are made from sapphires, are a startling blue. Lamps flicker in the notches on the walls. There are massive mahogany beams, blackened with incense.

Catharo jumps to his feet when he sees her. He has been lounging. 'My getter', her father calls him, the one who gets things done. She has seen him coming and going by her father's back door all her life, but she has never spoken to him. Though he lacks much in stature, he looks the sort of man who would enjoy breaking someone's arm and is powerful enough to do it.

'How did the guards let him past?'

'They are your father's men,' the high priestess says, as if this were her doing.

She turns to the getter. 'What are you doing here, Catharo?'

'Do you know who I am?'

'I have seen you. I have heard of you.'

He stands with his legs apart daring anyone to move him.

'No man is allowed in these gates.'

'Tell that to Alexander when he comes.'

'My father will stop him.'

'If he does, I'll leave.'

She spares a glance towards the temple gates, to the Agora just beyond. Carthage carries out its commerce out there, it is always full of melon sellers, crowds of pigeons, money changers, prostitutes, files of priests on their way to the temple of Baal-Ammon, tinkling bells. Today it is empty. The silence frightens her.

'You have to go.'

Catharo sits down on the edge of the fountain.

'Why are you here?'

'Your father worries for you, as fathers must, I suppose.'

'You are breaking the sanctity of the temple.'

'Better than someone breaks yours.'

'You think that if my father cannot stop Alexander with all his army, then you will save me on your own?'

'Yes.'

He sits there, unshakeable, immoveable. Catharo is not a man, he is a fact; if he is there, you cannot budge him; if he comes for you, you cannot stop him. That is what they say.

CHAPTER 16

'You have to hurry, sir.'

His lieutenant stands in the doorway, agitated. The Council have a few moments ago decided to give Alexander Hanno's head on a pike and sue for peace. They think to blame all on their general and make some arrangement with the lord of war. Well, it's too late for that. He has his war won, he has no need for treaties now, the walls will be down in one day, perhaps two, why accommodate when they can just crash in and take what they want anyway?

Hanno feels the floor shake under him as another great stone hurtles into the city from one of Alexander's catapults on the causeway.

His bodyguard insists that they leave. He thinks about going back for Mara but it is too late for that now, they simply don't have the time. He hopes that Catharo can keep his commission. He has never failed him in anything before.

Alexander's army appears as countless needle points of torchlight in the darkness. He sees something flare on the platform of a siege tower. An onager lobs a phosphorus flare over the harbour wall and the night explodes in a green dazzle.

His bodyguards have made plans to smuggle him out through the Macedonian lines, one final humiliation. But if he lives through this night he promises himself that he will settle with this Alexander one day. If anything happens to his daughter, then he will make him pay. He will not do it for Carthage. He will not do it for the Council. He will do it for every father who has lost a son or a daughter to this devil, this demon, this maker of widows.

Gajendra leads the column of elephants towards the causeway past the lines of siege engines, stone throwers and assault towers. They pass last night's assault troops as they head back to the camp to rest. Their faces are white from stone dust and exhaustion.

Look behind you and all is peace; smoke from a thousand breakfast fires drifts to the south, carried on the morning's zephyr. It is pleasantly rural, a patchwork of walled estates and paddocks for sheep, goats and cattle, though the animals that grazed there have long gone to feed Alexander's army. Camel trains move in from the desert, an endless line of them with supplies for the army. His ships ripple in the heat haze. Gulls fight over the rubbish on the beach.

But look ahead and you are afforded a vision of hell. Black smoke blocks out the horned mountain behind the city, it even blocks out the sun; infantry swarm up fixed banks of ladders in columns of four; the whole city is aflame. The air is acrid from last night's incendiaries and the charnel house stench on the wind leaves an acid taste at the back of the throat.

From inside he hears the inhabitants singing to

Melchert for salvation. Olive oil is burning in the warehouses.

Last night they broke through; one wall came down and the infantry streamed through. They heard the sounds of the battle all last night. The elephants bellowed, restless, agitated by the death they smelled on the wind.

He wouldn't like to be a citizen of Carthage right now.

The priestess is trembling, outraged and afraid. Catharo ignores her and stretches himself on an altar, like a cat claiming some warm spot. When he hears Mara's voice he opens his eyes and sits up. He regards his charge and his charge regards him.

Catharo is a wild dog; you give him a scent and he will follow it; you put him on a chain and no one will come past. He is freakish and dull and vicious.

His head inclines. He says, in a voice that is supposed to be respectful, 'So has my lady changed her mind?'

'Has it occurred to my father that I am happy to die here?'

He gives her a brutish shrug.

'I do not want you here.'

'But I *am* here.'

'You must go.'

He shakes his head.

She stabs her finger into his chest. It is hard and unyielding. She might as well lecture the wall. 'I don't want to live.'

'You don't have a choice.'

They hear a noise carried on the wind. It is the sound of the rams on the gates, a double heartbeat that sends a concussion through the body. With each blow the walls of the temple blur and white dust trembles from the joining in the stones.

Alexander is on his way. Tanith will not rule here much longer.

A clear blue hot morning. Men are dying. Seeing the sun set today is not certain.

CHAPTER 17

Colossus lends his shoulder to the gate, testing its strength with his head. It creaks and bends. He puts his shoulder to it, rocking it back and forth, but it is iron and the hinges creak but they do not break. Perhaps his pride is wounded for suddenly he goes up on his back legs and pounds it with his forefeet. The archers in the *howdah* shriek, thinking they are about to topple off. The strappings hold, the doorway gives way with a crash and the soldiers stream past them and into the city.

His job done, Colossus betrays no sign of wishing to do more. Once inside the gate he finds an acacia tree and helps himself to breakfast.

Gajendra might order him to continue along the street but decides against it. There is no glory to be had in a street fight. Colossus strips the tree and then sets about the roof of an empty melon stall, which has been thatched with palm fronds.

The gateway is set into the city's defensive wall and is topped with a walkway. A guard lies with his head on the stairs, his brains bleeding down the stone. Why didn't he just surrender? Perhaps he did. Alexander's men have been three months besieging this city, they are in no mood to parlay any more.

The soldiers are flooding through the gate, eager for women, gold, anything they can get their hands on. The city is alive with screams. But he and Colossus have a little oasis away from the looting and killing, which Gajendra wants no part of. Neither, apparently, does Colossus. He lumbers around the square looking for something else to eat. But if there were anything to eat in this city, Carthage would have eaten it. They have been starving for weeks now.

There are sparks in the air, ash falls like snow. Who has set light to the city, the defenders or Alexander's storm troops? Perhaps both. He knows they are well out of it. Street fighting is no place for an elephant. Colossus thinks so too.

This is another side to war; there is no glory here, they are acting like bandits. He does not like to hear women and children scream.

She is standing by the pit where she gave her baby up to Tanith. It has occurred to her that she might find consolation there also. Catharo rushes in and she says, so I suppose now you have come to save me. The city is lost, he tells her. You must come with me.

'Is my father slain?'

'I don't know.'

'I would rather the truth.'

He draws a breath, does Catharo. He is a sullen fellow and not given to emotion but it seems the licence on his patience has expired. 'Listen here. I do not care enough about you to lie to you. I should not care to spare your feelings, believe me. Your father may dote on you, but the reason mystifies me. You are a spoiled brat who has had some misfortune but a spoiled brat just the same. I shall protect you with my life because I have given my word to your father. Are we clear? You are to come with me now, and if you obstruct my purpose I shall as soon tie your hands like a prisoner and drag you out of here by your hair. I am bound to protect your life but if you suffer in the process of that, it's all the same to me.'

She stares at him, astonished not as much by what he says as the length of this speech. She had not thought him capable of more than three words.

She hesitates so he grabs her by the wrists and drags her out of the shrine.

The street is clogged with starved skeletons headed for the docks or the gates, clambering over and around the broken carts and debris of discarded furniture that others have left behind.

People claw at each other. She sees a woman go screaming under a cart. Men are elbowing old women in the press, even children are trampled. Militia push through the crowd, the last brave men in Carthage determinedly making their way to their own deaths. Catharo surveys the chaos and drags her away from the gates. They run across the courtyard to the back gate.

She hears war drums, and then a shuddering boom from the other side of the city.

'What was that?'

'The elephants are breaking down the gates. The soldiers are coming.'

He leads her down narrow alleys, his fist locked around

her wrist; he is so strong she thinks he will pull her arm out of its socket. He ignores her protests. The streets between the Byrsa and the hill of Tanith are a warren, but he knows his way around like a cockroach, every crack and byway.

She looks up at the bleached colonnades of the palaces; the gilded rooftops of the Parliament shiver in the heat mirage of the fires burning below. She thinks she sees the glint of iron helmets.

They come out at the docks, but it seems everyone in Carthage is there.

'What now?' she asks him.

There are boats but never enough for everyone that wants to leave. Some are already heading out to sea, people lunging to get on board, the crews fending them off with gaffes. One is overloaded and capsizes there in the harbour blocking the channel.

'I had a boat waiting,' Catharo says.

'Where is he then?'

He points. 'Over there, that skiff heading out past the breakwater. He must have thought we're not coming.' He hurls her arm away from him as if he's throwing something at her.

'You've broken my arm,' she says.

'Don't tempt me.'

There is no way through the crush. There are just a handful of boats left at the dock anyway, and those that have not pushed away are dangerously overcrowded.

Men are fighting, a woman goes down right in front of her with blood streaming from her nose. Even while she is on her knees men trample her as if she isn't there.

Catharo grabs Mara again, now her other arm, dislocate both perhaps, so it doesn't seem strange to the casual onlooker.

'We will try the west gate,' he says but when they get there it is worse. The militia have lost control and there is nothing passing through or around it. An ox cart has turned on its side, blocking the road and there are shops burning.

Catharo turns and runs back the way they have come, pulls her along another alley. A child is sitting on the cobblestones crying and she wants to pick him up but Catharo shouts, 'Leave him!' He rushes her past.

They hear horses in the street. She looks back and sees Alexander's cavalry streaming past, their swords drawn. 'Don't worry about them. It's the infantry you have to watch for. Those cocksuckers won't leave anything standing.'

She gapes at him. She has never heard that word before. She is shaking all over. She thought she'd be braver than this.

He kicks in the door of a shop. It is a tailor's, and there are bolts of cloth and scissors lying around on the benches. He shuts the door behind them and bars it. He picks up the scissors.

'Come here.'

'What are you going to do?'

'Your hair's got to come off.'

'What?'

'You want to be raped? I mean, not just once. You'll get passed around an entire regiment looking like that. We have to disguise you, girl. Look at you. Bitch though

117

you are, the Greeks won't care and the Persians are used to it. You're a nice-looking piece and they'll be through you a squadron at a time. You want to die, that's one thing. You'll not die that way. I gave my word to your father.'

Reflexively she reaches up and touches her hair. Yes, what did she think? That death would be clean and easy?

He grabs handfuls of her hair and chops through it with the scissors. In moments her hair is on the floor at her feet but he still isn't satisfied, keeps cutting until it is shorter than his. When he has finished she runs her hand across her scalp. She isn't a woman any more.

He rummages through the benches, finds a tunic and throws it at her. 'Put it on.'

'What?'

'What good is short hair if you're still dressed like that? Put the tunic on. What are you waiting for? A servant to do it for you? I won't look, don't worry. I have to find you something for your feet.' And he disappears into the back of the shop.

He comes back with a pair of boy's tough leather sandals. 'They'll fit you near enough. You're lucky the tailor had sons.'

He looks her up and down.

'What are you staring at?'

'You look like one of those dancing boys they pay double for down at the docks. I don't know I've done you a favour. They may bend you over a barrel anyway, knowing those fucking Greeks. Get the sandals on. We'll hide upstairs. We have to stay out of the way until the bloodlust is over. When they've got tired of killing we can come out again.'

He leads her up the stairs onto the roof. They crouch down under the parapet, listening as the screaming gets closer. Catharo peers over it to look into the street. 'They're coming! Macedonian bastards.'

CHAPTER 18

THE WAREHOUSES DOWN at the docks have been burning for days. They sleep on steps or on rooftops in the lulls, leaping over parapets to move on when the soldiers get closer.

She is hungry. She is thirsty. She wishes now she had jumped into the black arms of Tanith when she had the chance.

Above her the Byrsa is mostly in shadow. It is growing towards evening. She hears the tramp of hobnailed boots and peers into the narrow street below. She sees another building shimmer and tumble in a cloud of dust. The soldiers are clearing the tenements as they advance. They will not contest Carthage; they would rather pull it down, brick by brick.

They hold shields over their heads as they batter down the doors, prising away shutters with their swords and then scrambling into the dark interiors to dispute with angry skeletons who fight back with chair legs and kitchen knives.

Above them women and children hurl capstones and pans of boiling water.

The alley has been barricaded with ceiling joists and hunks of limestone. The soldiers scramble over them while an old man flings bricks from an upstairs window.

Catharo nudges her urgently. He points below. Two sappers have levered away the main doorframe. She feels the tremor through the roof. He grabs the piece of timber that has been their lifeline for two days and throws it over the alleyway to the next building and they scramble across. Moments later the tenement they had been hiding in comes down in a choking cloud of dust.

When it clears she sees more soldiers moving up the street through a mirage of heat. A catapult bolt deflects off the parapet in a shower of sparks. She screams and leaps back.

Below her an old man runs into the street on fire, screaming. Catharo pulls her away. He will not give up. He still says he will get her out of this, but she doesn't see how.

Torches move along the black defiles of the city. Gajendra supposes that he should be used to the smell of death by now, but he isn't. The thick smoke is making him nauseous. The elephants don't like it much either. Colossus trumpets in protest. It's as if they know what is happening here.

The streets are full of bodies; women, children, old men flushed out by the flames and the sappers, charred and crushed, some of them still moving or moaning. The street cleaners are dragging them out of the way of the cavalry with their hooked poles without bothering to check.

It is night but there are so many fires, the city is no darker than it might be at a particularly fiery sunset.

He sees two young boys crouching in the moon shadow; they have been cornered by four soldiers. They are laughing about it. One of the boys has a dagger out and the bigger one has taken shelter behind him.

Finally one of the soldiers decides it's time to be about their business and draws his sword. He lazily chops at the boy's head. What happens next is dazzling. The kid darts inside the blow and slices the man's neck, taking the sword from his hand before he is even dead.

It is so quick the other three just stand there astonished, and while they are busy being surprised he has made after the one nearest him, slashing his hamstring and putting him down.

The other two rouse themselves. They have armour and he has none; they back him against the wall. Gajendra wills the bigger boy to grab a sword and help his companion, but he just stands against the wall, not moving.

This is no good, Gajendra thinks, and marches over. The boy is on the ground now, still parrying blows with the sword, but there is blood leaking out of him everywhere and strong as he is he looks beaten.

'Stop!' Gajendra shouts at them. One of the attackers turns, an ugly veteran, with a scar across his nose and sprays of fresh blood across his face. In his present mood it's clear he would as happily put his sword in Gajendra as the boy on the ground. Neither of them are much pleased. One of their comrades is dead on the ground and the other is making mewing noises like a cat and clutching at his hams.

'Who are you, dog breath?'

'I'm the man with four bowmen behind him keeping him from harm. Who are you?'

Gajendra is hoping his archers are still there, but he

cannot afford to turn and look for them. Judging by the looks on their faces someone or something is backing him up and has given them a scare. He hears the tinkling of a bell and smiles. It is Colossus.

'Leave them, they're my prisoners now.'

'He killed our comrades!'

'No, he killed one of them. The other one's just keeled over now. When I tell Alexander he will not be pleased. Four of you against a boy and you couldn't dispatch him? What are your names?'

They say something, a curse he supposes, and walk away.

He looks over his shoulder. Colossus has flared his ears in warning. Now the danger is passed he settles again.

Gajendra goes to the boy, who is still reaching for his sword even as he's bleeding. He kicks the sword out of reach. He bends down and is astonished to discover that it is not a boy at all. It is a man, or a fiend of some kind; it is short, has a beard, a tattooed face and a nasty attitude. He slashes at Gajendra with his dagger and then passes out from loss of blood.

The taller boy is still cowering against the wall.

'Well, you're no hero.'

No answer.

'You might have tried to help him.'

'Is he going to be all right?'

'I don't know. Look what they've done to him and you did nothing to help. What was I supposed to do?'

'At your age I'd killed my first tiger,' he says to the bigger boy.

123

'With your breath?'

Gajendra stares. I have just saved this wretch's life and here he is insulting me. I can see we are going to get along famously. His archers finally show up.

'Do what you can for these two,' he tells them. 'They're my new waterboys,' and he walks away.

CHAPTER 19

THEY ARE NOT much to look at, as prisoners go. The smaller one is an uncommon fellow; a crooked little man with a tattooed face and as wide as he is high, and all of it muscle. He lies there, spreadeagled like a sacrifice, snoring and bloody.

He is not much to inspire, but what man is when his head is half stove in and he has bled all over himself? He has a wound the width of four fingers in his shoulder and down into his chest. Not much on an ordinary man, Ravi says, but he's only ten fingers high anyway.

The boy is not much more. He is delicate with snake hips; the next strong wind will blow him away. A bottom like a peach. He can only be trouble one way or the other. He would fetch a good price on the auctioneer's block as some rich man's private pet. There is high colour in his cheeks and blond curls. The Macks would pass him around like a wine jug if they got hold of him.

He is huddled against the wall, one hand laid on the bloodied dwarf. What an extraordinary sight. He is trembling. Do I look so fearsome? Gajendra puts a hand to his face and realizes he is covered in blood and elephant grime.

'Who are you?' he asks the lad.

The boy vomits on the ground. Ravi makes a face. 'Oh that's it,' he says. 'Spew everywhere. We find one good place to sleep and now we have his stink all night.'

'He can't help it. We shouldn't have given him so much food. He probably hasn't eaten anything for days.'

Ravi sighs. For all his truculence he is the one who walked through the dark to get the plate of stew for him.

The boy wipes his mouth with the back of his hand. 'My name's Mara.'

'And who's he?' Gajendra asks, pointing at the little fellow.

'That's my uncle. His name's Catharo.'

'Your uncle? Your uncle's a dwarf?'

'Don't call him that. He won't like it if he hears you say that.'

'Well, he's mine now so I'll call him what I want. And a "thank you" would not go amiss.'

'What do you wish me to thank you for?'

He hears Ravi take a breath at his insolence. 'For saving your lives,' Gajendra says.

'What made you think I wish to be saved?'

Until now Gajendra has been inclined to like him; now he wonders if he shouldn't have left them both to the mercenaries. He could have been buggered by half the irregulars and several squads from the phalanx by now. Was it too much to ask for a little gratitude, in the circumstances?

'What were you doing there?'

'My uncle is a merchant. We were running away from the soldiers.'

'A merchant?' Ravi says, astonished. 'What does he sell? Ugly potions?'

126

'What are these tattoos on his face?' Gajendra says. 'He looks like a bandit.'

'It is a custom where he is from.'

'So why do you not have them?' Ravi looks at Gajendra. 'There's something wrong here. He's the worst liar I have ever met, and that includes the carpet salesmen in the Babylon market.'

'What is your trade?' Gajendra asks Mara.

'We have an olive oil press in the city. We are just ordinary people.'

No, that's not right. There is something spoiled about him; and his uncle is no merchant. You didn't learn to fight like that pressing olives.

Gajendra squats down. 'You know we could just give you to the slavers. I would turn a tidy profit... for you, anyway.'

'Do whatever you wish.'

Ravi is disgusted. 'Just get rid of them. They're not worth the trouble.'

What is it that stays him? He should be dismissive of the boy's arrogance but somehow he admires it. If he had grovelled, he might have decided against him. There was something attractive in this show of defiance from a boy with arms like twigs.

'You could sell that one to a circus.'

'If he lives.'

'Which he won't, if his colour's any guide.'

Gajendra stands up and sighs. Ravi is older and wiser and probably a better judge. But he wasn't the new captain of the elephants. 'No, I'll keep them for dung larks.'

Ravi doesn't approve. 'That's just what we need. Two

more elephant boys. Even the tuskers can't shit that fast to keep them all busy.'

'What would you have me do? He's dying and the boy's a pansy. Someone has to help them.' Gajendra coughs; the air reeks of blood and smoke. 'Besides, did you see the dwarf fight? He has a big heart.'

'He'll be dead by morning,' Ravi says.

He bends down to examine him. He remembers the first time he saw such wounds after the battle against Alexander at the Jhellum River. They said the river turned red that day. He had thought he would never get accustomed to seeing men with arms torn off and their guts out. But you do.

'Three siglos he makes it.'

'Done.'

He lies on the straw, his skin grey. You would not think such a small body could hold so much blood. She finds a bucket and some water and wets a cloth, wipes his face. The whole square is filled with sleeping soldiers and some men are whimpering in their sleep all around her, even the ones who aren't wounded.

The stench is unbearable. It makes her want to be sick again. She wraps a scarf around her face and tries to take shallow breaths through her mouth. The fires are still burning down at the wharves.

I wonder what they will do to me if they discover I am a girl, she thinks; it will be worse if they know I am a priestess and the general's daughter.

This latest development confuses her. Why did this… she could not even remember his name, except that it was foreign sounding ... why did he save her? And what was he doing in Alexander's army? she wonders. He doesn't look Greek. Perhaps he's Persian. He terrifies her.

Catharo opens his eyes. 'Don't tell them who you are,' he whispers.

'I cannot stand this. You should have let me die.'

'Don't be such a ... coward. After all this ... you're going to live. I'm not taking these wounds for you ... for nothing.'

'What if you die?'

'Then you're in real trouble ... aren't you? But I'm not going to die. That's why your father employs me. I'm indestructible.'

Finally she sleeps, but only fitfully. She is in her husband's house. Her son totters towards her. She holds out her arms for him and he waddles towards her on fat legs.

Then he falls and she cannot catch him; he has fallen through the earth, into the Tophet in Tanith's temple.

The dream wakes her. Her heart is racing and she is sweating. She watches Carthage burn. She hears a building fall nearby, sees a glow spread across the sky. Catharo lies quite still and she puts out a hand to check for breath on his lips. She expects he will die tonight.

She wonders what has happened to her father; has he escaped the city or have they captured him? Her captors do not seem to know or care.

They are lying under one of the arcades around the market square. There is a red glow in the sky over the docks where they have torched the granary. The Agora is full of drunks, toasting their victory. Shadows dance around the walls. The whole city reeks of death and smoke.

Somewhere people are screaming and she can hear the

ring of horses' hooves and the clash of iron swords; the fighting must still be going on somewhere. They are still bringing in more and more wounded, who lie moaning and shouting, unattended.

She closes her eyes and puts her face against the brick of the wall. This is what you get when you are too much of a coward to end it when you should.

CHAPTER 20

THE NEXT MORNING Gajendra goes down to the wharves to see what is happening. They are taking away the slaves; he watches women and children being herded into the squares, ready for the day's auction. Their captors' names have been scrawled on their bodies in blood so they can get paid. It's good business and lines of them stretch right the way to the docks.

He trips on a severed limb. Even the air stinks of charred flesh. He just wants to get out of the city and back onto the plain so he can breathe again.

He has put the two prisoners with the elephant boys. Not much they can do for the one with the tattoos; they have soaked the worst of the wounds in honey, bandaged him as best they can, the rest is up to him. He hopes he doesn't die; a man like that, he could have his uses.

The pretty boy is a strange one. If it had been Gajendra's uncle skewered like that he would have wept and talked to him, tried to coax him back to the living. This one just sits there staring at the sky.

The boy looks up as he approaches; still not much gratitude there, in fact he looks at Gajendra down the end of his nose like he is a slave walking into his bedchamber without begging leave. In the daylight he looks even worse than he did last night; his skin is white as milk and he is as skinny as a twig. He imagines he was one of those high-born little princes permanently attached to his mother's skirts.

The little fellow looks dead. Then he gives a snore to prove he's not. But his condition does not inspire confidence. Gajendra remembers how his father died, the smell of rot, the reeking sheets, shouting nonsense. Death was an unpredictable fellow; you never knew what he would do next.

'How is he?'

'The same.'

Gajendra crouches down. 'This one's your uncle, you say? Where's your mother and father?'

'They are both dead.'

'How?'

'My mother of a fever. My father – Alexander killed him.'

'Well, you're lucky. Pretty boy like you, if it wasn't for this Catharo you'd be on the slave blocks over there, that's if you were still alive after they'd done with you.' He pinches the skin on the little fellow's face and he groans and twists. A good sign if he can still feel pain. Gajendra stands up again. 'Here,' he says, and throws the boy a shovel.

'What is this?'

'I didn't mean you for decoration. You may have been a little prince before but now you're just a dung lark and I'm your new boss.'

'What am I supposed to do with this?'

'The boys will show you. It's not difficult. You muck out the elephant dung and shovel it into that cart over there. When it's full you take it and dump it somewhere.'

The new boy dropped the spade on the ground. 'I'm not touching that.'

Gajendra grabbed the boy's hands. They were soft like a girl's. 'You've not done a day's work in your life, have you?'

He doesn't answer.

'How did they let you get this way?' He picks up the shovel and pushes it at him. 'Do it or I'll give you to the Greeks. You're going to have blisters somewhere by the end of the day, and I promise you, you'd rather it was on your hands.'

Mara stands there, like he'd never seen such a thing before. 'You can't talk to me like this.'

Gajendra cuffs him smartly round the ear. 'I'll talk to you any way I like. Now get to work.'

The boy goes off, sulky, then stops and turns around. 'Is the temple burned?'

'Which temple?'

'Tanith.'

'I don't know the names of all your gods. Who is he?'

'It's a she. Tanith is a goddess.'

'Look, you lost the battle. Get used to it. Your city's gone, so is your old life. It's the way of it.'

'What happens to us now?'

'I'll treat you well enough if you don't give me any trouble. Learn to look after the elephants and the rest of the time just get out of the way.'

'We're... slaves?'

Gajendra wants to cuff him again. How can anyone be so dense? 'Of course. What did you think, I'd make you captain of the infantry?'

'What if I try to escape?'

'I don't care what you do. Run away if you like. I'll give you five minutes on your own out there. You'd better pray your uncle gets better, son, you've got some growing up to do.'

And he walks away.

CHAPTER 21

S HE HAS NEVER been around animals much, unless you count the peacocks in her father's garden. She has certainly never seen an elephant close up before and she is appalled. The noise they make is terrifying, they all stink and every one of them is the size of a house.

Ravi stands there watching her, slapping the elephant hook against his thigh. 'What are you doing?'

'Mucking out.'

'You don't look like you know which end of the shovel to hold. What's wrong with you, boy?'

'I'm doing the best I can.'

'A girl could do better.' He pinches the flesh of her arm. 'Look at you. You need to toughen up.'

She would hit him with the shovel but she does not know which end to hold. Damn these people. She has had enough.

'Don't stand *there*,' he says and shoves her to the side. 'You stand behind him and he can't see you. He'll squash you like an ant.'

'I can't do this.'

'Why not?'

'Look at me! I'm not used to this kind of work.'

He slaps his knee and laughs so hard she thinks he is going to fall over.

Don't let him bait you. It doesn't matter about the names he calls you. Keep your head down and don't ask for trouble.

When he's done laughing, Ravi grabs her hands and examines them. They are raw and blisters are starting to form already. It's only the first morning.

'Piss on them,' he says. 'It will harden them up.'

My father would have you horsewhipped if he heard you, she thinks. He'd as likely piss on *you*. She cannot believe anyone would think such a thing, never mind say it aloud. This is impossible. She wishes she were dead.

'How old are you?'

She hesitates. 'Fourteen.'

'No wonder you look like a girl. Maybe you'll get some muscle when your balls drop.'

'When do we get some rest?'

'Rest? That's just one elephant. You haven't started yet. Gaji's soft, he should take the whip to you.'

Am I not sweeping up this monster's droppings fast enough? Take one cart of it away, there is always more. 'How's Catharo?' she asks him.

'That fucking dwarf? He's alive. Cost me three siglos. I bet Gaji he wouldn't make it through the night. He's a tough little fellow.'

'Why did – what did you call him?'

'Gaji.'

'Why did he save us?'

'I don't know. He's like that. You never know what he'll do. Like this one,' and he slaps the monster on the side. 'So be careful of him or they'll be sweeping you up and putting you in the cart. That's why he has a bell round his neck, so you know he's there. Be nice to him, he has a temper.'

'Has he killed many men?'

'Colossus? He's not so bad. Just don't make him angry. The last captain we had took to him with the bull hook and he went crazy. If it wasn't for Gaji he would have destroyed the whole camp.'

Later that day the order comes to get the elephants out of the city. She straggles behind as they march them over Alexander's causeway. She cannot believe it has come to this. The other dung larks, as this is what Ravi calls them, push her around and taunt her in some language she does not even know. When Catharo dies, she will be on her own. There has to be a way out of this.

They take the elephants down to the lake for their bath. The elephants love the water, Ravi tells her. When we can, we bath them at least once a day.

They form up a procession, each elephant holding the tail of the one before. The water is torpid and brown; the elephants plunge in trumpeting and the boys set to work with the pumice, scrubbing them like naughty children.

The one they call Colossus is a massive beast with ragged ears and a scarred hide. He makes a great trumpeting as he sinks to his haunches in the river, spraying water joyously in the air with his trunk. Up close his skin does not even look alive; it is so grey and withered it is like something you might find hanging cured upon a wall. He is enormous; the height of two men and the size of a small palace.

But it is his eyes that astonish her. They watch her

intently, not with the brute indifference of a beast of the field but as if he knows what she is thinking.

She stands dumb, exhausted, at the bank, every bone and sinew creaking. She cannot take much more of this. Will no one in this place show her kindness?

Colossus reaches out for her with his trunk, and at first she is too frightened to move. He leaves a trail of slime all down her face and her chest and she yells in disgust, and plunges into the river to get it off.

She sinks to her knees in the shallows, drained. She can't do this. She's not built for it. Her whole family is dead and she is a slave. Even these dumb monsters abuse her. She shouts at the elephant, who just yawns as if he is laughing at her.

'I shouldn't have let them go on the ship alone,' she says. Her husband would not let her come because she was so sick with the unborn baby. 'I'll only be away three weeks, four at most,' he had said. That was a rich joke for the gods. How they must hate us up there.

There were days after her baby died that she woke in the morning feeling light, sometimes even happy. But then she would remember and with each remembrance she tried to reach for sleep again, huddle inside her dreams like she was hiding from some intruder in her house. There were too many days when she'd longed for oblivion; now her father's dwarf and this wretched Indian have snatched it away from her.

They are around a bend in the river and cannot be seen by the others, though she can hear the shouts and laughing as the waterboys scrub their elephants. A great tree limb floats past in the water and she grabs it.

'Hey! Hey!'

It's heavy. It's as much as she can do to swing it, but she does. She slams it into the monster's haunch. 'Colossus! Is that what they call you? Well, come on then!' She hits him again, as hard as she can. 'Come on! They say you don't like being hit.' She swings again. 'Look at me! See what I'm doing?' She swings a third time, slamming the heavy limb into his rump. 'Come on! Where's this famous bad temper? What's wrong with you? Come on!' She hits him again and again, until her arm muscles cramp and she drops exhausted back to her knees, sobbing.

The massive trunk snakes out towards her. She closes her eyes. This is it. Make it merciful and quick, she thinks. Instead the beast wrenches the tree limb from her grasp and sends it spinning end over end to land with a splash in the river.

She feels a rubbery trunk curl around her body and pick her up. He deposits her on the river sand and stands over her, staring at her with one sad pink eye. She notices his eyelashes for the first time, how thick and wiry they are, and how his wrinkles criss-cross his skin. She reaches out to touch him but he turns and wades away in the direction of his fellows, blasting water over his back as he goes.

It is a dull morning, grey and hot. The clouds suffocate and are greasy pale like the dead. But how brightly Alexander shines; how eager his blue eyes. He glitters like a newly minted coin.

There is a huddle around him, as always, he is the air that others breathe. Nearchus is there, he looks like a hawk with that beak of his and hunter's eyes, hazel and vicious.

A harried man with badly aligned teeth and his hand on his sword.

At his signal they all retire a step, their heads craning.

Alexander is praying before Baal-Ammon, offering a skinned beast; at least he hopes it is a beast. He smiles as Gajendra enters, as if to say: here is the man I have waited my entire life to see.

'Ah, elephant boy! You know this god? His name is Baal. My advisers tell me that really he is Zeus, in another form. He is the god of the thunderstorm.'

The god stands, arms outstretched, hands pointing to the pit where sacrificial victims are burned. The temple is strangely bare. Perhaps it has been looted. There are a few benches, a gorilla skin hanging on the wall. Frankincense burns in mounds as big as ox carts.

Baal makes the other generals look small and peevish. He has a thunderous expression, while these men just look like schoolboys who cannot get what they want.

'They give their firstborn to the gods, they say, in times of war and famine. I wonder how many firstborns gave their lives needlessly to stay me? If they had but known. You cannot ask a god to work against his own son.'

He gets to his feet, jumps up beside Baal on his plinth to mimic his frown. There is a shudder through the corps of those who attend him. This blasphemy shocks them. You should not even mock a god you do not believe in, for you never know.

'Do you not think I should make a fine Baal, elephant boy? I think I should like to be asked for my favour a hundred years from now. To have someone pray to my statue, now that is something to be wished for, isn't it? We are here for but a short time but we may be remembered forever if we live this life with courage and ambition. Do you not think so?'

Alexander laughs and jumps down to the marble. There is such restlessness about him today, he cannot stay still for a moment as he talks. He takes out his knife and stirs the incense coals with the edge of the blade, breathing it in.

'Some men say that I am Hercules brought back to life. What do you think?'

'I don't know much about him.'

'He was a god. Do you think I'm a god?'

He can feel the other generals' eyes on him. If Gajendra says yes, they will set on him like a pack of wolves. Alexander seems to be the only one who cannot feel the tension.

'Come on now, answer. I rule half the world. I am invincible in battle.'

'But are gods not immortal?'

'Perhaps I am immortal. Until a man dies how can anyone be sure?' His flatterers laugh. No one else. 'My father saw my mother consorting with Zeus, did you know that? In the form of a serpent. Gods are shape shifters, elephant boy, or they are in our world.' He pats him on the shoulder, like a son, lowers his voice. 'Nearchus wants your head, you know. He says you are uppity. An uppity Indian.' He laughs. 'Nothing worse.'

'Why would he say that?' Gajendra says, staring at Nearchus.

'Oh, he means nothing by it. Do not take offence.' He steers him away from the generals. 'You should congratulate him. He is to be married. I am giving him one of my harem, as thanks for his steadfast duty. A girl named Zahara.'

Gajendra feels the blood drain from his face.

'Now have you heard? Antipater has bought off Athens and Corinth. He is gathering an army against me, he plans to go against me at Sicily. Did you know that?'

But he is not listening. Alexander is marrying Zahara to Nearchus?

'Come, boy. I asked you a question. What do you think of Antipater's plans?'

'There has been talk about the camp.'

'Some say it is all your fault.'

'Mine?'

'If you had not informed me of this plan to poison me, then I should not have crucified Iolaus and had Kassander put in a cage.'

'But then you would have been dead.'

'Is that all you can say in your defence?' he says and starts to laugh. The corps laugh dutifully along also. 'So then I suppose you wish me to reward you. Did you like the way they died?'

Zahara was meant for him! This was not how it was supposed to be. 'Who, lord?'

'Come on, elephant boy, keep up. Iolaus and the captain of the elephants! What was his name?' He snaps his fingers for memory.

'Oxathres,' one of the generals says.

'Yes. Oxathres. You never liked him, did you?'

'I hated him.'

'Well, there you are then. He took two days to die. A

142

long time. He did not look as strong. I should have wagered three hours, the most. You?'

'I thought he suffered overmuch.'

'Overmuch? But he wanted to leave *me* to die by inches. He set the stakes, not I. How did you feel seeing your captain wriggling like that? Undignified. They die of suffocation, you know. The pain is secondary.'

'It scared me.'

'Scared you? Why?'

'I should hate to die that way.'

'A man should never be afraid of death. Look it in the eye, stare it down, invite it in for wine and welcome. Pain is nothing. Are you scared of pain?'

'I don't know.'

'Then what is it? I wonder. I saw your face that day. What was it about it that troubled you so?'

Did Alexander really pick him out? His entire army was packed into the *maidan*. He surely could not make out one face among thousands, unless he registers every man instantly – like a god.

'It seems you have many talents. I cannot turn my back on you for a moment. If you are not taming wild elephants, you are discovering plots against me. Now you are talking to elephants.'

'Talking to elephants, my lord?'

'That is what they say. That you whisper in an elephant's ear and it will do anything you say, as if it were your own chamberlain. Is it true, elephant boy? Do you talk to elephants?'

'Not in that way. I just do what every *mahavat* does.'

'If you are like every *mahavat*, I would not have made

143

you captain. A question. We leave for Sicily within the week to face Antipater and his Greeks. My generals say that we should leave the elephants behind, that they are too expensive to feed and too difficult to transport. What do you say to that?'

'I say that if you have a weapon that is certain to confound and defeat your enemy, then you should use it.'

'Ah, but they do not think so. They say we won here because the enemy had never faced elephants before. Next time they will be ready. Antipater is not stupid, he will have reports of my battles in India and at least the advice of those soldiers I sent home with Kraterus – some of the ingrates deserted, did you know that? The bastards fought against your Rajah at the Jhellum River, they know the tactics I devised for fighting them. You know what they were?'

Of course he knew. Colossus still had scars on his legs and flank from wounds he had taken there. His *mahavat* had died there. It was the Jhellum that forced the Rajah to make peace with Alexander and give him two hundred elephants as part of the treaty. It was how he and Ravi and the others came to be in Alexander's employ.

Of course he knew.

The Macedonians encircled them first, using archers to pick off their *mahavat*s, and then his slingers attacked the elephants' eyes with a volley of darts. When the tuskers were half blinded and had no *mahavat* to help them, the infantry worked as a team, the bravest distracting the elephants by chopping at their trunks with a scimitar while their comrades chopped out the hams at the backs of their legs with axes.

It was brutal but effective. Gajendra doubted that any other army but Alexander's might be quite as successful. It took iron discipline to do what they did. As it was, the Silver Shields had taken frightening losses.

'Do you have a remedy to this?'

Gajendra looks him in the eye. 'I do.'

'Go ahead then. We are eager to hear it.'

The generals stand there with their arms folded. This Indian is going to tell them how to make war? This should be good.

'First I would not use elephants against infantry. As you say, a well-trained phalanx will not be as easy as the Celts and Gauls we fought outside Carthage.'

'What then?'

'I would put them on the flanks and pit them against cavalry. Horses are terrified of elephants. They cannot make a successful charge against them. But I would disguise the move. I would make an oblique attack from the centre across the enemy's front.'

Alexander stares at him for a long moment, then laughs and punches his shoulder. 'My little elephant boy is a student of war!' He turns to his commanders. 'Who would have thought?' He laughs again. 'What else would you do, my little general? Show me.'

He grabs Ptolemy and Perdiccas and his other generals, pushes them around like counters on a money changer's table. They flush, appalled, but they can hardly protest.

'Here, you are my new Elephantarch for the day,' Alexander says. 'Tell me who should go where.'

'What are the forces ranged against me?'

'There have been many defectors among his

145

Macedonians, gone over to Kraterus, and he is forced to fight on two fronts. So his army is mainly Greeks and mercenaries. My spies tell me he will have these as well as half of Leosthenes's men as well.'

'Leosthenes?'

'He commands the largest army of mercenaries in the world. He put himself out for bids. I should not stoop so I left the auction to Antipater.'

'So how many?'

'Forty thousand. Perhaps fifty.'

'Cavalry?'

A casual shrug. 'Five thousand. But *Greek* cavalry. We shall have four thousand, my new phalanx and my Silver Shields. Twenty-five thousand, plus our irregulars.'

Alexander pushes Ptolemy to the centre, as the phalanx. 'Here is Antipater's phalanx.' He grabs Perdiccas, and pushes him in front of Ptolemy. 'There! And here, Perdiccas, be the archers. Where shall Antipater place him?'

'They will be with the infantry. Archers are worthless against heavy cavalry; no bow is effective beyond a hundred paces, twenty-five if the wind is off the sea. I should use my own archers on the backs of the elephants where they are not nullified by speed.'

'An elephant can only carry one archer, perhaps two.'

'An elephant should carry at least four or five.'

The generals shake their heads and mutter. They don't like it; they like the old ways.

Finally Perdiccas says, 'It will slow the elephants down.'

'How?'

'The extra weight.'

'Do you know how many men an elephant can carry on its back?'

Perdiccas doesn't. He would like to thrash him. A gyppo talking back! Alexander beams.

'If you don't know how many, then how do you know it will slow him down?' He turns to Alexander. 'The *howdahs* need to be bigger, so you can have four archers or slingers in there. Instead of wood, you use hardened leather, to make it lighter and you give the archers lighter armour too. Then you have something no other army has – a mobile artillery.'

Alexander turns to Nearchus. 'You hear that, my friend? What a lieutenant you have here!' He shoves Lysimachus out next to Perdiccas, as Antipater's cavalry.

'Seleucus, you shall be the right wing. And Nearchus is Antipater. There, you have your enemy. You are outnumbered two to one. What shall you do?'

'First I should better armour my elephants.'

'Better armour them?'

'To protect their legs against infantry. I can design the plates for you and your smithies can make them. It is not difficult. It's just hooped iron tied together with leather thongs. You need heavier trunk and face armour, also.'

'Why are we talking so much about elephants?' Lysimachus grumbles. 'We know what they can do.'

'But they can do much more,' Gajendra says. 'If I were Alexander, I should use my elephants as a shield.' He walks up to Ptolemy but then turns towards Lysimachus. 'If your enemy sees the elephants, he is focused on the elephants. He may not think there are also several squadrons of cavalry behind them. He will not think you will go against cavalry because they are too quick. But the horses don't know that. They will turn.'

'Stand back, Lysimachus,' Alexander says, and he does as he is commanded.

'I should halt my elephants here, for the job is done. There is a break in the line. You are behind me with your Companion Cavalry. The mass of infantry are to our left. But if I am Alexander I should ignore them.' He steps past Perdiccas and Ptolemy, stands nose to nose with Nearchus. 'Here is Antipater at the rear. I should apply my violence here.'

Nearchus and Gajendra stare at each other.

Alexander claps his hands and stands between them. 'An excellent discourse. My elephant boy may make a fine general one day. It is decided, then, the elephants come with us. Can your beasts travel by ship?'

'It is difficult.'

'How difficult?'

'They must be manoeuvred up a plank to the ship. They are unhappy about it.'

'But you can do it?'

'I can do it.'

'You have managed elephants on a ship before?'

'Of course.' A lie.

'Good. Give me the details of what you need for the new armour and we shall set to work on it, as well as new *howdahs*. We shall have more archers on each beast. Gentlemen, we are going to Sicily!'

They are not all as enthusiastic as Alexander. As Gajendra leaves, the other generals position themselves so that he must squeeze through or else shove them aside. They look like lions hungry for supper.

'Jumbo fucker,' one of them murmurs as he passes.

CHAPTER 22

Z AHARA PASSES, A covered wagon taking her and the rest of Alexander's harem along the waterfront to one of the triremes. He only sees her eyes, the rest of her face is hidden behind a veil as she sits huddled in the back with the other girls. There is an escort of cavalry so it is barely a glimpse.

'In bed she'll just lie there.'

He looks around sharply to see who has spoken. It is Mara. The boy has this look on his face, like he knows what he's talking about.

'What are you talking about, cherry boy?'

'That's the trouble with beautiful women. They think if they lie there and sigh it's all a man deserves. She'll want a ruby for every kiss and a diamond for every entry.'

Gajendra cannot believe a slave would address him like this. He sees the other dung larks look at him to see what he will do. It sets a bad example, this. One of the other waterboys answered back to him yesterday and he had to thrash him to keep the rest of them in line. So why does this fresh-faced little mucker have special privileges?

Two other boys wheel away their handcarts filled with elephant dung. He pushes Mara in their direction. 'Get back to work.'

If this continues, he shall have to start carrying a whip. He's too soft with these boys. He stops and looks along the docks. They are unloading the women onto Alexander's trireme. There is an ache in his chest. This has ruined his day.

They are trying to get the elephants on the ships. Mara watches Gajendra coax them down to the dock one at a time; he only ever uses the bull hook to guide them, touching their trunk now one side, then the other, talking to them all the time in a language she has never heard before.

Finally he mounts the one called Colossus, and guides him towards the landing dock. It fascinates her to watch him, murmuring a continuous stream of orders in that strange language, tapping the elephant by the ear with the rod or touching him with the hook, all part of this same arcane communication.

Catharo is with her. Two days ago she thought he would die; but already he is walking again, one arm useless, the rest of him weak as a newborn lamb. The captain – Gajendra, she now remembers – has let him be. He may still have one foot in the Shades but the other elephant boys are yet wary of him and they have stopped their bullying; the tattoos on his face scare them, and he snarls at anyone who comes close. You don't expect it from a little fellow.

There is a sharp wind, raising waves on the inner harbour but unsettling the animals. Elephants may like the water, but the sea is a different proposition.

She watches Gajendra lead Colossus forward. It is not just one movement but a series of clicks with his tongue and nudges with his knees and feet as well as the hook. She allows herself to admire him. It is every bit as skilful as the best riders in her father's cavalry.

They have constructed a stout walkway of flat beams. Colossus eyes it suspiciously, flares his ears in alarm and turns away. Gajendra is patient. He leads him back. Colossus trumpets and circles. At the last moment he turns away again.

'This is impossible,' Catharo mutters at her shoulder. 'They will never get this stupid beast on the ship!'

'He's not stupid.'

Colossus circles again and one of the waterboys is almost trampled under his hind legs. After five attempts everyone is shouting and cursing and covered in dust and sweat and stinking of elephant.

Alexander appears on the wharf, with his usual coterie of staff officers, hangers-on, yes-men. He goes nowhere without them. Someone must lick his boots and tell him how like a god he is. 'Having trouble, elephant boy?'

'It will be all right, my lord.'

'What's going on here?' Nearchus asks him. 'What's the delay?'

'Colossus won't go aboard.'

'Well, what are you going to do about it?'

'We'll get him there.'

'You'd better. We have to be under sail tomorrow night. I want the army landed in Sicily within the week.' He rides off, leaving Nearchus behind in charge of things.

There is a hole smashed in the jetty where Colossus has stomped his foot. They try and control him with long pikes and ropes but it does no good. He is getting angry with them; he yanks on one of the dock stanchions with his trunk then butts it with his enormous head; the whole dock starts to sway. In a moment he will run amok.

She looks at Gajendra. He is sweating. Even he looks frightened now.

Nearchus has lined the docks with soldiers carrying javelins, bows and axes. If he does too much damage they mean to take him down.

Mara has no experience with elephants but the answer to the problem seems clear to her. If the beast is frightened of the sea, then make him think he is still in the forest.

She steps forward. 'You cannot do it this way!'

Gajendra looks at her, wide-eyed. 'You have a better idea, pansy boy?'

'Yes, I do.' I may not be as strong as you, she thinks, but at least I'm not weak between my ears.

He has Colossus let him down. He grabs her by the arm and leads her away, out of earshot.

'Tell me.'

'He's afraid of the water. So don't let him see it. Cover his eyes. Then hang awnings on the ship so he can't see the water even when he's on board. Cover the deck with bushes and trees and dirt. And reinforce these boards,' she said, jumping on the deck. 'A big animal like that needs to feel solid earth under its feet.'

He hesitates. He follows her reasoning but frets over the delay such precautions will take. But what choice do they have?

It takes another half a day to cart in enough dirt to throw on the trireme, shroud them with canvas awnings, then have a detail of slaves carry bushes and small trees down to the dock. The soldiers stand around, laughing and making ribald comments.

The carpenters have strengthened the dock and covered it with dirt, like the ships. Gajendra looks on, his face a mask. He has staked his pride and his position in the hierarchy of the elephant squadron on this. If he cannot get these elephants on the ships, and Alexander leaves without them, he will be just another shitkicker the rest of his life.

He drapes silk curtains from the headdress that Colossus wears to battle. Now he lets them fall, so his eyes are covered, and leads him back down to the dock, tapping behind his ears with his hook to guide him.

Colossus sniffs the air with his trunk and moves slowly, not quite trusting the ground underneath him, but when he feels the dirt and bushes either side of him he gains confidence. Mara wills Colossus onto the ship, prays that he does not stumble or baulk. She feels an affinity with him now. Why didn't he trample her into the mud of the river? Ravi had promised her that was what he would do.

Gajendra seems calm, but the sweat gleams on his face.

The waterboys crowd around Colossus, singing to him. Ravi sets his own elephant to follow and they both go tamely along the gangplank and onto the trireme. There is a cheer from the waterboys. Even some of the soldiers applaud, even though they have been mocking them all morning.

She catches Gajendra's eye. She does not expect effusive thanks. Just as well, for all he affords her is a reluctant shrug of the shoulders.

The boys use pitchforks to pile the hay in front of Colossus. He seems content enough now. Soon they will be on their way to Sicily.

CHAPTER 23

A FAIR WIND SNAPS the rigging and sends a thrill
through the canvas. There are rain squalls out on the
ocean. Gulls wheel in the air, hurled about by the wind.

She remembers the night she looked out of her window
in Megara and saw lightning flicker over the sea. She wonders now if it was the same storm that took her husband
and son. She had felt something clutch at her stomach and
thought it was her unborn child moving, but perhaps what
she felt was her husband saying goodbye.

The elephants stagger as the ship see-saws on the swell.
Colossus and Ran Bagha trumpet pitifully. She fears they
will snap their chains, but there is no one to help Gajendra
quieten the beasts as all the waterboys are clinging wretch-
edly to the side.

Mara watches the dark clouds scurry across the face of
the moon and dares the gods to claim her. Do it, damn you;
send the ship over and let me be free of this wretchedness.

But the plaintive trumpeting of the elephants makes her
forget her own pity. She hauls herself along the deck to
their enclosure. She has never seen two more thoroughly
miserable animals.

She starts to talk to them. She knows they cannot understand her, but if you can talk to a horse, you can talk to an

elephant is how she reasons it, and she has seen her father talk to his horse more tenderly than he ever talked to her mother.

Besides, if you beat something with a stout piece of wood and ask it to kill you, and it won't, then there's a good chance it won't stamp on you in a storm either.

She does what she used to do to her little boy when he was sick, pats him and sings to him; and then she rubs the widest part of this peculiar long nose, even though it is like rubbing sandstone. She tells him it will soon be over and what a brave lad he is.

After a while Colossus stops his trumpeting and the other beast follows his lead. They put their trunks in each other's mouths, perhaps for comfort. They are even strange creatures in the dark, when all you know of them is the smell and that curious rumbling they make. She has never before heard of a beast that can talk with its vitals.

'There, my big man, don't be afraid. It's going to be all right. The captain calls it just a fair wind. Soon you will be on dry land and we will find you some trees to eat.'

Colossus seeks her out with his trunk. After he is done she is covered in slime but by now she is too wet and too seasick to care.

Gajendra staggers across the deck. It is his first time on the sea. He needs to go to his elephants but another spasm sends him rushing for the side. The spray on his face feels cool. He shivers and burns at once. He kneels, wiping the bile from his mouth, and then staggers back to where Colossus and Ran Bagha are riding out the storm in their chains. He sees the new dung lark standing there under Colossus's front legs, fearless of the tusks or of being trampled. Perhaps he has underestimated the boy.

All right there for now, but he'd better not leave him alone once things are calmer, the sailors would be after him. Too pretty for his own good, that one. But he had hide, you had to give him that. The other waterboys wouldn't go near the tuskers when they were like this. But this one is talking to them like they are unruly children needing a good scolding.

One big wave and Colossus will crush the new boy against the gunwale. He'll pop like overripe fruit.

'What are you doing?' he shouts at the boy.

'Someone has to do it. Last time I saw you, you had your head over the side crying for your mother.'

Gajendra cannot believe his ears. The pansy boy thinks he can talk back to him now? 'How did you know how to get them onto the ship?'

'It was obvious.'

'Not to anyone else.' He drags him clear of his elephants. This is his job, not some dung lark's.

Just then the ship pitches on a wave and they are thrown together; the lad puts out a hand and catches his arm as if it were the most natural thing in the world that Gajendra should be expected to stop a slave from falling onto the deck. Mara lingers there on his arm long enough to confirm his suspicion that the boy would not mind it if he were given to the sailors for entertainment.

He shrugs him off.

'You have a way with them.'

'I don't see how. They are like horses that have mated

158

with a public building. I have never seen anything so big or so ugly.'

'No, you love them. It's in your face. At least you're good for something. You're pretty much useless for anything else.'

'Is that your way of thanking me?'

'For what?'

'For telling you how to get them on the ships.'

'I don't remember that. As far as I can recall, it was my idea.' He is not about to make himself beholden to a slave.

There is no more to say on the matter. His stomach rebels again and he rushes for the side. When he is done he looks back and sees Mara there again, gripping the rail, whispering to his elephant, telling him everything is going to be all right.

Gela, Sicily

The infantry go ashore in boats. They march into town and overwhelm a small garrison of Greeks after a short skirmish. Now the navy is landing horses and supplies. They bring the triremes into the docks to land the elephants.

Alexander is already there, supervising the landing, sending out scouts, ordering the Silver Shields into a defensive line around the town. He now occupies the small fort overlooking the harbour. A goat-skin vellum map has been placed on a trestle table.

He has planned a route through the mountains to Syracuse. He wants to surprise Antipater. It is as if the greater he is outnumbered the more eager he is to start the fight.

It seems Syracuse was on the verge of civil war anyway. The present tyrant had been disputing ownership of the city with some democrat called Agathocles, who represented the poor, of course, but had put aside his principles long enough to map out a deal with Alexander.

So Antipater and the tyrant, Sostratus, have now discovered a firm friendship.

Antipater has brought with him an army mainly of Greeks from Corinth and Athens, good for disporting with little boys and philosophy, Alexander tells them, but hopeless in a fight. He has forty thousand infantry. It will just make more corpses, he says, for numbers do not matter against a well-drilled army.

'And after we have won I will take back my Empire, and Corinth and Athens will have to deal with me.' His navy, he tells them, has established a blockade. Antipater and the tyrant of Syracuse will have to treat or fight. There is no backing down now, for anyone.

Nearchus walks in, stamps to the water pitcher, and splashes water on his face. He scowls when he sees Gajendra. 'What's he doing here?'

A real son of Macedon: fierce, xenophobic and impatient. Alexander seems amused at his irritation. His officers rush to console him for this slight. The generals watch the Persians fuss around their general with looks of savage contempt.

'I asked him here. He is your second in command and he knows elephants better than we. It may serve us to listen to him.'

'Are all your beasts landed safely?' Nearchus growls.

'They are.'

'I still say we hardly need them. Our cavalry are enough for this rabble we're against.'

'I made you Elephantarch because I thought you would appreciate their uses. Gajendra here has suggested that you could take command from a *howdah*, it would give you a better view of the battlefield, and you could use drums and flags to signal your intentions. It is how the Rajah of Taxila does things, apparently.'

Nearchus looks as if he will have apoplexy. He may be general of the elephants but he does not intend to go near one.

'Besides, if these elephants are not such a formidable weapon, why did you have me turn back after the Jhellum River? We would be at the end of the world by now and ruler of it. But you and the rest of the Companions said the next king had four thousand elephants and we would be no match.'

It still rankles with him, it is clear. He will get his revenge on all of them for stopping his inexorable advance on the unknown. The generals look accusingly at each other. Alexander feigns not to notice. Divide and conquer, that is his way.

Their king stabs a finger on the chart. 'This is where we are. Agathocles tells me that Antipater is disembarking his army at Syracuse as we speak. I should like to join battle with him before he has had a chance to choose his battleground. He will think the elephants will slow us. I should like to prove him wrong. Are we ready?'

'Should we not wait for our blockade to take effect?' Perdiccas says. 'If we draw his navy out to sea and destroy it, Antipater is finished.'

Alexander looks at him as if he has stepped into something foul. 'Where is the glory in that?'

'But you have spent half your treasury on the new fleet,' Ptolemy reminds him.

'So that I should not be at a disadvantage when I am on the land.'

'But what if Antipater will not leave Syracuse?' Nearchus says. 'Must we endure another siege?'

'I know Antipater. He will not hide from me. If he wants Macedon to accept him as king, then he knows he must defeat me, not hide from me.' He grins. 'Besides, I have his son.'

There are nods around the table. They are agreed. Gajendra grins: this is his chance, too. One good battle is all it will take.

CHAPTER 24

ALEXANDER SENDS FOR him. The guard escorts him through the camp and past Alexander's pavilion to a field almost a stade away. At first Gajendra thinks his general is feeding some wild pet, the way he teases and coos before dropping a well-gnawed bone into the cage.

Gajendra's nose twitches. It is Kassander. He has stayed alive these four seasons, somehow surviving the journey from Babylon and the sea crossing. He is kept in a wooden cage that is dragged everywhere that Alexander goes.

He is not in the fettle he once was; rolling around half starved and sunburned in one's own excrement can detract from one's enjoyment of life, or so it seems to Gajendra. He does not recognize the man he saw striding so defiantly to his execution that morning in Babylon. How he must have wished for crucifixion these last months.

The clothes have rotted off him. The smell would stun a hyena. He is skin and bone, a skeleton with sores.

'Ah, elephant boy!' Alexander says.

'My lord.'

'Tell me, how are my elephants?'

'They are well now they are back on dry land.'

'There was some difficulty getting them aboard but Nearchus has told me how it was finally achieved. You

163

made the ships look like a jungle! That was inspired. An idea of his own invention, is this so?'

So the bastard wishes all the credit. He wonders how to answer; he wants to spit. Yet the irony does not escape him. Really, the credit should go to the pansy catamite.

'You hesitate. Don't tell me a Macedonian general would try and take credit for another's virtue?' He laughs, and his crowd laugh along with him. Here is a man with ten shadows and ten echoes.

He turns around. Kassander howls and claws at the bars. It seems a bone and a piece of gristle is not enough for his dinner, especially after so long.

He tries not to retch. You did this, Gajendra, he is there because of you.

'I had a tutor once,' Alexander says. 'He found me burning incense to sweeten my room while I studied my books and when he caught me he thrashed me for it. He told me I was being wasteful. "When you conquer the spice regions you can throw away all the incense you like," he said. "Until then, don't waste it." So when I conquered Gaza I sent him eighteen tons of frankincense and myrrh. Do you think I made my point?'

'And you made him a very rich man.'

'Well, I didn't want to be vindictive. But you see what I'm saying. Nothing is ever in the past. Whatever has been done to us, it is there with us, for always. It speaks to us, urges us to present action. Doesn't it, elephant boy?' He smiles then, as if he can see into his soul. 'They don't like you, you know.'

'Who, my lord?'

'The other generals.'

'What have I done to them?'

'You have offended them.'

'How?'

'By not being born in Macedon. A grave error for one so young and ambitious. And you are ambitious, aren't you?'

'I want to be like you.'

'That's part of it. But there's something more, isn't there? You will tell me one day. I will divine it, somehow. What do you want, elephant boy?'

'Everything. I want to be a general. I want to conquer the world at your side.'

Several of his sycophants find this amusing. He silences them with a glance. 'Ride at my side? On an elephant? You should hardly keep up.'

'The elephants are a means to an end.'

'Go on.'

'I want a beautiful woman in my bed. I want a horse like yours. I want my boot on the other man's neck.' His voice has risen. Alexander, at least, does not seem to think his ambitions are either shallow or stupid.

'What should I get in return for such an embarrassment of riches?'

'Loyalty.'

'I can have loyalty at the cost of a few nails and some pieces of wood. Ask the men who saw your captain crucified. They won't let me down now. I didn't make him suffer from ill will. It was just tactics. You understand that word, don't you? Tactics.'

'I do.'

'Tell me more about it.'

'It is when you deliberately show your enemy your back and then watch him in the mirror.'

Alexander stands very close, holding his gaze. 'I know you. I know who you are. You know that, don't you?'

Gajendra nods.

'You can lead elephants but can you lead men?'

'You have to understand the nature of both before you can get them to do what you want.'

'I saw you when I promised Zahara to Nearchus. What is she to you?'

He does not answer.

'You like them, do you? Women? I mean, apart from breeding.'

He nods. Alexander's lip curls in disappointment. He feels he has given the wrong answer. 'Well, there is nothing to be done. She is a princess and you are an elephant boy. It was foolish of you to dream.'

Alexander returns to Kassander. He picks up a hock of beef that a servant holds out to him on a silver tray and starts to chew it. The thing in the cage thrashes and howls, trying to grab it from between the bars, but Alexander stays a finger's breadth out of range. The crowd snicker, amused.

'I remember once going into my father's study as he was writing a letter, addressed to an ally of his. The man who was to take it for him was waiting outside in an anteroom; I knew him, he was a friend of his. Do you know what it said? It said: *Kill the man who brings you this missive.* What do you think my father did?'

Gajendra shook his head.

'After he had sealed the letter he went outside, put his

arm around the man and asked him to stay for dinner. They stayed up all night drinking wine and telling jokes. They parted on the best of terms.'

'Why are you telling me this?'

Alexander puts an arm around his neck, draws him in and kisses the top of his head. 'Promise men the world but your thoughts belong to you. It's a lesson you would do well to learn.'

That night, in his sleep, he is back in the Taxila valley. There are monkeys screaming in the trees just outside their hut. His mother and sisters are pounding rice in the yard. He hears their chatter, and he opens his eyes with a start but it is just the canvas whipping in the wind.

Every day it's harder to remember his mother's face. He just remembers her throaty laugh and the smell of cardamom. He should have done something to save her. Here in the dark he stands accused of cowardice; a little boy, nine years old, but he should have done something.

He can't remember how he came to be in Taxila. He must have known how to find his way even at that age, but now he doesn't remember how or how long it took him. He imagines a small boy wandering about the camp stealing food.

That seems likely. He doesn't remember the dacoits riding away or what he did next. Just ran, he supposes, in the way that a child does. An instinct for survival, children.

They have put the elephants in a great warehouse by the docks. Catharo sits in the shade of one of the godowns with his back against the wall. A strip of linen supports his left arm, the wound is healing well. It seems to her you cannot kill this man even if you cut him in half. Even the sea would choke on the bones and spit him back.

She wonders how old he is; it is impossible to know. He has been slipping in and out of her father's private study since she was a little girl. His size deceives; any man that calls him a midget finds himself on his back with his teeth scattered on the ground and his nose broken. He is like one of those dogs that hunt lion; he goes for the belly first and only when the entrails are out does he start to fight.

She has asked him from when she was a little girl what the tattoos on his face mean and always he has a different answer. There are thick rings on his fingers but she suspects this is not vanity but for fighting, the quicker to gouge out an eye.

He tears at some bread with his teeth and tips back the waterskin so that the water runs into his beard. Then he leans toward her, and pats her knee, as if he is about to impart a gentle word. 'We have to escape.'

'What's the point?'

'I promised your father I would keep you alive.'

She is quiet for a time and then takes a deep breath. 'I would rather avenge him.'

'Avenge him?'

'You can do it, Catharo, if any man can. Let me help you. There is nothing left for me now. This way we do something for Carthage and for my father.'

'My charter is to keep you alive.'

'For what purpose? My father is dead and Carthage is destroyed.' She leans in. 'We have to get close to him.'

'No one comes close to him except the Companions, and he doesn't even trust his own that well any more. He put a spear through his best friend once after he had drunk too much wine.'

'We will use Gajendra.'

Catharo shakes his head. 'It's a ridiculous idea. Besides, I gave my word to your father.'

'My father could not have known we would be in such a position to avenge him, avenge all Carthage! Do you not listen to the waterboys? It seems our Alexander has taken the elephant talker under his wing. He nurtures him like a favoured nephew, they say. There have even been personal audiences. Fortune has given us opportunity. If I befriend him, I might get close to Alexander also.'

'Befriend? I won't let you whore yourself to that Indian!'

'Would it not be worth it to kill Alexander?'

'It is not a job for a woman to do! I gave my word to your father to protect you to my last breath. Enough! Go to sleep.'

He rolls over in the straw.

She looks at her hands; they are raw and bleeding from the work. There is dirt under her fingernails and it is ingrained in her skin. She stinks of elephant and their droppings. She has never felt so tired in her life.

She lies in the dark and listens to men farting and snoring around her. The few still awake talk of camp followers and wives and swap whoring stories. It seems there are places a man can put his erect organ she has never considered; certainly her husband had never wished her to welcome it in such places. She wonders if he ever talked of her this way. She cannot imagine it.

Oh, and now this young fellow speaks about a goat. A goat, really? And this other one about a whore without legs in Alexandria. He paid extra. This one goes to it with his sister; this one with a midget in Babylon: he claims he himself is so well favoured in nature that he had three of them end to end at once.

I have had one man my whole life. I swear, after this, I shall never want another.

She closes her eyes and hears her husband laugh as he plays dice in the courtyard with his brothers. Hasdrubal had such a pleasant laugh. They would love his company, the gods. He would take all their money at some game of chance but he'd shout them wine afterwards.

She remembers how he had kissed her that late afternoon as he and their son waited for the tide; and then, kneeling, had kissed her belly and said goodbye to their unborn daughter as well.

She puts a hand to her womb in remembrance.

It is all she can do not to scream aloud at the injustice of it. How the gods enjoy themselves at our expense.

Next morning Catharo insists on chopping her hair again to keep it short, but from what she has heard last night it shouldn't make any difference, it's all the same to most fellows; men who will have intercourse with cripples and goats will not play favourites.

But Catharo worries that if Gajendra discovers her true identity he will give her to the auctioneer and turn a profit.

If one of them sees you can't pass your water standing up it will be all over, he tells her.

He thinks about keeping her alive. All she can think of is how to kill Alexander.

CHAPTER 25

T HEY DRILL THE elephants all morning; there is *upasthana*, teaching the tuskers to rise over small palisades; *samvartana*, getting them to rise on their hind legs and take a giant step over a ditch. But most of their training is designed to get them ready again for pitched battle, to bear the noise of infantry sounding trumpets and banging swords on shields; and preparing the cavalry, getting them to bear the tuskers so they do not bolt from each other in a charge.

Afterwards the waterboys take the elephants to the river to water them and scrub them down. This is everyone's favourite time of day. The elephants trumpet and hose themselves and each other down while the waterboys scrub at them with brushes and pumice stones.

Gajendra watches how Colossus reaches for their new slave boy with his trunk.

Ravi comes to stand beside Gajendra.

'You want to know what I think? He's not his uncle. He's some sort of mercenary and he bought the boy from a brothel or an auction block. A freak like that is not going to get a woman or a boy unless he pays for it. Or else he's his pimp. An olive oil merchant! You didn't buy that, did you?

He's a merchant all right. And he'll do a fine trade from the Macks here, if he can get that pretty little thing out of your sight for an hour or two.'

Mara is giving Colossus a good scrub. He's better at that than he is at shovelling dung. The other waterboys complain that he wants a rousing cheer from the infantry and an extra ration at dinner for every lump.

'Still,' he concedes, 'he has a way with him with our tuskers. It's a rare gift.'

'It's no gift. He's always feeding them apples instead of mucking out the straw. If he keeps this up I'll send him over to the infantry.'

'You're jealous of him.'

'No, I'm not,' he grumbles.

It's not jealousy; it's something else. He watches how he pulls at the hair at the nape of his neck, like he is looking for a curl. Does he know he is being provocative? He has never been one for splitting the peach but there's something about this one that unsettles him.

And the boy won't leave him alone.

Mara wants to know everything, is on at Gajendra all the time, asking about the *ali baasawa*, the language he and Ravi use to control their elephants, wants to know about the *nila* points where the elephant is sensitive, the *dangupola* for controlling him, the *mara nila* or death points. He learns that the *sonda nala* is the top of the trunk and the *pasa dhana* is the knee.

Every day he pursues him with questions. Why do they turn more slowly to the left than the right? Why do they put their trunks in each other's mouths like that?

'You are a slave,' he tells him. 'Can you not behave like

one? For someone I could sell off to the highest bidder you are very sure of yourself.' He sees Catharo watching them. Ugly brute. 'He's not your uncle, is he?'

'Of course he is,' Mara says. But he can tell by his eyes; the boy is a terrible liar.

Gajendra is only slight, but it is all muscle. Her first judgement of him was wrong, he is not Persian but an Asiatic. She supposes some might call him handsome, he is clean-shaven, lithe and has an air of authority about him.

She watches him move among the elephants while they are getting scrubbed down in the river, examining each and every one, as gentle as if he were with his children. They seem to know him, too, reaching out with their trunks and feeling for him, like a blind man reading a face. He clicks his fingers for a boy to come and tend to some injury on one of the animals, scolds another for not fetching enough food. He talks to the beasts as if they were babies, cooing and chanting.

Today Colossus is, as always, the last to leave the water. Mara wanders away to find a bush to relieve herself. When she looks up, Colossus has followed her.

She hears Gajendra coming.

Mara turns. 'Go back,' she says and tries to shoo him.

He stops, trunk swaying, and trumpets at her.

Gajendra bursts through the bushes. 'What have you done to him?' he shouts at her.

'It's not my fault.'

'Have you taught him some secret signal? Why is he following you?'

'I don't know!'

'An elephant has one *mahavat*, only one, do you understand?' He taps the hook on his ear and Colossus turns reluctantly away.

That night Alexander orders elephants to be prepared for a wedding feast. Gajendra has a dozen of his tuskers painted in gaudy colours, even their toenails. They use reds and ochres and greens, with circles around their eyes and geometric patterns over their trunks and bodies, even headdresses like they would wear for battle.

When it is done he leaves Ravi in charge of it and retires early to the straw. Later he hears the sound of drums and flutes and tries not to think what is happening. Murder and jealousy curdle in him like bad milk.

It is like she is there beside him. He imagines the way her hip must feel with his hand resting upon it as she lies on her side, her sweet breath on his face. The longing is so urgent he groans aloud.

Finally he gets up in the night to retch into the grass and then he abandons sleep and instead he sits up all night with the elephants, staring at the sea.

CHAPTER 26

H<small>E HAS THROWN</small> himself down on his haunches on the riverbank and looks as if he has been told he is to die tomorrow. He scoops water over his head and stares at his reflection. She wonders at him. A good young man for the most part, she has decided, but overfond of melodrama in her opinion.

'Should I leave you to drown yourself in peace?' Mara asks him.

'What are you doing here?'

'I needed privacy.'

'Why don't you find a tree like the other fellows? Have you always been so precious?'

'May I ask what is wrong? Has one of our tuskers died?'

'You heard the celebration last night. Alexander gave our Elephantarch one of his harem.'

'What a very fortunate girl.'

He tosses a stone into the muddy water with great force.

'You wanted Nearchus for yourself?'

'Just leave me.'

'But that cannot be the reason you are here crying into the river. It's not the girl, is it? But how would an Indian meet a princess?'

'Not just an Indian. I am captain of the elephants.'

'A grand title but you have elephant droppings under your fingernails just like the rest of us. That's not going to get a princess in your bed.'

He gets to his feet. She can see he is thinking about thrashing her, and a crueller man would have done. Instead he says, 'Have you ever been with a woman?'

Mara shakes her head.

'Don't you ever think about a girl and feel like your balls are going to explode if you don't have her?'

'I have never had that great pleasure.'

'Did they do something to you? Really? You never thought about a woman until you can't sleep and your lingam just stands up all day long. Look. You see?'

Mara does not wish to see but looks anyway. 'Impressive.' Is that how my husband felt about me when we were married? Did he walk around all day like that? She should like to think so, but this initiation into the rites of men is a little daunting for so early in the morning. In Carthage she might be just rising from her bed and calling the servants to prepare her a peach and a warm bath.

'Is that how love feels to you?'

'It's a part of it. I suppose all you think about is boys, don't you?'

'Who told you that?'

'It's obvious. Ravi thinks you're a dancing boy. Is it true?'

So they all think she's a catamite. Well, that was predictable. Still, she supposes it is better for her esteem than that they think she is an out-of-work carter.

'Why am I talking to you like this? You're a slave and a bum jumper. What do you know of love, anyway?'

'More than you suspect.'

'I mean, here in the heart.' Gajendra punches himself in the chest to reinforce the impression of strong feeling. 'Not the false show you put on to dupe some customer out of his money.'

'You are the one who thinks I'm a catamite. I did not say that I was! I have never given love for money nor shall I ever!'

'What are you then, looking like that?'

It's a question that begs an answer and clearly she does not have one. Catharo would have them think anything of her but that she is a nobleman's daughter. 'This I know. There is more to love than walking around with a yard of stiff rope in your belly.'

'I cannot stop thinking about her. She is the most beautiful and mysterious creature I have ever seen.'

'There is nothing mysterious about a woman. Women are much like you are, only a very great deal smarter.'

'How can someone like you understand?'

'I know what it's like to have someone admire me for all my virtues and love me despite my worst faults. Will she do that for you? All you see is some mysterious object that you want for your own sake. But don't call it love. It's nothing like it!'

Gajendra is startled by his vehemence and does not know what to make of it. None of his waterboys would ever dare speak to him like this. Why is he tolerating this? But the catamite is not done yet.

Mara stands up close, so their noses almost touch. 'Has anyone ever told you that you are arrogant and self-obsessed, but the depth of your compassion far outweighs all your faults even though it shouldn't?'

'Maybe Ravi.'

'Then Ravi loves you. But if you've never had a woman say it to you then no matter how many holes you have stuck that… that thing in, then you are just like me. A cherry boy. And this Zahara whom you claim to love with such ardour? She is just a dream you have invented in your own mind.'

He turns pale. 'It's time to muck out the elephants,' he says, and walks away.

CHAPTER 27

ALEXANDER ORDERS THE army to march. He wishes to be at the gates of Syracuse before Antipater has a chance to prepare properly.

The Macks break down their eighteen-foot sarissas into two pieces, each squad of eight lashing them in one bundle and two men taking turns to carry them over their shoulders during the march. They decamp with their iron causia helmets strapped in front, their oxhide shoes hanging by rawhide laces around their necks.

The wagons, the women, the traders must follow behind as well they might. There will be just one pack animal for five men and one servant for ten. His forty elephants will follow single file, with their food and supplies.

It will not be easy. Every day an elephant needs enough fruit and fodder to fill several ox carts as well as enough water to create an inland sea. Somehow they will have to provide it or let the beasts forage for themselves, which will slow them down.

They had a saying in India: 'To take revenge on an enemy first buy him an elephant.'

He supposes Alexander will learn the truth of it soon enough.

*

That first afternoon, as they march east from the coast, they see a great mountain looming in the distance. The locals call it Aetna. An hour before sunset the order comes down the line to make camp.

There is a farm nearby. The farmer has been warned of their approach and knows the Macks will steal his pigs, so he has hidden them as best he can, locking them in a stone barn on the edge of a field. But one of the Macks hears them squealing and calls over his fellows and they smash down the door with an iron ram they have brought with them in case of a siege. The pigs scatter shrieking across the field and the soldiers run after them, laughing.

It is an hilarious diversion for all save the pigs and the farmer, until they reach the road and the elephants see them. Then the game becomes deadly serious.

Gajendra, walking beside Colossus, sees the pigs coming. He shouts a warning but he knows he's too late. Colossus flares his ears and turns to face them, trumpeting. Gajendra grabs Ravi, who is closest to him, and drags him behind a tree. The soldiers are still laughing. They won't think it's funny for long.

Colossus throws back his head and screams, ears flared, trunk raised high in the air. He takes off, and the rest of the elephants follow. Dozens of waterboys go down under their feet, caught up in the charge. He sees one of the *mahavats* stand in front of his elephant and order him to turn back with a sharp command and a whack with the bull hook. It is like trying to stop a runaway cart using pure reason. The tusker tramples him underfoot. He supposes the beast in its panic is not even aware that he is there.

181

Horses shy and run, the baggage trains are upended and tumble down the side of the hill. Carts are turned into lumber, iron-rimmed wheels pulped like twigs. He hears men screaming. There is nothing Gajendra can do about it until it's over.

His tuskers take off down the valley. It is chaos; shrieking pigs, shrieking men, shrieking elephants.

He waits.

When he finally steps out from behind the tree the elephants are gone. Bloodied rags and pieces of meat – once men – lie on the ground. The pigs are still squealing. Will no one shut the pigs up? Most of the carts are firewood. Men are walking around dazed.

He runs back down the column, finds one of the Agrianians, picks him out by his white tunic and tattooed face. 'Get your archers, kill these pigs now!'

The man is startled at having some Indian give him orders but he can see the sense in what is being said to him and shouts at his fellows to see that it is done.

Colossus has taken off through the trees into a narrow defile. Gajendra can see the treetops trembling as he blunders through.

He follows; it is not hard to find him. It is like a squadron of cavalry has crashed through the trees, flattening saplings and young trees. He runs until he is out of breath before he finally catches up with him, standing in an orange orchard, helping himself.

Gajendra puts one hand against the trunk of a tree, the other on his knee and bends over to catch his breath.

Colossus removes the leaves from a young tree, places them in his mouth and then snaps off the branch. As he finishes chewing the twig is ejected, stripped of the bark. He repeats the procedure several times until the tree is bare.

Finally the trunk angles towards him, detecting his scent. Colossus continues eating, but he continually turns his head and unfurls his trunk to satisfy himself that Gajendra is still there.

Colossus stamps his foot, as yet not completely satisfied that the foul-smelling devils with the curled tails are gone. There is nothing to do now but wait until he is calm again. Gajendra talks to him, sings him the song he likes when he is hurt.

Colossus blunders on through the orchard, selects another tree, gobbles a few oranges and strips the leaves. He allows Gajendra to move closer. He swings his trunk and sniffs the air again, checking for pig breath and pig smell. He seems satisfied. He plainly blames Gajendra for this upset, for he turns and bellows at him.

'Come on,' Gajendra murmurs, 'everything's all right now.' He takes another step closer and the elephant's trunk curls in defiance. He's not ready to come back just yet. Gajendra stays where he is.

There are footsteps behind him. It is the pansy water-boy, Mara. He stands there flushed and sweating. 'What happened? Why did they run?'

'They're scared of pigs.'

'The pigs? The pigs did this?'

Colossus pillages another orange tree; two shakes and it is half out of the ground by its roots. He scoops up the fruit with his trunk and puts them in his mouth very daintily, one at a time. He takes a step towards them and opens his mouth, as if he is laughing. It is a conciliatory gesture. Gajendra gathers more oranges from the ground and tosses them into his maw.

'When does an elephant learn to like oranges?'

'When there are no watermelons to eat. What are you doing here?'

'I was worried about him.'

'You were worried about an elephant?'

Mara walks up to Colossus. 'Bad elephant!'

'Bad elephant? Is that what you said? He's not a baby!'

'He behaves like one.'

'No, he behaves like an elephant. You teach him something and he'll do it, but the rest of the time he acts from instinct. Don't make the mistake of thinking he's human. He just does what nature taught him unless you can teach him otherwise. That's it.'

Colossus flares his ears again, disturbed by the raised voices. It is something Gajendra has never seen him do before. Why should he care if I shout at a slave boy? He steps towards him but Colossus steps back again, swinging his trunk, deciding if he will be led.

Gajendra hears them shouting up at the column, hears a pig shriek as an Agrianian archer hunts it down. They will be eating pork tonight but it is going to cost them dear. Alexander will not be pleased when he sees the dead laid out and what is left of his baggage carts.

Mara puts a hand on his shoulder as if they were comrades. Gajendra shrugs him off. He should send him to the slavers' block, get a fair price and get rid of him. Charity is all very well but this is sheer insolence. 'Can you persuade him back to camp?' the boy asks.

'As soon as he is settled. A big fellow like this, you can't bully him. He'll come when he's ready.'

Finally Colossus lets him close. He taps him on the trunk with his *ankus*. '*Aana*.'

Colossus reluctantly falls in step behind. 'You see,' he says to Mara, 'he runs from instinct and he comes back through training. There's your elephant for you. It's no more than that.'

When they reach the road, there is chaos. Two men have been dragged to the side of the road, dead. Five others have been injured. Three carts have been stamped into kindling, and siege equipment and sacks of vegetables and armour lie scattered up and down the road.

He finds Ravi. 'Where are the other elephants?'

'We've found half of them in the next valley. Those idiots,' he nods his head at the Macks gutting one of the sows, 'they think the whole thing is a lark.'

Ravi leads Ran Bagha back up the trail. Colossus is still skittish, he keeps stopping to sniff the air, he can still smell the pigs, he doesn't like them more because they're dead. Ran Bagha finds Colossus and puts his trunk in his mouth; they huddle for comfort. It is a strange sight, these two mammoth beasts so discomfited by a few porkers.

Someone has already started building a pyre for the two waterboys who weren't quick enough getting out of the way – or what's left of them.

Alexander rides back from the van with two of his officers. 'What happened here?'

He looks astonished more than angry. He has the usual

crowd with him: Perdiccas, Nearchus and some of his Persian bravehearts. The horses are skittish in the presence of the elephants. Even after all the training, you can keep them from bolting but they don't like being this close. They jerk at their reins and stare wide-eyed at the tuskers.

'The elephants took fright,' Gajendra says. 'Your soldiers let some pigs loose among them.'

'They are afraid of pigs?' a Persian says. 'What a wonder our new war machines are!'

Nearchus shakes his head. He can see him thinking: they gave me command of this lot. Did Alexander do it to promote me or humiliate me?

The Persians are muttering between themselves: they had these beasts at Gaugamela and Issus and what good did it do them? All they do is eat all the food and scare all the horses.

'Is there anything else your elephants are frightened of?' Alexander asks him. 'Should we tether all the sheep and mice on the island?'

'It's just pigs. They don't like pigs.'

'Let us hope they can do as much damage to Antipater's army as they have to mine.'

And then Colossus does something Gajendra does not expect; he flaps out his ears and takes a step towards Alexander, his trunk raised. Alexander's Arab shies away, nostrils flared. Even the general is surprised at this. He is not accustomed to belligerence from his own side, even an elephant.

Gajendra taps him with his *ankus* and Colossus subsides. Beast and man regard each other.

Alexander rides on.

The Persians cannot resist one final jibe. One of them leans down from his horse as he rides past, and shouts at Ravi, 'Oink, oink!'

Then he laughs and rides away.

CHAPTER 28

That evening they take the elephants down through the sheltering trees to the river. Colossus bellows his approval and wanders downstream. Catharo and Mara get to work with the pumice and the brushes. After the disturbing events of the afternoon, it seems he has recovered his temper. He is playful and sprays the thick green water on himself and on them.

He lumbers up to the bank and goes in search of a light meal. For all his size he is a delicate creature. His trunk encircles a clod of grass, sniffs at it then plucks it out of the ground. He taps it on his foreleg to dislodge the soil, then places it in the side of his mouth, just the roots protruding. He devours this morsel thoughtfully, before proceeding to the next.

Now some soldiers emerge from the tree-lined bank, an ominous presence; they say nothing, just watch. Mara knows what they want. She hopes that if she does not look up, they will move on, but she knows better.

The Macks are all twenty- or thirty-year veterans by the looks of them, seamed and craggy, some with grey in their hair. The leader is a bluff fellow with a scar across his left eye as if it were made of wax that had come too near to a flame and melted; another stares at her like a wolf considering breakfast. Back under the tree a third man, more furtive than the others, is fingering the blade at his belt and looks as if he cannot decide between buggery and slaughter. There's a younger one with a shrill laugh.

Her husband never looked at her that way, even when he had been away for months; it seems to her that some men hate the very thing they lust for. There's a poison in them and when it runs it goes straight to their crotch.

'What's your name, boy? Come on, don't be shy. We won't bite.'

When Mara ignores them, it just goads them more.

'I bet your pretty little arse is no virgin so don't come coy with me. Come over here, we're not beasts in the field, we'll take nice care of you. Here,' he says, and tosses a coin in the mud. 'Here's some silver for your trouble. You can't say we're not generous men.'

'I'd like to grease him up like a piglet and skewer him up to the lungs,' the one with the knife says. 'Come on, let's stop messing about with this, if he won't show us the proper favour we'll teach him to bow to Macedon, just like we were Alexander!' He grabs his crotch. 'I've got something right here he can pray to.'

One of them grabs her by the arm and pulls her out of the shallows. Mara puts out a hand to push him away; the smell of him is worse than anything else. She hears Catharo wading back through the shallows; this cannot end well now.

The Mack laughs when she struggles, this is what he likes. He grabs her in both arms and carries her back to the others.

'Are you looking for a fight, boys?' Catharo says.

'Who's that?' one of them shouts. 'Is he serious? I shit bigger than him.'

'I shit *prettier* than him.'

Catharo smiles. Until now his day has been tiresome. Mara has seen this expression before; it is the expression of a child when someone has given him a new toy to play with.

'Now give me back the lad. If he comes to no harm, neither will you.'

This is a huge joke, obviously. The big fellow pushes Mara away and puts his hands on his hips. He glances at his friend, sharing the joke. 'And what will you do, you little freak? Bite off my kneecaps?'

Catharo wades out of the river and stalks across the grass. He smiles. Picking up dung with his bare hands, scrubbing an elephant's back while he pisses on you, putting up with the stench and the disrespect, well, he doesn't mind this, it is all in a day's work. He is accustomed to hardship.

But this is what he really lives for: call him a freak and challenge him to a fight and you have made everything all right again. His face shines.

The big fellow does not understand what happens next. She might almost feel sorry for him. Catharo is fast and mean. The advantage every dog has is that it is fast, low to the ground and hard to hit; Catharo has these same virtues.

There is a blur of movement and the Mack is down, a knee broken, his male parts crushed, and Catharo is kneeling on his neck, deciding whether to break it.

Then everything is motion; the other three, appalled at what has happened to their fellow, draw their weapons and move in. These are seasoned professionals; fighting is their business also. They all have knives in their belts and know what they are about.

Catharo has his own knife, hidden in his leather tunic. He stole it from a Bactrian as soon as he had recovered from his wound. A soldier grows accustomed to fighting men his own size; fighting someone smaller is not necessarily an advantage, speed and getting underneath is everything. It is over quickly; two or three swift darting movements and one is down with his hamstrings cut, the other is squealing and clutching at his male parts, which are bleeding profusely.

But the other one is quick also and is behind Catharo with his knife raised. Her protector sees the strike coming but there is nothing he can do to defend himself.

A shadow passes across the sun. The man looks up and sees Colossus looming over him. The tusker wraps his trunk around the man's chest and casually dashes him against a tree. There is a dull wet noise, like throwing a watermelon against a wall. The man's head splits open.

Colossus drops him on the ground and stands over him, his trunk swaying, as if daring him to rise just once more. But there is no chance of that.

The waterboys come crashing through the bushes to see what has happened. They find Catharo standing there with a knife in his hand and three seasoned infantrymen in the mud bloody and screaming, the other pulped under a fig tree.

Catharo wipes the blade of his knife on the tunic of one and pulls Mara to her feet. Now she knows why her father valued him so highly. Even though it was done in her defence, it was a chilling display.

Four of the finest from Alexander's phalanx, men who can carry an eighteen-foot sarissa all day against endless infantry charges, and here they are spread over the river-bank like a hyena's lunch.

When he arrives, Gajendra stares at this scene in confusion. He wants to know how this happened. The waterboys mumble and stare at their feet; Catharo says they tripped on a rock. Some blame the elephant; some blame Catharo; some wit claims it is a ritual suicide.

Gajendra looks at Mara and points his finger. 'This is your fault,' he says and stalks away.

Nearchus finds Gajendra and grabs his elbow. He leads him along Elephant Row, out of earshot of the other *mahavat*s and waterboys.

'You heard what happened?' He looks harassed. As Elephantarch he will have to explain this to Alexander. He does not like the idea of some tattooed little Gugga killing good Macedonian soldiers. 'Who is the demon that did this?'

'Those men tried to rape one of my waterboys.'

Nearchus is mystified; yes, why is this a problem? 'Was he good looking, this waterboy?'

'Does it matter?'

'Perhaps he provoked it.'

'By appearing handsome?'

'Whoever did this to these men will have to be found. He cannot get away with this.'

'What will they do to him?'

192

Again Nearchus appears confused. He wonders that Gajendra should be so concerned. 'They will crucify him, I suppose.'

'Very well. I'll tell you his name. It was Colossus.'

'An elephant does not slash a man's hams or cut off his balls.'

'That depends on how badly he is provoked.'

'The men say it was a demon the size of a child. He has a tattooed face.'

'The elephant was protecting the *mahavat*. He did all the damage.'

'I don't need this sort of trouble.'

'There won't be any more trouble after this, do you think?'

'You have a point.' He shakes his head. 'Get rid of him.'

'Who?'

'The pretty boy. It's only a goad to the others.'

'He's good at his work.'

'At clearing up shit? You don't need to be tutored by Aristotle for that.'

At that moment they both look across and see Mara standing behind Colossus, his hands yellow with dung, up to his knees in mud, his mouth hanging open in exhaustion. It's like the boy has never done a day's work before in his life.

'He's useless and he causes trouble,' Nearchus repeats. 'Get rid of him.'

He walks away.

CHAPTER 29

A MIST OF COLD drizzle descends from the mountains in the west. Catharo wipes pork grease off his mouth with the back of his hand. Firelight throws shadows on his face. It is suddenly cold. In the distance lightning skims and shimmers over the volcano.

'We have to kill him,' she whispers to Catharo in the dark.

'Who?'

'Alexander.'

He doesn't answer her.

'I can do it. I just have to get close.' She imagines a knife and jerks it upwards with her right fist. 'He will have no armour and no sword. How hard can it be?'

'How many men have you killed, princess?'

'I am not a princess.'

'And you're no assassin either. But I am, and let me tell you it is no easy thing to kill a man. As a rule I have found that most would prefer to live rather than not and they will make a fight of it. Also you should know where to put the knife; a wounded man will fight like ten men and break your neck while he bleeds.'

'Will you not help me then?'

He sighs. 'The first chance we get, we will slip away. They

never guard us. If we can get across those mountains we can make for the garrison at Panormus. Carthage may be dead but there are still its colonies that will welcome us.'

'No.'

'No?'

'I told you what I plan to do.'

'Well, I can't let you do that, though it's just a silly girl's dream anyway. And if you won't go I'll carry you over my shoulder.'

'It won't be so easy to slip out if I'm screaming and struggling. I'm not leaving until Alexander is dead.'

'That was not what your father charged me to do.'

'My father is dead. You may think me a weak woman, Catharo, but if you do, then you have seriously misjudged me.'

She thinks of her husband waving to her as the trireme pulled from the dock, her little boy beside him, the gulls screeching around the stern. He never thought her weak. He told her that she had spirit and he listened to her counsel, as she would listen to his.

But then she thinks about the night her baby girl died, how she had taken her husband's knife and held it to her wrist, watched a tiny trickle of her own blood worm down her arm. But she couldn't finish the job. Her hand shook so hard she dropped the knife on the floor. And now you think you can walk up to Alexander and not flinch as you drive the point into his vitals?

She imagines she sees her husband smiling at her. Oh sparrow, you can't step on a snail without apologizing, you think you will slaughter the world's greatest warrior?

Catharo is right. I am too weak.

'Once you were so tired of life you hid in the temple,' Catharo says.

'I am still tired of life. It means I have nothing left to fear.'

'I will not let you do this.'

'Then you will have to work out a way to stop me.'

He puffs out his cheeks. 'You know your father's mistake?'

'You will tell me anyway.'

'He didn't beat you enough.'

'Are you threatening me?'

'You're not my daughter. But if you were, you would not have turned out so spoiled.'

'You don't like me, do you, Catharo?'

'It is not for me to have an opinion either way, princess. I am your father's man.'

'Why are you so loyal? He cannot pay your wages any more.'

'I never worked for hire. Not for your father anyway.'

'So what do you owe him?'

'That is our business. My business is to see you safe. Now my wound is healed I calculate I could walk it in six days. Twelve with you dragging behind. It's all the same to me.'

He says this without rancour. It is not meant as an insult, he simply makes his calculations aloud. She is about to tell him she can walk six days as well as him, but this is not true. She has never before walked further than the end of the garden.

But she will not have to find out if she is able to walk to Panormus. Despite what he says, she is going to find a way to kill Alexander.

CHAPTER 30

IT IS SOMETHING that Alexander would do: attack when you are supposed to be miles away and the enemy is not expecting you. Alexander's army is spread over miles, he is in the van with the cavalry, and the elephants take up the rear.

They do not expect to find Antipater until the next day.

All the same, Alexander has his cavalry sweep the valley in a broad W, using his cavalry and scouts. Somehow Antipater's men avoid the trap.

It is a hot afternoon, and some drowse in their saddles and those walking beside the column have their heads down, guarding their eyes from the bright sun, thinking about water and their dinner and rest. Gajendra feels the trembling underfoot and thinks it is an earthquake or the distant volcano. The riders come out of the sun, the first warning when they see sunlight flashing on their helmets and swords.

They close quickly, pouring out of the earth, like the dead rising on phantom horses. He suspects there is a gully that they have used for concealment. Already they are less than two bowshots away and the cavalry at the rear have no time to react, they are too far back.

They are making straight for his elephants.

Colossus smells them too. He stops, sticks out his ears

and faces the hills, his trunk testing the air. He bellows a warning to the other elephants.

'Turn them! Get them into battle line. Hurry!'

Suddenly the army is in motion. But it is panic and not orderly movement; no one has expected this. They are supposed to be attacking an enemy that is not ready for them, not be ambushed themselves. Some of the *mahavats*, those with presence of mind, scramble onto their elephants' necks and prepare to make a fight of it. But several of the tuskers have already bolted.

He looks up the line. Nearchus is at the van with Alexander, far out of sight. There is no one to save the tuskers except him. He sends a rider up the line to warn Nearchus but he supposes they will hear the commotion long before he gets there. By then it will be too late.

The archers are at the rear with the infantry, so he has to hand only a squad of Agrianians that might face the riders if they can form up in time. The elephants have no armour to protect them from a swift and concerted attack. He could turn them and run but the horses would overtake them. If they break the line they will be easy pickings.

The *mahavats* are milling around in confusion. He grabs one and shouts orders in his face. 'Mount your tusker, tell the others to do the same. *Do it now!*'

The man stares at him wide-eyed but it gets through. He does as Gajendra tells him. The marauders are already just a bow shot away. Gajendra forms a plan in his mind of how this might go. The key is the horses. How close will they come?

*

There is a wagon with spears, some armour. No time for the armour. Just grab the javelins and do what you can.

Keep the tuskers together, hold them close so they can't get inside. If we split them up they will pick them off. Put the rest of your men on the outside, to protect the flanks.

He grabs a spear and runs back to the line. No one has armour or even a helmet. He looks up to the van. There is movement there, Alexander has seen the danger now, but not in time.

The Agrianians, at least, know what they are about, they do not have to be told. They will have time to get off one dart before the riders are past them, and it is going to be difficult, hitting a rider on a fast horse. They will be in range themselves by the time they have a chance to loose a javelin, and they only have shields to protect them. In moments half these men he is shouting orders to may be dead.

He looks over his shoulder. Ravi has the elephants in a ragged line; Colossus is the only tusker without a rider. Another at the end of the line trumpets and scurries away. All the training counts for nothing, then.

He can feel the thunder of the hooves through his feet. The riders are Numidians, near naked but for their leopard-skin cloaks, black-skinned and bare-backed riders who are reckoned the best in the world. Where have they come from?

Carthage still has colonies on the north of the island, at Lilybaeum and Panormus. These boys have been sent down out of spite.

The Agrianians' wolfhounds are howling, straining

at their leashes. A volley of arrows hisses through the air, answered by the flash of their javelins. Some of the horses fall, a few riders, not enough to stop the charge. The Agrianians break, run back through the line.

He looks around to mount Colossus but it is too late. He is not of a mind to wait for him. He rushes out of the line to meet the threat. This is something the Numidians did not expect and the skirmisher line breaks and flows around him in a wave. The other elephants follow, whether their *mahavats* like it or not. It panics the horses and some of them shy on their back legs and bolt, terrified by the smell and size of the elephants.

Gajendra looks around. One rider gets through and is almost on him. He looks up just in time and sways outside the point of the spear and wrenches it out of the rider's grasp. The man screams as he comes out of the saddle, his horse galloping blindly on. Gajendra is on him instantly, has his knife in his hand and goes for the throat. He has never killed a man before, not close up, but there is no time to think about it. Gore sprays over his face and hands.

The man's eyes lock onto his as he dies. Gajendra freezes. For the moment he is too stunned by what he has done to get on with the battle. One thing to hurl a spear and not see where it lands; another to have a man's hot blood on your hands.

'Get behind me!' Catharo shouts when he sees the riders. He follows Gajendra to the wagon and finds a spear and a falcata, a hacking sword. He grabs Mara by the arm and tries to drag her clear. 'We're just dung larks!' he shouts. 'This is their fight, not ours.'

Mara looks around. Colossus has been separated from the rest of the tuskers. He charges at their attackers and their horses panic and bolt. One of the riders goes down but scrambles to his feet still holding a spear. Colossus trumpets in outrage as the spear goes into his unprotected shoulder.

Mara twists out of Catharo's grip, and runs towards the fight. She stops to scoop up a short sword from one of the fallen riders, now lying twisted and bloody in the grass. Catharo has no choice but to follow.

Gajendra hears a warning shout, high-pitched. He looks up and sees a rider coming at him, unhorsed and wielding a sword. The first blow nearly takes off his head, but he staggers back just out of range. The horse-less rider raises his sword again and Gajendra knows he is going to die.

It is a moment; he sees the future and it is filled with worms. But suddenly the man screams and falls to his knees. There is a dagger thrust into the back of his neck and as he goes down Gajendra sees the elephant boy standing behind him.

The light goes out of the man's eyes. He looks vaguely surprised.

Gajendra scrambles for his weapon and looks around.

The attack has been blunted, the attackers' horses have shied away from the elephants. But his tuskers have lost their line, and are milling about without order. Several have taken arrows and have blood streaming down their legs or their flanks.

He admires the courage of the men sent against them; a

handful have jumped from their horses and have gone after the elephants on foot. One has darted under the legs of an elephant called Futuh and placed his spear in his belly. Asaman Shukoh has trampled one of his tormentors under his feet and run away but another rider has remounted his horse and gone after him.

One of the *mahavats* has gone down with a spear in him and his elephant is standing over him, protecting him from further outrage, though he is clearly dead. Three of their attackers have chosen him as the likeliest target and are trying to get to his back legs with their spears and short swords.

He is trumpeting and running in circles on the spot, but he finally sets himself and charges one of the men and brings him down. But the other two dart in and hack at his hams with their scimitars. Shrieking, he turns on them and throws one aside with his trunk, but the other slices into him with his sword. Another Numidian hacks again at his hamstrings and the great beast trumpets in agony and falls.

Colossus has trampled another of his tormentors into the dirt together with his horse. He has a further spear wound in his left foreleg and this infuriates him even more. He captures one of his tormentors with his trunk and kneels on him.

Another has scrambled to his feet and is underneath him with a spear and would have placed it but Mara runs at him screaming, distracts him long enough that he makes for her instead of the elephant. Moments later Catharo hits him in the back running full tilt and brings him down. He rolls over and dispatches him expertly with a knife.

The dead man's compatriot runs at him, takes the little man with a spear. Catharo goes down clutching his thigh. He clings onto the spear shaft so he cannot withdraw it. It gives Gajendra time to run him through with a spear.

But the man does not die and Gajendra just stares at him, unable to finish the job. It is Catharo who crawls over and concludes the business.

Alexander and his Guardsmen are there now, galloping through the mêlée, and their attackers bolt towards the mountains. In truth, most have already fled, startled by Colossus's charge. Nearchus leads the cavalry in pursuit.

Their general walks his horse along the line of the column. If he is shocked by what has taken place he does not show it. He leans from the saddle to pat wounded men on the shoulder, laughs with his lieutenants over the bodies of the fallen enemy. The men still cheer him as he rides past.

The sun falls behind the mountains and they light torches and start campfires. No need to disguise their presence now. Someone knows precisely where they are.

Gajendra spits the dust out of his mouth. He looks for Mara and the other waterboy. 'Are you all right?' he says to Catharo, but he just grunts and passes out.

Ravi is there. 'Where's Hercules?' he says. He sees their pretty dung lark sitting on his haunches, crying. 'Well, a fine hero this one. He kills a man and then sits down to cry about it. They won't be building him a statue on Mount Olympus anytime soon.'

'I have never killed a man before,' Mara says.

'Well, you are in an army and this is a war and so it's inevitable if you think about it.'

'I thought it would be harder than that.'

'Not if you have a knife in your hand.'

'You saved my life,' Gajendra says.

One of the *mahavats* throws some water over Catharo to wake him up. The spear is still in his thigh and he sits up, grabs it two-handed and tries to pull it out. 'Leave it,' Gajendra tells him. 'You'll need the surgeon to turn it.' He uses a sword to lop off the shaft.

As the dust clears he sees two grey mounds lying in the dust, one of them still, the other shrieking in pain. Colossus stands over the stricken tusker, his head down, blood streaming from the spear wound in his shoulder.

Gajendra talks to him, telling him what a brave warrior he is and how well he fought. There will be extra rations for all the elephants tonight. But he is worried how many of the others ran at the first sign of trouble. How will they fare in battle against a determined cavalry?

Alexander gallops over. 'Did you lose only two?'

Only two?

'Futuh and Asaman Shukoh,' he says, resenting that Alexander doesn't know their names. Didn't they just bleed and die for him?

'Who organized the defence?'

'I did.'

'You did well. There shall be commendation in this.'

The other elephants, those that did not run, gather around their two fallen companions, like mourners at a funeral. They explore them with their trunks, comfort

Futuh as he screams, set up a bellowing you can hear all the way to Syracuse.

Alexander goes down the line, generals in his train, ordering more cavalry to the rear. The Invincible, King of Asia, has had the tables turned on him. He appears undaunted, more concerned with the fate of the dead tusker. 'Well, get him carved up, boys. We have food enough for the army now. Pork last night, tusker tonight. As long as we have meat, boys, we can march all the way to Rome!'

CHAPTER 31

THEY HAVE BROUGHT the wounded to a hastily erected tent and the physicians are at work, stitching wounds and taking out barbs with little ceremony. Men are screaming. It is hard to hear yourself think.

Catharo lies staring at the roof of the tent. It is clear he has suffered like this often enough that he now thinks nothing of it. Ravi was right: no merchant, no nephew, either of them. Not that Gajendra cares to unmask them. He doesn't like the little fellow but he is glad he is on his side, and he owes the catamite his life.

Catharo does not even appear to blink; you might think he was dead if it wasn't for the fingers of his right hand, which beat a kind of rhythm on the grass as he waits for the physician to attend him. He is a cheerful fellow, unperturbed by the agonies of others. Gajendra studies his body, what there is of it, sees that he has a collection of scars that would not have disgraced one of Alexander's oldest veterans.

Catharo makes a noise, something between a grunt and a curse, as they take out the spear. Me, I would have been yelling and trying to rip off the physician's head, Gajendra thinks.

'Another wound, Catharo, where did they ever find a place to put it?'

He scowls and says nothing.

'You are no merchant, are you? Who are you really?'

'I'm just a shitkicker with a spear in his leg. I don't have a past any more.'

'What do those tattoos on your face mean?'

'They say "Mind your own business" in Arabic, Greek and any other fucking language you care to name.'

'You fought well. I should be grateful but I'm just suspicious.'

'If I'd fought that well I wouldn't be lying here bleeding everywhere. But I fought better than you. You finish one combat and you stand there like you've struck down Zeus.'

'Your so-called nephew is just as brave a fellow and he has better manners.'

'If you can use a knife you don't need manners.'

He's not going to get far with this fellow. He leaves him to bleed and mend as best he can.

The camp is bristling with guards, and fires burn around the entire perimeter. The screams of a prisoner taken during that day's raid echo around the camp; Alexander has ordered him tortured out of pique.

Gajendra and Mara find Colossus chained to a tree. Some bales of alfalfa have been stacked in front of him and he is consoling himself with food. The arrow is still in his shoulder. He catches Mara's scent but like all elephants he does not see very well and has to confirm who it is with his trunk. He rumbles deep in his belly. It is both a greeting and a plea for help.

Gajendra gets to work. He feels Mara watching him.

'You don't have to be here, boy. Go and have your dinner.'

'I don't want anything. You know what they're eating.'

'Well, they couldn't leave him there to rot.'

'Will you eat Colossus if he dies?'

'This one's different.'

'How?'

'He's mine.'

'Such a fortunate elephant.'

Is he flirting again? He is standing too close. Mara puts a hand on his shoulder. He steps away.

'You saved my life today,' he says. 'I didn't think you had it in you.'

'Neither did I.'

'We'll toughen you up yet.'

'That's what I need. Toughening up. My father would be pleased.'

It is a curious remark. He stands by the beast's head, whispering to him. There are not many who will even go near him, let alone talk to him like this.

'What's he like?' Mara asks.

'Who?'

'Alexander.'

Gajendra considers. 'One of his guards whispered something to me, on the way from Babylon. He said Alexander sleeps with two things under his pillow: a dagger and *The Iliad*. *The Iliad*'s not just a story, it's his family tree. He believes himself descended from Hercules, part divine. He doesn't just rule other men because of the strength of his army. He conquers by right. He believes himself a god.'

'And the dagger?'

'To protect that part of himself that is not a god.'

'Do you think him divine?'

'He does things that are more than human. His idea of leisure at the end of a long day is a night march. His idea of dinner is a light breakfast.'

Gajendra works at the arrowhead, trying to work it free with as little fuss as possible. 'How did you learn to be a *mahavat*?' Mara asks him.

'From Ravi. It's called the *ali baas*. It's passed down, father to son, but he doesn't have a son.'

'What language is it you talk in?'

'I don't know. It is Ravi's language but all he can remember of it now are the words he uses for the tuskers.'

'And that's the only language they know?'

'It's not like Greek or your jibber. They know what to do when we say certain words but in a battle they can't hear us so most of it we do with our feet and with sticks. Or if I'm walking beside him I tap him under the eye to make him kneel, just here to make him stop, the back of his heel here to get him to raise his foot so I can climb up. But it's only an elephant's *mahavat* can do it, he won't do it for just anyone. He does it because he likes me and he trusts me.' He rubs his hide with his hand and pats him. 'Anyway, why do you want to know all this?'

'Perhaps I want to learn. To be a *mahavat*.'

'You think because one stupid elephant follows you about you can be a *mahavat*?'

'Who got him on the ship?'

Gajendra pokes Mara in the chest. 'Mind who you're talking to, waterboy.'

Mara pokes him back. 'You're a bully and a pig.'

When he gets over the shock of his impudence Gajendra laughs and pushes him, playfully, but it's a hard shove and he totters and falls over. 'Remember who you're talking to or I'll give you a hiding.'

Gajendra yells as Colossus wraps his trunk around him and shoves him out of the way. There is no doubt that he has taken sides. Gajendra is astonished. He has never seen an elephant do anything like this before. 'Well, well. He seems to like you.' He grabs Mara's hand and pulls him to his feet. 'All right, boy. We'll see what we can do with you. Maybe you do have talent.'

'For what?'

'For this work. At least the big fellow here seems to think so. Maybe I'll teach you a few things.'

'But how can you? I'm a slave, as you never tire of telling me.'

'And not a very good one.' The iron arrowhead is almost free. Colossus bellows again, but does not move.

'How's my uncle?'

'He's not your uncle, is he?'

'Is he going to be all right?'

'It would take more than one javelin to kill him. He fought well. A professional soldier could not have done better. For a humble merchant he knows how to use weapons.'

'I didn't say he was a merchant his whole life.'

'I would have thought the next time he sees a ledger of accounts it will be the first time.' He works out the arrowhead and a spray of blood splatters over him. Colossus shrieks and takes a step backwards but calms when Mara talks to him. It is remarkable how he can do this.

'Will my big boy be all right?'

'If you mean the elephant, yes. He'll be sore, but you can't kill an elephant with just one dart. Not in his shoulder anyway.'

'You care about him more than you pretend.'

'I need him. He's the biggest and the best. Aren't you, you big, bristly bastard?' He slathers the wound in honey to keep it clean. He looks at Mara, as if he's surprised to find him still there. 'Get back to your post. You'll have to work twice as hard now, I lost some of my best shit shovellers today. You're not much good at it, but you're all I've got.'

That night she takes Colossus down by the river with the other tuskers. A storm breaks over the mountains, and cloud tumbles down the valley like smoke, lightning sheets through the valleys. The tuskers don't mind the storm; they love the rain. Colossus seems none the worse for his wound. As Gajendra said, he's a tough one.

The storm brings on evening early. The other *mahavat*s retreat to the camp. Mara stays behind. Colossus is an immense presence in the darkness. He is restless. He rumbles, he trumpets, he snakes out his trunk and tastes her scent. It is as if he is trying to tell her something.

For all the terror he creates in those around him, he is a good-natured beast, even though his affection can be measured in pints of elephant slime. Once she would go nowhere without precious ointments and oils, smelling like summer. Now she reeks of elephant day and night and she has snot in her hair.

If her father could see her now.

'That's right,' she says, 'cover me in slobber. And Catharo still calls me princess!'

She pats his trunk anyway.

'How are you feeling, old fellow? If you're in pain you don't show it. You're like Catharo. Take his leg off and he just hops after you shouting threats.'

She could not have imagined this, a few weeks ago, before the walls of her city came down. For a long time she had not felt tired or angry or scared, and had no affection for anyone; now here she was cooing to an elephant. It has been so long since she has been touched, even the slimy pink tip of this strange beast's trunk feels like a massage with oils.

'I need a hero, old fellow, someone to watch over me tonight. Do you think you could do that for me?'

Colossus raises his left foot and stamps it down, the first sign that the stiffness in his shoulder is bothering him. He is still poking her with his trunk. Don't you have a water-melon for me? That's what he's saying.

'Did you see what I did today? He was black, did you see how black he was? They say they're not human, those fellows. But his blood was the same colour as mine, the same colour as yours. I didn't have time to think about it. I just did it. It was him or Gajendra. If I'd had time to think about it, perhaps I wouldn't have done it.' She makes a fist and jerks down. 'See! That's how I did it. Just like that. Me. A woman. And that's what I'd do to Tanith too, if she was here.' She stabs again. 'That's for taking my baby!' Stab, stab. 'That's for taking my husband and my son!'

She is crying. Stop it, get a hold of yourself, Mara.

The growling in Colossus's belly gets louder.

'What do you make of your Indian? He's a good-looking fellow, isn't he?' She runs a hand along his trunk, it is like stroking a rough stone wall. 'He reminds me of my husband. Did you know I had a husband? He would talk to me the way Gajendra talks to you, he knew where to touch me and what to say when I was angry or when I was afraid. He was my *mahavat*! But he didn't need to poke me, like your man does you. I would get angry when he told me what to do, but you know what, now he's not here, I miss it. Everyone needs someone like that, someone to whisper in their ear, someone who knows all about you, someone who never gets angry.'

She leads Colossus back to the camp. The elephants have been shepherded into a cypress grove. It is raining harder now, the thunder cracks over the mountains, but she throws down her blanket under the tree and under Colossus. If she goes over there to sleep with the other waterboys she knows what will happen; she will not risk it without Catharo there to protect her.

'If you decide to lie down in the night, remember I am here. I know once I asked you to squash me flat but I don't know that I want that any more. So I am going to trust you, old fellow. It's up to you. Goodnight.' And she lies down under her dark and bristled sky and listens to the rumbling of his belly and the swishing of his tail and feels safer and warmer under a bull elephant with a bad temper than she did for many months in the house of a goddess.

CHAPTER 32

BECAUSE OF THE attack there is nothing hot to eat, some three-day-old chunks of bread washed down with wine. Gajendra cannot sleep. There is something almost divine about thinking you are about to die and then finding yourself alive. He imagines this is why Alexander is as he is. Cheating death is a little like being a god.

At night it is as if you can see colours. Even the air tastes sweeter.

Ravi is in the straw, asleep, so he nudges him awake.

'What is it, what's wrong?'

'Nearchus has not come back,' Gajendra says.

'What do I care about that?'

'What if he doesn't return at all?'

'You're thinking Alexander will make you the new Elephantarch, aren't you?'

'I have been, in everything but name.'

'You're not a Mack. You're just an exotic, a foreigner, to them. Don't fool yourself.'

'He has Persians around him now. Why not?'

Ravi sighs in the dark. 'I am older than you, lad. I have seen so many men wrestle with their lives trying to force the gods to submit to them, to oblige their fortune so they have things just the way they want them. Look at your

215

Alexander. He wants a statue and his name in the histories. Can a statue smile? Can a man be happy after he is dead? The things that make you happy can be right under your nose and you just don't see them.'

'I know what I want.'

'Yes, but you're too young to know what you need.'

The clouds race across the moon. Rain leaks off the canvas and forms puddles where they sleep. The cured leather tent stinks when it is wet. Men are grumbling and snoring, shifting around in the dark trying to find a dry spot. He can hear the low rumbling from the tuskers; this is the weather they like. They will be into the puddles like ducks.

He sees one of the Agrianians take off his cloak and wrap it around his javelins to keep the damp from seeping into the doe-skin sleeve and swelling the grain. Then he curls up with his son and his wolfhound under a tree. A strange people, they'll freeze before they let anything happen to their darts.

The storm has flooded the high passes and left everything dripping. It was like this the night they fought the Macks on the Jhellum River, the river swollen and fast flowing, the men streaming back unrecognizable, covered in mud and blood. He was just a waterboy then.

Carthage had been his first battle. He remembers nothing about it now. It had lasted from noon till the late afternoon and it was as if it was a skirmish of a few hectic moments. What he recalls best is the terror that he would lose control of his own body and shame himself even before it started.

Once it began it was like he had smoked hashish; a vivid

and frightening dream swiftly forgotten once it was done. He had thrown his javelins wildly and did not know where they landed; it was Colossus who did the work, he had kicked and nudged and shouted but the big tusker did as he needed and carried the day. Yet afterwards he felt as he did now, like Zeus, like Hercules, like the greatest warrior there ever was.

Today had been different. It truly was a skirmish but in his mind it was never-ending, and no matter what Ravi says to him he cannot stop thinking about the man he killed with his knife. Why should it trouble his sleep? It was kill or be killed.

But every time he closes his eyes he sees the man staring at him, accusation and terror in his eyes.

'How many men have you killed, Ravi?'

'I don't know. You hurl javelins from an elephant's back, sometimes men fall. Who is to say if they die?'

'I was close up to that one today. I saw the light go out of his eyes. I didn't think it would be like that.'

'You think too much about it. Be grateful you're still alive. If it wasn't for the catamite you wouldn't be. He saved your skin today. I thought he would be hiding behind a bush somewhere. He has fire in his belly, that one, for all his pansy ways.'

'He touched me tonight.'

'What?'

'He's done it before. He... well, it's like he leans his head on my shoulder. It was like he wished me to hold him.'

'Did you bend him over?'

'You know I'm not one for that.'

'You missed your chance. Well, hero or not, he's going to be in trouble now. That little tattooed pimp won't be able to help him much with that spear wound in his leg. If the soldiers get him on his own they'll pass him round the regiment like a wineskin.'

'Then we should put him in the straw by us. I owe him at least that much.'

Torches are useless when the rain is this heavy. Gajendra fumbles around in the dark looking for Mara. He kicks the waterboys awake but none of them knows where he is.

He is about to give up and go back to the straw but while he is up and about and wet through anyway he decides to check on the tuskers, keep the guards on their mettle. Sure enough one of them is dozing against a tree and he gets a slap around the head for his indolence.

Gajendra sees what looks like a pile of rags under Colossus and he thinks he has massacred some other unfortunate in the night, but then the rags sit up and form themselves into the shape of a fool.

'What are you doing there, Mara? He could squash you flat.'

'Colossus won't hurt me. Will you, old fellow?'

He can stand up straight without crouching and his head doesn't even touch the tusker's belly. He rubs his eyes, very dainty. A real man would scratch his balls.

'An elephant only has one *mahavat*. Do you understand? Give him two and you confuse him. I don't want to find you out here again.'

'I'm not trying to take your tusker away. It's just I feel safe here.'

'You can sleep in the straw with me and Ravi. No one will touch you there.' He leads him back through the mud to their tent. A torch is burning inside and Gajendra sees Mara in the light and laughs.

'What is it?'

'Look at you. No one's going to want to bugger you now. Has Colossus been dribbling over you all night? You don't need him to stand over you, just sneeze on you. There's no Mack will come within an arrow shot of you today. You are the most disgusting thing I've ever seen.'

He doesn't see Mara's face, and it is a good thing. He is still laughing when he curls up in the straw.

CHAPTER 33

There is a river running through the tent and the straw has floated away on it. In the middle of the night they find a dryer spot under one of the carts but they are barely settled when they are kicked awake again by one of Alexander's sergeants. He wears a savage expression as if he has come to make an arrest.

'What is this about?' Gajendra grumbles, trying to keep fear out of his voice.

'Alexander wants you – now.' These Macks; it is clear he would rather slap him with his sword than be his escort. 'Where's the other one? The pretty boy?'

'He's over there.'

'Bring him.'

'What's happening?' Mara mumbles.

'We're going to see Alexander.'

'We?'

'Hurry up, he doesn't like to be kept waiting.'

Mara leaps to her feet and falls into step.

The rain has eased off a little. 'Make yourself useful,' Gajendra says. 'Carry the torch.'

They splash through the mud. Gajendra wonders what it could be. He hopes it's not about Catharo and the four soldiers he cut up. Or perhaps it's Nearchus, has he been killed on his foray against the raiders? His heart lurches between dread and hope.

Alexander is in his cups. He cannot sleep and is prowling his pavilion, agitated and nasty. 'Who is this?' he says pointing to Mara.

'He's the slave who saved the captain of the elephants,' the sergeant says. 'You asked to see him.'

He brightens, remembering his whim. 'Ah. So you're the fine fellow who saved my Indian?'

He stands close. He holds out his hand and a slave brings him another cup of wine. There is a shadow on their king's face. His lips are wet. His concentration is intense, like he is trying to see through billowing smoke.

'You're not long off your mother's teat, I should venture. One of his waterboys, are you? A fetcher and carrier? Or a dung pusher. In more ways than one by the look of you.' He takes Mara by the shoulders and pushes him to his knees. 'Kiss the royal foot.'

To Gajendra's surprise, Mara does it.

'What's a dung lark doing killing cavalry?' He turns to Gajendra. 'Where did you get him from, elephant boy?'

'Carthage, my lord.'

'Saved him from being filleted, did you?' He hauls Mara back to his feet. 'I heard you showed great valour. I am curious, why did you do it? What did it matter to you whether my elephant boy lives or dies?'

'I was trying to protect the elephant.'

Alexander makes a murmur, something between surprise and admiration. Mara has his complete attention now; this is something he has not considered.

'The elephant?'

'I have grown fond of him.'

Alexander drinks and the wine runs down his chin. He snaps his fingers and the royal cupbearer dashes from the shadows with a cloth to dab at it. 'Extraordinary. How do you grow fond of such an ugly creature?'

'They are much like horses. They have valour and loyalty.'

He looks at Gajendra. 'Is he mocking me?'

'It is true.'

He grunts and sways. Gajendra wonders at his little dung lark, and why he still stands so close to Alexander like this. Surely he doesn't intend to kiss him? He wouldn't put it past either of them.

He thinks for a moment that his king will raise a hand to stroke the boy's face. They hold the moment for long enough that Gajendra feels an unnatural pang. He does not wish to share his slave with anyone, even his commander. This unnatural jealousy takes him quite by surprise.

Then his general smiles, smacks his lips to taste the residue of the wine, and turns away.

'And you, elephant boy.' He turns his back on Mara so that he is facing his captain of the elephants. 'I've been watching you. You fancy yourself in a fight, don't you?'

'Yet you chose me because I know elephants.'

'You're an impudent creature. How did you feel after Carthage when Nearchus got all the credit for your efforts?'

'Did he? I didn't know.'

'Of course you knew. I saw your face. You were steaming about it.' Another gulp of wine. 'You did well today. As I hear it you organized the defence of the elephants on your own and you had them beaten by the time Nearchus came down the line. I think it's why he chased them, he was late for the glory and was rushing to catch up with it. But he's a popular fellow, you know. Among the troops.'

'He seems brave enough.'

'Too slippery for my liking.' Over Alexander's shoulder, he can see Mara step closer. He wonders why and is alarmed by it. 'You still want his wife, don't you?'

'Not just his wife. I want his horse and his commission too.'

Alexander laughs, delighted. 'You're too arrogant by half. You remind me of myself at your age. Except I have royal blood and you have… well, you're just a gyppo, aren't you?'

'Yes, my lord.'

'But you did well. I could have lost a lot more of my tuskers if you had not reacted so quickly.'

Gajendra tries to make out the look on Mara's face. If Alexander were to step back right now he would step on his dung lark's toes.

'I have underestimated you.'

'I don't mind that. It's happened before.'

His breath is on his face, sour with wine. 'You are hoping Nearchus does not come back, aren't you?'

It shocks him that Alexander can so plainly divine his thoughts.

'What happened to you, boy?'

'Happened to me?'

'Something impels you. What is it?'

'Ambition. Like every man.'

'No, it's more than that. If you lie, I'll know.'

Gajendra feels cornered. He doesn't know what to say to wriggle out of this.

'Where are your family?'

'They died.'

'Of what?'

'It was a fever. Half my village died from it.'

'And where were you?'

'I was lucky.'

'No, that's not it. There's something else.' Gajendra drops his eyes and Alexander grabs him by the chin and forces him to look up. 'Isn't there?'

Finally his general turns away. Mara steps back, just in time. For Alexander this is enough now. He has grown bored with them both. He needs someone else to entertain him until the wine knocks him out for a few hours.

His cupbearer splashes more wine in his cup. He gulps. It spills down his white tunic like blood. 'In two days we will stand before Syracuse. Do well and I will give you the world. Everything you ever dreamed of. It's all up to you now, elephant boy.'

The next morning Mara finds Catharo in a tent with the rest of the wounded from the previous day's skirmish; he is sitting up, even trying to stand, cursing the wound in his leg. A bloodied bandage is wrapped from his knee to his groin and he is shooing the flies off it.

He sees her and looks irritated. 'May I have my knife back?'

She reaches under the tunic where she has hidden it and slides it back to him.

'How did you know it was me?'

'I may not have had my own private tutor, as some, but I am not stupid. If you ever have to take to the streets, princess, you will make a fine pocket thief. When did you do it?'

'When you were lying on the battlefield.'

'I underestimated you.'

'A lot of people do. Mainly the men in my life.'

'Where's the elephant boy?' His eyes watch for a reaction. It seems he cares less about how she answers than if she can hold his gaze.

'He has taken the elephants to the river with the others.'

'Why aren't you with them?'

'I slipped away to see how you were.'

'I'm touched.' He taps the place where his knife is now hidden. 'Have you slaughtered Zeus's favourite son yet?'

She shakes her head.

'I hear you went to his tent.' He sees her wriggle and then smiles. 'You couldn't do it, could you?'

'I couldn't get close enough.'

He laughs at this. 'You were in his pavilion. How close do you need to be? Do you want to share his bath before you murder him?'

'I killed a man yesterday.'

'Yes, and I invaded Italy.'

'He had Gajendra on his knees. Did you not see me?'

'So you say. All I saw was you running towards the elephant.'

She cannot believe he had not seen it. 'Ask anyone.'

'You don't have the balls to kill Alexander, princess.'

'Keep your voice down!' She looks over her shoulder.

These men look like they are unconscious but it doesn't mean they really are.

'So, are you serious about this?'

'I thought you were pledged to protect me.'

'I've been thinking about what you said. You're right. Someone has to stop him, and he must pay for what he has done to our city and to your father, may he forgive me. But it's not a job for a woman, especially a pale little wonder like you.'

'You can't even walk. How can you do such a thing?'

'It's just a muscle wound. It's a bit stiff but the bone's not broken. You think I haven't had worse? I'll be up and about soon enough.'

There is not much of the little fellow but the attitude on him would make a thirty-year veteran look like a milk-sop. Nothing soft in this one, he has never wanted pity for his condition or shown any for anyone else's. Except her father, perhaps. Him he loved. She wonders what it is that has kept Catharo bound to him all these years.

'You know what they'll do to you if you succeed?'

'It was your idea, princess.' He makes a stabbing motion, underhand, twists the knife, then holds it to his own throat and draws it across the veins. 'There, that's how it's done. One stroke for him, one stroke for me, and we both go to Hades together, and we'll carry on with it there if he wants. But first I get you out of here, so there's no music for you to face. If you think you can kill a man, then you can walk to Panormus.'

'We should do it together.'

'It's my way or not at all. I have been knocked cold and run through twice so far on your account, but this I do for him.' He is sweating with pain and he sits down again. 'You were his whole heart, do you know that?'

She did know it; perhaps she had just chosen to ignore it.

'Your father did not know the trouble he would put me through when he gave me this commission. In the circumstances, a bloody end is inevitable.'

'I am sorry, Catharo. I have given you little enough gratitude until now.'

'If you want to repay me, then honour your father in your prayers. He was a better man than you gave him credit for.'

'You don't like me much, do you?'

'It's not for me to have an opinion either way on the matter.'

The physician comes in and pushes Catharo back onto his blanket and tells him to keep still, does he not know he has a fever and not enough blood left in him to fill a night jar?

Mara slips away. The sun should be climbing the sky by now but there are still thunderclouds around the mountains and more rain sweeping down the valleys. There is a rumour about the camp that this is Zeus come to help them. She imagines it was Alexander who started it.

The camp is in motion. The Macks look dark. Fighting Celts and Africans is one thing; soon they must make war on their own.

CHAPTER 34

THE FORWARD SCOUTS have found Antipater's army. He has moved out of Syracuse to meet him and his army is bolstered by more mercenaries from inside the city. They are now outnumbered by almost three men to every one of theirs, but they are just Greeks, the veterans say, and this is not news. They are always outnumbered. When you have Alexander as your general, numbers count for nothing. Besides, we have the elephants.

Elephants who still run away whenever they take panic, Gajendra thinks. Will they follow Colossus into the fight tomorrow?

The whole camp is in motion now. The sergeants are barking at their men, there are extra drills, a double line of sentries posted around the camp. There are grumblings around the campfires; what if there are fellow Macedonians in Antipater's army.

What then?

Nearchus is safely returned. It seems that the ambush was not laid by Antipater but by raiding parties sent out by Carthaginian colonies to the north. Another army is advancing through the mountains so Alexander must engage Antipater quickly if he is to avoid being caught in the pincers of two enemies.

Nearchus summons him to his pavilion; there is something different about him today. He does not sneer, at least not especially, nothing above the habitual contempt that the Macks reserve for any foreigner.

His living arrangements in the field are sparse: there is a bench with a water bowl and a camp bed. He has a boy to look after his horse and a sergeant to run messages. That's all. You don't feel like you've walked into a high class brothel, as you do when you are ushered into Alexander's pavilion. If he was back in his crease he would be ready to drink and wrestle greased pigs with the rest of the boys.

'How are our tuskers?' he asks Gajendra. It is 'our tuskers' now. A week ago he wanted to leave them in Africanus.

'We lost two. Three others took wounds, including Colossus, but nothing serious. They are still ready to fight. We've taken them down to the river and let them forage for a bit.'

'There's food down there?'

'Elephants will eat anything as long as there's enough of it.'

Gajendra imagines him with Zahara. All thumbs. It hurts to think about it.

There is a little wooden figure that Ravi keeps with him, an elephant carved from teak, and it has a hundred points marked on its body, and each point means something; you touch here to make him walk, here to make him angry, here to kill him, here to make him walk back...

With a man there is a point for jealousy, for helpless rage; it is right here in the pit of the stomach. That is what hurts right now. It feels cold and sharp, like he has been hollowed out.

Nearchus splashes water on his face, gets his own cloth to dry himself. How he must hate Alexander's affectations. 'I won't be humiliated in the field by some dumb animal.' He waits. 'You're meant to say, you won't be, general.'

'They just need more training. With all this marching we've been doing, loading them onto ships, there hasn't been time. You saw how it was even before we left Babylon. They just need more time.'

'With Alexander, time is something we don't have much of. Can't you just get these stupid beasts to stay in formation?'

'Elephants aren't stupid. They're smarter than... than most people.'

'Including me?' he says with a leery grin.

'I don't know. I've never tried to train a Macedonian.'

That was out of his mouth before he could stop it. He wonders what Nearchus will do. He is still for a moment and then chooses to laugh and clap him on the shoulder.

'He likes you, you know.'

'Who?'

'Alexander. Don't tell me you didn't know?'

Gajendra shakes his head and frowns to keep himself from smiling with satisfaction.

'He's grooming you for my position, you know that? You wouldn't mind that a bit, would you? I bet you even wish that I hadn't come back this morning. You would have hardly mourned my passing, am I right?'

'I'm just an Indian. How can I rise higher than what I am?'

Nearchus looks unsure if he is stupid or just pretending to be. He steps closer. The smile is gone and so is the good-natured banter. 'I don't know whether he wants you for his bum boy or his general. He likes you people more and more, you know. He doesn't trust his own kind any more.'

'He's my king now. I'll do as he commands.'

'Be careful of him. He'll take your soul, elephant boy.' Their eyes lock. Gajendra knows it is insolent but the challenge is there now, and something in him will not look away. Nearchus has drunk wine with his lunch. It makes him careless with his words. 'He loves you now. But he tires quickly of new things. He is easily bored. Just when you are most enamoured of him he will toss you aside.'

'He pays me for my work. I just do what I'm told.'

'I don't believe that for a moment.' He stands closer as if he is going to confide a secret. 'You know when we came through Egypt, I went with Alexander, down to Memphis. The priests gave him the crook and the flail, they called him Ra and Osiris. It's not just a game, you know. He really does think he's a god.'

He turns away, waves a hand in dismissal. Gajendra leaves, seething. *He likes you people more and more.* He talks to me like I am nothing and takes all the credit. If the elephants win the day, it is his genius; if they lose formation, he will blame me.

Does Alexander love me? Then let him love me more. He has promised me the world and that's the least that I want now.

This is how it will be:

She will say: Do you remember that day in the temple? You promised me that one day we would be alone, and that I would be yours. I was about to laugh at you but then

I saw the look in your eyes and saw that you meant it. But I never thought that it could ever happen.

He will say: I always knew you would be mine one day.

She says his name. Gajendra…

She whispers it; it rolls strangely off her tongue, like a prayer.

She will wrap her arms and legs around him. Her body coils. Her eyes glitter like diamonds in the dark.

His fingertips tease apart the fold of her robe. Her throat is warm, scented and a little damp from sweat. He can feel the bounce of her pulse against his lips.

The candlelight glows on her skin. Her breast is dusky and velvet to the touch.

From the raw stuff of his desire, from belief and from wanting, he will make his vision real. He smiles in the dark. His eyes shine.

This is how it will be.

They are with the elephants down at the river; last night's storms are just a memory, it is a hot afternoon, the scorching wind the locals call the *siroko* has been blowing from the south all day. Mara stands in the shallows, under the trees that bow over the river, watching as Gajendra and the other boys strip off their clothes and plunge in with the tuskers.

Mara starts scrubbing Colossus down with the pumice. Gajendra wades over. 'I've never seen you with your shirt off.'

'I get burned by the sun very easily.'

He shrugs; all the other boys had stripped naked, brown and gleaming. But then most of them were Indians like him.

*

Dusk is approaching as they walk the elephants back to the camp. The sun is about to dip below the horizon; the air is still, breathless.

He grabs Mara and pulls him aside. 'What did you think of our king?'

'He's shorter than I thought he would be. Was it true what he said to you?'

'About what?'

'That you want Nearchus's wife?'

'Everyone wants her. She's the most beautiful woman I've ever seen. Have you seen her?' He gets dressed, feels Mara staring. 'He seemed very taken with you. He likes boys, you know. You should have flirted more. Better a slave to a king than a slave to an elephant.'

He slaps at a mosquito.

Mara doesn't answer.

'You're a strange one, aren't you?'

Mara puts on his sandals, one hand against Gajendra's chest to do it. Like he's a tree. Or a lover. He could knock his hand away but he doesn't. 'What do you care about that?'

'You're right. I don't know why I even waste my breath on you.'

Mara seems to realize what he has done. He takes his hand away rather slowly, Gajendra thinks, his fingers lingering on his skin. He is both alarmed and intrigued.

There is a sudden light in those green eyes. The evening light on his flesh is arresting. Mara pulls at his hair, his short hair.

Then he leans forward and kisses him on the mouth.

Gajendra pushes him away. He could have hit him; he

233

decides to laugh about it instead. 'So that's what it is. You have a crush on me. Well, forget it. You don't need your dwarf to protect you, do you? He's just slowing things down for you.'

'Is that what you think?'

Something shifts in Mara's eyes.

Gajendra sighs, shakes his head. 'How old are you really?'

'I have fifteen summers.'

'The truth.'

A long breath. '… Twenty.'

He walks up to his dung lark, runs a hand down his cheek, so smooth, too smooth for twenty summers. Without warning he puts his hand between his legs. Her legs.

She gasps and tries to twist away but he stops her. 'Who are you?'

'If we were in Carthage, you'd be *my* slave,' she spits back.

'But we're not in Carthage. And if Alexander finds out about this, you'll be everyone's slave. He'll sell you or put you in with the rest of the camp followers and you'll earn your keep that way.'

She shakes her head. 'You wouldn't do that.'

'Wouldn't I?'

'You're a good man, Gajendra. You want to be like him, but you're not.'

'Why are you dressed like a boy? Who's that fucking murderous dwarf? Let me have the truth if you want me to help you.'

'I am a priestess of the goddess Tanith. My father is the

general who stood against you at Carthage. And that…'
She takes a deep breath. 'That… fucking… murderous…
dwarf who has taken wound after wound in my name is his
manservant and he must rue the day he ever set eyes on
me. Dressing me like this was his idea.'

Gajendra lets her arm drop. He walks down to the river,
stares at the sunset dappled in the water, gives himself time
to think. Then he walks back.

'Why were you not with your father under his
protection?'

'I refused to leave the temple.'

'What were you doing there?'

'I had had enough of life.'

'Enough of life? You are scarce old enough to know
what life is!'

'You are old enough to breathe, you are old enough
to hurt. That is all I can tell you. My father sent Catharo
to protect me as best he could when the city fell. To this
point he has done sterling service, don't you think, with
little enough gratitude from me. There, now you have it. So
what will you do with me now?'

He does not answer her straight away. He slaps at
another mosquito. Really, why did he act as if this was
news to him? He had already guessed half of it. 'One more
thing: why did you kiss me?'

'Because I wanted to.'

'That is no answer.'

'It is all the answer you will have from me. It was not
my plan or my intention. But it happened and now I am
ashamed of it. It is clear to both of us now that I would do
well as a camp follower.'

It was dark now and he could barely make out her face. 'I can protect you.'

'If I will be *your* camp follower?'

'That would be a reasonable bargain, wouldn't it? But no, that's not the agreement between us. I will protect you anyway. But you have to stop lying to me.'

'First I want to know why you would do that.'

'Because I want to.'

'That's not a good enough reason.'

'As you have said, it is all the answer you will have from me. Now I'm not staying down here to get eaten by the mosquitoes. If anyone asks you where you were you'll tell them the elephant captain has claimed your arse for his own, then no one will try and bend you over a table while your protector is laid up with his leg broken. No wonder you were useless at shovelling shit, princess!'

'I am not a princess.'

He shrugs. 'Well, you should have been.'

When Mara returns to the camp Catharo is back on his feet again. He has a stick to lean on for walking and an enormous linen bandage around his leg. 'Where have you been?' he asks her.

'I was by the river talking to the young captain.'

'What about?'

'I told him I needed a new bodyguard. I told him the one I had was an old woman who hid whenever there was trouble.'

'If he touched you, I'll fillet him from groin to chin.'

'By the time you're ready to fillet anyone again I

should be beyond child-bearing years. How is your leg?'

'What do you care?'

She puts a hand on his arm. It startles him. 'I am sorry, Catharo.'

It is too dark to see his astonishment but she hears it in his voice. 'For what?'

'For all the trouble you have been through in my name. If I am restored to my place in life I shall ensure that you are given a vineyard and a pension where you can live out your days in peace.'

'Who said I want peace? Why would you torture me with a vineyard? This is the life I like.'

'Shall I get you your dinner?'

'You are going to fetch me my supper?'

'I have been ungrateful to you in the past. I want to make up for it.'

'Why?'

'Because if someone is kind to you, you try and remember it and do the same for someone else. The Indians call it karma.'

His eyes glitter. He still has a fever from his wound. 'All right. See if you can get me an extra ration of bread. I haven't eaten for days.'

She kisses him on the forehead. He pushes her away, thoroughly alarmed. 'I know what you've been doing,' he growls. 'When I'm fit again, I'm going to kill him.'

That night she dreams of her father. He is frowning at her in the way that he did when she was a child. He had never needed to reproach her, he only had to look a certain way when he walked into the house to send her scurrying. It is as if he wants to say something to her, but in the way of all dreams, she cannot hear him.

CHAPTER 35

As gajendra lies in the straw all he can think of is that hot morning in the temple of Astarte in Babylon, Zahara about to settle that divine flesh onto the pillows her girls had set out for her on the temple stones; how she had blushed when they entered the wood; the heave of her breasts as she settled back against the tree and waited for his pleasure. Had he imagined it or did she look not displeased to have been chosen?

What might it have been like if he had taken what the goddess and his coins had promised? The thought makes him gasp aloud and he sits up in the straw. Ravi asks him what is wrong; he thinks perhaps he has been bitten by a snake. He snaps at him to go back to sleep.

Every time he feels drowsy he thinks of her and the thought rouses him awake again. He says to Ravi: I am going to check on the guards. Ravi grunts and turns over. The waterboys are snoring. No one cares what he does.

He prowls the camp like a ghost.

Ravi was right, he is the world's biggest fool. Does he really think he could ever have such a chance again? He aches for her in his bones now and, having refused what the goddess once had offered, he will be tormented by his impetuosity forever.

Alexander has asked for elephants to guard the royal enclosure. The elephants know him and allow him close, there is no trumpeting to warn the guards. The *mahavat* astride the nearest sounds panicked when he realizes someone is there and he calls out for the password.

'Ah it's you!' he says when he sees it is his captain. He says nothing as Gajendra walks past, and he gives the man no explanation for being there.

He knows he will not be discovered unless he gets close to Alexander's tent, for he has an extra ring of Companion Guards who would slit the throat of Zeus himself if he were to get within a hundred paces without express permission.

The women are in the great pavilion that once belonged to Darius. Alexander collects princesses like some men collect rounded stones. Oh that's nice, put it in your pocket, I'll look at it later, and never does. Alexander has left all but a few of the women in Babylon; he wishes to make it clear to his officers that it is his capital now, not Greece. He keeps just a few with him for the sake of appearance and as hostage against rebellion in the satrapies. They are also a useful form of barter, or reward.

Zahara was the diadem Nearchus earned at Carthage. In economic terms Alexander must see it as a bargain.

The men see none of this pampered flesh, of course; if they wish for female company they have gaudy camp followers in the baggage train to entertain them; here's a coin, now bend over this, there's a good girl. All they see of the high-born is a shimmer of silk slipping in and out of one of the covered wagons, and the rest is just their imagination.

Gajendra keeps to the shadows, avoiding the torchlight. If the guards find him he wonders how he will explain himself.

Nearchus salutes a guard and steps inside his pavilion. He must have excused himself early from Alexander's tent. He can still hear them; the Macks like to shout at each other when they're drunk, and he has even heard that at home they would rape bears after a few flagons of wine. It sounds unlikely, but they are an unlikely people.

He crawls on his belly to the side of the tent and lies there in the darkness despising himself for what he has become.

He listens to his Elephantarch take his pleasure. Is it a consolation that she does not call his name as she called his in his fantasy? Is it natural that a man should torture himself this way, listening to another man take what he longs for above all else, stay near enough that he hears him cry out in his moment of greatest release?

He crawls away on his belly; this is what he has become. Something that crawls; something he had sworn to all his ancestors he would never be again.

CHAPTER 36

I N THE DAYS that follow Alexander is uncharacteristically cautious. He halts the army ten leagues west of Syracuse and waits. Perhaps it is because he faces Antipater and he knows his man too well. He sends Nearchus and an escort as envoy. Gajendra and Ravi watch them ride out.

'What is all this about?'

'How should I know?'

'You are a confidant of the great general now.'

Ravi is mocking him and he has a point; he does know. 'It's a delegation to the oligarch at Syracuse. Alexander is offering terms.'

'What sort of terms?'

'He will ask for Antipater's head in a basket in return for not destroying the town. He will open the city to him. And annual tribute.'

'That is not terms.'

'They are Alexander's terms.'

'What do you think they will say?'

'I think they will send Nearchus's head back in the basket. That's what I think.'

'You wouldn't mind that at all, would you?'

'It is not for me to wish another man ill.'

Gajendra wishes this were true. But Ravi is right;

should Nearchus not return he fancies himself the next Elephantarch. Someone must lead the elephants into the next battle and he is the logical choice. Ravi had jeered at him in Babylon, but here in the wilds of Sicily his dreams are very close.

And if he can have the Elephantarch's baton, why not his wife as well? He is a heartbeat away from every dream he ever had, but for the good of his soul he will try not to pray for a deadly outcome to Nearchus's mission.

The pavilion has been fly-rigged open on all sides despite the baking wind so the men can see their generals at work. Soldiers cluster around outside, leaning on their spears, a few murmuring among themselves but mostly silent, intent. They are close enough that he can smell their sweat.

The Macks hate him until it is time for the battle. Then they remember they will be nowhere without him.

Alexander paces like a restless lion, his eyes on the table where the charts are spread. A lion, too long without a kill, sensing the wind, hungry.

There is no sign of Nearchus. Scouts ride in, bringing deserters bound and blindfolded. There are whispers that Alexander's spies have underestimated their enemy, that Antipater has an army a hundred thousand strong and that the harbour at Syracuse is a forest of masts, that it has taken three days just to land the horses.

Alexander looks relaxed. He wanders the tent with hands on hips, as if planning a wedding feast for his latest wife.

He tells us what his forward scouts have just told him; the truth is only a little less alarming than the rumours.

Antipater has with him fifty thousand infantry, and ten thousand horses. He has left Macedon largely unprotected, relying on his allies in the east to do his fighting for him. If he can defeat Alexander the crown is his, whatever happens elsewhere.

And he wants revenge for his sons.

Alexander is expansive. 'They outnumber us three to one, gentlemen; they are rested and they are well supplied; they even have a phalanx of Macedonians who are willing to betray their crease. So – shall we give up and go home?'

The generals laugh. It is good to see Alexander on top form again.

'We have surprised them with the speed of our arrival. He expected to find us still in Carthage, taking the sea air, I suppose. He cannot anticipate that we would have our elephants with us. If the attack on our tuskers had succeeded we might be at a disadvantage. Thanks to this brave young fellow here, they did not succeed.' He claps Gajendra on the shoulder and puts his arm around him, as if they had together held a pass against a thousand men. He knows it is theatre but feels flattered anyway.

With a flourish Alexander points out the rectangles and arrows he has made on his charts. 'Antipater has no experience of fighting elephants. All he knows is what he has heard from the soldiers who fought with us in India. He will think we will do as we did at Carthage and set them against the infantry.'

But he tells them that this time they will not do that.

'Carthage has raised another army from their city colonies in the north and they are three days' march from here. Antipater hoped to catch us between the horns of two armies but we have deprived him of that pleasure. The raiders they sent to harry us were Guggas, as we have discovered from the prisoners we took.

'Antipater's cavalry have never faced elephants before. You saw what happened when the Guggas attacked us with the skirmish line – their horses broke and bolted. They could not get close. In a battle they will turn and run.'

The seasoned veterans stand with their arms folded, looking weary with it all. He can see them thinking: this battle, perhaps one more, and we can all go home.

But for me, this is my chance, Gajendra thinks. This is my moment.

They hear a murmur in the distance, a susurration that comes like a wave towards them, like a ripple on a lake. A sentry rushes in.

'Nearchus has returned, my lord.'

And he has returned; at least, what is left of him. They have tied his hands to the saddle to keep him upright, but in truth it is just his pride that keeps him on his horse. His horse knows the way back to the camp, and now several of the guards rush out to grab its reins while others pull him out of the saddle.

Gajendra looks once then turns away. Dying in battle is one thing, this is something he has never wanted to think about.

As they help him down, he thinks Alexander might bend to comfort his former favourite, but he just sighs and turns away. 'There is our answer to our offer of treaty, gentlemen,' he says, and saunters back into his pavilion.

*

'You know what they are saying,' Ravi says. 'That he sent him out knowing what they would do. That he was getting too popular with the men so he wanted to get rid of him.'

'He could not have foreseen that kind of barbarity.'

'What was in the letter he gave him? No one knows, do they? Only Alexander.'

Gajendra thought about the story Alexander had told him about his father, Philip. *Promise men the world but your thoughts belong to you.* He doesn't want to believe it.

'It is what he always does. He attempts a treaty first.'

'Well, it's good news for you. Everyone says it now. His own people are tired of fighting and he wants someone young with energy and ambition to lead his elephants. Now Nearchus is out of the way it could be you. If we are victorious against Antipater...'

'We will win.'

'... then you will be his new favourite. At least, until he tires of you.'

'What do you mean?'

'You know what I mean. He'll use you and turn you and goad you and reward you and then when he has everything he needs out of you, the moment he thinks you are more popular with the soldiers than he is, then he'll do to you what he did to Nearchus.'

'He didn't do it! The Greeks did!'

'You know what I fear more, though? That it won't happen. That instead you'll become more and more like him until in the end I'll be sorry I ever found that little orphan boy wandering around the Rajah's camp and gave him the chance to make something of himself.'

Gajendra pushes Ravi in the chest. It is not intended as

a blow but Ravi trips and goes down. For a moment they are both too surprised to say anything.

Ravi shakes his head. 'You see,' he says. 'It has started already.'

CHAPTER 37

HE SHOULD BE accustomed to it by now; kicked roughly from his sleep in the middle of the night by one of Alexander's guards, led stumbling half asleep through the camp to his pavilion. The camp sleeps but Alexander's household is in riot; Alexander sits on a stool comforted by a wife.

He hears Ravi's voice: *you will be his new favourite. At least, until he tires of you.* The oil lamps hanging from the crossed metal spears in the entrance throw long shadows. Smoke from the pine knots burning in the brazier sting his eyes.

He barely recognizes his general. He looks haunted, and sitting there half naked he no longer appears indestructible. There is a purple scar on his leg where an arrowhead smashed his leg bone at Marakanda. They say splinters of bone still work their way out of it from time to time. And in the lamplight he can see the hollow where he was hit in the face by a stone hurled from the ramparts of some fort or other. He was blind for a while and could not talk.

He turns his head towards him. 'Boy, I dreamed about your elephants.'

Is this why he has him out of bed at this hour? Because of a dream? He relaxes and at once becomes resentful.

'What did you see in the dream, my lord?'

'Your elephant, the big one…'

'Colossus.'

'He spoke to me.'

Gajendra keeps his face immobile. 'My elephant spoke to you?'

'He said that I had overreached myself.'

'How is this possible?' one of his Persians says. 'A god cannot overreach.'

They look to him to agree. But Gajendra is not of a mind to join in. I did not leave my good sleep to come over here and kiss your arse, Alexander. 'Did the ele— did Colossus say anything else?'

'That I should fall at the feet of Hercules.'

'But you *are* Hercules,' says some other toady from the shadows. Alexander does not look as if this comforts him overmuch.

He pushes his wife away. He is tired of having his neck rubbed and her breasts in his face all the time, it is bothering him, like flies hanging around.

Ptolemy gives Gajendra a look. Tomorrow they must engage with their enemy. It will not do to have Alexander in this condition.

'This is not a bad dream to have,' Gajendra says.

'How can it not be a bad dream?'

'In India, the elephant is a lucky sign. When we dream of elephants it means good fortune.'

'Do your good luck elephants also tell you that you have gone too far?'

'It may just be a warning not to stretch your lines of supply. It just means that we should not rush into the battle, but take our time to confront the enemy.'

'But what about Hercules?'

Gajendra takes a step closer, his heart in his mouth. He fears he is about to overreach himself. 'You are not a god.'

Alexander's glance is not hostile, more curious. 'It would not do for others to think that.'

'The gods wish a sacrifice from you. That's all. To show that you are not a threat to them.'

His eyes are shining. Not a god, Gajendra thinks, but quite possibly mad. But it is enough. Alexander shrugs off the vale, leaves behind for now the underworld that waits for him in sleep and in death, forgets the terror of being forgotten. He smiles. 'You think that is all it is?'

'The elephant is a sign that you will win. Sacrifice to the gods and all will be well.'

'Yes, you're right. You're right!' Ptolemy rolls his eyes at how swiftly the general's mood lifts. Alexander claps his hands together and calls for wine. It is clear no one in his household will sleep now.

He stands up and stretches, his face radiant, then puts an arm around Gajendra's shoulder and leads him out of earshot.

An idea has dawned. He kisses the tips of his fingers and touches them to Gajendra's cheek. 'You saw what they did to my envoy?'

Envoy? I thought he was your friend.

He says, 'I need a new Elephantarch, someone to lead my elephants tomorrow. Do you think you can do it?'

'From a horse?'

'What do you know of horses? No, from Colossus.'

Alexander's fingers toy with Gajendra's tunic, like a

lover. He can feel the drum of his own pulse. All things are becoming possible.

'Help me be victorious tomorrow,' Alexander murmurs, 'and I will give you the whole world, anything you want.'

He holds out a hand for someone to place a wine cup in it. He takes a long draught and grins, his teeth red.

'I will not let you down,' Gajendra says.

'Of course not.' He turns his back as suddenly as he has enveloped him and waves an airy hand in dismissal. 'Everything is clear to me now. Go.'

He is ushered out again by the guards, into a firestruck night, and stumbles back to the straw. In the morning he will wonder if he has dreamed it.

But the next day he hears that Alexander has gone up the mountain just before dawn and made sacrifices by torchlight to the local gods, to prove to them that he is no threat.

Not that Alexander believes that, but never let the gods know what you're thinking.

Ravi finds him early next morning. He looks panicked. Gajendra is still in the straw, thinking about Alexander; then he sees Ravi's face and in that moment he knows what has happened.

'Gajendra! Gajendra!'

'What's wrong?'

Ravi pulls him to his feet and leads him out of earshot of the other *mahavats*. 'This boy, Mara. I just found him in the bushes, squatting. To piss. He's a girl!'

'Did she see you?'

Ravi stares at him speechless. The world shifts. 'You knew about this?'

'Yes, I knew.'

'How long?'

'Not long.'

'You're not screwing her, are you?'

'I thought about it. I don't think she'd let me. Or her bodyguard would kill me. She's quite high born.'

Ravi stares as if he has water in his ears. This shocking news has not had the reception he expected. 'Let you? Why didn't you just do it? She's a slave. And what's this talk about bodyguards?'

'You were right. He's not her uncle.'

'The dwarf – he's her bodyguard?'

'Have you seen him fight?'

'I can't believe you kept this to yourself.'

'The less you know the better.'

'But it's me – Ravi. Your uncle! You should have told me about this. Who is she?'

'She's a priestess of Tanith. She cut her hair and put on men's clothes to disguise herself.'

'A priestess! By the black breath of hell, this is bad business.'

'There's worse.'

Ravi did not look surprised.

'She's the daughter of the general who stood against us outside Carthage.'

Ravi is speechless. Finally: 'So why are you going along with it? She's a valuable hostage! Alexander would have you crucified if he knew you had deceived him about this!'

'Would he?'

The question takes Ravi's breath away. 'So now you think you're above everyone else?'

'Let me calculate the risk.'

'But why are you taking any risk? Because you feel sorry for her?'

'If someone finds out, I'll just say I didn't know. You're the only one who's worked this out.'

'And how long will you keep up this charade?'

'When that ugly brute who trails her around can walk again, I'll help her get away.'

Ravi shakes his head.

'So not a word, all right?'

Ravi sulks for a while, then says, 'If one of the other *mahavats* had found her, she wouldn't be so lucky.'

'I know that. It's only a matter of time. That's why I have to help her escape.'

'I don't understand. Why help her at all?'

'Because of you.'

'Me?'

'Do you remember how this hungry little orphan wandered into your camp once, when you were with the Rajah? You saw him getting kicked around by some soldiers for sport? You grabbed one of them by the ear, though he was twice your size, and told him I was one of your waterboys and you would set your elephants on all of them if they didn't clear off?'

'That was different. You weren't a priestess for one thing.'

'I was homeless and helpless. It's my karma now to pay back what you did for me.'

'Are you sure that's all it is? Because if you just

wanted to fuck her, you've gone to too much trouble.'

'I thought she was a boy. I would understand why you'd think that if I was one of these Greeks. Besides, you know who I want.'

'Not that, still! If I'd known how you were going to turn out that day I saw you, I would have let those soldiers do whatever they wanted. I should have just walked away, done us both a favour. What you are doing here, this is not the same. Taking you in was no risk for me. I needed another waterboy. But a girl like that is worth something to someone. A general's daughter!'

'Alexander will defeat what is left of Carthage, and Antipater as well, without hostages.' They hear the reveille. The camp is waking. 'Now get the waterboys up and about. We have work to do.'

Gajendra tries a fresh approach. As the new Elephantarch he will lead from the front; instead of archers Colossus will have a signal boy with flags in the *howdah* on his back so he can direct the others. He has some large drums mounted on its sides so he can still send his orders even if there is thick dust and the other *mahavats* cannot see the flags.

All that morning they drill the elephants; it is only Alexander's Companion Cavalry that can stand to be so close to them, and even that has taken many months of training. Some of the younger elephants are still not up to it; time and again, when the cavalry charge a few young bulls back up or turn out of formation, panicked, disrupting the others. By early afternoon Gajendra's nerves are ragged, his *mahavats* are cursing their elephants and one another. Ptolemy, in charge of the cavalry, is apoplectic. He rides off to tell Alexander that he must change his plans.

Gajendra calls the elephants back into line. They try again.

Late that afternoon, Mara finds him in an olive grove, on his knees, praying in front of a small stone god. He looks up, angry at being disturbed. 'What are you doing here?'

'What's that?' she asks him.

He has surrounded the statuette with flowers and some olives he has plucked from the tree. The god is like no god she has ever seen; it has many arms and a head like an elephant.

'It is Ganesha,' he says.

'It's an elephant. You pray to an animal?'

'Look, I may know your little secret, but you're still just one of my dung larks. So don't think you can talk to me whenever you like.' He picks up his god and hides him away in a pouch in his belt.

'Who is he? Your god?'

'Didn't you hear what I just said?'

'I am just interested. Won't you tell me?'

He shakes his head. 'He is the Lord of Beginnings and the Placer and Remover of Obstacles.'

'He does both?'

'He will clear the way to your desire if you ask him. He will put obstacles there, too, if he thinks you need to be thwarted for your own good.'

'Which obstacles do you wish him to remove?'

'If you are going to ask such questions you should grow

more brawn on you so you can take all the slaps on your head you are going to get.'

'It is a fair question.'

'Not from a slave.'

Gajendra stands up. He looks so sure of himself, she thinks. My husband looked like that the day he got on the ship that carried him to his death.

'All right, I'll tell you what obstacles I wish removed from my path. I want the colour of my skin to be no impediment to becoming one of Alexander's generals. I do not want Antipater's army to stand in the way of my hopes.'

'Why do you wish to be a general?'

'Because I want to be rich and feared and I want the girl of my dreams. I want the world. There, that's what I want.'

'Do you think that will be enough?'

'It will do to start.'

'The girl of your dreams. You have met her?'

'Perhaps.'

'And have you told her how you feel about her?'

He nods.

'And what did she say?'

'She wanted to give me my money back.'

She puts her hand over her mouth to try and stop herself, but it's no good, she giggles out loud and his face flushes a deep bronze and he looks as if he would like to thrash her if he had a good horsewhip to hand.

'You are in love with a dancing girl? The last time we spoke about this, the object of your affections was a princess. You continually seek outside your realm, if I may say so.'

'I am not in love with a dancing girl! I went to the temple

256

in Babylon and my princess was there also, as her duty to the goddess. I gave her my coins and we went to the wood behind the temple and that's when I told her.'

'You told her?'

'That I did not want to pay for her. That I wanted her for my own and that one day I would make it happen so.'

'You gave up your one chance to sleep with a princess?'

'Not my one chance!'

'What were you thinking?' she says, before she can stop herself.

'It will happen one day, you will see.'

'It is a simple enough transaction. Here's a pretty girl you might never see again. Bend over here, sweetheart, here's a coin for the goddess and a slap on the bottom from me by way of thanks. And you're on your way.' Gajendra bears this lecture, white-faced. 'Did you get your coins back?'

He shakes his head. 'If you tell anyone about this, you're straight to the auction block – after I've beaten you to a pulp, you and that dwarf of yours.'

'I won't tell anyone. Who would believe such a story anyway?'

'What is so hard to believe? Already I am captain of the elephants. My tuskers will win Alexander even more victories and I will be his most important general. Then I may name whatever token I wish from him.'

'Or tomorrow you could die in a battle or one of your tuskers might step on you. If you have a chance for pleasure you should take it. Life ends soon enough.'

'What do you know of life?' he snaps at her.

'I know that you have fixed your heart on a mirage.

When you discover she sweats and has a temper you are going to be very disappointed at spending your credit with Alexander on a fantasy.'

She turns on her heel.

'Before you go, there's something you should know. Ravi saw you. He knows you are a girl.'

She sighs and leans against the nearest tree. Well, it is a relief, in a way. It was ever only a matter of time before she was discovered. At least it is Ravi who saw her, and not one of the others.

'He spied you in the bushes. You will have to be more careful.'

She slumps to her haunches, puts her head on her arms. 'I am so tired of this.'

'You told me you became a priestess because you were tired of your life. What can possibly be so bad when your father is a general and all you have to do all day is lie in a bath and listen to your slaves tell you how beautiful you are?'

'I have lived ten lives for your one,' she says bitterly.

'I doubt that.'

She glares at him. How I would love to slap that arrogant look off your face. 'My husband had estates in Sicily. He went to visit them but I was too ill to travel with him. I was carrying his baby and I was sick every morning. He drowned three months before the birth of our daughter. Our little boy was on the ship with him.'

'Oh.' He has at least the decency to look shamefaced and lower his eyes. 'What happened to your little girl?'

'She died of a fever. I caught it too, but I survived. Countless times I wished I hadn't.'

'I see.'

'That's why I wanted nothing more to do with life. If you ever have a wife that you love and a son that is part of your own flesh then perhaps you will understand. You have to lose everything to understand what it is like.'

'And so you feel sorry for yourself?'

She jumps to her feet. She swings her hand at him but he catches her wrist. 'I have the right!'

'No one has the right. You must never give up. No matter what happens, no matter how hard things are, you don't give up. You never know if there is something just around the corner that will tip the balance back in your favour and give you back your life.'

She puts out a hand as if to steady herself. 'Is there?' Her fingers stroke the smooth skin of his shoulder. Their eyes meet. It is a moment of frank appraisal.

She takes her hand away abruptly and with a little gasp she tries to regather her composure, or what a priestess pretending to be a waterboy can pass off for it.

He takes her hand and puts it back. She strokes the smooth muscle on his chest. There, it has been said and better than words.

There is a look in his eyes. It is as if he has never truly considered this. He puts a hand on her hip, the other on her cheek. 'I have never felt this way before about a waterboy.'

She takes his hand, kisses the tips of his fingers and says, 'I don't believe you.'

The paleness of her throat beckons. He eases his fingers under her tunic seeking her bare flesh. The whole world is in motion; he licks the sweat off her cheek and cups her small breast. She makes a little sound, a moan, poised between longing and horror at her own betrayal. 'I can't,' she murmurs.

He was smiling, her husband, that last day on the dock. He blew her kisses. She had one hand on her belly and their growing child and she blew a kiss back. It was a bright day with a cool zephyr of wind, there was no warning of the storm, no premonition in her heart.

How could she leave him now? He was still out there, at sea.

Gajendra pulls back, confused. She wants to tell him just to hold her. She has missed a man's arms around her waist.

'You have to let go of them,' he says to her.

She shakes her head. 'He can see me.'

'You have to let him go,' he repeats. 'You have to let them both go. You can't follow them any more and they can't follow you.'

But she cannot let go. If she does, she must admit they are really gone.

Her husband. Her daughter.

Her son…

She would stare at him for hours when he was newborn, wonder at such tiny cuticles on his fingers, would smell his hair as if he was the richest perfume in Arabia. Hasdrubal would stand behind her, hold her and rock her in that easy way of his and she felt safe. But the world was not safe.

She feels the rumbling of the elephants, and Colossus trumpets somewhere down by the river. She puts her head on Gajendra's shoulder. A part of her aches to let go; another strives only to hold on.

'Let them go,' he repeats.

'Not yet.' He is right, they are gone, just as her father said. If she wishes for life, then she must betray the dead.

She cannot do it. He holds her anyway and she cries into his shoulder, a fool, a weakling. If her father could see her now, he would be ashamed.

But she must let go of him, too.

CHAPTER 38

SHE HAD RETURNED once to the Tophet, the place where she had given her child back to Tanith. She had stood on the edge, listening to the wind moan through the well. It sounded like despair.

She had been a priestess then for just three months but seclusion and devotion had not healed even the smallest part of her grief. The best parts of every day were those few moments on waking before she remembered; and those last few moments at night when she could welcome the oblivion of sleep.

There was a constant pain that sat just below her breastbone; it was as if she had eaten something foul. It ached in her all day, and she could not rid herself of it. Whenever she thought of Hasdrubal or her baby's smell, it grew worse.

So she had gone to the Tophet thinking to escape from the pain by tossing herself in the well; she had hovered there on the edge of the pit until her legs cramped, but she could not make herself jump.

She thinks about what Gajendra had said to her: *No matter what happens, you don't give up.* Was there still something in her that held out hope, even now?

Why should he say such a thing?

Life made no sense. They were all playthings of cruel

gods who brought death out of a blue sky to the unsuspecting. She could see no reason for any of it. Even Tanith laughed at her.

Don't ever give up.

But why not?

If she had jumped she would not now be a slave in the army of a man who had destroyed her home and everything she had ever known.

But if she had, she would not have met someone like Gajendra, who would try and change her mind and show her that there might yet be a brighter dawn.

Catharo is limping but he no longer needs the crutch they gave him. He looks at her accusingly, as her father used to. She cannot meet his eyes. It's as if he knows about her betrayal.

He is pale. He has spilled so much blood for her of late, endured so much, he must be all but empty of gore. Her father once told her that Catharo was indestructible; this morning, less so. She wants to tell him to lie down, to rest. As if he would listen to her.

Why is he so loyal? It is unfathomable. They are not even kinsmen. Her father told her Catharo is from some Balearic island, though others say he popped out of the earth from Hades. None of it accounts for this steadfastness to her father.

'You look pale,' he says. 'What has happened to you?'

She shakes her head and shrugs.

'From now on you will not leave my sight. You are still under my protection.'

'How many more wounds will you take for me, Catharo?'

'As many as it takes to keep you safe.'

'But why?'

He does not answer, just glares at her, as if she is the cause of all his troubles. And that is not such a strange thing to think, because she is.

She closes her eyes and imagines her father alive. Once she could not stand the sight of him; now all she wants is to see him one more time.

Shields, spears and javelins have been stacked outside the tents, men kneel in the dirt playing dice by the flicker of oil lamps. The flap to Alexander's tent has been left open; there's a guard but even he's lounging. There's a Persian carpet, a wooden chest with silver handles. His armour has been hung on a centre pole. It gleams in the glow of a lamp that swings from a ridgepole.

Alexander is sitting at a camp table; he is writing orders using a stylus on a wax tablet. As Gajendra enters he does not look up. It is so hot the wax is stripping off the board with every stroke and the words are difficult to read. How intense he is; how still. Does he even know I am here? He raises a finger to indicate Gajendra is to wait; yes, he knows.

Look at how he lives; now that he has to face Macedonian troops, he has decided to become a Macedonian again. He wears just a tooled leather breastplate over his tunic; there is a royal blue blanket laid on the ground for his bed. He is the complete military man again, just a single guard on the door and a rolled blanket for a pillow. If they should ban war tomorrow he would be lost.

Finally, he turns.

'You wished to see me, my lord?'

He stands up, stretches his back, so that Gajendra might admire his squat, blond physique. 'Do you know they say we're lovers?'

This is unexpected. 'Who says it?'

'Gossip. It is brought to me occasionally. Apparently because we spend so much time together. And because I am Greek, I suppose. But I have more important things to do than fuck. Don't people know this?'

The frightened little boy of last night is gone. He looks cocky again, a god once more. It is only the night that erodes his confidence; by day he is king of everything.

'Are the elephants ready? Tomorrow we go against Antipater.'

'We're ready.'

'I promise you will be in the thick of things tomorrow. That's what you want, isn't it? To be in the flaming heart of the battle. Test yourself.'

'Yes.'

'We must have our victory. That Gugga general, Hanno, escaped Carthage when we sacked it and fled to Panormus in the north. Do you know the city's Council tried to treat with me before the walls fell? He was to be part of their bargain. Why would I want to kill a brave man? Now they are in exile they have rehired him, and paid for another army. This is who is coming down to meet us. We will have to account for Antipater quickly before he gets here.'

'Surely Antipater will stall the battle until they are close.'

'You may understand battle, elephant boy, but you don't know the first thing about politics. Antipater will want to win this without the Guggas. This is not about land, it is about the crown of Macedon and who is fit to wear it.' He stands in front of Gajendra, straightens him up, adjusts his tunic, as if he is sending him off to make a good impression in the provinces. 'They tell me Carthage was your first battle.'

'I was at Jhellum. But I was only a waterboy then. I was behind the lines with the baggage train.'

'And killing? Close up, as you and I are now? Your first was when Hanno's raiders attacked your elephants, am I right?'

Gajendra nods.

'Do you dream about him? The man you killed?'

'Sometimes.'

'It seems unnatural at first. But it is in every man, this... lust. Any man will become a killer if you put a sword in his hand, you just show him how, give him a little skill and confidence. And the more we do it, the more battles we survive, the more we kill, the easier it becomes and the better soldiers we are.' He pats his arm. 'Such a need in you, isn't there? Such a desperate longing. Where does it come from? I wonder. How does it begin? Is a man born with ambition or does something happen to move him? What do you think?'

'I think it's in our nature.'

'No, you don't. You don't think that at all.'

He is so close. His breath is foul. Gajendra winces but tries not to look away. 'I am thinking of replacing you.'

'Replacing me?'

'With someone more able. Ptolemy tells me we cannot rely on your elephants in the thick of battle, that it will be as it was at Carthage, only this time we shall not be as

266

fortunate. He thinks you should be replaced, perhaps with someone who wants it more than you. Someone who is ambitious – by his nature.'

Gajendra feels the panic rising. 'No one wants this more than I do. I have trained for this, I have drilled my tuskers again and again! No one can lead those elephants like I can.'

Alexander shakes his head. 'You are incidental to me. When I need a thing done, I want it done.'

'Please. What do you want from me?'

'I want to know who you are, elephant boy. How you came to be here. I need to know all my generals, from their souls out. Do you understand?'

Yes, he knows what he's asking. He hesitates, but he knows he cannot afford to think about this too long. Alexander is not well known for his patience. 'I don't remember much of it.'

'Another lie. Perhaps Ravi will be my new Elephantarch?'

'I'll tell you everything.'

'You see? That's better. Now you have clarity. I'm your only friend, elephant boy. We should have no secrets from each other, you and I. Now tell me, what is this old *mahavat* Ravi to you?'

'He was kind to me.'

'Why?'

'I don't know. He found me half starved wandering around the Rajah's camp and decided to save me. Perhaps he never had a son of his own.'

'How did you come to be half dead?'

A fine, hot morning when they came. He was inside, listening to his mother and sisters pound the rice. What was he doing inside? Why wasn't he in the field with his brothers? He remembers now. He was sick.

He heard the dacoits shouting, felt the drumming of the horses' hooves through the ground.

'Ah, now we're getting somewhere. So, bandits attacked your village. What happened to your family? Don't tell me the bandits killed them all? Look at me, elephant boy, not the floor. If you are going to tell me, you might as well tell me to my face. These bandits, they killed your whole family?'

Their faces were fading now; sometimes he would lie in bed in the morning, in that soft place between dreams and waking, and try to picture them. But it was like trying to catch smoke. His father's face was almost gone now; he remembers betel-stained teeth and large bony hands. His mother's face lingers; but of his sisters, nothing at all.

'You're remembering now, aren't you?'

'My mother was threshing rice.'

'You were there? You saw everything?'

Gajendra winces. He can hear screams. He glances around, thinking they are real.

'What did you do?'

'I ran.'

'You ran away?'

'To my mother.'

'How old were you?'

'I was eight, perhaps nine.'

His two older brothers ran in from the fields, waving their arms, telling everyone to run. But there was no time to run. By the time they realized what was happening, it was too late.

'What did they do?'

'I couldn't stop them.'

'Of course not. You were just a little boy.'

One of the dacoits rode into the field and cut his brothers down, like he was harvesting rice. Two, three sweeps of his scimitar and they were gone. They must have screamed. Did they? He does not remember. His mother did, though.

'You can still hear them dying, can't you? You're hearing them now. Do you hear them at night, too?'

'Sometimes.'

'What are they doing? The bandits.'

'They have my mother and my sisters. They're holding them down. They're laughing.'

'And what is my little elephant boy doing?'

'I'm hitting them.'

'Hitting them? That was very brave.'

It is a lie; the little boy just watches. One of the men is laughing when he grabs him by the hair and pushes him to his knees. He tells him that he will give him the chance to save his mother and sisters.

'Did you try and save them?'

'They made me beg.'

'How did they do that?'

'Their leader said he wouldn't kill them if I would do something for them.'

'What did he make you do?'

He crawls, he cries, he begs, hands outstretched. When they laugh he thinks they are warming to him so he does it more. For the first time in his life he has an audience and while his audience laughs, his mother and his sisters are still alive.

Then they form a circle and piss on him, still laughing.

Gajendra is trembling.

'What did they make you do?'

'My mother was screaming.'

'You could see her face?'

'I could see her face.'

'And the men were laughing. They had you on the ground?'

'They pissed on me.'

'While they were raping your mother and your sister?'

'After.'

They have all taken a turn. Other dacoits are stealing the cows, everything they can find. The leader takes his turn to piss on him, too, and then he gives an order and they slit the throats of the women. They are going to kill him next.

'Leave him,' the chief says.

'Why didn't they kill you, elephant boy?'

'I don't know.'

Alexander strokes his cheek. Tenderly, he says, 'That torments you every night, doesn't it? Why didn't they kill me? Because I was a coward or because I was brave? You wanted to die with the rest of them, didn't you?'

He nods.

'You dread it, don't you, elephant boy? You dread being weak again. You dread being helpless. That's why you want this so badly. Then your mother and your sister will stop screaming inside your head, is that what you think?'

'Perhaps.'

Alexander sighs, and smiles. He kisses him gently on the lips. 'You are going to be a fine general. So now you are my new Elephantarch. Win for me, Gajendra. Tomorrow make me victorious.'

*

Gajendra finds Catharo hunkered down in the straw chewing on a stale crust of bread and staring at the mountains. He looks up, wary, when he sees Gajendra.

'You are going to get Mara away from here.'

He thinks there's a trick. He chews and swallows. 'What?'

'You can do that, can't you? It's your job, right, to protect her?'

He doesn't say anything, stares up at him with malevolent eyes.

'You are going to take her back to her father.'

'Her father's dead.'

'No, he's not. He is just over those mountains bringing another army.'

Catharo suspects treachery. Gajendra recounts what he knows from Alexander. 'Why are you telling me this?'

'Because I do not want her to come to harm. Perdiccas wants you both out of here anyway, after the trouble with the soldiers. It's nothing to me either way, so you might as well get away from here while you can.'

'Panormus is a long way to walk.'

'I'll get you horses. A few coins thrown the way of one of the sergeants in the baggage train for some old nags they don't need any more.'

Gajendra walks away, feeling better about himself. At least, a little better than he felt when he left Alexander's tent.

CHAPTER 39

'Your father is alive,' Catharo says without preamble. She murmurs something between astonishment and disbelief and sits down hard.

'The Hundred wanted to use him as barter, they say. He escaped to Panormus and those fuckers asked him to defend them again. He is three days west of here with another army.'

'How can you know this?'

'From this Indian boy. Our boss. It seems they got all this from the prisoner they took. Alexander has kept it quiet – he doesn't want the men to know they may have to fight two battles in two days.'

She draws her knees up to her chest. Too many shocks for one night.

One back from the dead, then.

She had abandoned all hope of seeing him again and it had grieved her that so many things had been left unsaid between them. Most of all, she wants his forgiveness. This news changes everything. Now she has a second chance, she is not quite so eager to die.

'I think the captain has a crush on you. Does he know you're a girl or doesn't he care? They don't seem to have much use for women round here.'

'Gajendra?'

'He has told me we are surplus to his needs and that anyway Alexander is still angry about the soldiers I killed and wants something done. He has arranged for us to get away. I can only think you have paid him in some way. Have you?'

'Of course not. What arrangement?'

'Two horses. Nags, he says, only used for baggage now, but he thinks they'll get us where we need to go.'

She imagines a reunion with her father, growing her hair again and getting the elephant stink off her.

It gives her a reason to live again. It is this Gajendra's fault, he has pulled her back from the edge. He has made her choose the living over the dead.

A messenger comes from Nearchus. He wishes to speak to his captain of the elephants.

His tent is dark. It is toward evening but there is not a candle burning. Gajendra wrinkles his nose at the smell of old blood. Zahara is there but as he enters she moves away from the bed, the gauze of her gown brushing his skin as she passes. Her scent is the only pleasant thing on the air.

Nearchus lies on a bed behind a curtain. His face is in shadow. The only part of him that is visible is his arm, which beckons.

A rustle of skirts and Zahara is gone.

A slave stands over Nearchus with a fan to keep off the flies. He can hear his former general breathing from the other side of the room.

Come and sit here, he says. It sounds like a goose

honking. He moves reluctantly. What does he want with me?

He watches the laboured rise and fall of Nearchus's chest. He cannot look at him; his eyes focus on the roof of the pavilion. A hand snakes out and grips his arm.

'So! Alexander's new beloved. You must be satisfied with the way things have turned out.'

'I never wished this suffering on you.'

'Still, it has worked in your favour. Be careful, elephant boy.'

'Of what?'

'Of your general and benefactor.' He laughs and blood bubbles through the bandage. They have bound up his head with linen so already he looks like the dead.

'Have they given you laudanum?'

'I can bear it. I still need my wits about me and the laudanum will take them away. You like her, don't you?'

'It is not for me to think one way or another about her.'

Nearchus laughs at this. 'Why does a man think he can slaver over another man's wife and not be noticed? Cheer up, son, when I'm dead perhaps Alexander will give her to you.'

There is so much copal burning in the censer it makes his head spin. 'You are not going to die.'

'That's the hell of it, isn't it? Death would have been kinder. I am sure Zahara thinks so. Hold my hand, elephant boy.' There is nothing for it but to do as he says. 'That's it. I can feel the strength in you. I shall need a little of that tomorrow.'

He pulls him closer. Gajendra tries to resist but his grip is too strong.

He mimics Alexander: 'Where is my Indian? Fetch my Indian. I want one elephant to guard my tent and another to sit under when it's hot. Fetch my Indian!' He drops his voice. 'Be careful of him. It is cold in the shadows when the sun decides to take its warmth elsewhere.'

'I did not ask for this to happen to you.'

'Yet you are responsible. Has he got you in his bed yet? He will.'

'I am more than a pretty boy, as you will all see soon enough.'

'Shall I blame Antipater for this or should I blame Alexander? I never learned what was in the letter until after it was delivered.'

'You cannot blame him for another man's perfidy.'

'But you can write a letter in such a way that a man's perfidy will work in your favour.'

'Why would he do this?'

'I'm sure you'll work it out. He has been looking for someone to love again since Hephaiston died. We always thought it would be a Greek. It seems he has gone native in more ways than one. Once it was just foreign soldiers, now he is recruiting the natives for home service as well.'

'It's not true.'

'Not yet. But it will be. You are to be groomed.'

He lets his arm fall.

'I thought you loved him,' Gajendra says.

'I thought he loved *me*. But Alexander's trouble is that he has everything, and the trouble with having everything is it's never enough. It has made him mad. He has a lion by its tail and as soon as he lets go, it will eat him. It will eat you, too.'

'I don't have to listen to this.' He gets up to leave.

'Do you know what happened when we were in Egypt? I was with him the day he went to consult the oracle of Zeus at the Siwa oasis. Three hundred miles across the desert we rode, we were lost once and the horses nearly died of thirst. Do you know what he wanted to know from the oracle? He asked if all his father's murderers had been punished to the satisfaction of the gods. Can you guess why it was so important to him to discover this from the soothsayer?'

Gajendra can guess, but he doesn't want to say it.

'He is terrified of dying, that man. What do they do in Hades to a god who has murdered his own father?'

Once outside, Gajendra draws the air in deep. The smell of dung and campfires and thirty thousand men seems almost fragrant now.

CHAPTER 40

IT IS DARK under the trees along Elephant Row. Colossus moves his trunk along the ground as he catches Gajendra's scent. He rubs the top of his trunk, feeds him some apples. The elephants sleep only a couple of hours a night. Like me, Gajendra thinks. But with them it's just the way they are.

They are restless tonight, they have set up an incessant rumbling. It's as if they know.

'Tomorrow is our day,' he whispers. 'You have to be brave and strong. If we win tomorrow Alexander will make us the heart of his army. His Elephantarch will be even more important to him than the captains of his cavalry. He will build his strategies around us.' He feels the rough skin quiver under his touch.

A sound behind him. He turns, a knife in his hand. Mara lets out a little gasp as the needle point draws a small trickle of blood from the soft white flesh of her neck. 'It's me,' she murmurs.

He pulls her away. 'What are you doing here?'

'I was looking for you.'

'Why?'

'I wanted to talk to you.' She slides her hand down his arm. 'I saw her today.'

'Saw who?'

'The most beautiful girl in the world. She was with the other women, they were taking them to the rear so they would be safe. I saw her with Nearchus. That is the one, isn't it?'

'Yes.'

'You will excuse me but to me she appears a little… bovine.'

'Perhaps it's just her eyes, then. There is no light in them. Have you not noticed? She will go where she is led, that one. Believe me, I have known many girls like it, I can sniff them a mile away. You should be bored with her in a week.'

'I could spend the rest of my life loving her.'

'Have you ever spoken to her? Apart from the negotiation about money, I mean.'

'Why?'

'You are young, Gajendra. Have you ever had a woman you haven't paid for?'

'Plenty.'

'Well.' She smiles. 'I think we both know that's a big lie.' She takes his hand and slides it around her waist. 'Catharo told me what you have done for us.'

'Is this my reward for saving you?'

'It would have made more sense to offer this before you found us the horses, if you think about it.'

'Yesterday I kissed you and you pushed me away.'

She is tugging at her hair again, he imagines she must have had luxuriant curls once, for it is a persistent habit of hers. 'Ravi told me what happened to you.'

'Ravi? He has a big mouth.'

'He loves you. He cares about you. Why didn't you tell me?'

'So you could feel sorry for me?'

'I let you feel sorry for me.'

'You tried. I didn't take up the invitation.'

She puts a hand on his chest. Above them the leaves rustle in the wind. The moon trails a filigree of black clouds.

'Why are you doing this?' He can feel her breath on his neck.

'You said to me that I should let go of the past in order to have a future.'

'But I may be dead tomorrow.'

'Then I should let go of the future, too, in order to have a past. If you die I should always regret not taking this moment.'

'What about your husband?'

'He was a good man, he would not want me to stop loving. I was punishing him, you know.'

'Punishing him?'

'I blamed him for dying. I wanted him to see me suffer down here. I imagined him up there with the gods, crying over me.'

She has lifted his shirt and runs her hand along his bronzed skin and finds the nipple. She frowns as if she has never seen such a thing before and then takes it in her mouth. The effect is startling. He gasps and claws at the bark of the tree.

When he catches his breath again, he says, 'What if he is watching now?'

She shakes her head. 'He is not watching. I have set him free. It's what you said to do, isn't it? It's what you meant.'

'Yes,' he says. 'It's what I meant.'

He lies her down.

'Gajendra,' she whispers.

Her body coils around him. He is stunned by this first glimpse of her flesh. He had not imagined her so beautiful. Her eyes shine. Who would have imagined such a moment?

He is overcome, wants all of her at once. She grabs him by the shoulders and pushes him away. 'I am not a door to be battered down. Have you never greased a lock? You tease it, Gajendra. If you are to make a woman a good husband one day I will have to show you.'

'I am willing to learn,' he says.

'Well then. Let us begin the lesson.'

When Mara returns, Catharo is sharpening his knife on a rock. He is stealthy about it; it will not do to have anyone see what he is doing.

'What are you doing?' she hisses.

'Alexander is coming to inspect the elephants tomorrow.' His face is a study in concentration. He wants it nice and sharp when he slides it between the ribs of a living god.

'But we're leaving here tonight.'

'*You* are. I'm staying here. Once you're gone, I'll be free to ply my trade in peace.'

'That's madness. He will be surrounded by his bodyguards.'

'That didn't save his father and it won't save him. I know what I'm about. It's not the first time I've done this.'

'It's suicide.'

'That's what I said to you but somehow you made it sound reasonable. I am persuaded.'

'They'll crucify you for this, Catharo.'

'I'll do it and fall on the knife afterwards.'

'What if you don't have time?'

'My life doesn't count compared to what's at stake here. Now get some rest. You have a long ride ahead of you.'

For a while she lies there, watching the stars wheel above her; she imagines it is the eyes of the gods, watching.

'Where were you tonight?' he says.

'In the bushes. I was unwell.'

'You were with the Indian.'

'Don't question me, Catharo. You are not my father.'

A noise from him, a grunt of irritation perhaps. She is growing fond of him and does not like to think that this time tomorrow he will be dead. It bothers her more than when she was contemplating her own end.

'Why did you not do it when you had the chance?'

'Do what?'

'That night you were in Alexander's tent, you had my knife with you, and I suppose now that you took it from me for that purpose.'

'I found it is not in my nature.'

'It was in your nature when you thought they were going to kill the Indian. You were handy enough with a blade then.'

'It is different to do something in cold blood than when you are panicked and there is no time to think about it. If I had not done what I did, Gaji would be dead.'

'Gaji now? Do you have a pet name for him as well?'

She feels her cheeks burning in the darkness.

'He reminds me of you,' he says.

'Of me?'

'He's arrogant, headstrong and young. Sometimes he's very kind. You might be twins.'

Twins? She hardly thinks so. 'I may be young but I'm not arrogant.'

He grunts. 'If you say so, princess.'

You must never give up. No matter what happens, no matter how hard things are, you don't give up. You never know if there is something just around the corner that will tip the balance back in your favour and give you back your life.

'Don't do it, Catharo. Keep your pledge to my father and ride out of here with me tonight as my bodyguard as you promised him you would. Let someone else rid the world of Alexander.'

'I've made up my mind,' he says to her and will say no more about it.

CHAPTER 41

As she creeps away, Mara hears them on Elephant Row. The sound they are making is like nothing she has ever heard; it seems to come from deep inside them, this rumbling, it travels through the ground and through the air.

They are grouped together, vast grey shadows in the dark, and as her eyes grow accustomed to the gloom she sees they have put their trunks in each other's mouths, as if for comfort. Colossus trumpets several times, a chilling sound.

She realizes they are frightened, and they are trying to reassure each other that it will be all right. They know the battle is coming, somehow, and like all soldiers everywhere they are thinking about pain and death.

From somewhere very close she hears howling and it sends a shiver through her. 'What was that?'

'Kassander,' Catharo growls.

The horses are where Gajendra has said they will be. Even in the dark she can tell they are miserable specimens. Still, they have four legs and it will be better than walking. 'Follow the north star by night and Aetna by day. When you are near the volcano you ride inland. Hanno's scouts will find you before you find him.'

'Come with me, Catharo.'

He helps her up onto the horse. 'I have served your father faithfully all my life and never questioned any order he has given me. But someone has to stop this devil and it will not be done on the battlefield. Even if I came with you, and got you safe there, how long would your freedom last, or your father's? This is the only way.'

There is no goodbye, not with Catharo. He slaps the horse's rump to set her moving and then disappears into the dark.

Alexander is wearing his antique armour, a metal breast-plate laced to a leather back plate. There are polished guards for his wrists and shins, a helmet with stiff red boar's hair under his arm. He stalks across the swept ground. He looks like Zeus himself coming down from the heavens.

The waterboys are busy with their pots of red and yellow paint, drawing circles around the elephants' eyes and patterns on their trunks and sides. He looks pleased when he sees this and agrees the beasts look more fearsome this way. Other boys are sitting astride their backs, rubbing in coconut oil to strengthen the beasts' nerves.

Alexander wanders down the line, examining each in turn, fingering the sharpened point on the iron protector they wear on their tusks, the tough leather they wear to protect their flanks, the new segmented armour on their legs. It will take the better part of the day to get them ready; they have them in the shade to keep them cool while the *mahavats* and waterboys do their work.

His guards lag; by the time he reaches the end of Elephant Row they are struggling to keep up with him.

Catharo fingers the knife he has concealed inside his tunic.

Gajendra accompanies Alexander along the line; this is an unparalleled honour. Alexander is reminiscing about Gaugamela, the first time he encountered elephants, when he faced the Persian king, Darius, for the first time. He is in high spirits. He claps Gajendra on the shoulder and tells him, for the sake of his retinue, that no army on the earth can stand against them.

The more timid beasts are given rice wine; it will get their blood up. There is none for Colossus; give him rice wine right now and he will tear down the camp before he even gets to the battle line.

The *mahavats* are laughing. It is amusing to see elephants drunk, staggering and spouting wine over each other, playful for now at least. But that will change, once they are on the battlefield, and they have the drums and the flutes around them, the noise making them mad, smelling the fear in the air.

'What is happening?' Alexander asks him.

'We are getting the timid ones ready to go to war.'

'By getting them drunk?'

'They are like men. Get some wine into a book keeper or a pastry chef and he thinks he is Hercules.'

One of the elephants roars, enraged, and charges at one of its fellows. The *mahavats* yell and tug on his ropes, using the bull hooks and canes to bring him back into the line. It has started already.

The beasts will soon be uncontrollable. Gajendra tells them to get the tuskers away from the wine, take them to their battle lines, have the archers mounted.

Alexander stops in front of Colossus. 'Why is this one not having any wine? The poor creature looks thirsty!'

Gajendra sees Catharo and for a moment he is surprised: what is he doing here? Last night he provided horses and a means of escape. Then he sees the glint of the knife, for just a moment, and he knows what is happening before he has even calculated how it has come about.

He puts himself between Catharo and his general. 'Don't just stand there,' he tells him. 'Get some of the others and fetch some wine for Colossus.'

He can see Catharo calculate; he must kill me to get to Alexander. Even if he kills me and is quick about it, the guards will have time to step in and dispatch him.

He hesitates.

'Quickly, you and you, go with Catharo and get the wine. Now!'

'You told us this one did not need wine,' Catharo says, standing his ground.

'I don't have to explain anything to you,' Gajendra says and slaps him hard across the face. Catharo reaches inside his tunic and for a moment thinks he will actually do it. But at the last he withdraws and with one last rueful look at Alexander he goes with the others.

Alexander is feeding Colossus oranges and seems amused by this activity. He holds out a hand for more. The waterboys laugh dutifully as he tosses them into Colossus's mouth, making a game of it. The King of the World's luck has held again; he should be lying slaughtered right now.

But he soon tires of the game and stalks away. 'Today

you shall make yourself a hero,' he tells Gajendra. 'They will build statues to you.'

Statues. What do I need with one of those?

Catharo and the other waterboys return with the buckets of rice wine. They are about to pour it into the tub in front of Colossus but Gajendra stops them. 'What are you doing? You want him to wreck the whole camp?'

'You said to fetch him wine,' Catharo says.

'I know what I said, now give it to one of the others. Siru. He needs the courage. No, let the other boys do it. You come with me. We're taking Colossus to the river.'

'But he has his armour on.'

'Don't argue with me, just do as I say.'

They walk Colossus down to the river in his battle armour, lead him under the shade of a fig tree, and Gajendra lets him drink but keeps him hobbled with the chains. When Catharo turns his back he slips his hand inside the man's tunic but all he finds is a silver medallion.

'What are you doing?' Catharo shouts and jumps back.

Gajendra stares at the medallion then at Catharo. He feels like a fool. He is sure he had seen the glint of a knife. Perhaps the strain of the coming battle is telling on him, too. 'What is this?'

'I stole it. It's mine.' He snatches it back.

'Why are you still here? Where's Mara?'

'She's gone.'

'You let her leave alone?'

Catharo shakes his head. 'You know who she is?'

'You haven't answered me, why are you still here?'

'I don't want to be on the losing side again.'

'What are you?'

'I'm a mercenary. I can see the way the wind is blowing and I don't want to go back. I'm a slave now but in time I'll do better here than I will over there.'

He doesn't believe him, but the trumpets are calling them to form up the lines. He hasn't time for this now. He hisses a command and Colossus lumbers out of the shallows, dressed for battle, iron clanking, leather gleaming with water.

'This isn't finished,' Gajendra says.

CHAPTER 42

GAJENDRA LEADS HIS elephants through the lines. The infantry are formed up in their phalanx, the brigade sergeants shouting, 'Plugs off, skin 'em back!', and the corpsmen strip off the oiled fleece covers from their sarissas, each the height of three men. It's a dangerous business just forming up for battle down there, the whetted edges lethal in close formation.

Trumpets are blaring, grooms boost riders onto horses' backs, they use their body weight to keep the beasts from bolting, they are high and need a firm hand. The forest of pikes springs into the air as the infantry rise from their knees. There is the smell of sweat and oil and iron. Nervous horses piss steaming yellow streams on the ground.

Gajendra looks left and right, sees the phalanx wheel in column and line without a word, in perfect unison. The gleaming spear line swings right then left. They are a terrifying sight. Suddenly the men beat their spears on their shields and shout their war cry:

'Alalalalai...'

The sound of it shatters the silence. It is terrifying even though they are on his side. He would hate ever to have to face them on the battlefield. As much as Alexander is brilliant, it was the phalanx that had conquered Asia.

The problem for Alexander is that Antipater knows him too well; he will anticipate him. But Antipater has his problems also; he has never before faced elephants.

Antipater has decided to stand his ground. His heavy infantry are in the centre, his cavalry in the wings, no innovation, a massive army three times the size of Alexander's and the Guggas on their way down from the mountains. It is up to Alexander to shift him or be crushed on the plain.

Reveal and conceal, Alexander tells them. He has shown Antipater a weakened right flank oblique to the centre, where Ptolemy is, inviting Antipater to attack him there.

Alexander rides along the line, the shoulder wings of his corselet unbattened; he won't dog them down until he's ready in the line. He's telling them all: look at me, I am utterly relaxed about this morning's little skirmish. Being outnumbered three to one is nothing to a god.

He wears an extraordinary helmet, with two great golden wings. He has his usual crowd of pages and staff officers clustered around him. This display is not just his monstrous vanity, though that is part of it. He wants Antipater to see him, to put his best cavalry regiments against him. This way he controls his enemy's moves as if he were issuing their orders himself.

He calls out to his sergeants by name as he rides the line, settles the more restless of his men with a gesture of his hand. His massive stallion is high, his tail up. Froth sprays from his muzzle and along his flanks. His hooves are the size of skillets, his chest armoured, seventeen hands high. Alexander rallies them to his cause, reminds them all that what they do this morning, they do for history. You are on the road to destiny, he tells them; no one has done what we will do, we are the first army of men to conquer the world.

'What do I care for Macedon? You fight for the gods, you fight for Zeus. I am Zeus!'

And he offends no one with his talk of foreigners and Greek gods; he says it all in Greek so none of the foreigners in his army can understand him. They cheer as loudly as the rest for the fine spectacle he makes.

Out on the left Ptolemy has begun to advance and has halted. Antipater has been invited to see the apparent weakness, but he knows Alexander's tactics of old and will not be drawn. Couriers from both armies dash along the lines; the sergeants stand out before their squares shouting instructions, keeping the lines to order.

Nearchus appears from nowhere, galloping alone from the line into the killing ground between the two armies. His disfigured face is concealed by his regimental scarf; he tears this garment free as he gallops. He cannot clearly be seen from where he sits but Gajendra knows what is now revealed; the nose and ears have gone and crusted dried blood has taken their place.

Nearchus raises his right arm; the hand has been severed at the wrist. He then elevates the battle standard in his left. He intends to ride without reins to hold. Impressive.

He wears no helmet and no armour, though his horse's headstall and frontlet are in place. He has only a light combat saddle.

'What is he doing?' Ravi shouts.

Gajendra thinks for a moment that he has come to steal his glory. Does he still think to command my elephants? But Alexander has made his wishes plain. He is the Elephantarch now, not Nearchus.

He rides back towards their line and raises the standard again in salute. Now Gajendra knows what is on his mind.

The two armies fall silent. Nearchus turns and rides straight at the enemy line. The archers and hoplites wait behind their palisade and let him come. Finally an arrow arcs from the line, then a volley. He does not fall.

There are shouts from their own infantry. Some of them seem to believe he might get through.

Another volley of arrows and he goes down, his horse as well. But there is yet movement as the dust settles. His horse rises slowly and starts to trot back towards their line. Then, unbelieving, they watch Nearchus rise too. He starts to stagger towards the palisade. Are they mocking him or honouring him by letting him come so close? Finally a last volley of arrows and he falls and lies still.

He remembers what Nearchus told him: *Be careful of him. You are his favourite now but it will not last.*

The riderless horse gallops back through the lines. The sweat dries on his back; he feels a sudden chill.

The size of their army is breathtaking. We are a wave and they are inviting us to dash ourselves on the rocks.

Gajendra is desperate with thirst; nerves and dust have turned his throat to chalkstone. Colossus flares out his ears, impatient to charge.

He looks out to the left: eight squadrons of Companion Cavalry under Ptolemy, and their Agrianians, halted on the plain; the Greeks would be pleading with Antipater to let them at him. But small as Ptolemy's force is, Alexander has insurance: two thousand light infantry, specially trained to fight cavalry and on double pay for doing it. They have no armour, just leather shields and a twelve-foot lance. They have been training since Carthage for this.

Now here it is. The Greeks charge their right flank, Antipater lured into it after all, or perhaps a commander acting out of concert. They will overrun Ptolemy, it is only a matter of time, but that is what Alexander plans to deprive them of.

Yet what he plans seems impossible.

He stands in the saddle and raises his sword. Gajendra turns and waves to the signal boy in the *howdah* and he raises the flags.

Alexander and his heavy cavalry transit to the front, his misdirection as he called it when they were gathered around his battle charts. Gajendra takes his squadron after them, revealing the mass of the infantry behind, then peels off to the right. Two movements, the elephants moving more swiftly than Antipater could have imagined. What will he make of this?

Now it is their nerves that will jangle.

Because he does not know elephants, Antipater cannot anticipate that they are as fast as horses over short distances. Maintaining such speed is not easy. He looks back and sees the archers in the *howdah*s clinging on. But his elephants are keeping their shape, none have peeled away, they follow Colossus in perfect order. They drive towards the cavalry on Antipater's left flank.

He wonders what Antipater will do. He is in a fix. If he moves to cover him he will lose the opportunity to attack on their weaker flank and he still has Alexander charging his infantry at the centre. He knows horses will not go against a well-ordered phalanx. He has just a few heart-beats to divine Alexander's plan.

Gajendra can imagine nerves at breaking point around the old general. They have the numbers but they no longer have the initiative. If he moves the infantry across to cover the elephants, Alexander may break through. If he doesn't, can the cavalry alone withstand the elephants?

Antipater will be doubting himself at every turn. Alexander could win this just with the legend of his own invincibility.

From up here the battle sounds like an earthquake. She can see nothing. The armies are too close to each other to make out what is happening. Gajendra told her it was the same for a warrior, even a general, that battles only made sense when you drew them out afterwards, in the sand – if you survived it – after talking to your fellows and some-times to prisoners. You were either too close or too far away, too scared or too confused to know what was going on. At the time it was just a blur, terror and desperation and instinct running together.

'You came back,' Catharo says to her and does not seem surprised.

'I thought I should find Alexander on a funeral pyre and you on a cross. Why didn't you do it?'

'This Gajendra found me out. I'm sure he saw the knife I hid in my tunic. Even when he confronted me later, he knew I was lying. A strange boy. He could have had me thrown in front of Alexander in chains but he chose not to do it. I thought I understood him, but I've not worked him out at all. Have you?'

She shakes her head.

'There is someone else I haven't worked out either. You, princess. I thought you would be long gone by now.'

'So did I.'

'Did you come back because of the Indian boy?'

'I don't want to die, Catharo, not any more. And I would like to see my father again and make my peace with him. But what is the point if I leave behind the very man who made me want to live again?'

'It's a curse, this wanting to live. It weakens the resolve.' He folds his arms. 'Well, that's it then. We're both trapped here now. It will be a long day.'

The ranks upon ranks of their heavy cavalry shimmer on the heat haze. All Gajendra can do is hold on. All they have against these thousands is these forty elephants, and for once Alexander has not yet teased a break in the line.

At this last moment he sees Alexander break off his advance and wheel his Companion Cavalry to the right and traverse the line towards them. His intentions are clear now. But if Antipater's cavalry hold the line they are lost.

But they have the wind at their backs, and this will be important.

He can see them now, the squadrons of heavy cavalry, pennants whipping in the wind, the serried ranks of the hoplites between them, in pot and plate, impenetrable lines of bristling steel. The archers are forming up; they will have the chance to fire one volley before they are on them.

Gajendra prays for movement and sees it.

A horse shies, then another. It is like a ripple spreading through the water, it starts from around the centre and moves outwards along the entire line. He has seen this in drills and in casual encounters, a horse's utter panic at the sight or smell of an elephant. The officers try to hold their mounts and cannot. The line breaks, slowly at first but then crumbles away as more horses bolt, terrifying their fellows.

The first volley of arrows whines down. The archers have miscalculated the speed of the tuskers. There are three ranks; the front row get off two volleys, the second one, but by then the third rank is already running.

The horses are shoving and kicking their way back through their own ranks, and when they find their way blocked they gallop over the top of the soldiers positioned between them. An infantry phalanx relies on order and discipline for its effect; once it is fractured the individual soldiers are powerless. The panicked horses create corridors through their ranks and Gajendra turns and points to his signalman, who is holding grimly to the sides of the *howdah. They must all follow me!*

And they do. Instead of attacking the entire flank along its length he leads Colossus through the widest gap, trampling anything in his way. There is scarce any resistance at this point in the line. The enemy's own horses have created chaos in their retreat and Gajendra's squadron punches a hole through Antipater's left flank.

He catches a glimpse of the famous golden helmet as Alexander follows them through with two thousand heavy cavalry coming in behind, flashing past them and ploughing into the rout.

But there is the danger that in the rush of victory they may push too far through the lines. If you were Alexander it wouldn't matter; Alexander is immortal. But Gajendra knows he must wait for the infantry following behind or there will be no one to protect the elephants once they are isolated from the charge. He turns and gives the order to the signalman in the *howdah* to pull back, but it is too late.

Ravi is in trouble.

Some Macks have surrounded Ran Bagha; they must have been veterans of the Jhellum River, he supposes, for they know how to fight an elephant. They target the *mahavat* first, one of their scouts whirling a sling above his head, bringing Ravi down with a stone. Archers take out the men in the *howdah*.

It would have been easier for Ran Bagha to retreat then, and leave Ravi there. Instead he stands his ground, one massive foot either side of his *mahavat*. He flares his ears, trumpeting his defiance.

Two of the soldiers run in and one is sliced clean through by his iron tusk; the other he catches with his trunk and slams him onto the ground. But an isolated elephant cannot last long against a determined attack from brave men. They have surrounded him now and it is just a matter of time.

Gajendra sends Colossus thundering over.

He knows he will be too late. Alexander's light infantry, his stingers, will not be far behind but they cannot get to Ran Bagha in time. Hard men like these Macks, they fight to the death, they will not run like a conscript or a mercenary. They are well drilled and know their business.

Ran Bagha catches two more of his tormentors with his iron-tipped tusk but already a third has slipped in behind with a battle axe and chopped his hamstring. He roars and swings to face his tormentor, all the while keeping himself above Ravi's stricken body.

The man raises his axe again and Ran Bagha swings with his armoured trunk and knocks him aside, like kicking a stone off the path. The man does not rise.

But now there is another, in behind him, his battle axe hacking again at his unprotected lower legs. A soldier is underneath him, thrusting up with his spear.

He roars and his back legs give way, crushing the soldier while impaling himself further on the spear. But still he holds himself up with his forelegs; if he goes all the way down Ravi will be crushed.

He swings again with his trunk and another soldier cartwheels across the ground.

They are attacking his eyes now, and looking for the gaps in the lamellar. But he won't go down. There must be at least a dozen Macks dead or wounded around him.

The soldiers see Colossus coming and wheel around to face him. He barrels into them, and they go down under his feet, screaming. He is in a rage and Gajendra does not have to tell him what to do. He uses his tusks and his trunk and his feet. Gajendra wonders at the courage of these

Macks for they try and stand up to him. Brutes, the lot of them, but they don't know the meaning of defeat.

As Colossus wheels around he uses his heels to give the order: *Let me down.* It seems to him that Colossus hesitates a moment but is too well trained to disobey. Gajendra leaps off and rushes over to Ravi, grabs him by the shoulders and pulls him clear just as Ran Bagha collapses. The ground shakes when an elephant goes down; you can feel it through your feet.

Colossus continues the slaughter unaided; he is a warrior for all his gentle ways with Mara. Now here come the stingers, rushing in and taking out the last of the phalanx.

Gajendra sinks to his knees beside Ravi. Colossus has finished with the war also and stands over Ran Bagha, searching for life with his trunk. Finally he raises his head and bellows.

Ravi's eyes blink open. He does not know where he is or what has happened; there is a dent in his helmet the size of a fist. Gajendra takes it off, there is a split in his head but his brains are all in there, his head has been given a good rattling is all. He would have been dead if not for his elephant.

The battle rushes over them like a wave, the slaughter continues somewhere else. They are calling to him from the *howdah*; he must lead the line again or the attack may yet falter. He runs back to Colossus and orders the signal boy to raise the flags.

They sweep into the remains of the phalanx a second time. He glimpses Alexander far ahead, in the thick of things, surrounded on every side, tireless in the way he swings his sword, laughing. It is the only time he ever sees him truly happy, when he is about death's work. Spray him with another man's blood and in his mind you pelt him with flowers; he feels fragrant and blessed.

The Gauls that Antipater has brought with him have dropped their weapons and armour and run. Only the Macks and Greeks stand their ground, but their lines are broken and it is simply a matter of doing the slaughter. After a time killing is just heavy labour; the soldiers will be exhausted tonight from wielding their swords all day. Antipater's men die in their thousands. Some of the Macedonians fought side by side with Alexander in India, but it must be done; these men have turned once and they cannot be trusted to be loyal again.

Impeded by their own baggage train, decimated by their own cavalry turning back on them, Antipater's thousands count for nothing. Once a soldier starts to run he can save himself or he can die, but he cannot hurt you any more. Many fall prey to Alexander's cavalry and the light infantry that follow in behind.

Behind the army the wives, the whores and the general crowd have been caught in the massacre and Antipater's baggage train is in ruins also; tents are just rags, carts no more than firewood. Whores stagger about stealing money from dead soldiers and offering their services to their new masters.

The day wears on, and the battle degenerates into bargaining; soldiers buy women with rings torn from dying men; prisoners are dragged behind horses for sport; captains and corporals stagger about draping themselves in plundered gowns and women's jewels.

It was supposed to be the great battle that would decide the future of the world. In the end it was no more than a skilled fighter grabbing a bully by the hair and pitching him out of the window.

CHAPTER 43

IT IS HARD work taking the armour off wounded elephants. They are distressed and it is a dangerous task. The leather armour on Colossus's flanks bristles with arrows; one has somehow found its way through and blood streams from his neck. The physician is the same one who tends Alexander; he is doing brisk business.

There is an air of celebration; men never drink so much or laugh so loud as when they have cheated death. Exploits are recounted in the disbelieving shouts of men who are trying to reassure themselves that they really are still alive.

The elephants are rewarded with food, mountains of it brought in carts and stacked in front of them to distract them while the physicians do their work. Later they are taken down to the river where the grime and blood can be washed off.

Most days they trumpet and spray water everywhere. But today the elephants are impatient with their handlers and several are hurt by their surly charges.

'Look at them,' Mara says.

'They have lost a comrade,' he says. 'They are wild animals but it seems to me that sometimes they act like men. They are angry with us. It is grief, pure and simple.'

'Where is Gajendra?'

He shrugs: he doesn't know.

She slips away to the battlefield. Kites circle screaming over the corpses. Soldiers are still trying to form up or are bent on looking for a spear they've left in someone's guts or drinking all the wine from their canteens.

She walks among the dead and dying, tries not to look too closely at what she sees. Twice she slips in blood pools. She keeps her hands over her ears so she does not have to listen to the things she hears. Why doesn't someone put these men out of their misery?

Ran Bagha is not hard to find, a massive grey mountain of flesh on the plain. Pennants flutter around him, placed there by other *mahavats*. Ravi sits alone and cross-legged. He does not look up at her approach.

She sits down beside him. They mourn together.

Alexander's sword is stuck to his hand with blood. A physician is stitching a gash in his shoulder with thread, a bowl of blood-stained water beside him. His general drinks another cup of wine and appears oblivious. Alexander's body is a patchwork of old wounds and cicatrices. He has scars on his scars.

His face is flushed with the glory of it. His armour lies on the floor, slimed with gore; both shoulder pieces of his corselet have been sheared away, and the facing of his breastplate is so battered he cannot identify the Gorgons that were so painstakingly worked into the gold.

His tunic is discarded also, a rag of blood and sweat. There is a cut on his head that is blackened with blood. His

303

physician now attempts to seal it with copper dog-bites and stitches.

Gajendra is cheered as he walks in. Hands clap him on the shoulder. He is not an elephant boy any more; he is the hero of Syracuse.

Alexander finally manages to detach himself from his sword and he stands and embraces him. There is a general euphoria. The dead are forgotten. How could they be so remiss as to expire in such a complete victory? It is plainly their fault that they are missing this celebration.

They have had word from their spies in Syracuse that Antipater has now proved himself inconvenient to his hosts and has been murdered. The oligarchs are suing for peace, and with Alexander's navy now blockading their port, it will come at a heavy price. The rebellion has been crushed. Kraterus will retake Macedon; Italy is next for Alexander, and then the world is theirs. Even the grumblers are silent now.

'Your elephants won the day,' Alexander says and gives him wine and a seat beside him. Blood still streams from his shoulder and mixes with sweat and grime. He is in his element. He takes a long breath, savouring the moment.

Gajendra has found his heaven also. No one is going to piss on him, not ever again. An elephant boy has become a general.

So why is it that all he can think of is Ravi and his beloved Ran Bagha? He imagines the flies will be at work already. Soon it will be the turn of the maggots and the worms. It was just a wild beast, not even one of the best warriors. They can buy and train another. A thousand men dead out there, what does one tusker matter?

'What shall be your reward?' Alexander asks him. 'Name it.'

'Zahara,' he hears himself say.

The smile falls away. Those standing close turn to listen.

Even Alexander seems perturbed. 'You will not give her time to weep?'

'She will not weep for him. She was just a trophy to him like any other.'

'Yet it would be best to wait.'

'You asked me what I wished for as a reward. I have told you.'

A chill silence settles on the room. Nearchus has earned a hero's death today and this smacks of disrespect. 'This is not right,' he hears someone mutter. 'Should a wife not be a widow for longer than a day?'

Even Gajendra is shocked by his own audacity. But he wants his due, what he has risked and worked for, and he wants it now.

Alexander smiles. 'So you can be ruthless after all. The elephant boy is a general.'

'It seems so.'

'They will not like it,' he says, looking at the other captains, those who cheered him hoarse a few moments before.

'I do not care what they think of me.'

Alexander is bleeding more heavily now. The doctor again attempts to finish stitching his arm. He pushes him away, and claps Gajendra on the shoulder. 'What are you all staring at? Is he not the hero of Syracuse? We shall give him his due!'

They are used to being bullied by Alexander but

305

they don't have to like it. All he gets is sullen looks. But Alexander just laughs and calls for more wine. He is a god. He can do as he likes.

CHAPTER 44

ALEXANDER HAS BLESSED the wedding; it is he who will sponsor it.

His pavilion has been decked out with flowers and garlands for the feast; there are censers burning to disguise the smell of the corpse fires further down the valley. Some of the guests are even still bleeding.

After the ritual sacrifices they retire to the pavilion for the feast. There is an air of forced gaiety; Alexander has commanded his own musicians to play for them. He has ordered general happiness and watches for glumness like his guards watch for assassins.

The men and women sit at different tables; Alexander sprawls at the heart of this grim celebration eating little and drinking much. His lips are wet, his eyes wild with dissatisfaction. He stews. Something nameless gnaws at him.

Gajendra remembers what Nearchus told him; he thought then it was just envy, now he wonders how much truth there was in it. He suspects that Alexander is using the wedding as a goad, is filling his own private agenda here. A god cannot be gainsaid; he will establish his will here for its own sake and flush out all doubters.

One of his lads tries to tempt him with a tray of sesame seeds mixed with honey but he pushes the salver away.

He grabs Zahara's wrist and drags her across the room to Gajendra.

'She has no father here, so I shall be the father.'

Gajendra stumbles to his feet, unprepared.

Alexander draws back her veil and thrusts her arm at him. 'I give you this woman, that she may bring children into the world within the bond of wedlock.'

'I accept her.'

'I agree to provide a dowry of three talents with her.'

'I accept that too – with pleasure.'

'There,' Alexander says. 'It is done.'

Some of Alexander's boys form up the procession and lead the way, holding torches. Others whirl ahead, dancing to the flutes and drums. There are even elephants, though Colossus is notable by his absence.

There is much shouting and laughter, though none from the generals. The din of music is so deafening it almost drowns out the screaming from the hospital tent. He lifts Zahara onto the ritual cart. The mules break into a trot.

Alexander leads the cheering. The Macedonians grudgingly join in. What choice is there?

Alexander has granted Gajendra his own pavilion, as befitting his new station as Elephantarch. It belonged formerly to Nearchus, as did the slaves. There will be no more sleeping in the straw or with the tuskers, no more washing in the river.

He lifts his bride from the ritual chariot and waits as carpenters rip off the axle. It is chopped and a pyre built with kindling and saltpetre. Zahara is handed a brand to light it. It is tradition; it signifies that she has taken a new home and will not now be returning to the old one. The Macedonians smirk behind their hands; but isn't this the tent she just came from?

Alexander posts guards at the door of the pavilion; her women remain outside with drums to scare away the underworld spirits.

He has his every desire fulfilled. This is the greatest day of his young life.

He would like Ravi to see this, Ravi who said such things could not happen to an elephant boy. But Ravi is still out on the battlefield sitting with his dead tusker and will come back to the camp for no man.

CHAPTER 45

*T*HIS IS HOW *it will be:*
	She will say: Do you remember that day in the temple? You promised me that one day we would be alone, and that I would be yours. I was about to laugh at you but then I saw the look in your eyes and saw that you meant it. But I never thought that it could ever happen.

He will say: I always knew you would be mine one day.

She says his name. Gajendra...

She whispers it; it rolls strangely off her tongue, like a prayer.

She will wrap her arms and legs around him. Her body coils, her eyes glitter like diamonds in the dark.

His fingertips tease apart the fold of her robe. Her throat is warm, scented and a little damp from sweat. He can feel the bounce of her pulse against her lips.

The candlelight glows on her skin. Her breast is dusky and velvet to the touch.

From the raw stuff of his desire, from belief and from wanting, he will make his vision real. He smiles in the dark. His eyes shine.

This is how it will be.

*

She takes off her clothes and lies under the sheet. There is a glimpse of honey flesh, the heady scent of Arabian perfume.

He draws back the sheet to gaze at her. Her beauty is breathtaking. This is perfect.

He lies down beside her; she is silky, compliant. She allows him to kiss her. He explores what he has so long desired, every soft place, every curve, every delightful rounding of the flesh. He waits for her to respond.

But he cannot wait; he must possess what he has ached for. He puts his arms around her and pulls her towards him. Perhaps I can shake it out of her. He mounts her, disappointed and enraged.

It is over quickly.

Is that all there is to dreams?

He rolls away from her and lies quite still as the sweat cools on his body and his breathing slows to its normal rhythm.

'Do you remember me?'

'Remember you?'

'The young man who came to the temple that day. You came to make sacrifice to Astarte.'

'That was you?'

'Do you remember what I said to you?'

'I was too shocked by what you did. What did you say?'

'It does not matter now.' He sits up, angry with himself, with her, with the world.

'Who is Mara?'

'What?'

'You said "Mara". I heard you.'

'Did I?' He puts on his tunic. 'When?'

'As you were loving me. You spoke the name twice. Where are you going?'

'Outside.'

'But we are married now. Should we not share the same bed tonight?'

'It is clear you don't want me here.'

'Why would you think that?'

She means it, he thinks. She is present, and decorous. It is what is expected. How can she understand that she has not fulfilled her obligations? You wish her to long for you as you long for her, and if you explain this to her all you will get is an imitation of it.

She did not choose this union. You did.

'Did you have any fond feeling for Nearchus?'

'Should I?'

'No, I suppose not. I am being foolish.'

He goes outside, looks up at the moon, just a sliver of it in a dark sky. Had he really said Mara's name?

He has the woman of his dreams; he has reached the pinnacle he set himself, this should be a moment of exhilaration. So why is he thinking about a girl who looks like a boy and has elephant shit under her fingernails? He has pursued the sun when he should have instead felt its warmth on his back. He supposes he does not know his true nature at all.

He stares at the stars. He has everything he wanted and once thought impossible to obtain. He is awash in glory. How can absolute triumph taste so bitter?

He is so lost in this self-recrimination he does not realize there is someone in the dark, watching him.

When he sees the shadow, he reaches for his knife.

'A little late for that,' Mara says. 'I could have slit your throat, stripped your body and had you in a shallow grave by now. Was she that good?'

'Mara.'

'You finally have what you always wanted.'

'What are you doing here?'

'I think the worst thing you did was make me start caring again. I was all right before. I was numb. I know you thought you were doing the right thing but having good intentions is dangerous. Show care and affection to a woman you care nothing for and you might as well have used her and beat her in the first place and be done with it.'

'You are a slave, have you forgotten? Who do you think you are?'

'I am not a slave, you arrogant boy! I am high born. I am the daughter of a nobleman of Carthage, and you are the son of a rice farmer. Circumstances have put you above me but do not ever dare call me your slave again. Do what you want but I will not let you humiliate me further.'

'Humiliate you? I saved your life. And what are you doing here? Why did you come back?'

'I hate you.'

Slap her, hold her, what should he do? 'I have done nothing to cause you to hate me.'

'No? You made me want to live again and then you married this perfumed tart before she has even had a chance to bury her husband. You still had my smell on you! It is bad enough you betrayed me, but now you have made me despise you as well.'

He rakes in a deep breath, to try and control his anger.

'I will give you one more chance to leave here, tonight, you and that murderous dwarf. Then let's be done with this.'

'How was it for you? Tonight? Was it as you dreamed?'

'Your father is just over those mountains. You can have your freedom again.'

She moves into the light. The moon plays on her face as it darts between black clouds. 'You don't understand anything, do you?'

'What is there to understand?'

'You made me want to live again and then you left me. You light a fire in someone's heart and just walk away and you tell yourself you are bringing warmth into the world when all you're doing is making more ashes. I am sick of being left. My husband. My little boy. My daughter. Now you.'

He feels a chill along his spine. 'They did not leave you. Death took them. It was not their fault.'

'I don't care whose fault it was, the emptiness is still the same.' She puts her ear to the tent. 'I cannot hear her. Is she sleeping? Is she not lying awake for you, tremulous, on this her wedding night? Her sisters are still beating the drums. Do they know you are out here or did you slip out another way?'

'What do you want from me?'

'I want you to take back everything you said. I want you to go back to that night I touched you and I want you to slap my hand away and tell me I was nothing to you, just another dung lark. Then I want you to go further back and let the soldiers beat me and sell me on the block, for at least then I was numb and it would not have troubled me as much as this.'

'How could it have been different?'

'Am I just the spoils of war to you? I thought we were friends.'

'How can we be friends?'

'How can we not? We are alike, you and I. We know loss. We understand the elephants. You give me hope, I give you comfort. Isn't that what friends do?'

'You don't understand anything.'

'Let me see what I do not understand. I do not understand why you are out here in the dark sighing at the stars when the bride you have longed for since Babylon sleeps alone in your tent. I do not understand why you look so sour when Alexander has promoted you to the rank of his inner circle when that is all you ever dreamed about. You're right. I don't understand.'

She slips away into the dark. He does not try and follow her.

CHAPTER 46

IN TAXILA, WHEN the elephants were not required on campaign or for training, they were left to forage for themselves during the night. In the morning the *mahavats* would go out to find them in the jungle; the bells helped. But Ravi had never put a bell on Ran Bagha. He always seemed to know where to find him. It was as if there was a voice inside telling him where to look.

Gajendra experiences this same feeling tonight.

He cannot sleep; he goes to Elephant Row but cannot find Colossus. Several of the elephants are missing, and the waterboys mumble incoherent replies when he demands to know where they are. At first he panics. If Alexander finds out about this, he will lose his position as Elephantarch as quickly as he has gained it.

But then he realizes – he senses – what has happened.

He had seen it before in India; he had never known any other animal except for an elephant do it. A young female elephant had died after being mauled by a tiger and for days the other elephants would not leave her. And every year after that they came back to the same place, looking for the bones. It was as if they were grieving.

Ravi had showed him this curious ritual. They had

hidden in the jungle, out of sight of the herd, to watch. By then most of the bones had bleached or disappeared.

'It is like they understand what death is,' Ravi had whispered. 'Tell me one other animal that knows what a grave is!'

Gajendra walks across the battlefield. Most of the bodies have been stripped and dragged away, but debris still litters the grass; he trips on the shoulder piece of a corselet in the dark. There are discarded scraps of uniform everywhere.

He hears his tuskers before he sees them. They are not trumpeting or shrieking; it is the rumble from their stomachs that alerts him that they are there. They are gathered around Ran Bagha.

Ravi sits cross-legged at his head. There are two other silhouettes. As the moon skims from behind high clouds, he recognizes Mara and Catharo.

He sits down and watches. He makes no move to join them and supposes they have not seen him. He is downwind, so the elephants do not catch his scent. He would like to join them but feels he has no place there.

He listens to the elephants and the wind rustling in the grass. He reconsiders.

A vast grey mountain lies among the ruins of the battlefield. The corpses have long ago been hauled away by the carters, but the elephant is a different proposition. They may have to burn him where he lies. And they will have to do it soon; he has lain out here for two days now in the hot sun and as the gases build up inside the giant body there is a danger he will explode.

Ravi will not leave him. He sits there in the sun, head

bowed, and if the waterboys did not take it in turns to bring him water from the river he would have died from thirst. He has not eaten; he has hardly moved.

Mara and Catharo are with him. No one comes to order them back to camp. Gajendra is too busy with his new wife to chasten his waterboys, she supposes. Besides he wants us to escape. He is giving us another chance.

But she will not leave Ravi; and Catharo will not leave her, does not even grumble about it any more.

Flies cluster around the dried blood on Ravi's scalp. He will not go to the physicians to have the wound tended. He just sits there cross-legged and stares at the massive corpse and rocks back and forward.

Mara sees a knot of riders approach from the camp. Sunlight reflects on their armour and hurts the eyes. She knows they are officers by the way they ride. As they get closer she recognizes Alexander in the lead.

He jumps down from the saddle and stands with his hands on his hips. 'Well, this is a fine pass. What do we have here?' He walks around the beast and then looks down at Ravi. 'He's starting to smell, lad. Time you moved on.'

'He gave his life for me.'

'Well, then we shall remember him fondly. In the meantime I wish you to remove back to the camp. We need good Indians to replace the *mahavat*s I lost in the fight.'

'What will you do with him?'

'What would you have me do? Build a mausoleum?' He sees Mara and Catharo. 'What are they doing?'

He does not seem perturbed that they do not answer. Instead he turns to Perdiccas, watching from his horse. 'I want the foot,' he says.

'The foot?'

'I shall need a footstool. I heard the King of Taxila had one. If it's good enough for an Indian it's good enough for me.'

'You will cut off his foot?' Ravi says, in a daze.

'Not just his foot, we will have his ivory, too. By the black breath of hell, he stinks!' He turns and is about to remount his horse. Mara comes out of her daze, grabs the knife that Catharo has concealed in his tunic and rushes him. Alexander hears her coming, turns unhurriedly to face her. He registers no alarm, even when he sees the knife flash in the sun. A man who has spent his whole life in battle is accustomed to having drawn blades thrust at him.

As she brings the knife down he casually steps aside and knocks her down with a fist. At the same moment he wrenches the knife out of her hand, waving aside his guards with a flicker of annoyance. I do not need wet nursing, the look seems to say.

Catharo is a different proposition. He is not expecting this; the little fellow hits him on the run and takes him out at the knees. Alexander goes down, winded, and drops the knife. Catharo snatches it up and is about to slash Alexander's throat in the same movement when one of the bodyguards reacts and takes him down with his spear. Catharo screams and grabs the shaft, which has smashed his thigh, the same one he wounded just days before. This time it smashes the bone. A man, even one as brave as Catharo, cannot stand on a broken leg. He falls to the ground.

Alexander is on his feet in an instant, takes out his sword and plunges it through Catharo's chest. He then turns on

Mara. She tries to get up. He kicks her over again and puts his sword at her throat. 'Don't hurt her! She's a girl!' Ravi shouts before he can administer the killing stroke.

Alexander stands back, frowning. He strides over to Ravi and squats down on his haunches. 'What did you say?'

'I said don't hurt her, lord. She's just a girl.'

'A girl?'

Ravi nods.

'Did your Elephantarch know about this?'

Ravi shakes his head, no, but he is a very bad liar. Alexander gives a nod of the head, signal to his bodyguards to take the prisoner away. He looks down at Catharo's lifeless body in disgust. Mara knows what he is thinking: how did a fellow like this become so useful with a sword? If it wasn't for his bodyguards he would be bleeding into the dirt right now.

This will bear looking into.

CHAPTER 47

S HE IS LYING on the ground at his feet. She has been beaten, but not badly, not yet.

Alexander looks up as Gajendra enters, and says, 'You heard what your elephant boy did to me? Only he's not a boy, is he? Did you know?'

He thinks about lying. There no longer seems any point. He nods.

Alexander strikes him once, with his fist. It is like getting kicked by a horse. He goes down.

'Why did you keep this a secret? What was it? Did you feel sorry for her?'

He gets up slowly. 'I imagine that I did.'

'You haven't fucked her, have you? I gave you a woman. Was that not enough for you? A princess I gave you. What is this scrawny wretch here? What could possibly be the attraction?'

He does not answer.

'So what shall we do with her? She came at me with a knife. I think we should crucify her, don't you? It would not do for others to think that they can test me with a blade and not suffer the consequence.'

'Please,' Gajendra says.

He freezes, his back turned, and looks over his shoulder. 'What did you say?'

'Let her live.'

'Let her *live*? You want mercy for her?'

'Yes.'

'Why? Why should you care if she suffers and dies?'

'I don't know. I have grown fond of her, I suppose.'

'Fond of her?' Alexander decides to laugh. This is a wonderful joke. 'How fond?'

'She only did this because of the elephant.'

'The elephant?'

He sees her look up at him, through her bruises. She is bewildered that he is arguing for her.

'She loved Colossus as you love your horse.'

'A horse is different.'

'Not to her. She was enraged, I am sure of it. She did not plan to do you harm. It was a moment's madness.'

'But if she had been quicker I should have a knife in my back whether she planned it or not. How badly do you wish my leniency, elephant boy?'

'Just please let her live.'

'Get down on your belly, then.'

He knows what Alexander is about to do and only hesitates for a moment. He is committed. He drops to his knees, then lies flat, his forehead touching the carpets. From here, he sees that Alexander's sandals have blood on them. He wonders whether it belongs to her or to Catharo.

'Beg me.'

'... Please.'

'Say it louder. Say it like you mean it.'

'Please, don't hurt her.'

'Again.'

'Please let her go. I beg you, my lord. Have mercy on her.'

Alexander draws up his robe and Gajendra feels his warm stream on his head and shoulders. He can hear his mother and sisters wailing again.

I am helpless, I am nothing. I am a worm, and there is nothing I can do to save anything I love.

'I didn't hear you. Say it again.'

'Please let her go…'

Alexander finishes and adjusts his robe. 'I am disappointed in you, elephant boy. I thought I saw something in you.' He bends over and whispers, 'You stink of piss. They have all seen you grovel now. You'll never walk among generals again. You'll always be just a piss-ant.'

'Let her go.'

Alexander sighs. 'All right. If that's what you want. Now get out.'

But even as he scrambles to his feet he knows this promise is a lie. Grovel all you want, elephant boy, he's going to kill her anyway.

Once, as a small boy, he had picked up a spider and put it in his mouth. One of his sisters had dared him to do it. She said he would not eat it and he had sworn that he could. As soon as he did it, she screamed and begged him to stop. She had even fallen on her knees and cried.

It had tasted foul, worse than he had ever imagined, but he had done it anyway. He could feel it biting him as he chewed. That night his tongue had swollen up and he could not breathe. His mother thought he was going to die.

His sister thought it was her fault. She prayed to Kali and asked to be punished herself if only her little brother would live. Perhaps Kali had answered her. A few days later the dacoits came; that's why he was sick in his bed and not with the others.

So he was responsible for what had happened to his family and to him. And all because of a spider.

Or all because of his pride.

CHAPTER 48

T<small>HE NEWS HAD</small> spread through the camp: the hero of Syracuse was disgraced.

Ravi finds him sitting alone by the river. There is a mist rising above the water but with the heat of the new day it burns off and he can see Syracuse in the distance, Aetna beyond. A heron fishes in the shallows.

He puts his arm around Gajendra's shoulders and leads him down into the river and scrubs Alexander off him.

'He is going to execute her,' Gajendra says.

'He'll do it slow so that you have to watch.'

'You think so?'

'You know him better than I do. What do you think?'

His limbs are shaking. He cannot stop them, it is like they belong to someone else. He tries to tense his muscles to still them. He does not want anyone to see him like this, even Ravi.

'I'm going to get her away from here.'

'How? Overpower Alexander's entire army?'

He stands there, streaming water. An idea comes to him. 'I don't have to overpower them. I just have to distract them. Will you help me?'

'When have I ever stopped you getting me into trouble before?'

'All you have to do is get me two good horses.'

'Oh well, that's all right then. I thought you might ask me to do something that would have me tortured and killed.'

'I know someone. You just find him and pay him, he'll know what to do. I've done it before.'

'No wonder you're in trouble, Gaji.'

'Packhorses will do. As long as they have four legs. You'll do it for me?'

'I suppose so. I was growing fond of her too. What are you going to do?'

'I'm going to set fire to Alexander's camp.'

There is just one guard outside the tent where Mara is being held. She's only a woman after all, and who is going to take her? He has drawn the duty as punishment from his squad sergeant for sleeping at his watch and now he sits slumped on the ground, resenting it.

He stands up, though, when he smells the smoke. He can hear the elephants trumpeting from somewhere on the other side of the camp, a commotion with the horses. When he sees the orange glow spreading up the sky he starts to panic. What is he supposed to do with *her*?

Then he sees Gajendra.

He knows the captain of the elephants from reputation and wonders what he is doing here. He has heard how Alexander made him grovel and then pissed on his head when he found out about the woman. Should he salute him or jeer at him?

He does neither.

'There's a fire, the elephants have got out!' Gajendra shouts at him.

Now he hears the elephants bellowing, hears screams. The tuskers are out of Elephant Row and are running amok through the camp. They will trample the army and be half-way back to Carthage by the time they have the fire out. In the fireglow the soldier's face is a study in confusion.

'Someone has unshackled them,' he says.

'Yes, it was me.'

The elephant hook hits the lad on the back of the head, under the helmet. He falls face down into the dirt.

Gajendra takes a smoking torch and goes inside the tent. Mara is curled up on the ground, bound hand and foot. One eye is swollen shut where they have beaten her.

She sits up, startled, and backs into the corner, expecting more maltreatment. 'It's me,' he tells her. He does not waste time explaining to her what is happening. He scoops her up in his arms. She is as light as a bird. He carries her out and runs off into the darkness.

Ravi is waiting with the horses. 'Did you have any trouble?' he asks him.

'That sergeant tried to raise the price on me at the last moment. I had to put a knife to his throat to get him to keep to our arrangement.'

'You have a knife? Here, let me have it.' He slashes through the bonds at Mara's wrists and ankles. She whimpers. They had bound her tight, and the ropes come away bloody.

'Help her on her horse,' he tells Ravi.

'Where are you going?'

'I'll be right back.' He runs off into the dark; it isn't hard to find what he is looking for, he just lets his nose lead him. It is a dangerous notion for what he is looking for has been placed close to Alexander's pavilion. But it is unguarded, as he thought it would be, for everyone has gone to the fire.

Kassander yips and snarls in his cage. Gajendra comes closer and bears another look. By the light of the torches he can see that it may be no mercy setting him free; he is covered in sores and all manner of filth, his beard is down to his belly and his eyes are as wide as a madman's. He cannot imagine what will become of him now.

He seemed so assured that day he had met Oxathres, in his red cloak and fine tunic.

You have the means to deliver it?

My brother is Alexander's cupbearer. What do you think?

But he owes him this much, at least. He slips the latch on the cage and throws it open. At first, Kassander does not move. He cowers in the corner, thinking it is a trick. It is only when Gajendra steps back that the cunning returns to his eyes. When he finally makes the decision to escape he is a quicksilver shadow, one moment there, the next vanished into the dark.

Gajendra silently wishes him better fortune, a quick death at least. Anything is better than dying as some man's plaything.

He leads back to the camp. Men are running everywhere, pointlessly, not knowing what to do; the smell of smoke is overpowering. He cannot hear his tuskers trumpeting any more, though. They must have escaped. It will be days before they round them all up again.

*

Ravi is waiting with the horses, trying to keep Mara in the saddle; she does not seem yet to understand what is going on.

Gajendra mounts his own nag. He is no horseman but he has ridden enough times to know how it is done. It is strange to have a saddle and no ears to hang onto. Mara's horse staggers and she sways and nearly falls. Even with her sparrow's weight on his back he looks as if he has been asked to carry a siege engine.

Pack animals both of them. If the sergeant hadn't sold them, they would have been in the soup by the end of the week.

'Go well, my friend,' Ravi says.

'Until we meet again.'

Ravi grips his hand. 'You're doing the right thing.'

Behind them, the camp is in uproar. Men are rushing around in panic, some trying to get away from the fire, others running from the elephants. No one pays them any mind. When a man is caught between a mad elephant and a good roasting he could be carrying away Alexander's pickled head in a jar and no one would stop to look, let alone draw their sword.

They gallop away, through the drifting smoke. He sees a few brave souls rushing the other way to help fight the fire. Not many.

Mara, weak from the beating, can barely keep herself upright. Gajendra holds the reins, leading her horse behind his. Well, I let you piss on my head, Alexander. You thought you had me beaten. But it was just misdirection, as you call it. A feint. You were a good tutor. I have learned well.

*

329

The fire has grown bigger than he intended; it has lit up the plain and the orange glow of it is reflected on her face. He stops to look back. Mara seems to have recovered a little. She has taken back the reins, at least.

She puts her hand on his arm. He thinks she is about to thank him. Instead she says, 'We have to go back.'

He stares at her; he knew it, she is mad.

'Go back?'

'I cannot leave Catharo to rot in the sun.'

'Catharo's dead.'

'More reason to save his honour.'

'Save his honour? I am trying to save your life!'

'I will not leave him. Go without me if you must. But my father did not raise a wretch who will leave her champion to be eaten by carrion crows!'

He admires her then, as much as he would like to slap her off her horse. Perhaps she will do the same for me one day. I, too, would like someone to save me from the birds.

He supposes there is nothing for it but to go back.

In the dark it might have been impossible to find him; with the glow of the fire spreading across the sky the battlefield is lit like early morning. He sees a huge silhouette near the brow of a low rise, what is left of Ran Bagha after the crows have been at their work. Catharo will be very close by.

But getting Catharo's body is not going to be so easy. Alexander has posted two men to protect the ivory tusks, which have yet to be removed.

He'll crucify me if I get caught, Gajendra thinks. I will be three days dying because of this madwoman.

The air is ripe with dead elephant and the guards have

been forced to stand some way off with scarves over their faces. They might have been dozing but the fire has woken them. They are too scared to leave their posts so they just stand there, gawping, pointing to where the flames have taken hold.

There are just two of them: are they veterans or recruits, Macks or Persians? It will make a difference to the outcome.

They leave the horses some way off, in the shadows, tied to a solitary olive tree. They creep closer. 'So Mara,' he whispers, 'do we say, good morning men, we just want this body, sorry to trouble you and now we'll be off? Is that your plan?'

It is clear she doesn't have a plan. It is down to him then. Typical.

'You will have to distract them,' he says.

'How?'

He shrugs.

'You want me now to play the tart when for all these months I have convinced everyone that I am a boy?'

'By the look of it, they're Greeks. They won't mind what you are as long as you show willing.'

He can feel her trembling. If it was daylight she would not look the seductress, not with this swollen face and bleeding wrists. But every woman is beautiful in the dark, or that is what they say, and there is no choice. This was her idea. He would rather leave Catharo where he is, but if she insists, then she will have to do her part.

He waits in the shadows. She stands up, takes a breath and starts to walk towards them. She affects a provocative sway of the hips, a parody of a Babylon streetwalker, which makes him almost laugh out loud.

These men are very little use as guards; they are both so entranced by the progress of the fire in the camp that she is almost on them before they realize she is there. They shout in alarm when they finally see her approach and run for their weapons.

He could not truthfully say that Mara has any talent for harlotry; the sum of her artistry is to hitch up her tunic and show the boys what is on offer and ask for a gold coin donation. It still astonishes him that they do not consider more carefully, yet it has been his experience that when men find themselves in these situations wishful thinking will take over. They assume she is a camp follower, so short on business that she has needed to leave the comfort of her own tent to find work, when any fool knows that when you have an army camped on your doorstep not even a dog is safe.

But they are young and they are bored from a long night sitting too close to a decomposing elephant. And they are Macedonians; in the crease, they are reputed for their brawn and not their brains.

But he'll give them this: they are quick about it. One is already on top and the other yelling encouragement by the time Gajendra can get into position. They have handily left their weapons, together with helmets and some clothes, to one side. The one looking out for his friend does not even turn around; the first he knows of Gajendra's presence is when the shaft of his own spear strikes him on the back of his head and down he goes, unconscious before he even hits the ground.

The second is immediately of a mind to rise and scramble for his sword, but Mara wraps her arms and legs around him, impeding him. Gajendra swings again but because the boy wriggles and throws up an arm it takes three clouts and a knee in the vitals before he is subdued.

When it is done Mara jumps to her feet and aims another kick at him, for good measure. Then she turns and slaps Gajendra around the face as well. 'Why were you so long? He had almost violated me!'

She arranges herself, her back to him. He hears her sobbing. He puts a hand on her shoulder, thinking to comfort her, and she shoves him roughly away. 'Just get Catharo,' she says.

CHAPTER 49

THE FIRE STRIPES the bodies of the two soldiers with ochre. He does not think he has killed them. He hopes not, they were only doing their job. It is the first time he has fought without weapons, and without an elephant to compensate for what he lacks in size.

Catharo lies in the shadow of Ran Bagha's corpse; the smell is unbearable and he does not linger over an examination of the body. He throws one of the soldier's blankets over him and picks him up. He is surprised at the weight of him for such a short fellow.

He throws him across the saddle of his horse. Mara is already mounted and ready to leave. Her tunic is torn and she has to tie a knot in the shoulder to hold it together. There are fresh scratches on her arm and her throat. But she herself looks composed; how quickly she is the general's daughter again, waiting for her champion to do her will.

If I were ever to marry her, he thinks, it will be a fiery wife I have claimed for myself. At least with the elephants they flare out their ears to warn you when they are going to charge.

The glow of the fire has dimmed by the time they reach what Gajendra judges to be a safe distance. The moon has appeared between high scudding clouds and he can hear the sea breaking on the shore. A pink glow is spreading up the sky to the south. They still haven't put his fire out. Alexander won't be best pleased.

They stop just above the beach to rest. He lifts Mara from the saddle and puts her down in the sand. The moon is bright enough to distinguish shapes from shadows.

He says, 'We are safe here. We can find somewhere to bury him in the soft sand.'

'No. We are taking him back with us to Panormus if we have to. My father will want to see the body.'

He sighs. He thought that was what she would say.

'Why are you doing this?' she asks.

'I don't know. You're useless at mucking out and you answer back. You have too much to say for an elephant boy never mind a woman.'

'You had everything you wanted until you walked into Alexander's tent and pleaded for my life.'

'Did you really try and kill him because of an elephant?'

'He wanted his leg for a footstool. Did you know that? Did you see? They forgot about the ivory but they took his leg off so Alexander could amuse himself.'

He sits down on a rock. His earlier elation has evaporated. A small victory such as this is not salvation. He hears Alexander in his head: *Do not think to win the battle, think to win the campaign. Think not to win the campaign, think to win the war.*

'I'm nothing again. You know that? When I was with Alexander I feared no one. I could stop the dreams.'

'It's just fear, Gajendra.'

'Just fear? Alexander is never afraid.'

'Of course he is. He is afraid there might be something on the other side of death greater than he is. He can't take his army there.'

'Would you really have killed him?'

'I have never hated so much. I couldn't see for spite. If he had not turned at the last moment I would have stuck that knife in him as far as I could make it go.'

'We had best keep riding.' He helps her back on her horse. She is still bleeding from where they beat her but she does not make a single complaint. An elephant boy on a horse. A general's daughter fighting her father's adversary. What a strange pair they make.

He dares not risk a fire. They huddle under their blankets for warmth. Her eyes are needle points in the dark.

'What will you do now?'

He wraps his body around her. Shivering and scared, he still burns for her; warm and scented, Zahara left him cold. He runs his hand along her thigh.

She knocks it away. 'I gave myself to you once in a moment of weakness and now you think you are my husband and can demand possession whenever you wish?'

'It will keep us warm.'

'I was a slave then, I had to submit. Now I am a general's daughter again. I can make you wait.'

'We are not at Panormus yet.'

She laughs deep in her throat but grips his hands and squeezes them. 'Just hold me.' The wind moans through the valley. He spoons into her. 'I will miss your elephants,' she murmurs.

'Not as much as I.'

She turns her head, kisses him over her shoulder. 'What will you do, Gaji? If we do find my father?'

'I don't know. What about you?'

'My old life is gone. My future is as uncertain as yours.'

'We will find some way to survive.'

'Yes,' she murmurs. 'Yes, I suppose we will.'

He has been promoted from being not quite her husband to having a place in her future. He nuzzles the back of her neck, where the smell of her hair is musty and sweet.

His fingertips seek out bare flesh. Her skin is cold but there are warm places and she gives a little moan. Even fugitive as they are, all things now seem possible.

They have slept beyond dawn; the sun has thrown a lemon stain above the hills. It is cold and his muscles are stiff and sore.

He feels the drumming of horses through the earth before he hears them. He thinks it might be that dream again, and that he is at Taxila, asleep on the floor of the hut. But then he comes fully awake and realizes that the hoof beats are real.

He jumps to his feet and looks for them in the early morning dark.

Get up, he says to Mara, and she says, it's still night, I'm not your waterboy now.

He pulls her, protesting, to her feet. He can see them now, silhouetted against the rising sun. They were headed south, but now they see them and change direction.

'We might be able to outrun them,' he tells her. He pushes her towards her horse. Were they Alexander's men, deserters, bandits? With any luck they would never have to find out.

'What are you doing?' he says to her. She is trying to haul Catharo's body towards the horses. Is she mad?

'We can't leave him here.'

'Of course we can. He's dead!'

'I won't leave him for the wolves.'

He tries to pull her away. She shrugs him off. 'I won't leave him!'

So there is nothing for it but to drag Catharo over to the horses and throw him across his own Arab. He covers him quickly with a blanket. And all the time the riders are getting closer.

Mara is a poor rider, even less expert than him. She keeps the reins too tight, unsure of herself in the saddle. And the poor nags they are riding are no match for the good horses of their pursuers, especially weighed down with a corpse. He looks over his shoulder. This is hopeless.

There are four of them, Bactrians by the look of them, and they know their business. They spread out, ready to encircle them.

They reach a creek and that slows them further and he realizes they will not make it. Her horse baulks in the riverbed; but it doesn't matter, two of the Bactrians have already leaped the banks and are trotting towards them, through the shallows, grinning.

CHAPTER 50

ONCE THEY HAVE them surrounded the Bactrians relax. There is no longer any reason to be desperate about it.

Their leader is a big man with a nose that makes his horse look handsome. A face like a leather bag, ill repaired, and no tooth that is not at least part rotten. He knows the type: they will run face first into walls just to make themselves look more fearsome.

'So who are these fine fellows?' he says and walks his horse up to them. No one yet has produced a weapon. In such a situation there is no need.

Gajendra studies the ragtag of men with him; if they were just bandits he would be more hopeful but these men look like mercenaries, professionals. They will be happy with such unexpected bounty because violation and murder are set into such men's souls like iron rusted into a wall.

They are deserters, from someone's army; he doubts it is Alexander's for he takes care to keep them well paid and well fed. They may have come from Syracuse hoping to find employment at Panormus. They speak rudimentary Greek with bad accents; he supposes men like this don't even speak their own language very well.

'Where are you headed?' Horse-Face asks them.

'Panormus,' Gajendra says and then, taking an enormous risk, he adds, 'This is General Hanno's daughter. There is a massive reward offered for her safe return. I hoped to claim it.'

There is stunned silence and then the horsemen all pound their saddles with their fists and guffaw. Horse-Face gives a nod and one of the riders grabs Mara and pulls her off her horse. 'Looks like a boy to me,' he says, 'but we'll soon find out.'

'Leave her!' Gajendra tries to put his horse between her and them but he is no horseman and only succeeds in losing control of the horse. After they have finished laughing at him one of the men draws his sword and hammers the hilt into his face, knocking him to the ground.

He lies winded. He cannot breathe. His mouth and nose are clotted with blood and he has to roll onto his belly to spit it out.

The men find this amusing. Meanwhile they have dragged Mara from her horse. 'Come on, boy, get up,' Horse-Face jeers at him. 'Let's see you make a fight of it.'

The brute gets off his horse and aims a few leisurely kicks at him. He hears Mara screaming, curses mainly, but they haven't really tried to hurt her yet.

Horse-Face stands, legs apart, right in front of him. Gajendra crawls forward, hand over hand. Never mind that he laughs and dares you to fight like a man. Keep your head down.

Poor Mara. For a general's daughter she has borne a lot of rough handling this last year, and now here are four men intent on violating her as a girl or as a boy, depending on their fancy. He shuts out her screams, it distracts him.

He thinks he has broken some ribs when he came off the horse.

'Please don't hurt us,' he says. 'Take our horses, take whatever you want, but please don't hurt us.'

Horse-Face likes that. 'You hear that? He's offering us the horses.' Another kick. 'If we wanted them we would take them, but I wouldn't even carve these nags up for the pot. Are you sure that one is a girl?'

There is consternation among them, however, when they find Catharo's body across his saddle. This is unexpected and alarms them. It is a perfect distraction.

When your opponent thinks he has won, this is your time to strike, he hears Alexander say. He concentrates all his will on bringing his knee up so that he is ready to spring and then reverses his grip on his knife; there, in pissing range now, if this fellow were a bandit.

He is on his feet in an instant, his head smashing the man's nose – he could hardly miss – while his knife plunges to the hilt under the breastbone. Catharo could not have done better.

Even before Horse-Face has finished his dying, Gajendra has the man's sword in his hand and has lopped off the left arm of the man pulling on Catharo's corpse. He does not delay to deliver a final blow. In his experience a man who has lost a limb in such dramatic fashion quickly loses his appetite for fighting.

He concentrates instead on the two men bending over Mara. They are covered in scratches; she has made a good fight of it. She clutches onto the soldier who is on top

341

of her and keeps him from rising. Twice in one day; it is becoming routine.

While the other one fumbles for his weapon Gajendra swings down with all his strength and the edge of the sword cleaves the man's face from scalp to chin.

The one on top of Mara screams in horror and punches her twice in the face to get away. But she has delayed him enough. Gajendra dares not swing the sword a second time in case he hits her; instead he lunges with the point. He is inexpert but he takes the man through the centre of his chest. He puts a foot on his breastbone to extract the sword and then dispatches the other, who is still lying on the ground bleeding and howling for his mother.

He has never known such cold rage. He is even sorry it is over. He would chew their bones with his teeth and spit their gristle in the mud if he could. He is of a mind to mutilate them even though they are dead, but that would serve no purpose. They are not the bandits who raped his mother and sisters. But they might as well be.

There are things he suddenly remembers now of that day; he was not sick after all, the episode with the spider was months before. He had actually run inside and covered his ears when his mother and sisters were screaming. The men had come in later and dragged him out again. By then, they were already dead. Why hadn't they killed him as well? It was what he had never understood; how arbitrary it all was, savagery and mercy all at a whim.

He wonders now at how he could have forgotten this telling detail. Until this moment it seems he could not bear to think of it.

Mara is on her knees, spitting blood and sobbing. He

goes to comfort her but she waves him away. She does not wish to be touched, even by her rescuer.

He hesitates, then reaches for her a second time. She relents and hides her face in his shoulder and clings to him. There is blood on her face. Look what they have done to her.

A thought comes to him: what would have happened to him if the dacoits had not come that day? He would be ploughing a field with an ox cart. He supposes.

Instead he is here.

He pulls the stopper from a waterskin and washes the blood off her face as best he can. As if she was not beaten enough. Her father will think he did this, if he recognizes her at all.

'It will be all right,' he whispers. Perhaps it will. Who knows? He hasn't given up yet.

He looks down at himself. He is covered in blood, too, some of it his. Just like Alexander, then. The elephant boy has learned his lessons well. And now they have four fresh horses and they can leave the two nags behind.

She clutches him like she is drowning and howls.

CHAPTER 51

HANNO STRIDES OUT of his tent. His scouts have brought in two prisoners and at first he assumes they are deserters, most likely from Antipater's army. The news has already reached him of Alexander's victory at Syracuse.

He watches the slow approach of the horses. A captain leads the escort up the slope. The two captives do not wear armour. One is a young man, Persian looking, in a rough and blood-crusted leather tunic; the other is a young boy, in rags, slumped over the saddle, with rope burns at his wrists and ankles. He has been badly beaten by the looks of it.

His men pull him from the saddle. He cannot stand unaided and they let him slump to the grass. The other prisoner goes to help him, cradles his head and appeals for water.

'Who are you?' Hanno says.

The Asiatic looks up and addresses him informally. 'Are you Hanno?'

He thinks to strike him for his impertinence but something about this scene disturbs him. His worst fears are confirmed when his soldiers haul a corpse from one of the horses and uncover it. 'Catharo,' he murmurs.

But this isn't right. He looks back at the Asiatic, who nods.

'Mara,' he breathes, when he realizes the bleeding wretch at his feet is his daughter. His little girl! One eye is swollen shut. Her lip is ripped and swollen, her hair is butchered, there is a pulpy bruise over her cheek the size of an orange.

It will not do for his men to see him weep. His hand moves to his sword. Who is there he might kill and vent this rage on? 'Alexander,' he says.

He bends to pick her up, bawling for his physician, and carries her into his tent. Gajendra is allowed to follow. Someone hands him a waterskin. He gulps at it gratefully, then slumps onto his knees, exhausted.

CHAPTER 52

Hanno is a big man who contrives, on this first occasion at least, to appear very small and pale. The unexpected reunion with his daughter has shaken him. If he were a horse you'd say he had been worked too hard by a man overfond of the whip.

He has just come from burying Catharo. They lit a pyre for him. Now the general stands uncommonly grateful to this Indian who has saved his daughter but probably seduced her in the process.

The last year has been wearing on the nerves of even a patient man.

'She says I have you to thank for her safe arrival here,' he says.

'Yes.'

'No false modesty from you then.'

'I killed four men for her. As I am not trained for it I think it remarkable and I intend to get full credit for it. Last night I had unpleasant dreams about it. Killing does not come easily to me. I did it for her.'

'Four men?'

'They misjudged me, you see.'

Hanno takes his point. 'I promise not to do the same.'

'Your man Catharo was the bravest fellow I have ever

seen. I hope you're going to build him a statue somewhere. He died trying to slay Alexander for you.'

'Would that he had succeeded.'

'Well, he did his best. I have seen thirty-year veterans with fewer scars on him than your man.'

Hanno goes to the stand and splashes water on his face. 'What were you with Alexander?'

'I was his Elephantarch.'

'And what is that?'

'I was chief of the elephants.'

'An officer?'

'You are surprised because I am Indian?'

'I am surprised because you are so young.'

'Alexander was younger than me when he won his first victory.'

He steps close. 'Can you tell me how to defeat Alexander?'

'Yes.'

He frowns. He has not expected so blunt an answer. 'Why would you do such a thing?'

'If I do not show you how to do it, my life is forfeit. Alexander never forgets a slight, and cheating him of his prisoner he will regard as a deadly insult. That, and I set fire to his camp.'

'That was you?' For the first time since the interview began, he looks amused.

'It was not done in malice. I needed to create a distraction.'

'How do I know I can trust you?'

'Ask your daughter.'

It is a brave thing to say. Hanno looks for a moment

as if he would like to pulp his head in his fist like a plum. He decides to smile instead. 'If you ever hurt her, I will tear out your balls by the roots and feed them to my horse.'

'You will never find the need.'

Hanno grunts, not utterly convinced. 'Your arrival here has caused much discussion.'

'I can imagine.'

He scratches his beard. 'Some call you a spy, others think you could change our fortunes.'

'Is this all your army?'

'As you know, Carthage is not a race of warriors. Most of our army were mercenaries, and mercenaries by their nature cost money. Carthage now is just a few forts and colonies on the north of this island. Even to raise an army this size will probably bankrupt us all.'

'Well, I suppose numbers do not matter that much if you employ the right tactics.'

'Before you got here, my generals favoured retreat back into the mountains, to the safety of our wall of forts there.'

'If I was one of your generals and recognized my deficiencies so would I.'

He is amused. 'Really? Are you a general now?'

'I am almost ready,' Gajendra says with such sincerity that Hanno looks startled. 'Now you have me here, you could perhaps win the campaign, if not the battle.'

Hanno leans on the table. 'Where did you learn such conceit?'

'From Alexander. If he were not so sure of himself he would not have come this far, and in that, at least, we are alike. I know his mind, general. There is no one outside of his close circle who knows it better. I can make a difference here.'

'As you say, this is not much of an army. I had a much larger one at Carthage and he decimated it.'

'You played into his hands.'

'I have no intention to do so again. We came here at Antipater's urging, he wished to catch Alexander in a trap. But he moved before we were ready. He wanted all the glory for himself.'

'Perhaps. But Alexander rather forced his hand. If he had not come out to meet him he would have penned him inside Syracuse while he dealt with you. It was much discussed among his own generals. Anyway, what is done is done. It is time now to deceive the great deceiver.'

'What is it you want, Gajendra?' Hanno says, calling him by his name for the first time.

'Once I could have answered that question exactly. Now I shall be happy if I live long enough to see Alexander dead.'

'You must want more than that. Every man has a price.'

'I could say that I want your daughter in marriage, that I want elevation to the nobility, a villa, an estate, a vineyard. I can imagine a fine life for myself, if I wish. But tomorrow has its own way of finding us, it seems. For now I would just want your gratitude and favour and later I shall work out what to do with it. If I live.'

'If we all live.'

Hanno smiles. From this year of exile, of despair, he now sees hope. He sees, too, a place in history if he is the one finally to vanquish the invincible. The light comes back to his eyes.

'So. Tell me how it can be done.'

She wakes to the murmur of insects, her father talking in whispers outside. She is lying on a camp bed, there are linen bandages around her wrists and ankles, her face drums with pain. She touches her face but it doesn't feel like her own. Her lip is swollen to twice its normal size, one eye is closed, she cannot bear to touch her own cheek.

Some women come in, fuss over her. She sends them away.

She can hear her father outside interrogating the physician. Is she in pain? Is she going to be all right? Are there bones broken? Is she missing teeth?

The poor man can hardly keep up with so many questions.

Did you give her laudanum? Why not? What do you mean she will not take it?

He hasn't mellowed then, she thinks. The tent flap bursts open and he stands there silhouetted against the volcano. He holds out his hands to her, palms up, as if to say: I'm sorry, this is all my fault.

'I thought I should never see you again.' He has lost weight. Once he was a big man; now he just looks very tall. 'Everything is going to be all right now. I am sending you to Panormus.'

As if that will fix her situation, his. She is not going to Panormus, or anywhere, and she steels herself for the fight. She missed him so much these last months; now a few moments in his presence and she wants to run back to Alexander and execution.

'Who did this to you?'

'Does it matter?'

'The Asiatic, he treated you well?'

'No. You should have him executed. Look what he did to me.' She holds out her hands to show him the yellow filth under her fingernails. 'I have blisters. Dirty nails. And *calluses*. It's all his fault.'

He doesn't understand she is making a feeble joke. He looks bewildered.

He kneels by her bed. For the first time he looks old to her. She notices the grey in his beard, the lines around his eyes. 'So who is this Gajendra?'

'Alexander was about to execute me. He saved my life.'

'Why? What is he to you?'

'We had become close friends.'

'Friends?' He presses his lips together until they are white. She can imagine what he is thinking. Bad enough some foreigner has violated his daughter, now he has to thank him for it.

'The boy claims to be Alexander's Elephantarch? A grand word. The boy says it like he's King of Persia. What is such a thing? I have never heard of it.'

'He is not a boy, or at least you did not think so when his elephants walked over your phalanx outside Carthage. He was surely not a boy when he killed four men to bring me safe here.'

'He does not exaggerate then?'

'He may look young but so does Alexander. Gajendra is a warrior, father, like you.'

He strides around the tent, agitated. Then he falls on his knees again, takes her hand and presses it to his heart. He starts to weep. She has never seen her father cry before and she is too astonished to speak. It is like seeing one of the marble gods in the temple step down from his plinth and start walking around.

She strokes his hair, feels the wetness of his tears on her arm. She had never imagined he cared for her so much.

Finally he stands up, turns away from her, embarrassed at this display of emotion. 'We have given Catharo to the flames with all honour.'

'Good. It was the least that he deserved.'

'It was brave and honourable of you, what you did. To bring him back.' He wipes a hand across his face, in control again. 'Was it a good end?'

'It was quick.'

He nods. 'That's good, then. He had surely suffered enough, judging by the scars on him when we buried him. There were fresh wounds on his thighs and his chest. The little fellow was just a patchwork of them.'

'They were all gained in my name and in your service.'

'How did he die?'

'He was trying to defend me. Alexander dispatched him with his sword.'

He hangs his head, trying not to imagine it too vividly.

'What was it between you?' she asks him. 'Why was he so loyal to you?'

He sits down, then stands up again. He looks as if he is about to tell her, then goes to the basin in the corner of the tent, and throws water on his face instead. 'There are some things it is better not to know,' he says at last.

'Perhaps that was true once. Now I think I deserve an answer.'

'It is not easy to explain. I am not sure you would understand.'

'Try me.'

He sighs, turns his back again. 'You know, of course, that your mother was not the only woman in my life.'

'I had guessed it.' There is a long silence. 'He was my brother?'

'Did he look like your brother?'

'Lying down he could have been anyone's brother.'

'Well, he wasn't yours. But his mother was one of my mistresses. She died of the same fever that took your mother, many years ago. Catharo was her boy, by another man who left her when he saw the misshapen son she had given him. She always worried what would happen to the little fellow if she died, and I swore I would look after him. In that, I kept my promise.'

'How old was he then?'

'Just a lad.'

'Yet I never saw him.'

'Of course not. I raised him elsewhere.'

'You trained him, too?'

'Well, I had him trained. He welcomed it. He had a warrior's instincts and as he grew – or as he didn't grow – he became the perfect candidate for many of those requirements of office that needed to be performed without official sanction. Who would suspect that such a harmless-looking little fellow was lethal? He loved me, I think, because I kept my word to him. I imagine he looked upon me as his father, or the closest anyone had ever come to it.'

'Well, he repaid your kindness.'

'He did his job and now I will make sure you are safe.'

'You cannot do that.'

He must have known that she would say this. He puffs out his chest. 'I will find a way to beat Alexander.'

'I am not going to Panormus.'

'I have ordered it. That's the end of the matter.'

'I am staying here.'

'That's just impossible.'

'The two men I love are here. If you die here, or Gajendra dies, what is there for me in Panormus? I need to be close to the men who are important to me.'

'He means that much to you?'

'You both do.'

He seems to deflate. 'You're right, I cannot beat Alexander. He has the best army in the world and he out-numbers us two to one. I don't know what to do. If we retreat he will only come after us, at his leisure. We cannot escape – we are already in exile.'

'You must never give up,' she says. 'No matter what happens, no matter how hard things are, you don't give up. You never know if there is something just around the corner that will tip the balance back in your favour and give you back your life.'

'You really think so, Mara?' He sits down on the bed, puts his arms around her and holds her, gently. He kisses the top of her head. 'I cannot believe I have you back. No matter what happens, then, we will live or die together now.'

*

The generals are gathered around the chart they have thrown across a bench. They stare at him as he walks in. He would imagine friendlier faces at his own execution. He can read it in their faces; he is too young, too unschooled, too foreign to be of any use to them.

'Who's this?' one of them says.

Hanno leans on the table. 'He's my adviser.'

Gajendra regards his former enemies; they regard him. Neither is much impressed. It is like a gathering of crows, waiting for their quarry to stop shuffling about so they can pick out the juicy bits for dinner.

Alexander would not have done this, he thinks, he was never one to stand back and let other men insult his charges. He would have his arm around me now, stand right in their faces, dare them to be uncivil.

Hanno's authority is not as certain.

Gajendra studies the chart, the planned dispositions. The generals watch him, arms folded. They are waiting for some brilliant plan, he supposes, as if that alone would defeat Alexander. But he knows whatever they do, Alexander will adapt.

Gajendra has some stones in his fist and he drops them there, places them at strategic points.

'Here is Alexander, here his cavalry, here his heavy infantry, here his elephants, this is how he will line up against us. But expect this to change almost immediately battle commences.'

He has exhausted almost all his pile of stones before he sets out their own positions. It requires not nearly as many pebbles.

'He has that many soldiers?' Hanno asks.

'Those mercenaries who survived the rout at Syracuse have gone over to him.'

'Then we're fucked,' someone says.

Gajendra nods. 'In a conventional battle you might as well fall on your swords and save the Macks the trouble.'

A few chuckles. Some of them appreciate his candour at least.

'The first thing you must do is show him how you intend to win. Because he will be wondering.'

Several of them turn to Hanno, and one asks, 'You are not still contemplating going against him without Antipater?'

'I have sent couriers to Antipater and the oligarchs at Syracuse, asking them to return to the field and attack him in a concerted pincer movement, allied with us.'

'But Antipater is dead! They had him executed!'

'Alexander has agreed terms with Syracuse!'

'He does not know we know this,' Hanno replies. 'The couriers have been ordered to defect, or feign to. No doubt Alexander shall arrange for us to receive a missive from Syracuse, under Sostratus's seal, agreeing to participate in a joint attack. Alexander will think we have been duped. If he thinks he can destroy us here it will save him the cost of a long campaign in the west of the island.'

He smiles at them, thin-lipped. This stratagem was Gajendra's idea.

'There are several other things we must do,' Gajendra says, and all heads swivel back to him. They are frowning now, seeing themselves drawn in to something they wish no part of – a fair fight.

'We shall need someone to take Hanno's place on the battlefield. A decoy.'

'Take my place?' Hanno says. This has not been mentioned before.

'This man must wear your armour and ride under your standard, take up your position behind the line, as most generals would.'

'Why?' someone asks.

'It is a baited hook, to lure Alexander into a trap. One final thing: we shall need pigs.'

They stare at him in utter disbelief. 'Pigs?'

'As many as you can get.'

There is stunned silence. The wind whips at the pavilion.

Never did even the Macks have this much enmity for a common Indian. They give Hanno their opinion of him and his plans at the top of their voices. How can we trust this boy? He has spent the last two years probably taking it up the arse from the King of Macedon and that's the closest he ever got to his inner sanctum.

And no one can go against elephants! Everyone knows that. Even Alexander almost lost a battle against them in India. They ran through our infantry at Carthage and chased off Antipater's cavalry just a week ago.

He thinks we can beat them with a few pigs!

You can't trust Asiatics. They'd sell their own mothers if there was a profit in it. My weight in gold he's a spy!

The generals crowd around and compete to shout each other down. If this is the calibre of men Hanno surrounds himself with, no wonder they won so easily at Carthage. He would like to remind them of it, but thinks it is not politic to do so. He keeps his own counsel and waits.

Hanno lets them shout themselves hoarse and when they have worn themselves out he holds up his hand for silence. But one of them still has to have the last word.

'Why are we listening to him? He is Alexander's spy!'

Hanno makes Alexander look like an hysteric; he keeps his arms crossed and his face still. Nothing gives away what he is thinking. His eyes flick around the room. He reminds Gajendra of a hawk, with those deep black eyes. They are the only thing in his face that moves.

Hanno nods at Gajendra, gives him leave to speak again.

'If you run back to Panormus,' Gajendra tells him, ignoring the rest of the rabble, 'then you know what will happen. He won't forget about you. He'll come back at his leisure with a superior force and tear down the walls of your forts and towns and crucify any that survive and take your women and children as slaves. You know this.'

'He has a superior force now,' another officer says.

'Why didn't Antipater wait for us?'

Why are they still talking about Antipater? he wonders. Isn't Antipater dead, by their own admission? Gajendra, the elephant boy, is losing patience with the high and mighty. What a stupid bunch they are. 'What Antipater did or did not do is no longer our concern. All we have is our present circumstance. And if you run away from him now, you gain nothing. Here you have one advantage. You can choose the terms of the battle.'

'No one can beat Alexander,' another braveheart says from the back of this inglorious huddle.

Gajendra does not look at them; he looks at Hanno. 'I can,' he says.

'With pigs?'

'Yes, with pigs. We will deploy them here. You will need soldiers to shepherd them. We have to direct them to the right spot.'

'You cannot beat Alexander with pigs.'

'No, you are going to defeat him in single combat, by the grace of the gods. The pigs will only unsettle his initial plans.'

'I don't understand,' another worthy says; at least he is honest about it.

'We have to do something about the elephants; your men will not be able to stand against them, they do not have the training or the discipline, and your horses will bolt. So we'll drive the pigs among them to scatter them. The elephants are terrified of pigs. This will serve a dual purpose. Firstly it will take away one of his greatest weapons, and secondly it will force him to take the opportunity to advance that we shall present to him. We will fight this battle on *our* terms and not his. Once the elephants turn it will create panic and we must make it appear that this is our chief strategy. We shall misdirect. We break our line, lure him in, and this, good men of Carthage, is our best chance to rid the world of Alexander.'

'What if the elephants don't run?'

'They will run.'

'But why would such a massive beast be afraid of a pig?'

'Why are some men afraid of spiders? Does it matter? They are afraid. It is a tactic that has never been used against them before. That is why it will work.'

'How do you know this?'

'Because I used to be the general of his elephants.'

And that finally shuts them up.

CHAPTER 53

S HE LOOKS SO different now. She wears a diaphanous gown and has ladies attend her, while her guards keep at a respectful distance. There are bangles on her wrists and at her throat. She has a wig, with blonde ringlets. She is still skinny, but is a little more rounded at least and smells of patchouli instead of elephants.

The bruises on her face are healing, though it will be a while before she looks as pretty as she did when she was just a dung lark. But the transformation is nevertheless astonishing.

'There you are!' She dismisses her entourage who wait for her at the temple gate. She takes his hand with the familiarity of a wife and leads him out of earshot. 'My father this morning could not break bread without some officer or another bursting in and decrying you for a charlatan. I could hear them shouting though my tent is some hundred paces distant from his. What have you been doing now?'

'I have been advising them on tactics. His men of war have been telling him to run away and hide. They don't like it that I have told them how they might actually win a battle. Their knowledge of warfare goes no further than tactical withdrawal.'

'Well, when Alexander is the opposing general, all men take pause.'

They have found a deserted temple. Leaves rustle across the marble and weeds grow through the cracks.

'Look at you!' he says. He pretends to examine her fingernails for elephant dung. 'This is more like it. No more breast binding, I see. And what is this gown? Are you trying to seduce me?'

'I could have you as my slave, you know. One word in my father's ear, confirm his officers' worst suspicions of you. I need a boy to run my bath.'

'This one would get in it with you.'

Her fingers stroke his cheek. Their eyes meet. 'Can the elephant boy really beat the god of war?'

The shadows of clouds race up the hill towards them. They are as fast as mounted raiders. The rain explodes with unexpected force on the marble flagstones like a barrage of stones. They run across the temple forecourt to the tabernacle to take shelter as the storm races up the valley. The filmy gown clings to her. He looks beyond the gates where the soldiers and her ladies have taken shelter under the trees.

He pulls her inside. Almighty Zeus is unimpressed, he lies on the floor of his tabernacle, fractured, one arm outstretched.

There are rats running behind the altars and the courtyard is littered with debris. 'They say his father wasn't Philip at all, but Antipater,' Gajendra says. She does not answer. 'You're supposed to appear shocked.'

'I never revered him as you did.'

'Revere? Is that what I did?'

'If I were a god and I wanted to destroy a man, do you know what I would do? I would make everyone else bow to him.'

'Nearchus told me that Alexander was behind the plot to kill his father. They had argued and Philip hinted that he would disown him. He married another woman and had a son by her, then told Alexander the baby would be the next king. I suppose that's not much of a hint, is it? Alexander said his real father was Zeus but most others thought it was Antipater. Whether your wife cheats with a god or with another man, I suppose it's still cheating.'

But Mara is not interested in Alexander's history any more. She steps over the threshold and looks around. 'What happened to this place?'

'Struck by lightning, or so they say. People here took it as a sign and cleared out. It's his symbol, you know, lightning. Zeus is the god of thunder around here.'

On cue, the tabernacle is backlit with a bright flash that trembles along the distant mountains.

The light is greenish. She stands on tiptoe and whispers, 'When did you first know that I was not a boy?'

'It was impossible to tell. There were so few clues. When I did discover it, it was quite a disappointment.'

He tries to kiss her and she bites his lip. He pulls away, laughing.

'After all this is done, you will come back to me, won't you, elephant boy?'

He slides a hand into her gown. She catches her breath and leans back against the wall. 'If I conceive here, I could say the father was Zeus.'

'He may have the blame as long as I have the pleasure.'

The breasts she had tried once to keep hidden are now pushed forwards, inviting caress. 'See here,' she says, 'on such a day the whole world is damp. Where to find a dry spot?'

From here he can see over her shoulder into the forecourt. Her people are still huddled under trees outside. While it rains like this, no one can see them.

'You'd best be quick, elephant boy,' she whispers. 'This downpour can't last forever.'

He smells fresh rain. Her skin glows in the storm light. Her shoulder is bare and he kisses it.

'Enough of that. No tenderness from you until after you have defeated Alexander. I couldn't bear it. You promise me you will win.'

'It is up to the gods, Mara.'

'I will not lose every single thing I have ever loved.'

He pushes inside with his hips and her eyes go wide. She puts her fingers on his lips to quieten him. 'Are you frightened?'

'Of course.'

'You do not appear to be frightened. You look very calm.'

'Men are frightened of different things. Some are frightened of pain, others of disfiguring wounds. Others are scared of death.'

'And you?'

'I am scared of not appearing brave in front of other men. I am afraid of my own cowardice.'

She strokes his hair. 'I am afraid that you will not come back.'

'I will bring you his leg as a footstool.'

'No trophies. Just come back to me, Gaji. I don't care if you are not brave. Just come back. It seems I have grown a little fond of you.'

CHAPTER 54

HANNO RIDES UP to him. He has his helmet under his arm. He wears plain armour, nothing to mark him as anything other than another cavalry officer. It is Gajendra who has on the plumed helmet, the red cloak, the high-stepping Arab with silver trappings. Another dream he has fulfilled, though not as he had once imagined it.

The whole battlefield is in motion. The atmosphere is charged. If fear could condense on the air, a man might not be able to breathe. It is in the eyes of the men, even the horses; a soldier drops his weapon, a horse rises on its hind legs, a man pisses where he stands.

They are all thinking the same thing: this is Alexander we are fighting. We are doomed.

The infantry plunge the butt of their spikes into the earth and drop down to one knee, their bronze and oak shields slung across their chests. Boys run in and out of the lines with waterskins of wine. Beside the hoplites are the Iberians with their bossed wooden shields and javelins. They have little in the way of armour, just some buskin boots and a woollen cloak. That is not going to help them much if they come up against the Macedonians' sarissas.

'This is madness,' one of Hanno's generals says. They

will not let this go, these men. Too late for anyone to change their minds and still they grumble about it.

'Get to your positions,' he tells them, brooking no further discussion. He turns to Gajendra. 'You think this will work?'

'That is up to the gods. We cannot win the battle, you understand that? Today has but one purpose.'

'I know it.'

Another storm is moving in off the sea. He feels the ground quake under the next roll of thunder. He can imagine what Alexander will make of this.

Could there be more gloom? Hundreds of Hanno's men have deserted during the night, though not as many as he had supposed. Mercenaries are sometimes more loyal than conscripts. They maintain a sort of professional pride, while conscripts look to the main chance.

Alexander has formed up his army on the plain below. He can see the spear points glitter for a moment as the sun appears through a rare break in the clouds. The grass has been soaked by the rain and glows emerald green. It looks pretty now. Soon it won't.

Hanno steps his horse up beside him. 'I wish to thank you, Gajendra.'

'What for?'

'For bringing my daughter safely back. She has told me everything you did to help her. I shall be forever in your debt.'

Gajendra smiles. 'You may regret saying that if I ever call in my marker.'

'Well, I think it is my creditors who should be more concerned today than my debtors. Goodbye, Gajendra.'

'Aren't you supposed to say – I will see you after the battle?'

'It's likely as not one or both of us will be dead. Do you not think so? Let's not jolly ourselves along. We know what has to be done.'

'And your couriers?'

'They have done their job. Alexander had them flogged for their disloyalty and then paid them five gold coins and a guarantee of mercy to return here and tell me that the oligarchs of Syracuse had agreed to my terms.'

The standard bearers and signal corps cluster around. Hanno puts on his helmet, a plain thing, bronze, with face pieces something like a beard. All his officers have them.

'You will get no credit for this afterwards. History only remembers the generals, even when they go in disguise.'

'Oh, I think history will remember me in some way if this goes for us today,' he says and grins.

'Take care, my boy. My daughter seems to think something of you.' And he rides away. Gajendra, surrounded and cramped on every side by bodyguards and couriers, has never felt so alone.

CHAPTER 55

ALEXANDER HAS PRESENTED as Gajendra thought he would. The elephants – his elephants – are at the centre, the stingers in between, the phalanx at the rear. The cavalry are at the flanks, at the oblique, of course, but not static. Alexander will never present to the enemy a static line; already he is on the move, his light cavalry crossing to the right, further weakening his other flank and inviting attack.

There will be light infantry, Agrianians, Iberians, hidden somewhere in the hills, there will be a trick or two to play.

There he is, a flash of gold, Alexander in his gorgeous armour, moving down the line, his flag bearers and officers riding behind him as he inspects the lines, cajoling, encouraging. He will be in his heaven. He has never seen him bad-tempered before a battle. Without war, Alexander could not exist. His only fear, Nearchus once told Gajendra, was that he would reach the end of the world and everyone would have surrendered.

Whatever happens today, he will miss him. But it was like standing too close to the sun: you were either burned to a crisp or you froze.

'Always attack,' Alexander told his generals once, as they gathered around his table before they defeated Antipater.

'Attack makes men bold; defence makes them timorous. Always attack, even when you are outnumbered and out-manoeuvred. Always.'

So now I present you my defence, Alexander, but it is a feint, misdirection. You see how well I have learned?

Does he know I am here? He will suspect. But he still thinks me an elephant boy. If I was Perdiccas or Ptolemy he might be more cautious, but I'm just an Asiatic, an infe-rior, and he will underestimate me.

He thinks we are holding the valley waiting for Antipater; he thinks we are relying on the caltrops we have spread in front of our infantry to blunt his attack; he thinks he can hypnotize us with the elephants.

Cloud shadows race across the grass. Another hour and the storm will be on them. They will be fighting this battle in the mud; Colossus would like that. But it will also slow Alexander's cavalry; so in this instance the god of thunder may not be such a good omen for his intentions.

Gajendra concentrates his mind on the gods: hold off your rain for just a little longer. Let him race to the heart of us. We will embrace him, enfold him. Bring your dagger and your bite here, my king. We will die together.

We feint, we provoke.

How will he provoke them today? His feint had been to make Alexander think Hanno was unsuspecting of Syracuse, that he was not privy to any private arrange-ments between the oligarchs and Alexander. He thought Hanno was unprepared to face his entire army.

He will provoke them first with his oblique; here he is flooding his cavalry to the right, inviting them to attack his left flank. Gajendra has never seen this before, standing with him, and realizes what a tempting target it makes.

The whole field is in motion now. The elephants are coming up, the noise is the thing, the infantry will feel it through their feet, they will hear the battle cries and the unison of their marching and it will shudder through their bones. He can feel it even through his horse. They are a fearsome sight, these Macedonians, they have been drilled to the point that they could fight this battle in their sleep.

He can pick out Colossus now at the head of the battle line. He smiles at the thought of him. Look at how proud he is to be out at the front! He holds his head high, his massive forelegs come down to shake the earth, he appears to double in size with each advancing stride. There is one last warning shriek and then he curls his trunk between his tusks, and then resumes in silence.

Gajendra must carry this off today without hurting his elephants. He will not see his boys come to harm, not a single one of them.

Alexander: *We must ask ourselves with our every stroke how our foe will counter. All tactics shall seek to provoke a breakthrough in their line.*

This is where the answer lies. He must not think about what Alexander is doing now or what he will do next; this is about what he will do an hour from now, two, when the battlefield looks very different. He must think many moves ahead. That was the master's lesson; today will show whether the student has been apt.

They come at them like a wave; not the phalanx of Silver Shields, not the cavalry, not the elephants; it is the camp

370

followers, swarming out in their thousands. A gasp runs through the serried ranks of the hoplites behind the palisades. What are they doing?

No one asks Gajendra what is happening, but if they did he would have told them; he may be the only one on this side of the lines who is expecting this. He expects it because Alexander has told him this is what he will do if ever this situation arises.

After the battle of Carthage, Gajendra had asked him this very question: 'What if, instead of sharpened wooden spikes, they had seeded their front with those spiked metal balls, those caltrops, to impede our elephants?'

'I would respond with greed,' he had said.

'Greed?'

'I would send a man to the rear, to the whores and the cooks and the carpenters and the hangers-on, and offer a silver coin for every caltrop brought to my quartermaster by hand.'

'No one will risk his life for a few coins!'

He had laughed at that. 'You are so young. It's almost touching how innocent you are.' His lips had curled into a smile. His mouth was ugly; it was always a surprise, how ugly his smile was, when the rest of him was so very pretty.

Hanno is watching proceedings from a hill above the temple of Zeus, far to the rear. A courier is sent all the way back to ask for orders. The response is then too slow to be effective. By the time the archers have been told to deal with these irregulars, half the field has been cleared.

What surprises him is how brave these whores and cooks are. Even when the first arrows slice in and their neighbours start to fall, they still remain, gathering armfuls of the spiked metal balls, either in sacks or in their arms. A few flee; after the second volley so do many more. But even then some remain and a handful who have fled change their mind and return for just one more.

It is only after the fourth volley, when a hundred or so tarts and barbers lie twitching in the grass, that the field is empty again. By then, most of the caltrops are gone. If the elephants advance now, there is little between them and the palisade.

For a while silence prevails.

The thunder growls in the high passes. The wind whips at the clothes of the dead and wounded lying in front of the timbered palisade.

Gajendra admires how fine his elephants look. Colossus is worthy of his name; he is immense. He has never stood with infantry before and faced a squadron of elephants and now he understands why soldiers are so terrified.

He imagines Ravi on his shoulders. He feels a twist in his gut. It should be me up there.

Ravi starts to bring them forward; has Alexander made him the new Elephantarch? The whole line is disciplined and moving at the oblique. He sees the stingers jogging between them, brown-skinned and lithe. He feels a surge of pride; he trained them well.

They are downwind and he can smell them. Out on the flanks the horses catch their scent too and skitter in their places.

He hopes Hanno remembers all he has told him and does not deviate from the plan. He has some gutless time-servers on his staff; he supposes when the army is picked by a council, you have to work with what you have. But if he lets them interfere, then this will be a bloody rout and none of them will get out of this with their lives.

The host is bearing down. They are engaged now and nothing will save them but Gajendra's devices, which seem increasingly frail, even to him, as the time comes closer.

There is movement in the front ranks. Men run through the lines with flaming torches and spears. Alexander will not like this; he is to face the unexpected on the battlefield. He prefers the initiative.

Here are the pigs; there are hundreds of them brought up on chains, at the trot. They run through the phalanx and are only released when they are out beyond the palisades. The men prod them with their spears and flaming torches to make them run. They set off across the field towards the elephants. Some of them have been soaked in pitch and have been set on fire so they will run faster than the rest. He never ordered that. He did not think it necessary.

For a moment nothing happens. The pigs run, both armies watch. Some of the porkers run in circles, others turn back in the direction they have come, confused. But that is the reason he has specified there should be so many; he needs just a portion of their number to flee straight at the elephants for them to be effective. This is what happens.

And now there is chaos.

The trumpeting of the elephants is deafening. They raise their trunks and squeal in terror and Alexander's line crumbles and breaks at the centre. The elephants back up at first, despite the desperate efforts of their *mahavats* to keep them in line, and then they turn and dash through their own lines, trampling everything in their path. *Howdahs* topple and are crushed under the feet of other tuskers running behind. The infantry scatter.

He can hear men screaming on the wind.

He feels sorry for his *mahavats*. When an elephant loses its mind there is nothing to be done; you would have better luck ordering the tide to turn or making an avalanche to stop dead on the side of a mountain. They leave a trail of bolted horses, crushed infantry and dashed flags in their wake.

Carthage cheers. They sense victory.

What happens next is entirely predictable. Even as the hoplites give their battle cry and rush through the palisades, Gajendra thinks ahead to the next move after the next one. A lesser general than Alexander would panic. But Alexander will instead be pulling on his helmet and looking to gain advantage from this reverse.

The whole line is in motion now, the infantry running over the open ground to the ragged gap left by the departed elephants. The tuskers' rout has left a gaping hole in the line, piles of bleeding rags that once were men littering the ground behind them.

The squares of the phalanx have been scattered. If they were Greeks or Persians they might have dropped their weapons and fled, and it may have degenerated into a massacre. But these men are Alexander's Silver Shields, scarred veterans of Issus and Gaugamela and the Jhellum River, some are fifty or sixty years old, and they have seen it all. They rapidly re-form. By the time the hoplites arrive, they will find them unchastened by this reverse and ready to do murder.

His horse twitches underneath him; if it were Colossus he would know how to calm him but this beast is as foreign to him as riding a camel. A horse should be smarter than its rider, the Macks said, but you should never let him know that.

Well, this one does not have to be told. He knows already.

The hoplites arrive at Alexander's phalanx and face a serried rank of eighteen-foot-long sarissas. They cannot fall back, neither can they break through. The easy victory of just a few breaths ago now looks like a serious misjudgement by the captains on the line. Instead of leading a rout they are stalled by the points of the Macedonian spears and have themselves left a break in the line behind.

Alexander brings Ptolemy and his heavy cavalry to engage the Numidians on the left and charges through the gap with his own cavalry. He has seen Hanno's colours now, indeed he has looked for nothing else.

There is just a squadron of bodyguard cavalry between him and me, Gajendra realizes. And as he thinks I am Hanno, this is the moment he has waited for.

Although he is expecting Alexander's attack, it is the speed and ferocity of it that startles him. He has seen him do this at Carthage and at Syracuse, but when you are behind him, it is impossible to appreciate how demoralizing it might be to see his heavy cavalry coming straight at you.

Gajendra's bodyguards ride out to meet him but the force of the charge breaks their ranks almost immediately.

He can see Alexander clearly now, his plumed helmet, the beautiful golden armour. They fight like Furies, these Macks. He cannot but admire him, even as he wishes him dead.

Hanno's cavalry try to hold them, but it is soon clear that there are not enough of them. The first stragglers arrive, galloping hard. It does not take much to win a battle; once an army turns, it is like a crack appearing in the wall of a castle. After that everything is then concentrated on that one point, and after months of siege it is all over in hours.

One moment you are at the rear; the next you are in the front line.

Until now he has been still, he does not want to snatch the lure too soon; but now he realizes that the lure is in danger of being taken sooner than he thinks. He turns and orders the retreat. The standards and certain of his body-guards follow. He does not know what happens to the rest; they are swallowed up in the mêlée.

He wishes Hanno and his generals were here, he would like to shout in their faces: *See, I told you what he would do.*

But then perhaps they would shout back at him: *Yes, you can lure him, but now can you stop him? Can anyone?*

It is chastening to see how quickly heavy cavalry can decimate infantry if they are not properly organized. These Greek hoplites he has, they are not the Macedonian phalanx, and the Celts and Gauls are simply no match, for all their bearskins and tattoos and beards, they just scream and die along with everyone else.

They are no match.

Alexander himself has just one focus; he has seen

Hanno's battle standards and he intends to confront him personally. For Alexander a battle is not just about victory, it is about personal glory. He will be determined that this time Hanno will not escape. He leads the charge from the front; he always said that a general could not commend his men to valour if he himself sat behind the lines on a fine horse with a servant holding a shade umbrella. Not that he had ever been tempted to be that sort of king.

He is shocked at seeing that golden armour so close, so soon. The breastplate on Alexander's horse has been pierced repeatedly and the animal has a chunk out of its hindquarters that would make a steak big enough for three men. Its chest and forelegs are stiff with matted blood. Yet still he comes, maddened by pain and rage, and Alexander seems no less crazed.

Gajendra leads the retreat, the ragged remains of Hanno's bodyguard trailing behind. He sees the temple on the knoll above, the glimmer of the sun for a moment catching a soldier's armour somewhere on the ridge above it. He hopes Alexander does not see it, too.

'Hanno!'

He thunders onto the crest saddle below the temple ruins, hears Alexander call him out. He turns his horse to face him. The battle now has deteriorated into scores of single combats, but it is this one that will carry the day. Gajendra hurls his javelin and it strikes Alexander's shield and bounces harmlessly away; Alexander responds with his own. It strikes Gajendra's breastplate and snaps off, but the force of it is enough to take his breath away and knock him off his horse. He lands on his back in the grass.

He struggles to his feet, wondering why Hanno is

not here to help him. He draws his sword and looks for Alexander. Alexander charges at him, but he does not use his sword, he batters him with his shield until he goes down again.

Gajendra knows he is no match but is disappointed he has not put up a better show; but then he supposes there are few bravehearts who can say they have not been bested in combat with this demon.

Alexander does not dispatch him immediately. Instead he leans down and rips off his helmet, for Alexander will show mercy to any man who will ask for it, if he has fought bravely.

It is the only time he has ever seen Alexander confused. 'Elephant boy?' he says.

CHAPTER 56

ALEXANDER'S MOMENTARY CONFUSION gives him a moment's respite to roll over and vomit. He has never fought from the back of a horse before. These Macks make it look so easy. He is stunned, exhausted. He spits blood. Where is that coming from? Falling from a horse in full armour is a chastening experience.

Ptolemy arrives and leans from his saddle looking similarly bewildered. 'What is he doing here?'

Gajendra tries to crawl away. Alexander puts his foot on his throat to stop him.

He thinks he intends to choke him to death. But no, he is just giving himself leave to think, to piece together what is happening. Gajendra knows now he must break his promise to Mara; he is going to die now and there is no help for it. He thinks how bitter she will be. For some reason of her own she has loved him, and as she said, everything she loves always dies.

Still, when he is dead he will be glad to get out of this armour. He is too weary to fight on; the fall from the horse has crushed his spirit. Everything hurts.

He looks up at the knoll and wills Hanno to make his entrance now. His advice to him was to wait until Alexander was fully committed. How more committed must a man be than to be off his horse and scratching his head in bewilderment, next to his enemy's battle standards?

'What have you done, elephant boy?'

'I did not just do it for me, I did it for Nearchus.'

'Nearchus?'

'He warned me. I should have listened. He should have listened to himself.'

'By the black breath of hell, what is he talking about?' Ptolemy shouts. 'Kill him, Alexander, and let's get out of here. This is no time to be off your horse berating this lunatic!'

Alexander kicks him again. He sees the sense in what Ptolemy has said. He raises his sword. 'Well, elephant boy, you want a reckoning with the gods, you shall have one.'

Just then he hears yelling from the ridge above and looks up, sees Hanno and his cavalry swarming down the slope. It gives Gajendra a moment to scramble away out of range. Alexander looks faintly irritated by this turn of events. He points his sword at Gajendra. 'I will settle with you shortly.'

He picks up a javelin from the ground and hurls it at the first of Hanno's cavalry. It takes the rider in the breastplate and bounces off, but the aim is so perfect that it knocks the man off his horse and sends him tumbling to the ground.

Gajendra shakes his head in astonishment. The man is not human. Perhaps he is a god after all. Does he never miss his aim?

Without breaking stride Alexander jumps back onto his horse and he and Ptolemy ride to spring the trap.

The two ranks of horses collide. Alexander's enthusiasm for the fight is undiminished. One of Hanno's officers wheels his horse around and comes at him from behind; he swings wildly and his sabre almost crushes Alexander's helmet. He slumps in the saddle but recovers. Now Perdiccas is there and his spear takes Alexander's attacker out of his saddle.

Alexander shakes his head like a wet dog. His head must be bone right through. It is true, then. You just cannot kill this man.

Gajendra's body is racked with pain but he concentrates his will on standing up and getting ready to face Alexander a second time. Just one of us can walk off this field today, and I promised Mara that it would be me. He staggers to his feet, searching for his sword, any sword.

The rain sweeps in, blinding him. As the lightning arcs across the sky, he sees Hanno's men are in retreat and Alexander is still in the saddle. His plan has worked but Alexander, the god, is bigger than his plan. Zeus has spoken. The omens were true after all.

Gajendra sways on his feet. It is hard to breathe, and his vision has blurred. He has found a sword and buckler, though, and has again dropped to one knee to gather himself. As Alexander approaches he raises himself to stand.

That he should do so seems like an irritation to the great king. He hammers his sword into Gajendra's buckler and sends him back onto his knees.

'I treated you like my own son. I would have given you the world if you had wanted it. All I asked was your loyalty!'

Gajendra tries to rise but he hammers him again with his sword and forces him down to his knees once more. He half rises and staggers backward towards the temple. He imagines Mara, kissing him in the storm light. He blinks away the image, tries to concentrate. Alexander can kill him whenever he wants to. But first, it seems, he wishes to make his point.

Alexander removes his helmet and throws it on the ground to register his disgust. 'Why did you do this?' he says.

'Do not think to win the battle … think to win the campaign. Think not to win the campaign, think … to win the war.'

'This was your plan?'

'When you die, you Greeks will go back to fighting among yourselves and leave us alone.'

'*You Greeks?* Who are you fighting for now?'

The sword hammers on the shield again; he will pound him into the dirt like a nail at this rate. Get it over with, Alexander.

He reels backwards against the temple gates.

'This cannot be over a woman, can it?'

'You pissed on my head.'

'It *is* over a woman!'

He retreats as Alexander batters him with his sword again and again. Finally he has enough of it and summons what strength he has left and hammers his buckler into Alexander's face and thrusts with his falcata, tearing through the composite of his corselet and finding the flesh between his ribs and the inside of his left arm.

Alexander staggers back, his face registering his outrage that an elephant boy would dare to stab at the royal person. He puts his hand beneath his armour and when he takes it out it is covered in blood. He stares at it in disbelief.

Gajendra runs across the courtyard, slips on the wet stone and goes down again. The fall from the horse has damaged something inside. The pain seems to be everywhere. It is hard to breathe. He rolls on his side and vomits.

Alexander shakes his left arm, as if he can hurl aside the wound in his side like a stray insect. 'What a soldier you make,' he says. 'Not a mark on you, and you are rolling around the floor like you are dying. Come on, elephant boy, get up and let's make a proper fight out of it, then.'

He cannot feel his arms and he cannot hear Alexander's voice any more. His sword feels as if it weighs as much as his horse. Alexander is standing over him. His lips are moving so he must be saying something. His teeth are black with blood and dirt.

Alexander stabs down, but it is not a killing stroke, he hasn't finished talking yet. Alexander likes to talk and he has plenty to say when he feels like it. The battle is over. What is to be established here is the more important question of why he is not properly loved.

Gajendra writhes as the point of Alexander's sword goes in. As his general stands back he slithers away. Of all the telling moments of his life is this how it will end, down here on the floor again, like a worm, like a snake?

He rolls his head to the side and sees Zeus lying down there with him. It can happen to me, Zeus seems to be saying, it can happen to you.

He is lying in a pool of blood but it does not appear to be only his. There have been other combats fought in here today. One of Hanno's officers lies outstretched, his spear at his feet. It is a short, stabbing spear with a four-square iron point.

He concentrates his will on crawling towards it. Inch by inch, now, never mind about what he is saying about you. When your enemy thinks you are beaten is when you are at your most dangerous. Isn't that another of his lessons? Alexander is still ranting, now he rolls him over with his foot, the better for him to hear the rest of his speech about loyalty.

Gajendra's fingers close around the broken shaft of the spear.

Now as Alexander raises his sword to deliver the killing stroke he steels himself for one final effort. He grasps the spear and thrusts upwards, seeking the vital flesh below the lip of Alexander's breastplate. But he hasn't the strength to do it and Alexander seizes it with his left hand and forces it out of his grip, his fist so far up the shaft that their fists touch.

It is then the world turns black.

When he opens his eyes there is chaos. The stone gate crashes in and he hears an elephant trumpeting. Colossus stands in the courtyard, ears flared, clearly very angry. Somehow he has lost his *mahavat* and the archers in the *howdah* are shrieking and clinging on for their lives.

Alexander is thus delayed in killing his elephant boy. 'What have we here?' he says, turning around. 'Have you come to rout my enemies or protect your little elephant boy?'

Only Alexander would stand bare-headed before an enraged elephant with nothing but a sword and buckler. His soldiers would come and help him but they are too far away and his bodyguard are engaged by Hanno's men, who have regrouped for a second attack.

For the moment the King of Macedon is on his own.

Colossus raises his trunk and charges.

Alexander reaches for the javelin he has just wrested from Gajendra's hand and hefts it in his right hand. He aims for Colossus's eye.

Gajendra rolls onto his side, finds the dagger at his belt and plunges it into Alexander's calf. Alexander screams and the javelin falls easily wide of its mark. He turns and stabs down with his sword a second time. Gajendra cries out in pain.

Colossus picks him up with his trunk and hurls him across the courtyard. He slams against the temple wall. A lesser man would have died; but Alexander, the god, the immortal, lies still for long moments, then shakes himself and gets to his feet, dazed, and looks about for his sword.

Colossus charges a second time. He swipes him again, sending him sprawling across the marble where Alexander lands against his fallen idol, Zeus.

No ordinary man could survive such punishment; but Alexander is no ordinary man. He lies on his back, his right hand feeling for his sword. Giving up the search, he rolls onto his side and starts the slow climb to his knees. He leaves a smear of blood on the marble.

Colossus takes him a third time, charging with his tusks, which have been sheathed with iron tips. The force of the charge is enough that the tip of one tusk penetrates Alexander's golden armour and pierces him through, pinning him to the wall of the tabernacle. Colossus shakes his head like a dog with a rat and Alexander lands on the altar, leaving gouts of blood on the stark marble.

Ptolemy is first on the scene and shouts his dismay; their king is dead. Even Hanno's men leave off their fighting and stare in disbelief. It is a scene so improbable that no one can quite believe it.

Ptolemy rides his horse into the temple to try and retrieve his body but Colossus will have none of it. He charges and Ptolemy retreats. But even that is not enough, for he barges now into the Companion Cavalry and scatters them. In moments he has cleared the field. He turns and trudges slowly back to where Gajendra lies stricken. He nudges him with his trunk, rolling his body, looking for life.

Lightning cracks around the mountain.

Hanno climbs down from his horse. He knows the battle is lost, but they have done what Gajendra has promised, they have killed the man who called himself King of the World. Their reprieve is temporary. Alexander's cavalry will regroup; his own army is in rout. Only the thunderstorm and the confusion that will inevitably follow Alexander's death will save them now and allow some of them to escape with their lives.

His men are trying to retrieve Gajendra's body but the monster elephant will not let them close. They hesitate and look back at him for orders. Well, he is not leaving the boy here. Gajendra didn't leave Catharo and he will not leave Gajendra.

Does he try and kill the elephant now?

Mara appears from nowhere; she is supposed to be at his camp on the other side of the mountain, with the supply train. It does not surprise him that she has defied his orders and come here. She rides to the temple gates, or what is left of them after Colossus finished his rampage. She jumps down off her horse and pushes his men out of the way.

She walks straight towards the crazed elephant.

'Kill him! Kill the monster now!' he shouts.

His men reach for their javelins, the two bravest run in with their swords.

CHAPTER 57

Mara slips on the blood pooled underfoot. She gets up and runs at Colossus who flares his ears and roars at her.

'*Ida!*' she shouts at him. '*Ida!* Step aside!'

His trunk snakes out and tests her scent. Then he lowers his ears to let her know it is safe and steps back.

She kneels down at his feet and cradles Gajendra's head in her arms. There is gore everywhere, over her hands, over her dress. Once again, she is standing over the pit. She sees the goddess reach up for him, all black blood and greed, but she pushes her back. This one is mine, she tells her. I am claiming him back.

They leave the Greek Colossus where he has fallen. His generals are coming for him now, she can hear the thunder of their horses. Let them fight over what is left on the earth. She will settle for this simple victory over Tanith, for children again, and a husband for her bed. It is not much compared to what Alexander had conquered, but today he is the one lying on the marble, cold and dead, and she will be the one riding away, wiping the blood off her hands, and smiling.

CHAPTER 58

Panormus

H E LIES ON a litter, in the sun. They have brought him out here because she has said he needs the sun. He can smell the sea. The fountain court is sweet with lilies, and a fountain bubbles at its centre. There are cages of bright birds.

A shadow passes over the sun. He squints. 'Mara.'

'You are much improved.'

'It is a trial even to breathe.'

'You call yourself a warrior! One little scratch and you moan about it for days.' She examines the bandages. It is the first day there is no fresh blood.

'Do you require anything?'

'I do not have the strength, I am afraid.'

'I meant water. Or fruit.'

'Oh.'

She sends a servant running for both. She strokes his cheek. 'Your elephant does nothing but eat. It would be cheaper to house a regiment of Celts.'

'He is all right?'

'Listless. In his way I think he enquires after you.'

He coughs and grimaces in shock. 'What news of the world?'

'They are building a mausoleum for Alexander in Egypt. Ptolemy has taken the body there and Perdiccas has taken advantage of the situation by trying to turn the army against Kraterus. You see, it's started already. They have quite forgotten about us. We are safe here until it's settled.'

'It will never be settled.'

'I know. That's why my father wants to build another army.'

'To what purpose?'

'To take back Carthage.'

'What is left of it.'

'What is knocked down can be built again. While Alexander's generals squabble among themselves we can grow strong again. We cannot spend our lives perched on this rock hoping the world will forget about us. One day our enemies will come looking for us again, when they have decided on a new king.'

He leans up on one elbow. 'Armies can be had with proper alliances. Carthage always used mercenaries.'

'What we will need is something to sway the battles in our favour next time.'

'Elephants?'

'And someone who knows how to train them, how to lead them. Do you know of anyone?'

He shakes his head. 'The only one I know has no wife. It's important, you know, for a general to have a wife. It's lonely work, training elephants. He has told me he won't have anything to do with war until he has mastered the arts of loving. It seems reasonable.'

'And supposing that can be arranged?'

He hears a bellow from somewhere close by. 'Is that Colossus?'

'He is becoming unmanageable. You had better get well soon.'

'He could be in musth. We'd better find a wife for him as well. If you want an army of elephants, it would be a good place to start.'

He touches her cheek with the back of his hand. 'I thought he had killed me, that he had stolen this moment from me.'

'We have a destiny to fill, Gajendra. As do our children and their children to follow. Alexander's Empire will be nothing compared to theirs.'

She leans over and kisses him on the cheek.

'What was that for?'

'For not leaving me. If you had died I would never have forgiven you.'

He manages a smile, making the effort seem greater than it is. 'I shall have you barefoot and pregnant in months.'

She cuffs him around the cheek. 'Watch who you're talking to, elephant boy.' And she walks away, with an extravagant sway of her hips that promises much.

AFTERWORD

AS IN EVERY work of fiction, the events described in this book never happened. But when you're writing historical fiction about real people, lines become blurred. As every history book will tell you, Alexander the Great died in Babylon in June, 323 BC. He did not attack Carthage or invade Sicily, though he did contemplate such a campaign before his death.

Most historical novels are based on fictional events that are overlaid on real events. So 'Colossus' might not perhaps be described as an historical novel – just a story of what might have happened if Alexander had lived. It is vested in one of the parallel universes that quantum physicists tell us exist side by side with ours.

But this does not mean it is totally fictitious. I used a number of sources to form my impressions of this alternative world. For those who wish to know more about Alexander the man, I would recommend Peter Green's excellent *Alexander of Macedon*. If you want to know more about the actual history of Carthage you could refer to Richard Miles' *Carthage Must Be Destroyed*. John M. Kistler wrote a fascinating book about the history of war elephants, and Jeff Champion's *The Tyrants of Syracuse* will explain more about the politics of Sicily long before it became famous just for being the birthplace of the Corleone family. All novels are speculation. My interpretation of Alexander is my own, based on a reading of his life, rather than pure imagination.

Whether he would have turned his attention to North Africa, had he lived, is of course open to much debate. The only thing I am convinced of is that should he have lived beyond 323 BC, his medical and mental history precludes the possibility that he would have lived to see ripe old age.